D0238757

The Burma Legacy

ALSO BY GEOFFREY ARCHER

Sky Dancer
Shadow Hunter
Eagle Trap
Scorpion Trail
Java Spider
Fire Hawk
The Lucifer Network

THE BURMA LEGACY

Geoffrey Archer

CENTURY · LONDON

Published by Century 2002

1 3 5 7 9 10 8 6 4 2

Copyright © Geoffrey Archer 2002

Geoffrey Archer has asserted his right under the Copyright, Designs
and Patents Act 1988 to be identified as the author of this work

This novel is a work of fiction. Names and characters are the product
of the author's imagination and any resemblance to actual persons,
living or dead, is entirely coincidental

This book is sold subject to the condition that it shall not,
by way of trade or otherwise, be lent, resold, hired out,
or otherwise circulated without the publisher's prior
consent in any form of binding or cover other than that
in which it is published and without a similar condition
including this condition being imposed on the
subsequent purchaser

Century Books
The Random House Group Limited,
20 Vauxhall Bridge Road,
London SW1V 2SA

Random House Australia (Pty) Limited
20 Alfred Street, Milsons Point, Sydney,
New South Wales 2061, Australia

Random House New Zealand Limited
18 Poland Road, Glenfield,
Auckland 10, New Zealand

Random House (Pty) Limited
Endulini, 5A Jubilee Road, Parktown 2193, South Africa

The Random House Group Limited Reg. No. 954009
www.randomhouse.co.uk

A CIP catalogue record for this book
is available from the British Library

Papers used by Random House are natural,
recyclable products made from wood grown in sustainable forests;
the manufacturing processes conform to the environmental
regulations of the country of origin

ISBN 0 7126 82465 (hb)
ISBN 0 7126 82961 (tpb)

Typeset by Deltatype Ltd, Birkenhead, Merseyside

Printed and bound in Great Britain by
Mackays of Chatham plc

To Eva, Alison and James.

Acknowledgements

I am indebted to several authors whose books helped me to understand present day Myanmar and the Burma of the past.

Aung San Suu Kyi's *Letters from Burma*, Rory Maclean's *Under the Dragon*, and Shelby Tucker's *Among Insurgents* provided potent illustrations of life under military rule in the 1990s.

Richard Rhodes James' *Chindit*, Philip Stibbe's *Return Via Rangoon*, George Macdonald Fraser's *Quartered Safe Out Here*, Eric Lomax's *The Railway Man* and Theodore F. Cook's *Japan at War – An Oral History* all, in their different ways, revealed the suffering of those who fought the Second World War in Burma.

I also owe a debt of gratitude to the Burma Star Association and to Arthur Titherington for sharing his painful memories of being a prisoner of the Japanese. Sincere thanks too to Martin Smith for his invaluable advice and assistance prior to my research visit to Myanmar.

The Andaman Sea, Thailand
Thursday, 30 December 1999

A GLEAMING MOTOR cruiser carved a white scar across the vivid blue sea, its throttles wide open. The man and woman on the bridge gripped the grab-handles as it hammered through the curling wake of a white-hulled ferry on passage from Phuket to the paradise islands of Phi-Phi. Scanning the ship's decks through binoculars they saw passengers watching them with envy. But the image the tourists had of them – a relaxed, well-off couple enjoying a vacation in the privacy of their own boat – was a lie. This was no pleasure cruise.

The real name of the bare-chested man at the wheel was Sam Packer, but his business card described him as Stephen Maxwell, a Singapore-based investment adviser. In reality he worked for British Intelligence. Beside him, wearing a yellow bikini, was Inspector Midge Adams – cover name Beth – a narcotics officer with the Australian Federal Police. They'd met for the first time that morning and were still wary of each other.

After a day of searching, they'd finally located their quarry, but the man they were after was an hour away from them. Fearing he might move on before they had the chance to catch up, they were squeezing every ounce of speed from their craft.

Their target was a man called Jimmy Squires, a former sergeant in the SAS, who'd turned to narcotics trading after leaving the Queen's employ. It was the Australians who were leading the operation to catch him – the market he served was in their backyard, the druggie hangouts of Sydney and Melbourne. MI6's offer to help put Squires out of business was in part the returning of a favour owed to the Australian Federal Police, but it was also to do with national pride. The SAS, the jewel in the UK's military crown, had a reputation to maintain. If one of its dogs went feral, the beast had to be culled.

Packer had been scrambled to Phuket that morning. Only when he landed in Thailand had he discovered the 'Inspector Adams' he was to work with was a female. And despite her petite shape, attractive blond hair and dark brown eyes, he hadn't welcomed the arrangement. The last time he'd worked closely with a woman, she'd nearly got him killed.

The Australians lacked the evidence they needed to put Jimmy Squires behind bars. The purpose of *this* operation was to find some. Cash was the key. If they could trace its passage from the addicts back to the supplier, Midge Adams would have her case. The usually effective, electronic systems for money tracking had failed to come up with the goods, so now they were trying the direct approach. Hoping to trick Squires into telling them where he banked his loot.

The scheme was entirely Midge Adams' idea. Packer considered it dangerously naïve and almost bound to fail. In the few hours he'd spent with her, he'd been troubled by the intensity with which she talked about the drug-runner. He suspected a personal motive behind her need to nail the man. And when self-interest intruded in a case, mistakes tended to follow.

The Andaman Sea shimmered in the relentless December sunlight. A bimini over the bridge protected them from its afternoon heat. The area they were powering through was a playground of turquoise waters and white sand beaches, which drew millions of tourists a year escaping from cold northern winters.

Packer altered course a few degrees to avoid a long-tail skiff which was slicing through the waters towards them, its slender lines at odds with the lumpy V-8 engine thundering away on its steering pole. The Thai boatman had two Europeans as fares. He nursed his craft through the waves, helming it towards some dream island, with the panache of a gondolier.

'You married, Steve?' Midge had spoken little in the last hour. Her accent was broad and she eyed him from behind dark glasses. Steve. From the moment they'd met she'd been meticulous about using cover names.

'No, Beth. I'm not.'

'Partner? Live with someone?'

He half smiled. 'Getting personal all of a sudden . . .'

'Always like to know the score.'

'Well, for the record, I have a girlfriend back in London.'

She stared ahead again. 'But you're living in Singapore.'

'That's right.'

'Tricky. What's her name?'

'Julie.'

'Ever see each other?'

'Not often enough.'

A few days ago Julie had threatened to give up on him unless he relocated to London soon.

'Offering to fill the gap?' he asked.

'Tcchh!' She turned away, opened a bottle of sun cream and started applying it to her shoulders.

'What about you?'

'I live with someone in Sydney.' It was a woman she rented a room to, but she wasn't going to tell him that.

'Can I help?' He pointed at the bottle.

'No thanks.' She gave him an old-fashioned look. 'And, just for the record – and since my assessment of the accommodation arrangements on this little ship tells me we'll be sharing a bed tonight – when I work with guys it's strictly no touching. Under *any* circumstances. Okay?'

'Just trying to be helpful.'

'Yeah, well, as my old granny used to say, give a man an inch and he'll stick the rest in.'

Sam smiled. 'Some granny.'

'Opened beer bottles with her teeth.'

He laughed. '*That* you're making up.'

Midge pulled a tense smile. It was the first one he'd seen on her. And it was an improvement.

Sam Packer's knowledge of the Golden Triangle heroin trade had been superficial until this morning – his normal focus being the profits from arms, not drugs. Midge had briskly filled him in on the ethnic-Chinese Wa tribes who controlled the Shan border area of Myanmar – formerly Burma – shipping heroin through China and Thailand to the wider world. And in particular she'd told him about a man called Yang Lai whose distribution network they suspected Jimmy Squires was attached to. Suspected. That was the problem with the Australians' case. They had nothing strong enough to convince a jury.

The event a couple of days ago which had triggered this attempt at entrapment was the opening of a small suitcase containing wads of cash. The yacht broker in Phuket, who'd received the $280,000 in payment for a luxury powerboat, had tipped off Thai Customs and they'd called the Royal Thai Police money laundering squad. The cash itself had proved clean, but when the name of the boat purchaser – Vincent Gallagher – was fed into a database at the Narcotics Suppression Bureau, it had come up as a pseudonym used by Jimmy Squires.

The sun disappeared behind a line of cloud, turning the sea slate-grey. As they raced towards the main island of Phuket, the water had become less open. Dark humps dotted the surface now, limestone outcrops jutting from the water like thumbs, and longer, flatter islands of finely ground coral where night fishermen had bamboo huts under the coconut palms for sleeping in during the day.

'Tell me,' Sam probed, 'the name Midge – is that on your birth certificate?'

'No way. And I never let on what is.'

'So how come you're called that?'

'Because when I was little, I was small for my age. And nasty with it. Anybody got in my way, I bit them.'

'Charming . . . ' He pursed his lips. 'Grown out of the habit I hope.'

'Don't bank on it.'

She leaned over the chart. There was a warm, oily smell to her, which Packer found irritatingly arousing.

'Where are we?'

He touched a finger to the paper.

'This the fastest we can go?'

'Yep.'

'How fast's Jimmy's boat?'

'No idea.'

They'd picked up the chartered craft from the same marina Squires had motored from the day before. Midge had confessed that although she spent a lot of time *in* water back home, being on top of it was alien to her. Sam had given her some basic instruction in crewing.

She leaned back in the white leather seat beside him, placing her feet on the rail. Nice feet, Sam noticed. Slender and straight-toed.

'Your boss wasn't lying when he said you liked boats,' she commented. 'I've been watching you.'

'Wanting to be sure you were in safe hands?' He glanced sideways at her and raised an eyebrow.

'Something like that.'

'Sailing's my thing, not power.'

'You own a yacht?'

'Used to have a fifty per cent share. But I had to sell it. Work. You know . . .'

'Never leaves you time for the things you want to do. Would you do more of it, if you could? Big time cruising, that sort of thing.'

'Like a shot.'

'What has to happen to make it more than a dream?'

'Enough money, enough time and the right woman to crew for me.'

'Julie . . .?'

Sam shrugged, not wanting to get into that again. 'Tell me about Jimmy Squires. Everything you haven't already told me.'

She looked away, staring at the horizon. 'Oh, he's straight out of a casebook. A boy who never knew his father. Brought up in an orphanage, then by foster parents. A right tearaway when he was a teenager. The file said he created a one-man juvenile crime wave in his home town.'

'Where was that?' The background file Packer's own employer had provided had been woefully sparse.

'Somewhere called Ripley? Yorkshire, I think. He did car theft, vandalism. The usual. Then some kindly probation officer steered him into the army to keep him out of jail. He was a tough nut, but they found he was bright too. Demonstrated a readiness to kill and a talent for survival. A shoe-in for special forces, I guess. But then he turned bad.'

'And bought a quarter-million-dollar ego-trip with the proceeds.'

'Amongst other things.'

It'd be a bloody great stamp in the passport, Sam realised. Barnado's boy makes good. An 'up yours' to every bugger who'd ever tried to put him down. The question was whether he'd be stupid enough to brag about it when they caught up with him. *If* they did . . .

'Remind me – when did he leave the SAS?'

'Two years ago when he turned forty. Been in uniform since the age of seventeen. His marriage broke up a year before that.'

'SAS men don't get home that often.'

'Then you and him'll have something to talk about . . .'

'Thanks.' He didn't need reminding. His affair with Julie had been relatively new when he was posted to Singapore nearly a year ago. Going three months. And he'd only seen her twice since then.

He asked Midge what had brought Squires to this part of the world.

'The Thai military recruited him – they were looking for men with jungle experience to show Karens living near the border how to spy on drug caravans.'

'Why bother with Brits? They must have dozens of their own who could do that.'

'One reason was historical. The Karens fought with the Brits against the Japs in World War Two and still have a high regard for them. The other, would you believe it, was *integrity*.' Midge's voice was heavy with irony. 'They thought SAS men were incorruptible.'

'Christ. How many did they hire?'

'Two. The other guy alerted the Thais to the fact that Squires wasn't playing by the rules anymore.' She shook her head in amazement. 'I thought those fellers were loyal to each other unto death.'

'Shows you haven't read the books they write. How did you lot get involved?'

'When the Thai's Narcotics Suppression Bureau put a watch on Squires, they logged frequent trips to Australia. So they alerted us. We put him under surveillance in Sydney and Melbourne, but the bastard was too good. Gave our watchers the slip. However ... by some remarkable coincidence his visits always seemed to be followed by an influx of Burmese heroin.'

Sam glanced to port. The sea was dotted with pleasure craft now. He looked enviously at a yacht under full sail. Midge noticed.

'More your style?'

He nodded. They were nearing a large land mass.

'Phuket island?' Midge asked, pointing.

'S'right.'

She leaned forward, moving a finger up the chart. 'The marina's here, right?'

'You've got it.'

A Thai narcotics officer on the quayside had radioed thirty minutes before to say that Squires' boat the *Estelle* was coming in to have a dodgy water pump replaced. A tip-off they'd desperately needed. Until then, they'd spent the day rushing from one sun-baked anchorage to another in a fruitless search for him.

Suddenly a beep shrilled from the console in front of them.

'Shit!'

'What's that?'

Sam grabbed the throttles and yanked them back to neutral.

'Oil pressure.' He pointed to the gauge. The needle had sunk to zero.

'What's that mean?'

'Don't know, yet.' He pulled the stop button and the engine died.

'For Christ's sake, Steve! What're you doing? We've got to get to that marina.'

'No oil, no can do.' He spun from his seat, slid down the companionway steps and stomped into the saloon. Before leaving harbour that morning he'd been given the briefest of tours of the boat's machinery space. He unclipped the engine covers and peered inside.

Midge followed him down. When she reached him he was reading the dipstick.

'Bone dry.' He opened the spares locker. 'But we're in luck! There's a five-litre can here.'

'They forgot to top up before we took the boat?'

'Or else there's a leak.' He leaned into the engine space again. There

6

were black oil smears down the engine block. 'Could be that the rocker cover wasn't screwed down properly.'

'Meaning . . .?'

'That I might be able to fix it with a spanner.' He looked in the locker, found a large, long-handled wrench and applied it to the loose securing bolts. 'Better get back on deck and keep watch. Make sure nothing runs us down.'

He poured the fresh oil into the engine, cleaned up and restarted the diesel, checking there were no more leaks. Soon they were on their way again.

'Fix you a drink, skipper?' Midge asked, her eyes betraying a trace of admiration.

'I could murder a mug of tea.'

She headed down to the galley.

Fifteen minutes later there was a further message from the marina. The *Estelle* had called to say she'd be alongside at four-thirty.

Sam smiled with satisfaction. 'We'll only be twenty minutes behind him.'

'Well, well, well,' said Midge. 'Perhaps there *is* a God.'

Ten minutes later they arrived at a guano-smeared post marking the entrance to the channel which led through mangrove clumps to the marina. The water here was like brown soup. Sam reduced speed to a point not far above the 5 knots allowed. Midge sat tensely beside him, as more long-tail boats sliced past, their fisherman owners waving giant prawns in the hope of a sale.

The channel narrowed. Ahead, the river was flanked by mangrove roots as spindly as spider-legs. Then, round a bend, the concrete harbour entrance came in view, just as the police radio crackled one more time.

'*Estelle in berth B23. If you quick, you take the space next.*'

'Okay,' Sam grimaced. 'Let the performance begin.' Uneasily he watched Midge pick her way to the bow and cleat on a line in the way he'd shown her earlier in the day. Her hair was bunched in a pony tail and as she moved about, it flicked from side to side. She'd pulled on a clingy, low-cut tee-shirt over her bikini top.

The sinking sun had burned a hole through the clouds. Sam squinted into it to identify the marker posts at the ends of the pontoons. Spotting the one for row B, he saw the *Estelle* six slots up, the name in big gold letters across her broad stern. Two males were on deck, busy with ropes. Two women lounged in chairs on the aft sun deck. Sam swung the boat into the row, cut the revs and turned into the empty berth alongside.

'Port side to, Beth.'

Midge looked baffled.

'Left side alongside,' Sam explained.

She moved to the rail with the bow line in her hands as he eased the hull against the finger pontoon, reversing the prop to prevent the bow crunching the quay.

'Jump!'

She hopped onto the finger, yelping as it dipped under her weight. She grinned sheepishly up at the bridge of the *Estelle*, then steadied herself and took the rope forward to the main pontoon, staring down at the mooring ring as if it were the most complex piece of technology she'd ever seen.

'Tie it anyhow, Beth,' Sam told her, favouring his voice towards their neighbour.

She fed the warp through the ring, then sat holding it, giving a good impression of not knowing what to do next. Out of the corner of his eye Sam saw the man they'd come to seduce step down from his boat.

'Give you a hand, darling?' Jimmy Squires' voice was like raked gravel.

'I'm so stupid with ropes,' Midge simpered, handing him the warp.

The former SAS sergeant had curly fair hair, blue-grey eyes and a small v-shaped scar on his left cheek. There was nothing obviously threatening about him, but even bears looked cuddly, Sam reminded himself. He watched to ensure the man knew what he was doing with the lines, then cut the engine and stepped off the boat to secure their stern warp. As she received her lesson in knots, Midge leaned forward to give Squires a look down her front.

'I'm pretty new to boats,' Sam heard her gush. 'Haven't got the hang of things yet.'

'Anytime you want coachin', darlin' . . .'

On the aft deck of the *Estelle* one of the women was plumpish, the other as trim and pretty as Thai girls were meant to be. Sam gave them a friendly nod, then climbed onto the foredeck to attach a second mooring line, passing the end to the man on the pontoon.

'Reckon I owe you a beer for that,' he said.

'Now you're talking . . .'

Sam went below, brought out a four-pack from the coolbox, then held out a can to Squires.

'Steve and Beth.'

'Nice to meet you.' Squires took the beer and ripped off the ring-pull in one smooth movement. 'I'm Vince. The bloke up there . . .' He pointed to the powerboat's high flying-bridge, '. . . is Nige. And the girls are Vicky and Jan. Their real names are a mile long and unpronounceable.'

His eyes radiated a cool intensity, but he looked at ease with the world. Midge was standing so close she was almost touching him.

'Where've you come from today?' Sam asked, raising the can to his lips.

'Ko Racha Yai,' Squires answered. 'Diving. You do any of that?' He indicated the air bottles secured to the side of the *Estelle*'s sundeck.

'Only snorkelling.'

'That's good too . . . Fantastic fish. Water's gin clear down there. This marina's a sewer. Only came back in because the pump in the shower packed up. You girls need your luxuries, don't you, darlin'?' He smiled condescendingly. 'What about you? Where've you been?'

'We only picked the boat up this morning. Trying her out. Came back in for some more provisions.'

'You won't get out again tonight,' Squires commented. 'The tide's too low.'

'I know.'

'Here for the Millennium?'

'Seemed a good way to celebrate.'

'Where do you live?'

'Singapore. We work in financial services.'

Squires turned his gaze on Midge. 'Don't tell me you're a money-brain too?'

'That's right. Any time you want your assets checking . . .'

Squires' chuckle was like a drain overflowing. 'I think you'll find them in good order . . .'

The sound of feet on the pontoon made them turn. It was the mechanic, toolbox in one hand and a small cardboard spares carton in the other.

'Been waiting for you, you little bugger.' Squires clapped the young Thai on the shoulder, then swung a leg onto the *Estelle*. 'Thanks for the beer. I'll return the compliment later. Hop over in about an hour if you feel like it.'

'Mind if we leave the timing loose?' Sam replied. 'Not sure how long things'll take ashore.'

'If you're here, you're here. If you're not we won't be offended.'

'Thanks.'

Sam did a final tidying of the bridge then went below. Midge had preceded him and sat flopped on the saloon berth with her arms spread across the back.

'That felt too easy,' she whispered.

'Yes.'

They looked at one another. Then Sam glanced at the bulkhead clock.

Midge nodded. 'I'll get some more clothes on.' She stepped down into the cabin and started pulling things from her bag. Sam concealed the Thai police radio handset in a drawer, then stuffed a wallet in his pocket.

By the time they stepped onto the pontoon, the clouds had cleared completely, but the sun was well down and had lost its heat. Beneath a thin, long-sleeved top Midge was bra-less, Sam noticed. Her tanned legs protruded from skimpy yellow shorts, and she moved with the fluidity of a cat.

The pontoon ended at a long quay. On the far side was a yacht club with a toilet and shower block. Next to it a restaurant, a café and a small supermarket. Because their initial connection with Squires had gone so smoothly, Sam felt things could only get worse, a suspicion that intensified when he sneaked a glance back down the pontoon.

'Shit . . .'

Nige was ambling along the decking behind them.

'Probably just needs the loo,' Midge suggested under her breath.

'Or keeping an eye on us for his master.'

They walked on.

'Oh my God . . .'

Sitting in the café was the plain-clothes policeman who'd radioed their berthing instructions. Dark trousers, striped shirt, portable VHF set on the table in front of him, he might as well have been in uniform.

Midge looked away in despair. Too late to shoo the man away. Nige was right behind. They walked quickly past the café and pushed open the door to the shop.

Thirty minutes later they returned to the boat carrying plastic bags of provisions, including a couple of bottles of overpriced Australian fizz. The sun had set by now and the sky was darkening. As they walked down the pontoon they could see Squires' lean face watching them from the deck of the *Estelle*. They sensed his suspicion, but when they drew near he held up a long glass, clouded with condensation.

'Hot work! What you need is one of these.'

'Great! Be over in a minute.' Sam swung the bags onto their own deck.

'What's your poison, Beth?'

'I'm a beer girl, Vince.' She gave him a cheery grin, trying to radiate a confidence she didn't feel.

'Beer for you too, Steve?'

Sam gave a thumbs up.

They stowed the shopping below, squeezed the wine bottles into the tiny fridge, then locked up again before stepping across to the other boat.

Jan, the prettier of the Thai women, gave Midge a warning glare. The other held out a limp hand for them to shake.

'How long you guys got for your vacation?' Squires asked, handing each a can of Singha Draft.

'A week,' Sam told him. 'Escaping the concrete of Singapore and smelling real air for a change. You?'

'Same idea. Poodling around for a few days, seeing the new century in.'

'What sort of business are you in, Vince?' Midge asked.

Sam flinched at the directness of her question.

'This and that.' The ex-soldier narrowed his eyes. 'Know this area?'

'First time here.' Sam took a swig of his beer.

For a while they chatted about anchorages and inlets, the price of prawns and which islands had provisioning and restaurants. A second beer followed the first, but Sam noticed Squires had moved onto soft drinks. Nige and Vicky took little part in the conversation, while Jan seemed more than a hanger-on because Squires kept turning to her for approval.

After a while Nige got restless, nudging Vicky until she got up and stepped into the saloon.

'We're eating soon,' Squires announced. 'Sorry we don't have enough to ask you to join us.'

'No problem,' said Sam, making to stand up.

'No rush,' Squires insisted. 'It'll be a while before she serves up. Finish your drink and tell us more about the two of you. Finance, you said. Doing what, exactly?'

'Investment management,' Sam replied, trying to give the words a mystique they didn't deserve. 'Private clients. People who want to use their money cleverly. Which means not losing it to the taxmen.'

'Or explaining where it comes from . . .' Squires suggested, playfully.

'We . . . we have to make sure it's in a useable form,' Sam cautioned.

'Of course.'

Tempting smells of hot ginger began to waft up from the galley below. Vicky emerged clutching cutlery which she plonked on the table.

Midge rested her hand on Sam's arm. 'Time we left these good people to their dinner, sweetie.'

Squires stood up. 'Nice to know you. If you're partying tomorrow night, give us a call on the VHF to say where you've dropped your hook.' He took Midge's arm as they stepped onto the pontoon. 'Give us a chance to get to know each other better.'

'Mmmm . . . I'd like that.' She put a leg up onto their own boat.

'You two been together long?' His eyes swept over her body like an airport scanner.

'A while,' said Sam, uncomfortably realising it was a detail they hadn't discussed.

'Nearly a year,' Midge added.

'See you in the morning then. Before you head off.' The drug-runner climbed back over the rail onto the *Estelle*.

Down in the saloon, they flopped onto the sofas, hunching forward so they could speak without being overheard.

'Now I know what fledglings feel like,' Midge whispered eventually. 'When a cat gets hold of them.' She tilted her head back and let out a long gasp of relief. The exposed ridge of her throat had a purity to it which Sam found disturbingly erotic.

The smell of the food on the *Estelle* had made him hungry. Midge read his mind.

'Try that restaurant next to the yacht club?' she suggested.

'Absolutely.'

Going ashore again would take his mind off the fact that in a couple of hours he'd be sharing a bed with this disconcertingly well-put-together woman, but with physical contact strictly taboo.

Friday, 31 December
Millennium Eve

Sam was woken by the daylight streaming in through the cabin window. Instantly alert, he sat up and peered out, fearing their neighbour might have slipped away in the night. But the *Estelle* was still there.

He swung his legs to the floor and listened. Rigging pinged against a mast nearby, signifying a breeze. Its sound triggered a yearning to be under sail.

The space where Midge had lain was empty. He found her in the galley making coffee, still wearing the tee-shirt and briefs she'd slept in. The sight of her neat behind and slim brown thighs as she stuck bread under the grill brought him fully awake.

'Been up long?' He rubbed his eyes. The bulkhead clock said 7.15.

'Half the bloody night. You were snoring like a walrus.'

'Sorry.'

'How does Julie put up with it?'

'Elbows me in the ribs and I turn over. If you hadn't been so against laying your hands on my body . . .'

'Yeah, yeah . . .'

'Any sign of life next door?'

'Nope.' She turned and looked quizzically at him. 'Who d'you reckon sleeps with whom over there?'

'Jimmy has Jan,' said Sam firmly.

'You'd think. Only he's not getting any. That guy was gagging for it last night. And why itch to make out with me if he had that little Thai poppet to play with?'

'Maybe you've got a better bum.'

She raised a contemptuous eyebrow. 'Seriously, I don't get the impression Jan's his playmate. She's more like a minder.'

'And Vicky?'

'Does the cooking – and anything else Nige wants. Looks to me like he found her in some bar. Not a very classy bar at that.'

'Thai police have anything on them?'

'Nothing useful. They tailed Jimmy to the airport, which is where Jan joined him. But they don't know who she is. The name on her ticket didn't fit anything on official records.'

'So,' Sam murmured, taking the coffee Midge offered him, 'where do we go from here, Inspector?'

'Whatever happens, we stick with him.'

'And if he doesn't tell us where he's going?'

'Then I'll have to make it clear I just can't bear to be parted from him.' She set her jaw, her eyes steely with determination.

After they'd breakfasted and tidied the saloon, she handed him the wrench he'd used on the engine.

'I found this on the floor. Don't want to nag, but it probably has a home.'

'Leave it by the cooker and I'll put it away in a while.'

They washed, put on shorts and fresh tee-shirts, then went on deck to top up the water tank from a hose on the pontoon.

It was well after nine before Squires made an appearance, leaning over the rail of the *Estelle*'s sundeck. When he spoke, there was a coolness to his voice that made them both uneasy.

'Off shortly, are you?'

'We were just talking about that,' Sam hedged. 'What about you?'

'The girls have gone shopping. Nige and I plan to relax until they get back. He's still in his pit, lazy bugger. Then we'll see. Might go north to Phang Nga, maybe over to Phi-Phi. Jan's got a friend visiting today.'

Sam's antennae twitched. There'd been no mention of a visitor last night.

'We still going to be able to toast the Millennium with you guys tonight?' Midge checked, stepping onto the foredeck and spreading out a towel to lie on.

'Maybe.' As Squires watched her apply cream to her legs, he smiled like a man who'd spotted a trap but who reckoned falling into it might be rather pleasurable. He turned his attention to Sam again. 'By the way, Steve, I was interested in what you were saying last night.'

There was something distinctly disingenuous about the way Squires said it.

'Anything in particular?'

'How you preserve confidentiality when you're hiding clients' money . . .'

It was as if Squires was testing him on his cover story, but he played along. No alternative. He talked about nominee holdings and anonymous accounts. Squires listened hard, putting in questions every few minutes.

'Interested for yourself?' Sam queried.

The drug trader half-smiled and shook his head. 'For a friend.'

It always was. 'I'll get you one of my cards. You can pass it on to him.'

A charade, but it couldn't be *him* that ended it. As he turned to enter the saloon Squires called after him.

'While you're at it, give me one of Beth's too.'

Sam rummaged in his bag for the visiting cards they'd printed the previous day. Then he felt the boat rock slightly. He looked through the window. Jimmy Squires had come aboard. Midge had sat up and was making room for him on the deck.

Sam re-emerged with the cards in his hand. Midge shot him a glare that said to leave her to get on with her seduction, so he climbed up to the bridge and pretended to busy himself with charts and the pilot book. Over on the *Estelle* Nige had surfaced. He was facing away from them, his eyes on the shore. Sam followed his gaze and saw the women returning. Squires had spotted them too and was hunching forward in anticipation.

Jan's 'friend' turned out to be male. An oriental, dressed in a white polo shirt and dark trousers. He strode purposefully towards them, scowling at their foredeck as if there was something seriously amiss there which needed dealing with immediately.

Sam sensed things were about to go horribly wrong. He saw the alarm on Midge's face and watched her pull her knees to her chest in an instinctive move to protect herself. He guessed she'd recognised the man.

By the time he'd clattered down to the deck, Squires was on his feet. Midge too, clutching the towel to her chest.

'Scuse me a minute . . .' she whispered, trying to slip away.

Squires hooked an arm round her and pinned her to his side.

'Don't disappear, darlin'. This bloke spends a lot of time in Singapore. You'll have things to talk about.'

The man approaching them looked more Chinese than Thai. A hard, square face with slicked back hair. He marched along the line of boats like a military commander, a small leather attaché case under his arm.

Midge began to panic. 'Get off me!' she snapped, struggling to escape Squires' grip. But the drug-runner had no plans to let her go.

Sam sprang forward and wrenched Squires' arm from her shoulders. Midge ducked away and stumbled across the deck towards the saloon. The former soldier bunched his fists.

'I don't know who the fuck you two jokers are, my friend . . .' He raised his right hand as if to give it to Sam full on the nose, but instead the fingers formed into the shape of a pistol which he jabbed against the middle of his forehead. 'But if I come across you again, you're dead!'

Holding his gaze for a couple of seconds, he turned away and hopped onto the pontoon, a hand snaking out to greet his guest.

Sam ducked inside the saloon, heart pounding. Midge was scrabbling through lockers. 'Handset . . .' she hissed. 'Where the fuck's the . . .?'

Sam pulled the police radio from a drawer and gave it to her.

'Tell me . . .'

'Know his face.' She turned the set on. 'From photos in the files. Works for Yang Lai, the guy I was telling you about. Golden Triangle. He's number two or three in the organisation. Name's Hu Sin. And for some reason I can't explain, the bastard seems to know *me*.'

From outside there was an explosive roar as the *Estelle*'s engines started up. Sam heard feet on the deck and spun round.

Hu Sin filled the doorway. In his hand was a gun, its barrel extended by a silencer.

Sam stopped breathing. Midge had the handset to her mouth, but couldn't speak, transfixed by the pistol levelled at her head.

Packer backed against the galley counter, remembering the wrench they'd left on the worktop. Fingers closing round its shaft, he lunged forward, cracking it down on Hu Sin's arm.

The man yelped and the gun clattered to the floor. Midge unfroze and made a dive for it. His face twisting with pain, Hu Sin spun round and fled the saloon. The policewoman grappled with the pistol and took aim.

'Leave him!' Sam snapped. 'He's not the one you want.'

They heard the clunk of feet on the finger pontoon as mooring lines were freed. Then the engine noise declined as the *Estelle* reversed from the berth.

'Fuck!' Midge hissed. 'Fuck, fuck, fuck!'

'*How* does he know you?' Sam growled, furious at coming so close to death for a cause she'd told him so little about.

'*I don't know* . . .' she howled. Then she caught herself, put a fist to her mouth and closed her eyes. She'd remembered.

Through the wide stern window of the saloon they saw the *Estelle* accelerate away. Jimmy Squires was at the wheel. On the cruiser's aft deck Jan and Hu Sin stood side by side, the man talking on a mobile phone, the woman clicking with a long-lensed camera.

Sam turned his face away. Theirs was a photo album he had no wish to grace.

2

They had their bags packed within minutes. The charter agent
looked outraged when they returned the boat keys and asked for a taxi
to the airport.

'But, this is New Year Eve,' he protested, as if no sane person would
abandon plans for a millennium celebration.

Their haste to get away was being driven by Midge.

'Hu Sin was on the phone. You saw. Yang Lai's mob won't waste time.
People who get in their way don't live long.'

At the airport they hid in a crowd of European tourists, then got lucky at
the check-in. An extra flight had been put on for the busy Bangkok run
and within minutes they were boarding an Airbus.

They spoke little on the flight, but by the time they landed in the Thai
capital an hour later both had recovered their composure.

'It was that twat of a narcotics agent at the marina café,' Midge muttered,
as they walked through the terminal to the baggage collection. 'Might as
well have had a label on his head.'

With their luggage on a trolley they queued at an agency desk to find a
hotel.

'*Two* rooms,' Midge stressed, to the surprise of the girl behind the
counter.

They took a taxi to the centre, checked in to an anonymous tourist
monolith and began the painful process of reporting back to their
respective headquarters, agreeing to meet up later.

Sam was startled by his controller's lack of concern. The man was a dry
Ulsterman called Duncan Waddell.

'It was an Oz operation, Sam. From what you've just told me, no mud
will stick to the firm.'

'That's hardly the point, Duncan. Jimmy Squires . . .'

'They'll catch him eventually,' Waddell interjected. 'And when they do, our concerns about the man will be history. Essentially he's their problem, not ours.'

Clean hands. All that mattered to a bureaucrat.

'Anyone who threatens to kill me is *my* problem,' Sam snapped.

'You're off the case, and that's an order. Look, the main reason for getting you involved was that we owed the Aussies a favour. You did the deed. Now we're evens.'

But Sam wasn't. And he wouldn't be until Jimmy Squires was sorted out.

After finishing his call to London, he went into the streets and found one of the internet booths that dot the centre of Bangkok. He dialled into his email and downloaded a couple of messages. One was from Julie wishing him a Happy New Year. The other had been sent by his controller just after he'd left Singapore – a more detailed background file on Jimmy Squires. He printed it, checked there were no copies stored on the computer, posted a reply to Julie saying he'd try to ring her later, then logged off.

It was early evening before he and Midge met up again. She came to his room and her eyes suggested she'd been crying.

'Problems?' he asked.

She screwed up her face, making out it didn't matter.

'Gave me a roasting, that's all.'

'I'm sorry.'

'I'll get over it.'

He told her about his email. 'There's some personal stuff on Squires. Comments from his former mates. Adds a little colour.'

'I'd like to see it.'

He handed her the printout. 'Basically it says he was never happier than sleeping in a ditch. Had a reputation for putting up with any amount of shit and terror so long as there was a good piss-up and a willing woman at the end of it. But a little out of his depth in the real world. And not used to handling big sums of money.'

'Times have changed, then.' She frowned down at the sheet of paper. 'What's all this about him being fascinated by military history? World War Two in particular.'

'Simply that his views on national characteristics are pretty much formed by the past. All Germans are Nazis . . . Japs are torturers. That sort of stuff. Half the UK population thinks that way.'

'And the people who use his smack are cockroaches, I suppose . . .'

'Yeah.' Once again her bitterness flagged some personal motive in her quest to nail the man. 'Don't worry. You'll get another crack at him.'

'Unless he gets his crack in first.' Her face was pale and drawn. 'I have to be honest, Steve. He's got me scared, him and Hu Sin.'

Sam wanted to give her a big hug and tell her it'd be okay, but feared she might sink her teeth into his neck. She handed the email back to him.

'Tell you what,' he suggested, 'why don't we find some cosy bar where they do food, and forget all about it for the night. It's New Year's Eve.'

'I don't want to go anywhere. Just for tonight I've lost my nerve.'

'Then let's get some booze and a takeaway and we'll eat here in my room.'

She agreed to that and he took himself off to a nearby shopping mall to get in supplies. On his way he paused by an international call centre, thinking of ringing Julie. Then he remembered Bangkok was seven hours ahead of London. She'd be at work. Better to wait until after midnight his time and try to catch her at home before she went out.

Three quarters of an hour later he and Midge started on the first bottle of Australian Chardonnay, with CNN's world coverage of the Millennium celebrations flickering on the TV in the corner. Midge ignored it. She was fidgeting.

'You asked why Hu Sin knew me,' she said eventually, thrusting fingers through her hair, then clenching them as if trying to tear the stuff out by its roots. 'I'll tell you why. I got photographed a few weeks ago. Walking into a government building in Bangkok. There was a Narcotics Bureau seminar going on. Meant to be covert, but *somebody* found out about it. The cameraman rode off on a motorbike.' She let out a long sigh. 'And here comes the confession. I didn't take it seriously enough. Should have changed my appearance afterwards. I've even kept the same bloody hair colour, Steve. Talk about unprofessional. They'll string me up when I get home.'

He reached across the table and squeezed her hand. 'Been there, done that.' He told her how he'd been snapped by a newspaper photographer in London a year ago and identified in the press as an MI6 agent. 'It's why I'm here. Sent to Singapore in the hope my face wouldn't be so familiar.'

'Thanks,' she said. 'I guess we all blow it sometime or other.'

They looked at one another across the table and knew what they had to do. The only possible way to see out a century that had ended so badly.

As they set about the task of getting drunk, easing the wine's impact with plates of chicken, prawns, noodles and rice, Sam did his best to lighten the mood by indulging in a little mild flirtation. This was a woman who'd shared his bed and shown no interest in having sex with him – a challenge, if ever there was. But Midge didn't respond to his gentle advances. Hardly noticed them, her mind firmly elsewhere.

Soon the TV in the corner began emitting whoops and cries as people closer to the international dateline began welcoming the new century. Midge glanced at the screen and raised her glass.

'To a better world,' she said sombrely.

'Fat chance,' Sam replied, emptying his again.

At 9.00 p.m. Bangkok time, it was Australia's turn to enter the year 2000 and they swung their chairs towards the screen. Midge hugged herself and bit her lip as the Sydney Harbour Bridge erupted with fireworks. A few moments later she fell apart, tears streaming down her cheeks. Sam moved his chair next to hers and put an arm round her shoulder. She sobbed into his shirt.

'Shit! I'm *not* going to *do* this . . .' She dried her face on one of the napkins that had come with the food, then cut the TV sound and turned her back on the set. 'Jee-sus! They're only bloody *fireworks*.'

As the hours ticked on towards their own midnight, she drank with a growing determination. Her conversation began to ramble. Sam got an impression of a life peopled by bosses out to get her and by male colleagues jealous of her success.

Before long the name 'Barry' began featuring in her babble. Sam soon twigged the man had been a teenage sweetheart, but was now dead. A 'loveable loser' she called him, someone who'd dropped out of the rat race just when she began winning heats.

'So your ways parted,' Sam suggested.

'I guess we had different expectations of life.'

'But you went on loving him?'

'Sure I did.' She chewed her lip again. 'Then he passed away. In a squat. Poisoned by contaminated heroin.'

'I'm sorry.' Now he understood why her pursuit of Jimmy Squires had become a crusade.

'It's history,' she insisted, but Sam knew it was her present too. He felt powerfully drawn to her. Women with tortured pasts were as tempting to him as caviar.

By the time Bangkok's midnight approached they were both extremely sozzled. When the hour struck and the city beyond the hotel windows began clattering with firecrackers, they slumped together in a Millennium embrace. Midge made no attempt to end it this time, so he kissed her. When she still didn't push him away, he put a hand on her breast and was encouraged by the sound of her breath quickening.

Her face was a blur to him. He cupped it in his hands and tried to articulate his feelings.

'Wanna go to bed with you.'

'I guessed.'

'Make love.'

'Not for a zizz, then?'

His brain was alert enough to realise that although joking with him she wasn't saying no.

'Historic moment,' he mumbled, hopes rising along with his relevant body part. 'Be able to tell your gran'children how you cebre . . . *celebrated* the great 2K. Did it with a bang . . .' He grinned at the silliness of his joke. 'Unique opportunity. Always regret it if we don't . . .'

He began trying to get her tee-shirt off, but his hands seemed to have lost their dexterity. She stopped him, her face twisting into a sloppy smile.

'I don't even know how old you are,' she said, as if it mattered.

'Gonna be forty this year,' he told her sombrely.

'Guessed as much.' She wobbled to her feet, keeping her eyes playfully on his, then groped her way to the door. 'Don' go away.' She stepped out into the corridor.

In his hormone-pickled mind he imagined she was returning to her own room for condoms, but she didn't return. After a few minutes he looked into the passageway. Her room was opposite and the door was closed. A Do Not Disturb tag hung from the handle.

The next morning when he eventually came round from a head-rumbling sleep, he discovered she'd checked out at dawn and taken a cab to the airport.

Not feeling up to a phone conversation with Julie, he sent her an email apologising for failing to ring her the night before. Then in the evening he flew back to Singapore. On the plane he reread the backgrounder on Jimmy Squires. It wasn't enough. Service record stuff. He wanted more. The inside track on the man. Everything, down to the size of his shoes. He knew a man in London who might help, an SAS officer currently running a desk in the MoD. He resolved to contact him.

His controller's cavalier attitude to the Squires case had annoyed him. The ex-special forces man *was* their concern. UK government had given the sergeant precious skills and now he was misusing them.

When he returned to his flat overlooking Singapore's Botanical Gardens, Packer plugged in his laptop and composed an email to Duncan Waddell, setting out reasons why he should stay on the case.

Then he remembered a message he'd left in his outbox waiting to be sent. A resignation letter he'd penned a couple of days ago in response to Julie's threat to pull the plug on him.

Things had changed. He opened the file and deleted it.

3

Singapore Airlines flight SQ 322 to London
The night of Wednesday 5 to Thursday 6 January 2000

HE HATED LONG flights, particularly at night. Seated on the aisle, he'd decided to ignore the movies and try to sleep, but with little success. He'd twisted his body into endless new positions, but each time he nodded off one of the two beer-swilling Scots sitting to his right would scramble over his legs to take a leak.

He was being summoned back to London, not because they'd responded positively to his email on Jimmy Squires, but to be briefed on a totally new operation. He'd protested strongly, but had been told once again that the former SAS man was none of his business any more.

The good side of going home was that for the next few days he would be with Julie. She'd sounded over the moon when he'd phoned her – having given him a hard time on the 1st of January for his silence on New Year's Eve.

In the row behind him a child began to cry. Sam groaned and conceded defeat, undoing the lap strap and standing up to extend his legs. A few others were doing the same. They passed in the darkened cabin like spectres seeking release from their earthly shackles. At the back of the plane where the aisle was wider he paused for a stretch, raising himself up and down on his toes. He looked at the rows of slumbering bodies. The woman nearest was elderly, but had her head resting on her partner's shoulder. It affected him.

It was a moment or two before he recognised the emotion fluttering weakly in his chest as envy. He was nearly forty. Halfway to a natural death and he'd still not experienced what these people had. A lasting partnership. A sense of belonging with another human being. He wondered what had united this particular couple. Brilliant sex? Or something mundane like a fondness for country walks?

He let his eyes wander up and down the aisles. Most of the passengers seemed to be travelling in pairs.

Settling into married life wasn't something he'd consciously avoided. Simply that he'd met few obvious candidates. His ten years as a Royal Navy officer had seen plenty of decent women putting themselves his way, level-headed creatures longing to envelop his life in soft furnishings. But he hadn't wanted them. The women who turned him on were the hard cases. The ambitious and dissatisfied. The unhappily marrieds. Those with a past.

Julie was one of those. And in the next few days he would have to make up his mind about her.

Sam knew that if he were to pop the question, she would say yes. And the auguries weren't bad. They managed to spend time together without getting on each other's nerves. They were more than compatible in bed. And he was pretty sure he loved her and she loved him. What held him back was the same thing that had stopped him in the past. The fear of choosing wrongly and regretting it for a long, long time.

Something else worried him. His own inability to resist temptation. If Midge had played along on New Year's Eve, he'd have felt no guilt. Would have treated it as a bit of fun, irrelevant to his relationship with Julie. But the state of marriage would demand different standards of him.

He looked down at the elderly couple again. The way their bodies propped each other up said 'trust'. And trusting anybody, particularly a woman, was something he'd never mastered.

He drifted back up the aisle. The Scots appeared to be unconscious – the alcohol had won.

Back in his seat, before he fell asleep again, it was Midge his thoughts kept turning to. His desire to know her better felt like a dull ache begging to be rubbed.

Julie had come into his sights fifteen months ago. She worked at a virology lab in the centre of London. He'd gone there to interview her about the murder of her father, an arms trader gunned down in Africa, and had been attracted to her immediately. By the end of his investigation they'd become lovers.

She'd refused to join him in the Far East when the Intelligence Service decided to re-base him there nearly a year ago – she valued her job too much and had a young son whose stability and security she was determined to preserve. So they'd continued the relationship at long distance, emails and phone calls backed by a couple of visits, one in each direction. But now Julie had laid it on the line – if they couldn't be together again soon there was no point in going on. She hadn't said what had brought things to a head, but he suspected it was Christmas – the fact that work hadn't allowed him to return to England to spend it with her.

The flight landed a few minutes early, but by the time the baggage came through it was well after 7.00 before he was on the road to London. A bright January day, with frost coating the embankments along the motorway. The cab driver was a chatty type, so Sam feigned sleep.

The flat where Julie lived and where Sam kept a few of his possessions was in Ealing, to the west of the city. His half share of the rent allowed Julie to live in more comfort than could be afforded on a Health Service salary. Her main expense was eight-year old Liam, the outcome of a short-lived college relationship. The boy lived with his grandmother in Suffolk, and Julie went there at weekends.

For him the flat was a statement too. A token of his commitment to returning to London and to her. It was in a large, converted Victorian house near the green, with a grey slate roof and wide sash windows. Sam paid off the driver, then pushed open the front door. Julie collided with him. Late as usual, she was hurrying for the tube.

'God, I've missed you,' she sighed, hooking her arms around him. He hugged her tight, feeling for her body beneath the thick coat. Her wispy brown hair smelled of rose petals. 'Oh God . . .' she moaned, pulling her head back and looking at him hungrily.

'Another ten minutes wouldn't make you any later,' Sam whispered.

'Yes it would. The professor's called a meeting for a quarter to nine. I'll have to run all the way to the tube as it is.'

'Tonight then.'

'I'll try to get back early.'

They kissed like honeymooners, then she tore herself away and hurried out of the door.

Sam entered the first floor flat. It was the only place in the world he could call home. He glanced into the living room. A small, tinsel-smothered tree stood in the window bay, almost devoid of its needles, the skeletal remains of the Christmas he'd missed. He walked into the bedroom. The duvet had been hurriedly tossed aside, the bed left unmade.

When he'd left for the Far East, he and Julie had had a rational, dispassionate discussion about sex. All very grown-up. But the thought that some other man might have been rolling in these sheets with her made his stomach twitch.

Sam Packer was tall and moderately stocky. His thick, dark hair had not yet begun to grey. In Singapore he used a gym to keep in shape, but this morning he felt spaced out. His body clock was seven hours ahead of London, mid-afternoon instead of breakfast time. He unpacked his bag and took a shower, then dressed in some of the winter clothes he'd left in the wardrobe a year ago. He walked into the small kitchen and made fresh coffee to take away the taste of the stuff on the plane. By the time he felt ready to face the world it was nearly ten. He rang his controller to check in.

'Welcome back!' Duncan Waddell had a much deeper voice than seemed right for a man of diminutive stature. The accent betrayed his Ulster upbringing. 'I thought we'd do our briefing over lunch, if that suits.'

'A scoff at the tax-payer's expense . . .'

'Tch! Careless talk. You'll have a Parliamentary Oversight Committee breathing down our necks.'

'D'you have somewhere in mind?'

'There's a Spanish restaurant in Pimlico that has little alcoves where we won't be overheard. I've booked a table for one o'clock.'

He gave the address and they rang off.

Sam had a couple of hours to kill before taking the underground into the centre of town. He paced round the flat, pausing to peer from the windows, then let his eyes fall on the things that were his in the place. A pair of armchairs in the living room, a few maritime prints on the walls and an old bracket clock that had once belonged to his father. He'd owned his own apartment for several years, until forced to bed hop when the address became known to people out to kill him. Most of his meagre stock of furniture had been in store ever since.

Sam had been told nothing about his new operation. Waddell had refused to say on the phone. The travel and the time shift had left him feeling out of touch, so he put on a warm coat and slipped out of the house to buy a fistful of newspapers. There were no world crises troubling his fellow countrymen, it turned out. The headlines were all about a 'flu epidemic.

Two hours later Packer emerged at the top of the escalator at Pimlico. It was five to one. The cream-painted terraces of Bessborough Gardens gleamed in the wintry sun. After the humid heat of the Far East, he found the crisp winter air invigorating. He walked west towards the restaurant his controller had chosen. Suddenly a hand on his arm made him jump.

'Well met!' It was Duncan Waddell, dressed in a long black coat with the collar turned up. They shook hands. 'Coping with the cold okay?'

'Nice change, actually.'

They strode on. 'Next turning on the right. Good flight?'

'Passable.'

When they reached the restaurant, warm food smells wafted up from the basement. Their coats were taken by a waiter who introduced himself without irony as Manuel and they were shown to their alcove. Waddell ordered a bottle of sparkling mineral water, then waited for the server to be out of earshot.

'Ever been to Japan?' he asked. He had a pointed, terrier face, and fired the question like a dart.

'No.'

'Interesting lot.'

'Yes?' Sam waited to be told what this was about.

'This culture they have. Honour and duty . . .' Waddell broke a bread roll and bit off a piece. His short, fair hair was showing hints of white. 'The need to expiate guilt about the past . . .'

'Are we talking about the guilt of a nation or an individual?'

'The latter.'

'Ah.' The first clue of where the conversation was heading.

'Tetsuo Kamata's guilt,' Waddell explained cryptically. 'You've heard of him?'

'Should I have?'

'If you'd been keeping up with your London press summaries . . .' the headquarters man chided. 'Walsall car factory? About to close with the loss of thousands of jobs?'

'Ah, yes. Read about it this morning. Some Jap manufacturer wants to buy it and produce cars for Europe.'

'That's right. The Matsubara Motor Corporation. Trying to nudge Toyota and Nissan aside for a bigger place in world markets.'

Sam's recollection widened. 'There was a picture in the *Guardian*. Some minister salivating at the prospect of jobs being saved. Marginal seat? By-election expected?'

'Exactly.' Waddell clasped his hands to underline the seriousness of the case. 'The government is setting huge store by this deal going through, Sam. It's not just the jobs at the Walsall factory, it's loads of others in the area that are dependent on car manufacturing. Tens of thousands will find themselves in trouble if the plant closes. You know the score . . .'

'So what's that got to do with you and me sitting here?'

'Tetsuo Kamata is the chairman of Matsubara.'

'I'd just about worked that out.'

'Problem is it's him and him alone who's insisting the new factory be in Britain. The rest of his board want it somewhere in the Eurozone.'

'Which might make more sense.'

'Financially. But that's not what Kamata's most concerned about.'

Their discourse was interrupted by the return of the waiter. They browsed the menu quickly. Waddell suggested garlic soup followed by roast suckling pig.

'They do it crisp as a biscuit here.'

'Fine,' said Sam.

'*Sopa de Ajo* and *Cochinillo Asado*, Manuel,' said Waddell in his best Spanish accent.

The waiter bowed his head and was gone.

'So . . .' Sam pressed, 'what *is* Kamata concerned about?'

'I'll tell you a little story. Oh, but first . . . any idea how old Kamata is?'

'Not a clue.'

'Nearly eighty.'

'Christ! No pensions at Matsubara?'

'Took over the reins of the company from his father. Won't give them up while he's still got strength in his arms.'

'What's his age got to do with anything?'

'A lot. The story starts in 1943 when Tetsuo Kamata was a young officer in the Japanese Army, carrying out his Imperial duty in Burma. His unit captured several British soldiers. You know about the Chindits?'

'Wingate's lot. Airdropped behind Japanese lines. Aiming to terrorise the enemy with sabotage raids. An awful lot of them died.'

'Exactly. A particularly low survival rate amongst the few who got caught. Sixty per cent of those imprisoned ended up being buried in Burma.'

They paused again as the soup was set in front of them.

'That's quick,' Sam muttered.

'They have a huge vat of it out there. Everybody orders it.' Waddell savoured the liquid with half-closed eyes. 'Last time I had this was in Seville earlier in the year,' he murmured.

'Holiday?'

'No. International security conference.'

'Getting around these days, aren't we?' Sam had always seen Waddell as a back office man. He tasted the soup too. 'But you're right. This is good. Go on about Kamata.'

'Well he was as brutal as any of them. Used to personally supervise interrogation sessions. Holding a hose over the face until lungs and stomach were filled with water.'

'Nice chap. His past is public knowledge?'

'It is now. The tabloids have been having a field day. Monster turned angel – all that sort of stuff. Anyway, as you've probably gathered, Tetsuo Kamata's most recent actions are motivated by the desire to make amends.'

'A late attack of remorse.'

'You could say that.'

'What brought that on?'

'Time, I think. Fifty years of thinking about it.'

'Did they do him for war crimes after the Jap defeat?'

'Absolutely. He was incarcerated in Rangoon prison until early '49. But when he got home, his war record was brushed under the carpet. As you know, in those days in Japan the gory details of what the Emperor's warriors did to their enemies were never discussed. Men returning from the prisons of the Far East were treated as war heroes, not criminals.'

'So Kamata junior slipped comfortably into the family business?'

'And rose steadily in the hierarchy, until he became chairman on his father's death in 1980.'

'War record conveniently forgotten.'

'Looked that way. But things began to change in Japan when Emperor Hirohito pegged out in 1989. People no longer felt the need to maintain a respectful silence about the war. Talked about it openly for the first time. And eventually – ten years later to be exact – this new spirit of openness filtered through to Kamata. He maintains he'd been racked with guilt for a long time but didn't have the courage to address it until the national culture changed. Anyway, he decided to try to make amends to those he'd maltreated. Did it anonymously at first with donations to British ex-servicemen's organisations. Then he got braver and decided to try telling his former victims in person that he was sorry for what he'd done. Those still alive.'

'That must've taken quite a lot of courage.'

'Worries about the afterlife were what was driving him, I think. Whatever, he was desperate for them to pardon him.'

'Fat chance! Or?'

'Some were prepared to forgive, but others refused to have anything to do with him. Which is what stung him into making a much bigger gesture. Towards the whole British nation. Just in time for Christmas . . .'

'Even if it amounted to financial folly for his company.'

'Exactly.'

'And his directors are letting him?'

'No choice. What Kamata says goes. While he's still *alive* . . .' Waddell fixed Sam with a meaningful look.

'I see.' At last he understood where this was leading.

The waiter reappeared suddenly. They'd finished their soup. He cleared the plates and scraped breadcrumbs from the cloth. Sam waited until he'd left before posing the obvious question.

'You're saying there's some doubt about how long Kamata will *stay* alive?'

'Yes.'

'Because of his age?'

'No. Kamata's surprisingly sprightly. A natural death is not seen as likely in the near future. No. The problem's of a different complexion.'

'One of his victims wants revenge?'

'Precisely.'

'But they're all geriatrics.'

'Doesn't matter.'

Sam pondered for a moment. There had to be a reason why they'd brought him back from Singapore for this.

'And this former victim – he's resident in my neck of the woods?'

'Resident, no. But since his target seldom leaves the Far East we're assuming that's where he might try to do the deed.'

'This is getting more far-fetched by the minute. Who is he?'

'Peregrine Harrison.'

'Never heard of him.'

'Usually known as Perry. He wrote a book about his experiences in Burma. Came out in the 1970s. Gave some vivid descriptions of the techniques used on him, with a particular reference to a certain unidentified Japanese Lieutenant who'd ordered the water torture and had him beaten senseless a few times.'

'How old is Perry?'

'Seventy-seven.'

'And full of piss and wind, no doubt,' Sam protested. 'You're not seriously suggesting he could hunt Kamata down?'

'He has the determination for it. In his book he was quite specific about what he hoped to see happen to his tormentor – if he could ever be traced. Wanted him strung up by his hands until the sun dried him to a husk.'

'But you said the book came out twenty, thirty years ago. Harrison must have mellowed since then.'

'Apparently not.' Waddell's eyes lit up. The suckling pig had arrived. 'Pretty as a picture.'

'Smells good,' Sam agreed. He was seeing his controller in a new light. Until now he'd thought him devoid of normal human appetites.

When they were on their own again, Waddell leaned forward, eager not to lose momentum.

'The point is this. It was only in December that Tetsuo Kamata had to go fully public about his past. After Matsubara made its surprise bid to take over the Walsall factory one of the old soldiers who'd been approached privately by him revealed what was behind the gesture.'

'You mean *we* didn't know Kamata's motive at that point?' Sam asked, surprised. 'Or his record?'

Waddell shook his head. 'Never occurred to anybody to check. Anyway, when the press told Kamata's story, Peregrine Harrison realised this had to be the man who'd tortured *him*. A man whose name he'd never known.'

'Must've been quite a moment for him.'

'It was. So much so that he wrote a letter to *The Times* about it. Arrived on New Year's Eve, but wasn't published. You'll see why when you read the last line.'

Waddell wiped his mouth with a napkin, then pulled a photocopy from his jacket pocket. Sam unfolded the sheet and held it towards the light. The first paragraph was stirring stuff. A call for Britons to stand up for principle and refuse to accept the blood-stained money of a Japanese monster.

'Can't imagine this'd cut much mustard in the working-men's-clubs in Walsall.'

'Dead right. What they want in the Midlands is work, and they don't care who's paying the wages. Pork good?'

'Excellent.' Sam read on to the end.

It would be foolhardy in the extreme for the British Government to support Matsubara's offer to take over the Walsall works. It is predicated entirely on the autocratic decision of one man. Remove that man and the Matsubara board will instantly reverse the decision, leaving the Walsall workforce in the lurch. And make no mistake about it, now that Tetsuo Kamata has finally owned up to his dreadful past, his sudden and bloody removal from this life can only be a matter of time.

Sam stroked his chin. 'I see what you mean . . .'

'That's a threat in anybody's language, Sam. People who know him say Peregrine Harrison is still as fixated about his torturer as he was fifty-five years ago. *And* . . .'

Waddell leaned forward with his knife poised over his plate

'. . . since writing that letter Harrison has disappeared. Gone to ground, Sam. Why? Why else but to lay a trap for the Jap?'

He put his cutlery down and sat back.

'Even if it kills the careers of several thousand car workers in the Midlands.'

'Perry Harrison's driven by obsession. Other people's wage packets don't rank high on his list of priorities.'

'And the fact you've summoned me back from Singapore to tell me all this means the firm's been told to stop him?'

'Exactly. The PM is adamant. Says it's a matter of vital national importance. It's not just the Matsubara Motor Corporation he's worried about. If we let a British national murder one of Japan's top businessmen because of something that happened over fifty years ago, the knock-on effect on Japanese investment in this country could be devastating. There must be hundreds of thousands of people in Britain working for Jap companies.'

Sam couldn't quite understand where his own particular talents and experience fitted in with such a mission. 'This is a police matter, surely.'

'Absolutely. But the PM wants us in on it too.'

'The key is to find Harrison.'

'Of course.'

'And it's the police who have the resources and the international connections. *I*, on the other hand, still have a highly significant narcotics case on my hands involving a rogue SAS man.'

Waddell spread his hands dismissively. 'You're overlooking something.'

'What?'

'Harrison is somewhat unconventional.'

'So?'

'So the PM felt an *unconventional* approach to finding him should also be tried – and he thought of you.'

'He asked for me personally?' Sam asked incredulously.

'More or less. He remembered we'd moved you to the Far East after you'd cracked open the Lucifer Network. And since it's highly likely that's where Harrison's gone, he thought you were the man for the job.'

Sam pushed his plate away. The food had been good but he'd suddenly lost his appetite.

'The Far East is a mighty big area, Duncan. Do we have *any* idea what country Harrison's in?'

'No. The people at the school aren't being very helpful.'

'*What* school?' The man was talking in code.

'Sorry. I've jumped ahead. Let me give you some history.'

He refilled his glass with mineral water and offered the bottle to Sam, who by now was thinking a real drink would be more appropriate.

'In the period immediately after the war Perry Harrison had a pretty bad time of it. His health was a right mess after a couple of years in the hands of the Japanese. Both physically and mentally. In those days the armed forces didn't have counselling. Stress disorders weren't recognised. The men coming back from the prison camps were supposed to put their awful experiences behind them and be thankful they were alive. Well, Harrison had a couple of nervous breakdowns. Even tried to top himself once. All this stuff's in his book – I've got a copy for you in my briefcase. Anyway, eventually he met a woman who helped sort him out. She was a nurse actually – at one of the clinics where they tried to unscramble his brain. He married her and became a schoolmaster – minor prep school, that sort of thing. Some place where you didn't need teaching qualifications so long as you were a bit barmy and looked the part.'

'What did he teach?'

'Don't know. Anyway, it didn't last long. He left his wife, and one child by then, and went back to Burma.'

'*Burma?* I'd have thought he wouldn't ever want to see the place again.'

'Oh he loves Burma. Brought up there, you see.'

'You didn't tell me that.'

'Sorry. Yes. His father managed a rubber plantation or something. Young Peregrine spent the first thirteen years of his life in Burma before being sent to boarding school in England. It was one of the reasons he volunteered to join Wingate's mob. He knew the country. Loved its people and was ready to do anything to free them from the Japs.'

Sam scratched his head. 'I thought the Burmese welcomed the Japs in. As a way of getting rid of *us*.'

'A lot of them did. But it didn't take them long to discover their new friends were even more arrogant and self-serving than their old masters.'

'So what did Harrison do when he went back to Burma? Did he plan to live there permanently?'

'I don't think Harrison's the sort who *ever* makes plans that are permanent . . .' Waddell pursed his lips, realising the same could be said of Sam. 'Bit of a rolling stone. Anyway, he got work with a timber exporting company and it wasn't long before he was shacked up with a Burmese woman. They had a couple of kids. Then a few years later, when Ne Win's lunatic regime plunged the country into socialism and began nationalising all the businesses, he left her too. Came back to England.'

'Fickle fellow.'

'Yes. But the women seemed to love him for it. His English wife welcomed him back, even after nine years away. Of course, the fact he'd inherited some money might have had something to do with it. Quite a lot of money actually. From an aunt he'd never met. But he only stayed with his wife for a year, just long enough to get to know their son who was about twelve. Then he buggered off again.'

'Burma?'

'No. Cambridgeshire. To found a sort of commune.'

'We're in the 1960s by now.'

'Precisely. Buddhism and free love. An odd cocktail. He used his inheritance to buy an old manor house with farm attached at a place called Bordhill. Surrounded himself with flower people. They produced most of their own food. Doing it organically long before the supermarkets picked up on the word. And he started a school for misfit teenagers. A sort of sixth form college with lessons in *life* instead of A-levels.'

'This is the school you referred to before?'

'Yes. They call it the Bordhill Community.'

'So it's still functioning?'

'It is. But catering for adults now rather than teenagers. There was some scandal in the early years involving sexual relations between the staff and the pupils. Harrison came close to being charged with corrupting minors. Some of the pupils were barely sixteen. So nowadays it's people in their late twenties and thirties mostly. Sad types searching for themselves.'

'Aren't we all . . .'

Waddell looked uncomfortable.

'The point is, Bordhill's something of a cult. Oh, reasonably benign by all accounts. No reports of people held against their will. But people stay because they fall under the spell of Perry Harrison. Women particularly.'

'Even now he's seventy-seven.'

'Apparently.'

'The people at the school aren't being co-operative, you said.'

'That's right. There's a woman called Ingrid Madsen who runs things. Danish, I think. She's told the police she doesn't know where Harrison is. The last time she saw him was the day before that letter arrived at *The Times*.'

'Convenient. What's being done to try to find him?'

'Everything you'd expect. Requests for help sent to foreign police and immigration services.'

'You're being open about it? Telling them we suspect he intends to take out Tetsuo Kamata?'

'No way. This Matsubara deal is extremely sensitive. Nothing's been signed yet. And if Kamata or his company learn there's a threat to his life, he might just decide to pull out. The government doesn't want anything public about this. No. We've said we want to question Harrison about his financial affairs.'

Sam shook his head. 'I have to say I still find the idea of a seventy-seven year old planning a revenge killing rather hard to believe.'

Waddell lifted his briefcase onto his lap and opened it. 'You won't when you've read his book.' He handed over a volume whose dust-jacket had a torn corner. 'It'll give you a flavour of the man. Look, first thing I want you to do is make some excuse to visit the people at Bordhill. See if you can glean anything the police didn't. Then we'll ship you back to your usual beat.'

'But *where*, Duncan?'

'That's the trouble. We don't know yet. We can pretty well rule out Japan. Kamata is hard to get at there. And Japan is a country Harrison detests. Never been there so far as we know. Not the likely scene for a killing. But Kamata travels in the area quite a lot. Still very hands-on. Matsubara has business interests in most countries in the region. We're trying to get a sight of his travel plans for the coming months. Through our commercial attaché in Tokyo,' Waddell added sheepishly.

'With minimal hope of success.'

'Quite. The Japs are a particularly hard lot to crack. Naturally secretive. Genuinely inscrutable.' He produced a manila envelope from his case and handed it over. 'This is some more background on Harrison and the school.' Waddell flicked out his arm to look at his watch. 'Heavens! I've a meeting in twenty minutes.' He summoned the waiter for the bill.

'You don't . . . you don't think you're imagining this threat?' Sam suggested tentatively.

'Unfortunately not.'

'But you seem to be basing it on three pieces of purely circumstantial evidence. An emotional letter to a newspaper, a book written twenty-five years ago, and the fact that we don't know where Harrison is. I mean, he might be visiting a relative in Scunthorpe for all we know.'

Waddell signed a credit-card slip, adding a precise 10 per cent for a tip. They got up and by the time they reached the stairs, the waiter had retrieved their coats.

Outside in the street a light rain was falling. Waddell produced a small umbrella from his briefcase, holding it over their heads as they walked back towards Vauxhall Bridge.

'No, Sam. I don't think we're imagining it. You see, one other piece of information emerged this morning. Two weeks ago Harrison set up a trust and put all his assets into it. The premises for the Bordhill Community, his remaining capital, the lot.'

'So?'

Waddell stopped and fixed Sam with a look that said *for Christ's sake start taking this seriously, chum.*

'The lawyer who prepared the deeds told us he gained the impression his client wasn't expecting to be around for much longer.'

Sam stared back obstinately. If he was to be forced into this mission, he would make them spell out the reasons for it line by line. 'And from that you deduced . . .'

'That for Peregrine Harrison, killing Kamata is so goddam important he's ready to die in the process.'

4

As he made his way back to Ealing on the tube, Sam flicked cynically through the pages of Harrison's book, unable to convince himself the threat was real. The way he saw it, the PM had told SIS to jump and the buck had been passed to Waddell, who'd put *his* name in the frame. Simple as that. Days, weeks of effort were about to be wasted. Then Peregrine Harrison would reappear, asking why all the fuss.

The cold weather was beginning to get to him. The thought of prowling around the windswept flatlands of Cambridgeshire looking for Harrison's Bordhill community did not appeal. Spending the next couple of days in bed with Julie *did*.

When he arrived at the flat he browsed through the file Waddell had given him, finding most of the contents merely duplicated what he'd learned at lunch. Then he opened Harrison's book again, *A Jungle Path to Hell*, and began reading it more seriously.

The opening chapter was written in the clipped style of a previous age, telling of a school leaver's excitement about joining the army in the late summer of 1940. Despite the recent and salutary lesson of Dunkirk, the war had still been an adventure to him.

My upbringing in Burma made me a natural for service in the Pacific and after basic training I was shipped out to Rangoon, considering myself a lucky blighter not to have been dispatched to the deserts of north Africa. A year later however, our belief that the Japs would never dare take on the British in Burma and Malaya received a nasty shock. They invaded with great strength, remarkable speed and with the tactics to outwit our own rather incompetent commanders. There began a retreat for us which involved trekking through a thousand miles of jungle before reaching the safety of India.

Harrison wrote movingly of the loss of hundreds of his comrades to disease and Japanese bullets during that withdrawal, and expressed a deep concern for his parents who'd been living at a hill station near Mandalay. He'd feared his father's determination not to yield his property to the invaders had put them into the hands of the Japanese.

Unfortunately my fears proved justified. When I eventually reached India I managed to trace some friends of theirs who confirmed my father's insane intent to defend his property to the end. Where they died, I do not know. Sadly their bodies have never been found.

Sam skim-read the next section in which Harrison stepped back a decade to dwell on his Burmese childhood. An idyllic upbringing by all accounts, with a mother who spoiled him, partly out of her own obsessive love, and partly to compensate for the aloofness of his father. Harrison wrote fondly of his early interest in Buddhism. He told of friends he'd made with Burmese of his own age – not common amongst the colonials – and about the attractively gentle customs of the country.

It was a place where children seldom seemed to misbehave. They had an extraordinary tolerance of one another, which even at that young age I found admirable. It proved a rude shock for me therefore, when, at the age of thirteen, I was transported from there and thrust into the mêlée of an English boarding school, where very different standards of behaviour applied.

Then the narrative jumped forward again to 1942. Harrison had been selected for the Chindits. He described forced marches through mosquito-infested jungles in north-east India, part of a gruelling seven-month training to prepare for survival in the Burmese bush. Their eventual insertion had been by glider, crash-landing onto clearings hacked out of the forests by advance parties of American paratroop engineers.

That first Chindit operation was certainly not short on daring, both in its conception and its execution. The Japs were rattled to discover that we British could fight a guerrilla war as well as them, but teaching them that lesson was done at great cost to us in resources and in lives. The sad truth is that the first Chindit deployment of which I was a part achieved little.

Sam heard the front door opening. He looked up from the book and glanced at his watch. Nearly six and Julie was back. He stood up and walked into the small hall. Hanging up her coat, she gave a little laugh of pleasure at seeing him.

Julie Jackman had grey-green eyes, shiny brown hair and wide cheekbones. She was wearing dark trousers and a red pullover. He hooked his arms around her waist and kissed her small, soft mouth. She yielded for a moment then pulled away from him.

'I stink of the lab,' she whispered. 'Want to take a shower.'

'We'll take one together . . .'

They kissed again, more slowly this time, savouring each other's half-forgotten taste.

'God I've missed you,' she breathed. 'Like . . . like absolutely bloody crazy.'

'Missed you too.'

Julie pulled her head back, her eyes full of questions. But they weren't the ones she asked.

'How was it – the flight back? You must be zonked.'

Trivial matters. To buy time. She'd been a little shy of him when they'd had their last reunion after months apart and she was so again. Made worse this time because of the ultimatum she'd given him by email a few days ago.

'What time of day is it for you?'

'Bed time.' He nuzzled her neck, smelling faint echoes of the perfume she'd put on that morning.

'You need a shave . . .' she giggled.

'Later.' He guided her to the bedroom. Just inside the door he lifted her pullover, her arms floating up in willing connivance. Then, as he was about to unclip her bra, she shied away, turning for the bathroom. He pulled her back, nudging her towards the bed.

'No . . .' With a shake of the head she extracted herself from his grip. 'It'll only take a moment.'

He peeled off his own clothes and followed her into the bathroom. Julie was reaching for the tap in the shower. He ran his fingertips down the ridge of her spine, then slid his hands round to cup her small, soft breasts.

She squirmed away and stepped into the cubicle, pulling him in with her. As their mouths found each other under the warm deluge, he reached down to her hips and lifted her up. She locked her arms round his neck and encircled him with her legs.

He guided himself into her and came within seconds, losing his balance and banging his shoulder against the tiles. Giggling hysterically, Julie clung on with octopus limbs, then with a whoop of alarm released her grip, splashing down into the shower tray.

'You'll have us both in A and E, you daft bugger. Broken arms, wet hair and you with a bent willy.'

They soaped each other down then hugged under the jets.

'Welcome back, my darling,' she murmured. 'And you still need a shave.'

When they were dry they poured glasses of wine and Sam ran an electric shaver over his chin. Then they lay on the bed making love again, slowly and lingeringly. Eventually, they fell back against the pillows. Sam's eyelids closed. By his body clock it was after midnight.

'Hey!' Julie nudged him in the ribs. 'Hey, you can't nod off on me! We're going out to dinner!'

'We are?' He opened one eye. The look of bitter disappointment on her face told him he was in trouble.

'We discussed it, remember? On the phone a couple of days ago.'

'Oh Christ . . .'

Today was Julie's thirtieth birthday. He'd failed to buy her a present, forgotten to book a restaurant, even, in his eagerness for sex, omitted to congratulate her on this landmark day in her life.

'You forgot,' she said limply.

'I'm terribly sorry. The jet lag . . .'

She turned away.

'Happy birthday, Julie.' He put a lame hand on her shoulder but she shrugged it off. 'Shit, look I'm sorry. Before I left Singapore I had it firmly in my head. But what with the journey back and my meeting . . .'

'Oh sure . . .' She gave him a look of petulant disdain. 'You haven't even got me a present, have you?'

He knew why she was so upset. This was what her absent father had done throughout her childhood – turning up to visit when the mood took him, forgetting birthdays, oblivious to what was important in *her* life.

'Wasn't sure what you wanted,' he mumbled, knowing it was a lousy excuse.

'Only what *you* wanted . . .' she muttered, getting off the bed.

'Look. I'll fix something.'

He sat up, but his head was a mess. If they went for a meal he'd nod off at the table.

'Julie . . .'

'Forget it.' She could see the state he was in.

'We'll celebrate tomorrow. I'll be better company when I've got my time zones sorted.'

She forced a smile and began to put some clothes on. 'It doesn't matter. Sorry I made such a fuss.' She stuffed her feet into slippers and began

40

shuffling towards the kitchen. 'I've got some supermarket curry in the fridge.'

Sam massaged his temples, racking his brains for a way to make amends. Time was his biggest problem. In a very few days the operation to find Peregrine Harrison would take him away from her again.

Then he had an idea. A way of combining business with pleasure. He got dressed and made his way to the kitchen.

'Tomorrow's Friday,' he announced.

'Ten out of ten.'

'Followed by the weekend.'

'Now you're heading for a double first.'

'What I meant was, why don't we go away somewhere? Oak-beamed hotel in the country. Crisp walks and log fires. Three rosette cuisine.'

Softening instantly, Julie looked up from the worktop. 'I'd have to see if mum can cope with Liam.'

'I'm sure she can.'

'Did you have anywhere in mind?'

Sam rubbed his chin.

'Well, yes, actually. Cambridgeshire.'

5

Friday, 7 January

THE NEXT DAY Sam was wide awake at five, his body clock still out of kilter. He got up quietly without disturbing Julie, made himself some tea, then got stuck into Harrison's book again.

The descriptions of the Chindit operations in Burma were gruelling. Jungle marches with massive packs on their backs. Perilous crossings of swollen rivers. Unreliable radios putting airdrops of fresh supplies in jeopardy. Then brief, bloody skirmishes with a foe best known for its willingness to die.

The name for Wingate's 3,000-strong guerrilla force was a corruption of *chinthe*, he learned from the preface – a Burmese word for the mythical stone creatures that guard Buddhist temples. Half lion, half dragon. One of the beasts featured in a chapter entitled 'Capture'. In it Harrison described how, after weeks of no contact with the enemy, his platoon had come under machine-gun fire from an undetected Japanese position.

We were at our lowest ebb and desperately short of water. The last two supply drops had failed. We were having to buy food from villages, which put us at great risk, since many of the local people were informers for the Japs. But, despite the poor state we were in, the men reacted well to the attack, despite several of them being immediate casualties. I called for volunteers to go with me in a flanking manoeuvre to try to flush the gunners out. We set off under covering fire from the rest of the platoon, but my section did not get far before we were spotted and attacked with grenades. Four of my men were mortally wounded and I sustained a nasty shrapnel wound in my side. Despite that, those of us who survived managed to withdraw to safe ground and regroup.

The following day they'd been ordered south to meet up with another battalion. Harrison had lost a lot of blood and was too weak to march, so his commanding officer had been forced to leave him behind.

I fully accepted the decision. The injury had sapped me of my strength. I hoped that if I could rest up for a few days I might have the energy to follow. Fortunately for me, Burrif Kyaw Zaw (Burma Rifles) volunteered to stay with me. He knew the area well and believed he could find us shelter in a friendly village. He hid me as effectively as he could in the ruins of an old Buddhist temple, guarded appropriately by a weather-beaten chinthe. *Then he set off, promising to return within six hours. A full day passed however, and I began to fear he had been taken prisoner, a fear that was confirmed when a Japanese search party pulled back the stones concealing my hiding place and captured me too.*

His treatment by the first Japanese soldiers hadn't been too bad. A medic had dressed his wound and apart from a few face slappings he wasn't harmed. But after being transported up the line to a field headquarters, things had taken a sharp turn for the worse.

My captors were determined to make me reveal where my unit had moved on to, but I said I would tell them nothing other than my name, rank and service number in accordance with the Geneva Convention. This made them very angry. At first they set about me with bamboo poles, beating me all over my head and body, including the area of the unhealed shrapnel wound. It was appalling and the attacks only ceased when I blacked out from the pain. Worse was to come, however. The Japanese Lieutenant in charge ordered me to be stripped and strapped to a bench. Then a hose was turned on my face. I could not breathe. Water filled my mouth and nose. I had a particular horror of being submersed. The origins of this fear were no mystery to me. At the age of six my well-meaning but ill-advised father had thrown me into a river in the hope that nature would teach me to swim. I had very nearly drowned.

As my chest and stomach filled with water I felt total panic and I am not ashamed to admit that. There came a point when I would have told them anything to end the torture. The irony was that because of the water in my lungs I was unable to speak. I remember beginning to hallucinate. I saw my mother walking towards me with her arms outstretched, walking on water like Jesus Christ. Then, when I was on the verge of unconsciousness, they turned the hose off, untied my bonds and rolled me over so I could cough and vomit everything from my insides. I was in a very bad state by then, so much so that the Japs decided there was no point in interrogating me again that day.

My lasting memory of that awful experience was the expression on the face of the Lieutenant in charge. It was not pleasure I saw there as the hose was directed at me. I do not even know for sure that the man was a sadist. What I saw was total disregard for my suffering. To him I was a creature with no more significance than an ant. And as a defeated enemy he felt he was entitled to do with me what he wanted. Long after that period of my captivity was over, his face would come back to me in my dreams. It does to this day. At the end of the war when I was finally freed from Rangoon Central Gaol I made myself a promise. That if I could ever identify and find that man, I would make him understand what he had done to me, whatever it took.

Sam read the last sentence again. This was the threat from a quarter of a century ago which his masters believed was finally to be carried out. He still wasn't entirely convinced, however. Tens of thousands of POWs must have made the same promise to themselves at the end of the war.

He heard the shower pump running. Julie was awake. The sky was brightening outside and the bracket clock said seven. He picked up his empty mug, then padded to the kitchen.

Deciding it would be a tactful gesture to make breakfast for Julie, he opened the fridge. The almost bare shelves reminded him she wasn't the most domesticated of women. He tried in vain to remember what she ate in the mornings, then began looking in cupboards for clues. Inside one was an unopened pack of muesli which he placed on the section of the worktop used as a breakfast bar. A carton of milk from the fridge, a bowl and a spoon completed his preparations. After an extended search he located some sliced brown bread for himself.

'Making yourself at home,' Julie remarked, coming into the kitchen in a towelling robe and wet hair. She went straight for the kettle. 'Oh good. Just boiled.'

'I've laid your breakfast,' he told her, feeling slightly smug.

She craned her neck from stirring an instant coffee and stared at the worktop. Her brow wrinkled. 'I don't,' she told him. 'You know that. Just a coffee in the mornings.'

'But the packet of Alpen . . .'

'I bought it for *you*.'

Sam swallowed. 'I never touch the stuff. *You* know that.'

They looked uncomfortably at one another, realising that the catching up they had to do wasn't merely in bed.

'This evening . . .' he began.

'I'll try to get off early, but don't expect me before five.'

'No problem. We can still be there for dinner.'

She looked at him sceptically. 'You do realise I won't believe any of this until it happens?'

'Oh ye of little faith . . .'

She picked up her mug and headed out of the kitchen, trilling, 'going to be late again . . .'

Sam ate his toast, then made a mug of coffee for himself. As he returned with it to the living room, he could hear the hairdryer going.

He picked up Harrison's book.

The Japs moved their headquarters soon after capturing me and took me with them. At first they tried to make me walk but I was in a bad way. In order not to hold things up they tied me onto the back of a mule. I kept looking out for Kyaw Zaw, the brave soldier who had remained behind with me when the Chindits moved on. His own capture had almost certainly led to mine, but there was no sign of him and I feared he must have been killed soon after revealing the whereabouts of my hiding place. I knew what terrible tortures he would have gone through and felt no bitterness towards him for giving me away.

Julie bustled into the sitting room with her coat on. 'What's the book?'

'An autobiography.'

'Of whom?'

'Peregrine Harrison.'

She screwed up her face. 'With a name like that I s'pose I should know who he is.'

'Not really. The book came out twenty-five years ago, and he's not made many ripples since.'

'I take it you aren't reading this entirely for pleasure.'

'Not entirely.'

She knew it was pointless pressing for details. The book was business. And Sam's work was a *closed* book to her. She turned for the door.

'Hang on a second.' Sam put the volume down and stood up. 'Is this goodbye?'

'Sorry.' She turned and kissed him perfunctorily, mumbling about being *very* late.

'We'll have a great weekend,' he told her. 'I promise.'

She gave a tight-lipped smile. 'See you tonight.'

He watched from the window as she half walked, half ran down the street towards the tube.

He got dressed and shaved, then returned to the book, keen to know how Harrison had spent the rest of the war. The man's detention in the

Central Jail in Rangoon had been gruelling. The prison was overcrowded and disease-ridden, with men dying almost daily from sickness and malnutrition. But although there were frequent beatings, often for the 'offence' of failing to salute a guard, the systematic torture he'd experienced at the hands of the unidentified Lieutenant was not repeated.

Sam skipped through to the post-war period. Harrison described his repatriation to England as a time of trauma and despair. With his own parents dead and his only sibling, a brother, in the colonial service in India, 'family' in England had consisted of elderly grandparents and a few aunts and uncles whom he hardly knew. On arrival at Liverpool docks aged twenty-three, he'd had no idea where to go or what to do next. Given his discharge papers, back pay and a rail warrant to wherever he wanted, he'd picked Gloucester because his maternal grandparents lived there.

The first few months in England were a desperate time for me. I felt stateless. Not belonging. Nobody wanted to know what I had been through. Nobody seemed to care. The war in the Far East had been too far away for them. Everybody I met had had their own bad experiences closer to home, with family members lost in France, or missing in POW camps in Germany. They simply did not understand that what we had been through at the hands of the Japanese was far, far worse. Our minds had been damaged, permanently in many cases. I myself became ill. My grandparents could not cope with my waking at night, screaming and shouting from the nightmares that would not leave me alone. They persuaded me to see their local doctor, but all the man suggested was more exercise and fresh air. I considered trying to get in touch with the men I had shared imprisonment with, for mutual support, but they had dispersed throughout the country and I did not have their addresses. It occurred to me too that contacting them might make it even harder to shake off the memories plaguing me. Throughout all of that time, I kept seeing the face of the Lieutenant who had tortured me, knowing that if he were still alive he would be feeling no remorse for the condition he had reduced me to.

'Until now,' Sam murmured.

He closed the book and stared at the cover. Bedraggled soldiers in bush hats standing in a jungle clearing, the image washed over with the rising sun of the Japanese flag. On the back was a photo of Harrison. Teutonic eyes set on some distant horizon, with a Buddhist temple behind. Handsome, chiselled features and a thick shock of fair hair. Not hard to see why the man had been worshipped by his women.

It occurred to him it might be *through* one of them he'd get to Harrison – if he could discover who they were.

The file Waddell had given him was on the dining table. Inside was a note from a Special Branch inspector, saying the Bordhill Community had proved as tight-lipped as a convent.

Outside it had grown darker again. Rain beat against the window panes. He powered up his laptop and plugged the modem cable into the phone socket. On the Internet Google quickly found him a site for Bordhill. There were photos of a rambling eighteenth-century manor house, a potted history, a brief personality page on Peregrine Harrison and outlines of the Buddhist-centred courses held there. It all looked appealing enough, with fresh-faced twenty-and-thirty-somethings extolling the virtues of meditation.

Then he clicked onto the *Telegraph* archive and fed in Kamata's name. Half a dozen stories came up about the car factory deal. He browsed them quickly and copied them to a file on the hard-drive. Then he searched for sites run for former PoWs. Plenty of stuff about regimental histories and torture methods, but no reference to Harrison or Kamata.

Finally he checked his email. There was one from Beth.

> *Sorry to walk out on you without a goodbye on Jan 1. Just seemed to make sense at the time.*
> *They're putting me through the grinder here in Sydney but I'll survive.*
> *Thanks for being so nice on NYE. And for the generous suggestion of how to best use that historic millennium moment! Don't think I wasn't tempted. Ah well. Another time, another place . . .*
> *Be nice to stay in touch.*
> *Beth*

Sam smiled, savouring the bitter-sweetness of the missed opportunity. He hit the reply key and typed.

> *Told you you'd regret it . . .*
> *Steve*

As soon as he disconnected, the phone rang.

'Hope I didn't wake you.'

Sam recognised his controller's voice.

'No chance. Been up for hours.'

'Brain still ahead of us?'

'Always is, Duncan. Always is.'

Waddell cleared his throat.

'Tetsuo Kamata's in town.'

'Didn't mention this yesterday.'

'Didn't know. It's a private visit. They're signing the Memorandum of Understanding today, for the transfer of the factory. Complete bloody surprise to us. The two companies had kept it to themselves.'

'I thought the sale was months away.'

'It is. But the MoU sets out the terms. Gives the Japs the right to look at the books. Make sure they're not buying more of a pig in a poke than they think they are.'

'We're providing protection?'

'As discreetly as possible. He doesn't know about it. The company's giving a press conference at noon at Brown's Hotel. First time Kamata's been seen in the flesh in this country. The media'll go mad. And I think *you* ought to be there. Get a feel for the man.'

'Fine, but I'll need a press card.'

'That'll be ready at eleven-thirty. I'll have someone meet you with it.'

They fixed a time and place, then Waddell rang off.

Sam stared out of the window, unhappy with the way the Harrison affair was developing a momentum of its own. He wanted it to die so he could get back to doing something about Jimmy Squires.

He remembered the call he was going to make. Checking his address book on the computer, he found the number and dialled it.

The desk where it rang was deep inside the Ministry of Defence.

Sam took the tube to Piccadilly, then dropped into Waterstone's. He browsed the travel shelves for a guide to country hotels, buying the one with the greatest number of sites in East Anglia. Then he sat in the café and read it over a double espresso. To his dismay the area within twenty miles of Bordhill seemed to be a culinary desert. In the end he plumped for a coaching inn half-an-hour's drive away, near the cathedral city of Ely. It promised an inglenook in the bar, a bedroom with a whirlpool bath, and a menu 'drawing its inspiration from the four corners of the world'. He phoned from his mobile and found to his relief they had a room free.

It was twenty past eleven. His appointment with Waddell's messenger was outside Green Park tube. A five-minute walk.

Stopping at a stationers to buy a small notebook, he reached Brown's Hotel at ten minutes to twelve. A board in the reception area directed him to a suite on the first floor where a burly security guard checked his newly minted press card. The suite was already crowded, with half a dozen TV cameras facing the platform. He found a seat to the side, squeezing in between two tensely expectant Japanese reporters.

At precisely twelve o'clock a flustered PR girl walked onto the podium to announce a delay. Mr Kamata's party was stuck in traffic but would be here shortly. When she stepped down again, the reporters each side of Sam spoke across him in Japanese.

At the back of the room TV producers paced, phones clamped between head and shoulder, reporting the bad news to their lunchtime bulletins. Time slots allocated to this story would need filling with something else if Kamata didn't show in time. Sam studied faces, fearing that by some dreadful coincidence he might stumble across the press man who'd ambushed him fifteen months ago.

At twenty past the hour the PR girl reappeared to announce the imminent arrival of Mr Kamata. The TV people switched on their cameras and the elderly saviour of the Walsall motor factory was ushered through the throng by a quartet of aides. He was tall for a Japanese, and for an octogenarian remarkably straight-backed. Sam watched him take his seat, studying this face that had haunted Peregrine Harrison's dreams, while trying to picture him fifty-six years ago in drab jungle fatigues. Kamata displayed signs of nervousness. Sam guessed he'd been warned of the viciousness of the British media.

The table was draped in the red, white and gold of the Matsubara logo. On Kamata's right sat a much younger Japanese. The name card described him as the company's Development Director. To the chairman's left sat a slick-haired Englishman who stood up and introduced himself as the chairman of Brassinger-Mulholland Public Relations.

'Ladies and gentlemen, welcome to this press conference. On behalf of the Matsubara Corporation I'd like to apologise for the late start, particularly to those with imminent deadlines.' He attempted a mollifying smile. 'First, I'd like to read a brief statement. Afterwards Mr Tetsuo Kamata, the chairman of Matsubara, will take questions. His answers will be given in Japanese and will be translated for you by his interpreter, Miss Kimura, who is seated at the end of this table.'

He indicated an attractive young woman dressed in a smart, dark suit, wearing oval designer spectacles, with a pearl necklace round her slender neck. She bowed her head.

Clearing his throat and glancing at the cameras, the spokesman began. 'The Matsubara Corporation is pleased to have signed a Memorandum of Understanding this morning with the Walsall Motor Group. It is the company's intention to complete the purchase of the plant and assets as soon as possible, so work can begin on adapting the factory to produce Matsubara cars in the UK. It is also the company's intention to re-employ as many as possible of the Walsall Motors workforce and to keep redundancies to a minimum. The signing of the MoU today means Matsubara can now have privileged access to the group's accounts and business records, a full examination of which will be necessary before the purchase of the company can be completed. Matsubara believes it *can* produce cars profitably in the UK, selling them both here and elsewhere in the European economic zone.'

Sam stared at Matsubara's Development Director looking for any sign of the disagreement he undoubtedly felt. The expressionless face gave nothing away.

'Matsubara's chairman, Mr Tetsuo Kamata . . .' the PR man nodded deferentially to the tense figure beside him, '. . . wishes me to state that he is particularly pleased to be forming this new bridge of friendship between Japan and Britain, which he hopes will be of real benefit to very many people in this country. Mr Kamata is now ready to answer a few questions.'

The PR man looked round, trying to identify who would be gentlest with his client. Hands shot up.

'The time available is strictly limited, so please keep your questions brief and to the point.' He aimed a finger at the reporter he'd selected, but it was too late. A pushy television correspondent had stepped forward.

'Mr Kamata. Do you recognise yourself as the same man who tortured British prisoners of war fifty-six years ago? A man for whom the sanctity of British lives was at that time of no significance whatsoever to you?'

The PR man winced and turned to his client. As the question was translated, the chairman's only reaction was to blink. Then, staring at some fixed point high up on the far wall, he began his reply. His voice was thin and reedy, the words coming out as a monotone. His answer was brief.

'War changes a man,' Miss Kimura translated in a strong, clear voice with an American accent. 'But fortunately once that war is over a man can change back to the way he was before.'

'Did you enjoy torturing British soldiers, Mr Kamata?' the TV man persisted. There was a growl of 'oh come on!' from further back in the room.

'Please,' the PR interjected, puce-faced, 'we're here to talk about the MoU and the rescue of a car factory.'

Kamata listened to the translation of the question. For a split second there was a flash of anger on his face, then he curbed it and began to speak. He was in control and had every intention of staying that way.

'The war in Burma was indescribably horrible,' Miss Kimura interpreted, a few seconds later. 'One hundred and sixty thousand Japanese soldiers died there. It was not something to enjoy. Men on all sides were reduced to the level of animals. But whoever they fought for, they believed that what they did was justified by their cause. Imperial Japanese soldiers had been trained to believe that their race was superior to any other. We were taught that enemy prisoners were sub-humans, not deserving of our respect. I appreciate that for people of your generation it is hard to understand the effect of such a culture and training on young minds. Today we know so much more about the other peoples in the world. We know how wrong those old attitudes were. And if we continue to forge international bonds such as Matsubara's link with the Walsall Motor Group, then it must surely make it impossible for such terrible things ever to happen again.'

Sam kept his eyes on Kamata's face while Miss Kimura did her stuff. The old torturer's eyes flicked from side to side, gauging the audience's reaction.

'Now,' the PR interjected quickly, 'a question about the MoU please.' He pointed to a grey-haired industrial correspondent from one of the broadsheets. 'Bill.'

'How certain is it that this purchase of Walsall Motors will be completed, Mr Kamata? Is there a danger that once you study the books you'll decide to pull out?'

Safer ground. But Sam had been impressed by the old man's blocking of the TV man's bouncers.

'It is our firm intention to complete the purchase,' came the stolid reply. 'We are not anticipating any unsolvable problems.'

A string of industrial questions followed, mostly about job numbers and guarantees that the company would stay in Britain if the going got tough. The replies were vague, citing the unpredictability of the market.

'Time for just one more . . .'

The reporter who raised his hand identified himself as a representative of *The Times*. 'This is your first ever visit to London, I believe, Mr Kamata. While you're here, will you be taking the opportunity to meet any of the former British soldiers you maltreated? To ask their forgiveness? I'm thinking in particular of Mr Peregrine Harrison.'

At the mention of that name Kamata flinched. His reply was a single word, uttered in English before the translator could take breath.

'No.'

The chairman stood up. His entourage encircled him protectively.

'Thank you *gentlemen* – and ladies,' the PR muttered. 'That's the end of this press conference.'

Cocooned by his staff, Kamata was swept from the room. Most of the press had their heads together, asking one another who the hell 'Peregrine Harrison' was.

TV producers clutching cassettes elbowed their way to the door, heading for satellite trucks. The Japanese journalists each side of Sam looked acutely uncomfortable and also got up. He followed them out, listening to the mutterings around him.

'Bet *he* won't call another presser in a hurry . . . '

'*How* many of our blokes did he kill . . .?'

'Have to admit he's got guts coming here . . .'

Yes, thought Sam. Plenty of guts. A written statement would have sufficed today. He suspected putting himself in the firing line had been a matter of face, however. If he *hadn't* come, he'd have risked appearing a coward, which would have been an intolerable humiliation for a former servant of Japan's god-emperor.

Half a century later the world had moved on. But for Tetsuo Kamata and Peregrine Harrison, it seemed, certain fundamentals had remained unchanged.

6

West London

SAM HAD BEEN back at the flat only a few minutes when Julie arrived. It was ten past five.

Smiling uncertainly, she hung her coat on a hook in the hall, then turned to embrace him, stopping when she saw his look of preoccupation. 'What's happened?'

'Nothing. Why?'

'Your mind's a million miles away.'

'No it isn't.' He kissed her cheek which was still cold from being outside, then, twinkling mysteriously, he extracted a slim package from his trouser pocket. 'For you. Happy birthday.'

'Oh . . .' She beamed with pleasure. 'You shouldn't have . . .'

Sam knew his life wouldn't have been worth living this weekend if he hadn't. The gift was wrapped in shiny red paper and tied with a white ribbon. He'd found it in a smart jewellers in Ealing on his way home from the tube.

Julie glowed. She'd always taken a childish delight in gift-wrapping. As she slipped off the ribbon and opened the dark blue box she gasped.

'It's beautiful!' She draped the bracelet over her wrist. 'No, but it really *is* gorgeous. *Thank* you.'

'You like silver, don't you?'

'I *love* it. More than gold – which looks tacky on me.' She held it up to the light to get a better look. 'And the stones are adorable. Sort of honey-coloured. What are they?'

'Forgot to ask,' Sam mumbled, kicking himself for missing an important detail.

'Never mind. It's absolutely lovely and I forgive you everything.' She kissed him on the mouth. Then she drew back suspiciously. 'Unless . . . Our weekend?'

'Soon as you're ready.'

'Amazing! Never thought it'd happen. A quick clean up, a few things in a bag and I'm all set. How posh do I need to be? Where are we staying?' She narrowed her eyes. 'Four stars? Five?'

'Not quite. More of a glorified pub. All the smart places I tried were fully booked.'

'Liar. I knew it'd be a pub. Smart isn't exactly your style.'

'Thanks.'

'Anyway, it's going to be great.' She walked into the bedroom, expecting to see a suitcase open on the covers. 'You not packed yet?'

'To be honest I only got back a couple of minutes before you did.'

'What've you been doing all day?'

'Seeing people. And fixing things up for our weekend.'

'Choosing pubs, you mean. *Very* arduous.' She opened the wardrobe and stared at the garments on the rail. 'Where is this place exactly?'

'Near Ely.'

'Nice cathedral. Haven't been there for years. This do?' She held out a maroon skirt. 'With a white top?'

'Fine.'

'I mean, I take it the place does have a restaurant,' she asked, hand on hip. 'You're not just treating me to a sandwich in the bar?'

'Certainly it has a restaurant. One which the book says draws its inspiration from the four corners of the world.'

Julie frowned doubtfully. 'Sounds like they can't make up their minds.'

'If it's dreadful we'll find somewhere better tomorrow.'

She laid the skirt on the bed, then put the blouse beside it and some clean underwear. 'If you feel like packing this for me while I wash, it'd save time.' She stripped to her bra and pants and stepped into the bathroom. 'Any particular reason for Cambridgeshire?'

'Not really.' Sam knew immediately his lie was a mistake, but it was too late. 'It's just a part of the country I felt like getting to know.'

The grunt from the bathroom told him she wasn't convinced. And she'd been right about his mind being on other matters. He'd dropped into the Ministry of Defence in the afternoon for a snatched cup of tea with his friend in the SAS.

'Contrary to popular belief, the Regiment is not stuffed to the gills with psychopaths,' the man had said. 'But there are a few. And Sergeant Squires was one of them. It never appeared on his service record but we took him off duties in Ulster because he showed too much enthusiasm for the job in hand.'

And Squires was now at large in the Far East.

With Midge on his tail.

The traffic out of London was hellish. On the motorway north, a light rain began to fall. The windscreen of Julie's Peugeot smeared with grease kicked up by lorries.

For the first hour of the journey she chatted intermittently, telling him about the gossip at the lab, her mother's rumblings about how it was time she became a full-time parent, and the trouble Liam was having making friends at school. Sam listened with half an ear while he thought about how to approach Bordhill in the morning. Then she asked him a question.

'Where've you been in recent weeks, darling? Or is that a secret?'

'Thailand.'

'Checking out the lady-boys?' she teased.

'No. On a boat.'

'With sails?'

Her question seemed oddly pointed.

'No. A stink boat this time. Several tons of plastic wrapped round an engine.'

'Disappointing for you.'

'It was work.'

'You were alone?'

'No. But I can't talk about that . . .'

'Sure. Sorry I asked.'

Julie fell silent. Sam realised she was watching him.

'Look,' she said eventually, 'I know I'm not supposed to ask questions, but are you going to tell me?'

'Tell you what?'

'About this weekend. I'm assuming your sudden recall to London and the fact we're going to the empty flatlands of Cambridgeshire are not entirely unconnected?'

Sam chewed his lip.

'So?'

'Okay. I confess. There's a place up here I need to take a look at tomorrow.'

Julie turned away, staring at the blur of tail lights in the slow lane. 'You'll be going there on your own, I take it.'

'Hey, come on!' He patted her knee. 'Essentially this is a weekend for you and me. Tomorrow won't take long. Actually I'd love it if you came with me.'

'What is this place?'

'A quasi-religious community. Buddhist. Started by the man whose autobiography I was reading.'

'Fine. But keep me out of it.'

Her reaction didn't surprise him. When he'd involved her in the investigation into her father's murder she'd nearly got killed.

'We can talk about it later.'

'You can talk until your teeth fall out, Sam, I'm not taking part in any more of your lethal games.' She folded her arms. 'And if you've brought me here as some sort of cover, then you can drop me at a train station and I'll go and see my son.'

'Julie . . .'

'Don't *Julie* me! The world you work in scares me stiff, Sam. I don't want to be a part of it.'

'Okay. But tonight we don't talk about work, all right? Not mine and not yours.'

Ely
8.45 p.m.

The Laura Ashley curtained dining room of the Waterman's Arms was only half full. Rachmaninov's Third played in the background, doing nothing to lift the sombre atmosphere of the place. The other diners spoke in whispers or not at all.

The menu was comically pretentious, with references to 'fresh caught produce from the rivers and seas', 'sun-ripened Mediterranean aubergines' and 'Basmati rice watered by the melting snows of the Himalayas'. Sam loved it because the absurdity of the descriptions had broken the ice. Julie giggled at the text, her laughter becoming ever more hysterical as she tried to control it.

The food arrived under silver domes which were whipped away with an awkward flourish by the school leavers employed as waiters. The dishes beneath were predictably bland, but with the help of some New Zealand Sauvignon, the evening slipped by, with neither of them talking about anything that mattered.

7

Ely
Saturday, 8 January

THE NEXT MORNING Sam awoke early again, his mind turning instantly to Perry Harrison. The little he'd learned about the man had heightened his curiosity. Julie stirred momentarily as he got up, then turned her back. He grabbed Harrison's book from the suitcase and took it to the bathroom, closing the door and switching on the light. The room was chilly. There was a robe hanging there, which he put on, then sat on the toilet lid to read.

In the chapter where Harrison wrote about the setting up of the Bordhill Community, he readily admitted his selfishness towards women. He blamed it on having had a doting mother who'd instilled in him a belief that the male of the species existed to be served. Sam noted that his fascination for the female sex seemed to be predominantly physical. Harrison even admitted that when setting up Bordhill, one aim had been to surround himself with beautiful and insecure young women, '*and then see what happened.*'

There was no shortage of such women in the sixties. As a nation we were emerging from the self-denial years of the post-war period into something else, but what that 'else' was nobody was terribly sure. Girls entering their twenties, and young men too, were seeking something they had been deprived of. To some it was spiritual enlightenment, to others it was the physical love which for many had been lacking in childhood. And to the confused young creatures who came to me at Bordhill it was frequently both.

I have to admit that for me the sexual act is something I need to carry out with considerable regularity. Only at such moments of physical indulgence can I truly escape from the demons inside my head. My thoughts are frequently of death, my own and that of the Japanese who maltreated me so damagingly in Burma.

Sam understood yet again why his controller had wanted him to read this book.

When I am in congress with a woman however, my mind and body are generating love instead of hate. Its effect is like morphine to a troubled soul.

In self-defence, lest the reader think me entirely selfish, I should add that my partners have also benefited from my attentions. I have genuinely tried to help them by bringing a degree of light and warmth into their lives which was not there before, and frankly I think I have succeeded. I believe too that despite such extra-marital sexual activity being contrary to the teachings of Theravada Buddhism, I have been able to combine it with the doctrine of selflessness which is integral to the Dhamma. It has always been understood by my partners that our physical liaisons must be for mutual pleasure and emotional release only. Not for one person to possess the other but as a way of reaching a higher state of consciousness by escaping from the prison of unfulfilled physical wants. Such 'selflessness' is not easy for women to achieve, but their struggle to attain it with me has usually proven a valuable therapy.

Although many Buddhists in Britain would say my approach to physical relationships is heretical, I would argue that it is more or less in line with the teachings of the Buddha. The Dhamma tells us that nothing in this world is permanent. That no long-term satisfaction can be gained from things physical or material, because they are in a constant state of change. It follows, therefore, that a possessive bonding between one man and one woman will often create unhappiness, because each is changing in different ways. It is easier for one individual to satisfy another individual sexually than in other areas, so I decreed when founding Bordhill that the community as a whole was to provide the emotional and social support we all demand. No individuals were to take on such a responsibility.

Harrison's version of Buddhist principles had produced casualties, Sam discovered. Several women had left the community in disillusion and one troubled creature had hanged herself in the barn where Harrison first seduced her.

That was a bad day for us all, but I felt no personal responsibility for her death. Scars on a person's character can be as misleading as they are on flesh. They conceal the extent of the injury beneath. We knew she was a woman who had been through bad experiences, but it was only at the inquest that we learned just how traumatic her childhood had been and that there had been two previous suicide attempts.

As Sam turned the pages, Harrison's idiosyncrasies kept popping up. There was a ban on Japanese cars or TVs at Bordhill, and in a radical diversion from the Buddhist edict that no harm should be done to any living creature, he'd told his students the atomic bombings of Hiroshima and Nagasaki were a fitting punishment for a nation so steeped in cruelty and barbarism.

Sam heard the bedsprings creak. Then the bathroom door opened and Julie stood there naked and bleary eyed. She shivered and hugged herself.

'I reached out and you weren't there,' she complained.

The morning was misty and damp. After they'd showered and dressed, they looked out from their bedroom window across an expanse of ploughed earth which was almost black. A hedge ran down the side of the field, punctuated by leafless trees, their trunks bowed by the wind which whistled unhindered across the open landscape. At the far end was the barely visible line of a drainage dyke. To Sam the terrain had a stark beauty. To Julie it felt grim and lonely.

After a breakfast of 'succulent Suffolk bacon' and 'farm-fresh eggs', Sam broached the subject of the day ahead. He knew it was unprofessional to involve Julie, but since she'd played a significant role in a previous operation, he reckoned she had an honorary status with the firm. He told her about the commune and about Perry Harrison's pursuit of the young women he'd recruited. What he didn't reveal was the reason for his interest in the man.

'What would I have to do if I were to come with you?' she asked.

'Smile and look interested.'

She looked at him dejectedly. 'You're a manipulative sod, Sam Packer.'

'Think of it like playing charades.'

'Makes it worse. I was never good at them . . .'

Bordhill was a tall-chimneyed manor house of weathered red brick, on the outskirts of the village of Sidgefield. It stood back from the road at the end of a gravel drive scarred by a ridge of moss and grass. Sam drove in. To their right was an orchard of gnarled apple trees. To the left, beyond a wire fence, a handful of goats and cows fed from bales of hay.

A parking sign pointed to a yard, which was edged on two sides by converted stables. Sam swung in, pulling up outside a door marked VISITORS. As he got out he heard the humming of machinery and smelled wood.

'I'll wait in the car,' Julie told him. 'So I can pick you off the floor when they boot you out.'

Beside the door was a window. The room beyond was a reception area. He saw a plain wooden table laden with literature. A shop bell attached to the top of the door-frame tinkled as he entered. He listened for approaching footsteps but there was only the same noise as before, which he decided was probably a lathe. At the back of the room a glass partition with a locked door separated it from a corridor.

He browsed the booklets on the table. One, entitled *The Bordhill Community – The Way to a Better Life*, included photos that looked as if they dated from twenty years ago.

There was a bell push which he hadn't noticed before. Seconds after pressing it, the glass door to the corridor was opened by a slightly overweight young woman in her late twenties, dressed in a long woollen skirt and a cardigan of some vaguely earthen colour.

'Yes?' She looked searchingly at him. 'Can I help?'

Her pale face was marked with pink blotches. Psoriasis or eczema, Sam guessed. She'd cut her dark hair just short of her shoulders. It was thick and curly and splayed out from the top of her head in an unruly triangle.

'Oh, hello.' Sam beamed. 'We wanted to find out about this place, my partner and I.' He pointed outside. Julie was sitting in the car with her arms folded. 'You run courses I understand.'

'You're not a reporter then?'

He feigned surprise. 'A reporter?'

She shook her head. 'It doesn't matter.'

'Any chance of having a look round?'

'Well, I'm not really supposed to, but . . . ' She stepped back into the corridor and glanced anxiously in each direction. 'What . . . how did you find out about Bordhill?'

'From the Internet. And from Mr Harrison's autobiography. I got a copy from the library.'

'Oh *that*. That was written ages ago. The place has changed a lot.' She stared at his feet. Sam had the odd impression she was trying to divine something from them.

'We're interested in learning more about Buddhism.'

'You'd have to work at it,' she warned. 'It's not exactly off-the-shelf.'

'We realise that. You've been here long?'

'Three years.' She sounded weary when she said it.

'Tell me something. Does Mr Harrison still live here?'

His question startled her. 'This is his home, yes.'

'Any chance of meeting him?'

'You sure you're not a reporter?'

'Nothing so glamorous. I work in the City.'

'Well anyway, he doesn't see visitors.' She still appeared flustered. 'Look, if we're to do a tour, you'd better bring your partner in.'

As Sam turned towards the door to the yard it opened and a tall, red-haired woman entered. She was older than the other and moved with an air of authority.

'That's all right Melissa. I heard the bell.' There was a foreign lilt to her voice. Sam assumed this was Ingrid Madsen.

'They're visitors. I was going to take them on a tour.'

'I'll look after it now.'

'Oh, but I'm quite happy to.' The red patches on Melissa's face intensified in colour. 'He's not a reporter.'

The Danish woman responded with a glare which drove Melissa back through the glass door. She locked it behind her.

'Now . . . How can I help you?'

'We wanted to find out about Bordhill. Thinking of maybe doing a course here sometime. It says on your website you welcome visitors.'

'Yes I know it does, but I'm quite busy.'

The woman spoke with Nordic bluntness. She stared at him for a while as if trying to decide whether he was genuine or not.

'Well all right. I'll show you quickly. Her too?' She pointed outside. At that moment Julie walked in.

'I'm Ingrid,' the woman announced, 'and I'm the head of this community.'

'I thought Mr Harrison was.'

She flinched, her doubts about him returning.

'He is our master,' she said carefully, her voice softening. 'He functions at a level far above the rest of us.' She opened the glass door into the corridor with a key attached by a string to her belt. 'And your names?'

'Geoff and Ginny.'

'Fine. We'll start with the workshops.' She locked up again behind them. 'We're a self-financing community,' she explained, ushering them into a work space. 'Part of our income comes from the sale of things we make.'

They were assailed by the smell of hot wax and Indian scents. Melissa was packing candles into small, brown cardboard boxes. She didn't look up. Ingrid Madsen hurried them on. In the joinery workshop next door there were new smells. Pine and beech.

'Furniture and toys,' she summarised.

A man working at the lathe smiled fleetingly at Ingrid. He had hooded eyes and moved with a rambling gait as he crossed the room to get another piece of wood.

'We sell the produce in our own shop,' Ingrid explained, leading them into the corridor again and unlocking one more door. 'In the summer we have many people coming here. We also supply to local stores. Fruit from the orchard. Vegetables. All organic. Cheese and yoghurt. We have goats and cows and hens.'

'We saw them,' Julie commented.

'Foxes are a problem here. They killed one of the kids just before New Year. You would like to buy something?'

They stepped into the shop. Julie was drawn to some Shaker-style chairs. 'Maybe,' she said.

'Later,' said Sam, not wanting to be distracted.

The Danish woman led them across the courtyard to the main house. 'You know something about Buddhism?'

'The basics. No more.'

'Then you'll know that what we revere is the wisdom of the Buddha. His understanding of life and of human nature brings a lot of comfort to those who embrace his teachings.'

The side door to the manor was old and of oak. Above it, carved into a stone lintel, was the date 1757.

'When did Peregrine Harrison buy this house?' Sam asked.

'About thirty-five years ago.' She glared suspiciously at him.

'I've read *A Jungle Path to Hell*,' Sam said, hoping it would explain his interest.

'But you're not a reporter?'

'Certainly not. Why do you ask?'

She didn't reply. Yesterday's Kamata press conference must have sent the hacks scurrying up here, Sam decided. He made a mental note to buy a paper.

Inside the house they entered a long corridor. There were kitchen sounds and the smell of baking.

'You make your own bread?' Julie asked, smelling the air.

'Yes, of course.' Ms Madsen smiled at her in a way that led Sam to believe she was fonder of women than of men. 'For ourselves. And we sell some too.' She pointed out the kitchen and the communal dining room next to it.

The exterior of the house had looked attractively original, but the inside less so. Whatever fine panelling, plasterwork and fireplaces it might have once had, most had been lost as a result of the house's various reincarnations. The place had a dowdy feel and there was little to suggest a living, vibrant community inhabiting it.

Ingrid Madsen took them into the main entrance hall and stood on the bottom step of a wide staircase, using it as a podium.

'I will explain a little about Buddhists. We believe in three fundamental truths. The first is *impermanence*. Everything is always changing, even if very, very slowly. We call that process *conditioning*. Even rocks are not permanent because they are worn down by wind and rain. The second truth is *unsatisfactoriness*. We human beings are never happy for long with anything that is conditioned. Thirdly, although we think of our innermost self as something about us that is permanent, it isn't. We too are always changing. Therefore we say there is no such thing as *self*.'

'How disconcerting,' Julie whispered.

'On the contrary, we find it comforting. Because once we understand that the cause of our unhappiness is our dependence on conditioned things like possessions, then we can learn to do without them and to strive for nirvana, which is an *unconditioned*, unchanging state where there is complete contentment.'

'Have you attained nirvana?'

Julie's innocent question provoked a scornful glare.

'Of course not.'

'Mr Harrison?'

'No. Not even he. We all strive to attain it of course, by following what we call the noble eightfold path. Right living, right thinking, right livelihood, right speech and so on . . .' She opened a door on the far side of the hall and revealed a class room. 'If you come to a summer school here you will learn all this. They last from two to four weeks. Would you be interested?' She directed the question at Julie.

'Um . . . quite possibly.' She glanced uncomfortably at Sam.

'We would teach you about the self-disciplines involved in becoming a Buddhist. And there are many. Then after further study, you could apply to join our community. Normally you would be expected to have some skills which would be useful to us. What is it you do?' Her eyes were like gimlets.

'Oh, nothing useful at all, I'm afraid,' Sam shrugged. 'Finance. Investment advice.'

'I see. And you, Ginny?'

'I work in a laboratory.'

'Ah.'

'Tell me, does Peregrine Harrison teach at the summer schools?' Sam asked, frustrated at her reluctance to talk about him.

'Not any more. He is quite old. We have several ordinates who can teach. And there are some tapes recorded by Perry which are also used in class.'

'He sounds a fascinating man. Is he here? I'd love to meet him.'

'That's not possible.' Her expression turned to stone. 'He doesn't see visitors. I will show you upstairs quickly, then I will take you back to the shop.'

She stepped briskly up the stairs, checking over her shoulder to see they were following. On the floor above she showed them another classroom, a library and an administrative office. Again, it was the emptiness of the place that struck Sam. Where were the inmates?

She was about to take them downstairs again when Sam spotted a door at the end of the corridor. It was controlled by a coded lock.

'What's in there?' he asked.

'Private quarters.' She shepherded them away from the door.

'Mr Harrison's?'

'You are *very* interested in him.'

'Because I found his book so fascinating. What he went through in the war – it's like having your character shaped on an anvil.'

'It made him understand the strength of the *dhamma*, the Buddha's teachings,' Ingrid said, conceding no ground.

At the top of the stairs Sam glanced back at the door at the end of the corridor, convinced he'd get nowhere with the case until he knew what lay behind it.

Outside again, they crossed the stable yard and Ingrid Madsen unlocked the shop.

'I'll let you choose something to buy, while I get you a summer school prospectus.'

Julie began to wander round, touching things and sniffing at perfumed candles. 'We've got to buy *something*. I like these straight-backed chairs. We could do with one for the bedroom.' She found a price ticket and turned it over. 'Oh dear. £170.'

'Find a scented candle and let's get out of here.'

Ingrid Madsen returned and handed him a booklet. 'This tells you all you need to know. And there's an application form at the back. There are still places available this coming summer.'

Sam wasn't in the least surprised.

Julie held up a jar of honey.

'They're two pounds.'

Julie paid up and Ingrid Madsen slipped the money into a deep pocket in her skirt. As she ushered them out of the shop, she locked the door again.

For an open, free spirited community, they seemed remarkably keen on locks, Sam noted.

'I wish you a safe journey.' She gave a perfunctory wave. 'And I hope you find the peace you're looking for.' Then she walked briskly away from them and disappeared inside the house.

'That's it then,' Julie murmured as he closed the car doors.

But Sam knew it wasn't. Melissa was peering at them through the window. Like an asylum inmate longing to rejoin the outside world.

The rain clouds from yesterday had cleared, leaving a pale blue sky, broken by white cumulus. They drove into Sidgefield, a single street village with a few dreary houses.

'I'm hungry,' Julie announced. 'There's a pub over there. Home-cooked food.'

'Fine by me.'

The car park was almost full. The pub had a beamed ceiling and most of the tables were occupied. They both chose salads from fresh-looking selections in a cool cabinet and settled by the window, overlooking a bare garden dominated by a children's climbing frame.

'So, did you learn anything from this morning's little escapade?' Julie asked eventually, frustrated by the fact he wasn't talking to her.

'Not a lot.'

'What's he done, this Harrison person?'

Sam shook his head. 'It's what he *might* do.'

'And?'

Sam shook his head again.

'You're not going to discuss it,' she sighed exasperatedly.

''Fraid not.'

The truth was he'd found the visit to Bordhill had done nothing to confirm the suspicion that Perry Harrison was planning a murder. On the contrary, the atmosphere of tension and secrecy at the place had made him wonder if there could be a domestic explanation for his disappearance.

After they'd finished eating, Julie suggested a walk. From the warning look in her eyes Sam realised she expected him to devote the rest of the weekend to her.

'Okay,' he said. 'I'm ready for a leg stretch.'

They drove out of the village and found a footpath. He stopped the car in the entrance to a field so Julie could check whether the track beyond the stile was too muddy for her trainers.

Sam felt close to her this afternoon, but suspected she'd want more from him in the next few days than he'd be able to give. There was a clock ticking in his professional life, and until he knew whether it was attached to a bomb he couldn't let up on it.

'Remarkably dry, considering,' Julie said, returning.

'What is?'

'The footpath, stupid.' She groaned theatrically. 'How about we tie a string round your mind and let *me* hang onto it for a while?'

'Not a bad idea.' Sam switched off the engine.

Beyond the stile the ground was almost flat and they walked across a lush meadow punctuated with the brittle, brown spikes of last summer's thistles. The path joined another which followed the meandering banks of a river swollen by the winter rains. Julie took his hand and smiled uncertainly at him.

It was a smile Sam knew well. The question lurking behind it was born out of having had a father who deserted her, and a boyfriend who'd disappeared after making her pregnant. How long before *he* left her too?

'What did you think?' she asked, as they followed the bank of the gurgling river.

'What – the pub?'

'No, dumbo. Bordhill. The idea of practising Buddhism. Giving up material things. Cold showers to damp down your dirty little urges.'

'I don't think *that*'s ever been an issue at Bordhill,' he commented. 'Anyway, religions are all the same basically. Telling people to be nice to each other and to put up with the lousy deal they've been given . . .'

'That's cynical.'

'Religions have good intentions but they become a means of control for the people who run them. And I don't think Bordhill's any different.'

A willow tree caused them to duck, its bare twigs cascading down towards the fast-flowing water. When they'd passed it Julie stopped and turned to him.

'Were you hoping to meet Percy Harrison today?'

'*Perry*,' he corrected. 'No. Hoping to learn what makes him tick, that's all.'

'And did you?'

Sam didn't reply. He put his arm round her shoulders and they began walking again. A flight of rooks was circling a clump of poplars a hundred yards ahead of them.

'You like it, don't you?' Julie's voice was heavy with resignation. 'It gives you a buzz.'

'What does?'

'The secrecy. The feeling that because you're who you are, you never have to be open with anyone.'

Her accusation jarred him. 'Maybe I've been at it so long I've lost the skills to be any other way,' he confessed.

'That's a terrible admission,' Julie whispered.

'What I meant was, they are skills I shall have to relearn.'

'If . . .'

If he was to change his way of life so they could have a permanent home together. That's what they needed to talk about. The trouble was, now, with most of his mind engrossed in a case, was a bloody awful time to discuss it.

'Julie . . .'

She turned to confront him, blocking the path. 'Okay. Tell me straight. How much longer do you think the Singapore posting will last?'

'Look. I really do want us to be together,' he breathed, putting his arms around her. 'And I'm working on it. Please trust me.'

But trusting a man was something Julie had never developed the knack of.

8

THEY SPENT THE rest of the afternoon in bed back at the Waterman's Arms.

Soon after six they began thinking about where to have dinner that evening.

'Nothing short of death through starvation would make me eat downstairs again,' Julie declared, propping herself against the pillows. 'Ely must be full of places.'

'It's Saturday night,' Sam warned, preparing her for the decision he'd made some time ago. 'The good ones'll be heavily booked.'

'So where then?'

'Actually I quite fancy that pub where we had lunch.'

'God!' Julie attempted to push him out of bed. 'You don't give up, do you?'

'They pay me not to.'

They were on the road by seven, and twenty minutes later he stopped the car at the end of the driveway to Bordhill Manor. Lights were on downstairs and at the right-hand end of the upper floor. He tried to remember if that was the wing with the locked door, concluding eventually that it wasn't. The section that housed Perry Harrison's private quarters was in darkness.

The pub was humming when they got there, with most of the tables taken. They found a perch next to the open fire, but quickly realised why it was free.

'We're going to melt sitting here,' Julie commented.

'I'll get us a drink.'

'Half of lager would do me fine.'

Sam looked at faces. He'd come here on the off-chance some of the Bordhill residents might be regulars. Most of the customers were elderly, however – retired people in pullovers and cardigans, dipping into their pensions for a Saturday night out.

At the counter, two ruddy-faced countrymen made way for him. The landlady was a stout, middle-aged woman with blonde hair, stacked up in a 1960's beehive. Sam paid up and carried the drinks to the table, holding a menu under his arm.

'Quick.' Julie pointed across the room, her face agleam with perspiration. 'There's a couple leaving.'

They hurried over and claimed the cooler table. She began browsing the menu.

'It's all meat here. Your Buddhist friends will be veggies. And I don't suppose they drink alcohol either. In fact, altogether, this wasn't the brightest of ideas, Mr Packer. How much does the government pay you?'

'Just choose something.'

She went for chicken breast in grape and muscat sauce while he opted for lamb chops. Sam returned to the bar to place their order, then headed for the toilet, not because he needed it but because it was an excuse to look at more faces as he moved through the further reaches of the pub.

A couple of minutes later he sat down again.

'Urinals full of monks hitching up their saffron robes?' Julie asked.

Sam curled his lips in a mock snarl.

She reached out to touch his hand. 'Actually, I'm beginning to quite like this place. Nice atmosphere.'

When the food came it wasn't disappointing either.

'Good choice after all, Mr Packer. You're forgiven.'

As they ate, Sam's mind was on those closed-off quarters at Bordhill. He resolved to call Waddell and ask for the burglars to be sent in.

'Do you . . . d'you know when you'll be returning to Singapore?'

Julie's question jerked him back to the here and now.

'No.' Suddenly he stiffened. From the far end of the pub a rambling figure had emerged.

'Who?' she mouthed, seeing his expression change.

'The wood turner.' Sam leaned forward.

Julie twisted her head to look. 'He's like something out of a Frankenstein movie. It's those hooded eyes.'

They turned their heads away as he passed.

'Anyway he's gone to the bog,' she whispered. 'Pissed as a rat judging by the way his legs splayed out.'

'If he's following the noble eightfold path, then tonight's his night off,' Sam commented.

'What're you going to do?'

'Discuss the price of fish with him.'

He waited until the man re-emerged, then stood up and followed in his wake.

At the far end of the pub was a doorway to a small room which he hadn't noticed before. In the centre was a billiard table. And leaning across the green baize was Melissa, her hands grappling with an outstretched cue as she aimed for a ball on the far side. She missed her shot.

'Oh *sugar* . . .' She swayed back from the table and plopped down onto a straight-backed chair. 'I'm useless at this, Toby.'

The carpenter took his position and despite his inebriation smacked the ball neatly into a pocket. 'Need longer arms,' he muttered.

Melissa picked up a drink. Clear liquid with a lemon slice. G and T, Sam guessed, the most recent of many, judging by her smudged expression. She gulped a mouthful, replaced the glass perilously close to the edge of the table next to her, then stared dejectedly at the floor.

Suddenly, for no obvious reason, her face crumpled. Sam saw her shoulders begin to shake. Toby saw it too.

'Don't start that, Mel, for God's sake.' He strode over to where she sat, picked up her glass and emptied it into a vase of dried flowers on a mantelpiece.

Suddenly her cheeks blew out and she cupped her hands in front of her mouth. Making as if to get up, she jerked forward and retched onto the floor.

'Oh, God, not again!' The carpenter lumbered towards the door, pushing Sam aside. 'Always doing this . . .' He made an erratic beeline for the exit and disappeared into the night.

'I was getting lonely,' Julie said, appearing at Sam's side. She'd brought his drink. 'Isn't that the girl who . . . ?'

'She's been sick.'

'I'll get someone.' She turned and headed for the bar.

Sam felt revolted by Melissa – the vomit down her pullover front, the livid skin eruptions. Yet she was an opportunity he couldn't ignore.

'Out, you!'

The voice came from behind him. The bar lady with the beehive marched in, Julie at her heels.

'You're banned. Don't come in here again, understand?' She saw Sam's questioning frown. 'Did the same last week. All over the carpet in the other bar. I warned her.'

'We know where she lives. We'll help her get home.'

'Don't put her in your car whatever you do. You'll never get the smell out. It's only five minutes to the manor. Walk'll do her good.'

Sam took Melissa's arm and helped her to her feet. Outside in the car park, when the cold air hit her, she jerked free and staggered backwards, desperately trying to focus on him. 'Do I know you?' she slurred.

'Geoff and Ginny,' said Sam. 'We visited the community this morning.'

'Bitch,' she hissed, swaying back and forth, trying to get them into focus.

'I *beg* your pardon . . .' Julie assumed the epithet was addressed at her.

'Who's a bitch?' Sam asked.

'Ingrid. S'all her fault.'

'What is?'

Melissa's cheeks puffed and she retched again. Sam handed Julie the car keys and asked her to get the torch which he'd left in the glove locker.

'Got to lie down,' Melissa mumbled. She dropped to her knees. 'Wanna die. Here and now.'

'You can't. It's the pub's car park. The landlady'll do her nut.'

Julie returned with the flashlight.

'Help me get her up,' he whispered. Taking an arm each, they pulled Melissa to her feet. 'Now. We're going to walk.'

The woman's breathing was as heavy as a pensioner's.

'How many did you have?' Julie asked.

'Dunno. Feel awful.'

Beyond the spill of the pub lights the road was pitch dark. Sam flicked on the light. 'Got anyone to look after you back at the manor?'

'They hate me. All of 'em. 'Cept Toby. An' even he . . .'

'Why do they hate you?'

'Cos I was closer to the Master than any of 'em . . .'

Sam was taken aback. Surely this unappealing creature hadn't been Harrison's latest lover?

'You said you *were* closer,' he prompted.

'Not there any more.'

'Where's he gone?'

She stopped and half turned her head.

'You a p'leeceman?'

'No. Why d'you ask?'

'They came an' asked *her* about it. Wanted to know where Perry was. But *she* doesn't know.'

'But you do?'

She straightened up, sucking in gulps of air to try to slough off the effects of the booze.

'I don't know *anything*.' The cold was clearing her head. The torch beam picked out frost on the road. 'S'alright. Find my own way now. Don' need your help 'nymore.'

She began walking again, weaving from side to side. Then she stopped and swung round.

'Ingrid thinks she can be leader, but she can't. Cos most of us supported the Master, an' she didn't.'

'Supported?'

'In the fight against the big cor-corporations . . . We were there, Perry and me. London. In June.'

Sam blinked. He'd read about the anti-capitalist protest which had degenerated into violence and vandalism. 'Are you still in touch with the Master?'

'You *are* a reporter, aren't you?' Her face screwed up with suspicion. 'Or a pleece'man.'

'No way.'

The lights of the manor were visible beyond the low, roadside hedge.

'Goin' home now.'

'We'll see you to your door.'

'No!' She lashed out at him and began to walk faster. 'Leave me alone. Rape!'

'She's bonkers,' Julie whispered, grabbing Sam's arm.

The torch beam picked out reflectors on the gate posts marking the Bordhill drive. Melissa reached them, lurched to the right and staggered up the gravel.

Julie hooked her arm through Sam's to stop him following. 'There's no point. Let's go back. I'm freezing to death out here.'

Sam stared at the house. The lights were still on upstairs, but at the *left*-hand end this time.

Someone was in Harrison's private quarters.

Ingrid Madsen?

Or could it be Perry Harrison himself – not missing after all, but in hiding?

9

Ely
Sunday, 9 January

THE REASON FOR the jumpiness at Bordhill Manor the previous day became abundantly clear when Sam read the Sunday papers. The story in the *Telegraph* was representative.

CONCERN OVER MISSING WAR VETERAN

Cambridgeshire police are worried about the apparent disappearance of former World War Two POW Peregrine Harrison, aged 77. He was last seen at his home on December 30th, the day before a letter from him was received at The Times, *attacking Mr Tetsuo Kamata, the Japanese saviour of the Walsall car factory.*

Mr Harrison heads a controversial Buddhist education centre at Bordhill Manor in Cambridgeshire. Yesterday a representative of his community told reporters they had no idea where he was.

The Burma veteran served with the elite Chindit force set up by Brigadier Orde Wingate in 1942 to operate behind Japanese lines. Many Chindits died in action and a few, including an injured Lieutenant Peregrine Harrison, were taken prisoner. Fellow veterans told the Sunday Telegraph *he has never forgiven his former enemy for torturing him and others during their captivity.*

In his letter to The Times, *which was not published, Mr Harrison suggested that now Mr Kamata had been identified as his one time torturer, 'his sudden and bloody removal from this life can only be a matter of time'.*

Asked whether this was being construed as a threat against the Japanese industrialist, a Cambridgeshire police spokesman said, 'Mr Harrison is an elderly man. We are concerned he may be unwell and in need of assistance. That is why we're trying to find him.'

A Downing Street source wouldn't comment on suggestions that now Mr

*Harrison's attack on Mr Kamata was public it could put the Walsall car
factory deal in jeopardy.*

*'The purchase of the factory is a commercial matter and nothing to do with
the government. As to Mr Harrison's whereabouts, the police are conducting a
missing persons inquiry.'*

'So what's your role in all this, exactly?' Julie asked after she read it. She
looked puzzled.

'To find him before he does any harm.'

'And the fact they've roped you in means they think he's gone to the Far
East?'

'They're guessing, but yes.'

She paused, thinking about it.

'You believe he *does* intend to do harm?'

Sam hesitated before answering.

'That's the trouble, Julie. I can't make up my mind.'

After a late breakfast, they checked out of the Waterman's Arms and set off
for Bordhill again, ostensibly to enquire about the well-being of Melissa,
but with the intention of having another chat with her. When they drove
into the courtyard, they found the shop closed and a board hanging on the
door saying the community was not receiving visitors. Sam had called his
controller the night before to request a search of Harrison's private
apartment. Now all he could do was wait for the results of it.

They lunched in the pub again in an unsuccessful attempt at hoovering
up useful gossip, then set off across the flat East Anglian countryside for
Woodbridge. Julie had persuaded Sam to take her to tea with her mother
and son on their way back to London.

The place where Julie usually spent her weekends was a converted
brown-brick mill, sited by the river from which it had once drawn its
power. Lawns stretched to the water's edge. As the car pulled up on the pea
shingle drive, eight-year-old Liam threw open the front door of the house
and ran to greet his mother. He stopped dead when he saw she was
accompanied by the other male in her life. Before being posted to the Far
East, Sam had managed to break down the boy's hostility towards him, but
the months of not being around had undone all his efforts.

They went inside to a warm welcome from Julie's mother Maeve, a
former nurse who spoke with a light Irish accent.

'You look lovely and brown, Sam. I suppose all you do is sunbathe and
play golf out there in Singapore.'

'That's precisely what they pay me for, Maeve.'

She laughed throatily. 'It's good to see you again, anyway.' It had been obvious for some time that she wanted his relationship with Julie to last.

While Maeve set out plates of cake and biscuits and poured tea into bone china cups, Sam squatted on the floor with Liam and challenged him to a Game Boy contest, which he proceeded to lose.

The time passed swiftly and before long Liam lost interest in the grown-ups, turning his attention to the TV. As soon as was decent, Sam suggested they make a move. Julie took leave of her son quickly, nuzzling his ear while he was still absorbed in his programme. The boy waved her away.

Outside, night had closed in. The headlamps picked out wintry hedgerows on the curving road to Ipswich. Julie was silent. Sam knew what she was thinking – that being a weekend-only single parent was a lousy way to bring up a child.

After a while she turned and thanked him for taking her to Woodbridge. 'It meant a lot to mum that you brought me over. Even if Liam isn't easy with you.'

Sam knew the visit had been for Julie's benefit rather than her mother's. She was testing him. Still trying to decide what sort of father he'd make, should they finally decide to settle down together.

For the rest of the journey to London, they talked very little. Sam's mind kept hopping back to Thailand and the unresolved case of Jimmy Squires. And he thought about Midge, a little guiltily.

They arrived back in Ealing shortly before eight. While Julie bunged a frozen pizza in the oven and prepared a salad, Sam took another look at Waddell's background file on Peregrine Harrison. The Special Branch had done sound, solid police work. Four close-typed pages. It was the section on Harrison's family he wanted to look at again. His English wife had died ten years ago, but they'd had a son, Charles, born in 1950. Like everyone else, he'd told Special Branch he had no idea where his father was. Hadn't even spoken to him for over a month.

Gave the impression he didn't care much either, the report concluded.

Charles worked as a barrister in the Inner Temple, it said. There was an office phone number and one for his home. Sam dialled it.

The call was answered by a woman with a deep, languid voice that conjured up headscarves, the countryside and the bark of hounds.

'May I ask who's calling?' she enquired.

'I work for the Foreign Office. The name won't mean anything to him. But tell him it's to do with his father.'

'Oh . . . Has something happened?'

'Not that I know of. Expecting something?'

'Um . . .' She sounded off-balanced by his question. 'Hang on and I'll get my husband.'

He heard the click of heels on a wooden floor as she walked down a corridor in what must have been a very spacious home. A few moments later he heard heavier footsteps returning.

'Hello?' A male voice, soft and inquisitive.

'I'm so sorry to trouble you on a Sunday night, Mr Harrison. My name's Maxwell from the Foreign Office.'

'What department?'

'I deal with international issues . . .'

'You mean some of your people *don't*?'

Sam ignored the sarcasm. 'Look, I'd be very grateful for a chat about your father. We're a little concerned.'

'I've already spoken to Special Branch.'

'I know. Any chance we could meet tomorrow?'

'I'm in court all day.'

'In your lunchbreak perhaps?'

'God, I only get about twenty minutes . . .' He broke off and Sam guessed he was calculating something. 'Well, all right. I shouldn't need to confer with my client unless things go horribly awry. It's at the Old Bailey. There's an Irish pub almost opposite called Seamus O'Donnell's. I could meet you outside it. About one o'clock? How will I recognise you?'

'I'll be carrying a copy of your father's book.'

'Heavens . . . I'd hoped it was out of print by now. All right. Until tomorrow then. But I should warn you, my father's a law unto himself. I don't think I'll be able to help.'

As he put the phone down Sam smelled burning. He walked into the kitchen.

Julie had the oven door open and was pulling out their smoking supper, conscious of Sam's eyes on her.

'There's something wrong with this thermostat,' she insisted, uncomfortably aware that her culinary skills could be listed on the back of her thumb. 'You're a man. *Do* something about it.' She slid the pizza onto a board. 'Anyway, it's not too bad. And charcoal's good for the digestion.' She smiled feebly at him.

Sam wondered if it mattered that the woman he was thinking of marrying couldn't cook.

Monday, 10 January

CHARLES HARRISON WAS unmistakably his father's son, even if Sam had only seen his old man in photos. The same lean features and indecent growth of fair hair. And the same intently searching eyes.

The lawyer strode across from the Old Bailey and pointed unhesitatingly at the book Sam was clutching.

'Mr Maxwell, I presume.' He projected his voice as if still in a courtroom. He had rid himself of his robes and wore a plain, dark suit over a blue shirt and golf-club tie.

'Good of you to spare the time,' Sam mumbled.

'That place is desperately noisy,' Harrison commented, pointing at the pub behind them. 'There's a Prêt-à-Manger round the corner, but it'll mean standing. How are your legs?'

'Should be up to it.'

Harrison strode ahead like a teacher. 'I've got about half an hour,' he explained, turning his head, 'which should be plenty since there's not much I can tell you.'

They entered the crowded lunch spot, selecting packaged baguettes from a refrigerated display and small bottles of water. Sam insisted on paying, then they perched at a chest-high, zinc-topped counter.

'Now . . .' Harrison eyed Sam like the trained interrogator he was. 'What sort of Foreign Office bird, are you, my *friend*? Maxwell's not your real name, I imagine.'

Sam flicked open his sandwich pack without looking up.

'I deal with security issues, if that's what you're asking.'

Charles Harrison nodded, pleased he'd guessed right. 'And the powers-that-be have been thoroughly rattled by my father's letter to *The Times*?'

'That and the fact nobody wants to tell us where he is.'

'In my case it's not a matter of *wanting*, I simply don't know. After you rang last night I phoned Bordhill. Ingrid Madsen's usually been straightforward with me, but this time she was abrupt, almost to the point of rudeness.'

'The press were on her back at the weekend,' Sam commented.

'So I saw. Downing Street stonewalling pretty effectively.'

Sam took a bite from his baguette. All around them office girls were gossiping, but out of earshot.

'Has he ever done this before? Disappearing.'

Harrison sighed. 'You see, that's where I'm not going to be much use to you. I really have no way of knowing, since he and I only speak once or twice a year. He may do this sort of thing every other month for all I know. Or maybe he's had a sudden onset of Alzheimer's and wandered off into the woods somewhere.'

'Is that a serious suggestion?'

Charles Harrison shook his head. 'Nothing wrong with his memory as far as I know.'

'You sound as if you're not too concerned.'

'It's not easy to care about a man who only ever made a token effort at being interested in *my* existence. Someone who made my mother's life an absolute misery.' He said it with vehemence.

'She died ten years ago?'

'Is it that long?' He sounded surprised.

'Did she stay in touch with your father to the end of her life?'

'No way. Wouldn't countenance it after he walked out on her a second time. Finally learned her lesson.'

'When did *you* last see him?'

'About six weeks ago.

'Where?'

'He was in hospital.'

'Oh?' This was news. 'Why didn't you mention that to the police?'

'They didn't ask the question. And *I* wouldn't have known he was ill if I hadn't let my teenage daughter goad me into dropping in at Bordhill on my way back from a job in Norwich. Said it was disgraceful how little contact we had with her grandfather.'

'What was wrong with him?'

'Old man's disease. Prostate. Although to get him to tell me about it was like squeezing water from a stone. For someone whose life has been driven by sex, he found the mechanics of it hard to discuss. Only when I tracked down his doctor did I learn he'd been made impotent by the operation. The cancer is fuelled by testosterone apparently. Stopping production of the hormone by cutting his balls off was the only thing they could do to prolong his life.'

Waddell's words came winging back to Sam – Harrison's lawyer thought his client didn't expect to live long. Now they knew why. And contrary to the conclusion his controller had come to, it had nothing to do with Tetsuo Kamata.

'How long did they give him?'

'The doc was loath to commit himself – you know what medics are like. But they were talking months rather than years.' The lawyer snorted with derision. 'Poor sod. No more injecting his worldly wisdom into his female students through their nether regions.'

'At seventy-seven, he can't have done much of that in recent years,' Sam remarked.

'Don't you believe it. Until the op he claimed to have the libido of a young man. Told me once that he hoped to die in the act with a woman young enough to be his granddaughter. He was being deliberately provocative,' he added, seeing Sam's raised eyebrows.

Sam fiddled with the cap of the mineral water bottle. If Harrison was terminally ill there could be a tragically simple explanation for his disappearance. He might have driven somewhere remote and piped the car exhaust through the window.

'How was he when you saw him? Depressed?'

'Hard to say. Still hadn't grasped what had happened I suspect.'

Sam scratched his head. 'I can't understand why the people at Bordhill didn't mention this to the police.'

'Under strict instructions not to, probably. And there's no reason why anyone other than Ingrid Madsen would've known. My father was quite remote from most of the residents.'

'Apart from the ones he was sleeping with.'

'Quite.'

'Any idea who his latest was?'

'None at all. The only woman I know at the manor is Ingrid, and I've always got the impression that when it comes to earthly pleasures she's not in favour of them.'

'It amazes me he got away with it for so long,' Sam commented.

'Masters write their own rules. Anyway, for my father, Bordhill Manor was never about religion or philosophy. It's about having people on tap to play his own private games with.' He looked at his watch, a reminder that their time was short.

'I'm trying to get a feeling for how his mind works,' Sam said. 'So we can anticipate what he might do.'

'That letter really got to you people, didn't it?'

'In the context of his disappearance we *have* to see it as a threat,' Sam said solemnly. 'I'm curious. When you were a child, how aware were you of what he'd been through in the camps?'

'Never knew anything about it until that book came out.'

'You astonish me.'

'I was only three when he abandoned my ma first time round and went back to Burma. Didn't really meet the man until he returned in '62. I was twelve.'

'Your mother . . . ?'

'Avoided mentioning him. Certainly never talked about his past.'

'So when he returned it was a bit of a shock.'

'Highly unsettling. Until then it had just been her and me at home. A family of two, with a few photos to remind me I'd once had a father. Then, suddenly he turned up. And instead of mum telling him to bugger off after dumping her like that, she welcomed him home. Settled him in front of the fire like he'd merely popped down to the post office. I felt thoroughly displaced. Particularly as my father had no knack with children. We had polite but meaningless conversations for a year which felt like a decade. And never any mention of what had happened in the war. Then he left again to set up the Bordhill Community. My hapless mother tried to pass this second desertion off as father having been called by God to live in a monastery. But I wasn't fooled. I could see the defeat in her eyes. He broke her spirit, Mr Maxwell. It was a bad time for us.'

'I can imagine. But surely, at that stage, your mother must have told you what the Japs had done to him? As a way of explaining his strange behaviour.'

'Nope. I'm telling you, it simply didn't feature in my childhood. Like sex, it was a subject one simply didn't discuss at home. It may have been because she didn't dare tell me about it. I was a rather precocious twelve year old, with very firm views. To me, the dropping of the atom bombs on Hiroshima and Nagasaki was a far greater obscenity than what the Japs did to the likes of my father.'

'So what did you think when he spilled it all out in *Jungle Path to Hell*?'

'I was shaken. Naturally. I was twenty-five when the book came out, my mind rather more open by then.' He took in a deep breath, as if trying to prevent some deep-seated emotions coming to the surface. 'Mixed feelings, you could say. The details of his childhood I certainly found fascinating, but I felt cheated having to learn it from a book.'

'Of course.'

'And the descriptions of the war in Burma, his capture, the torture and so on . . . it brought it all home. To discover someone related to me had been through all that and survived – well, you simply have to stand up and salute, don't you? Whatever your reservations about the man in question.' He squeezed his jaw. 'You've read the book? All of it?'

'Not all. But a lot.'

'I wonder if you can guess the part I found hardest to take?'

Sam said he couldn't.

'Learning I had two half-brothers. That he'd had two more sons by a Burmese woman after abandoning my mother that first time.'

'You never knew that?'

Harrison shook his head.

'Your mother . . . ?'

'Didn't know anything about it either. That's what resolved her never to speak to him again.'

'Not surprisingly.'

'He'd admitted having relationships during the decade away, but nothing about children. Nothing about having lived with one particular woman all that time, even going through a form of marriage with her.' Harrison exhaled through pursed lips. 'It was bigamy. My parents weren't divorced.'

'These half-brothers – you've met them since?'

'No. Don't even know their Burmese names. He uses English ones in the book. George and Michael.'

'Never tried to make contact?'

'No. Too far away, both culturally and geographically. I'm not a great traveller, Mr Maxwell. We prefer our summers in Cornwall or the Lake District. Only go long distances if we really have to.'

'And your father made no effort to put you in touch.'

'None. I have a feeling he felt bad about his Burmese woman. More so than he did about my mother. Tried to shut it out. But . . . well, his attitude to women is absolutely outrageous, as you know. He uses them with great selfishness. And yet they forgive him.' He tapped his fingers on the book which lay next to their sandwich wrappings. 'When this little time-bomb came out, the *News of the World* did an exposé on Bordhill. Tracked down a couple of young women who'd spent a few years there. Each told the same story of a secret and highly intimate liaison with my father, which ended when he moved on to the next young initiate. Both took it without protest and said they felt privileged to have been chosen by him. Now, that's *power*, Mr Maxwell, when you can get women to love you so unconditionally.'

'Enviable power,' Sam muttered. 'His women may have been forgiving, but what about your father himself? Any sign he's prepared to put the past behind him now he's nearing his end?'

'Not when it comes to the Japanese, no.'

'You ever discuss that with him?'

'In recent years, yes. I told him his refusal to buy Japanese goods was daft. But he wouldn't be shifted. He hates them with a passion and won't do anything to benefit them financially, or in any other way for that matter.'

'Is he still having nightmares?'

'Oh yes. The same dream every time. The face of the man torturing him. You know the worst thing for him?'

'The utter brutality of it?'

'No. They were fighting a war and dreadful things were done by all sides. No. What he couldn't forgive was that the Japs destroyed his self-respect.' The lawyer leaned forward, lowering his voice while strengthening its intensity. 'They reduced him to a level where he was forced to confront his own weakness, Mr Maxwell. Once, a few years ago in about the only moment of openness I can remember, my father told me he'd cried like a baby when they tortured him. Wept with self-pity and self-loathing. And that man, Tetsuo Kamata, had just watched. Looked down at him with utter contempt. That's what my father can't forget. They cut out his pride, you see. Systematically. Like excising a tongue. Something that could never be restored. That was the reason he had those breakdowns after the war, the ones my mother nursed him through. Because the Japs had made him feel completely worthless. And,' he added with one eyebrow raised, 'it didn't help that his fellow countrymen showed no interest whatsoever when he and his fellow POWs returned home. Oh yes. His hatred of the Japanese makes perfect sense to me, even if I wish he'd been able to get over it.'

'You believe he'll try to kill Kamata?'

Harrison pursed his lips and upended the mineral water bottle into the plastic beaker. He stared down at the bursting bubbles, warily watching each one as if it were a new piece of evidence he'd not expected.

'I don't know.'

'Could he do it?' Sam pressed.

Harrison flicked a glance upwards. 'He killed Japanese soldiers during the war. Used a bayonet on several of them. Hasn't got the same physical strength today, but you don't need brawn to end a man's life. You need brains and determination, and he's got plenty of those.'

'So where's he gone? If he were going to kill Kamata, where would he do it?'

The lawyer shook his head. 'Guessing's not my thing.' He looked at his watch again. 'Now I *really* have to go.' Leaning forward one more time, he added, 'I'll tell you one thing for free, though. Now he knows about his cancer, uppermost in my father's mind would be the realisation that he has to act soon.'

'Because . . .'

'. . . if he doesn't, *he'll* die before Kamata does. And he wouldn't like that, Mr Maxwell. Wouldn't like it at all.'

A s t h e y w a l k e d back towards the Old Bailey, Sam asked Charles Harrison if he'd known about his father's involvement in protests against the multinationals.

'No, but it doesn't surprise me. He'd join any organisation that meant fresh totty to get his hands on.'

With that final burst of cynicism he bade Sam goodbye and hurried back into the Central Criminal Court.

The sun had come out, but there was a cold wind. Sam continued towards St Paul's underground station, then took a diversion into a quieter side street to phone Duncan Waddell on his mobile.

His controller sounded out of breath and admitted to having run up several flights of stairs after going for a sandwich. Sam told him about Perry Harrison's terminal illness.

'Ah,' he exclaimed, sounding almost hopeful. 'You mean you've found him in a hospice somewhere?'

'No such luck. Has Kamata left the UK yet?'

'Still in London. Flying back to Tokyo tomorrow.'

'And after that? You've got his diary?'

'We're still working on it. His hotel room's been searched, along with those of his staff, but nothing was found about his future travel plans. Tokyo station is trying to recruit someone inside Matsubara.'

'It'll take too long.'

'And we don't have the resources, to be honest.'

'What about the search of Bordhill?'

'That's being worked on.'

Sam heard shouting in the distance. He swung round to see where it was coming from, but the street was boxed in by offices which blocked his view.

'Duncan, I need a full breakdown of everything the Matsubara Corporation does. And a list of the countries it's involved in. Every last tentacle, down to the smallest subsidiary.'

'We're collecting that already. I'll email it to you. What are your immediate plans?'

The shouting was getting closer. Chanting too.

'There seems to be a demo. I'm somewhere near St Paul's.'

'That's the anti-global mob,' Waddell told him gruffly. 'The City police have pulled hundreds of extra men in on overtime. Don't you *ever* read newspapers?'

Sam ignored the remark. 'Perry Harrison took part in the last protest in June. Did you know that?'

'Nothing surprises me with that man.'

'Think I'll go and take a look.'

'For God's sake, he's hardly likely to turn up there . . .'

'No, but some of his friends might. I'll ring you in a couple of hours.'

Melissa Dennis sensed that today's demo would end up being a waste of time. The turnout was poor and the atmosphere lacked the electricity of the last time she'd marched against the global corporations. She kept wondering if it would have been different had Perry been with them, but she suspected that even his enthusiasm and inspiring words would have failed to lift the glumness that hovered over her and her companions like a cloud of midges.

Three of them had driven up from Cambridgeshire that morning. Toby had hardly spoken to her since the incident on Saturday, save to remind her precisely what had happened at the pub in case the alcohol had wiped it from her memory. And the other man in their group, with whom she'd never had much in common, was a moody schizophrenic, whose stability depended on remembering to take his medicine.

So the morning had consisted of a rather silent drive south, followed by a miserable plod through the cold, damp fumes of London's streets. Today, however, she didn't mind the surly silence of her immediate companions. Welcomed it even, because her mind was far too busy with plans to want to be distracted by idle chatter.

The procession rounded a corner and she spotted the dome of St Paul's. She had half a mind to break away from the demo and pop into the cathedral for a rest and to get warm. And to give the pain in her insides a chance to ease up.

Sam walked towards the noise. Emerging onto Newgate Street and facing north towards the tall, grey towers of the Barbican he saw the head of the procession approaching, its banners and floats tailing back. A police incident-control van crawled a few feet in front, an officer watching the crowd from inside a perspex bubble on the roof.

The protest looked small and unthreatening. Sam stood at the kerb as it passed, studying faces and banners. Some slogans were rants against the Big Mac, others were old-fashioned Marxist dogma. Their target list was wide – globalisation and almost anything bad that could be attributed to men with million-pound salaries.

Several of the faces were middle-aged and bucolic, looking uncomfortably rustic alongside those with spiky hair and studs. He searched their ranks for Melissa, his memory of what she looked like distorted by images of her puke-smeared pullover. She was shorter than Julie, he recalled. Less than five foot eight, therefore. Hair dark and unruly, eyes greyish.

A phalanx of banners proclaiming the evils of GM foods passed him by. Then the crowd began to thin. He glanced right. A second police van was bringing up the rear. If this was the demo, they'd had a wasted day. Wouldn't even make the TV news. No windows smashed. No paint daubed. And no Melissa.

Sam began jogging towards the head of the parade to have another look. Then, all of a sudden, he saw her. At a bus stop, sitting droopily in the shelter, the seat beside her empty.

'Hello,' he exclaimed, sitting down next to her. 'Fancy seeing you here.'

She shot him a glance that bore no sign of recognition. The eyes, he noticed, were a sort of blue.

'Sorry?'

'I'm Geoff, remember? Ginny and I visited Bordhill at the weekend. And we helped you home from the pub on Saturday night.'

'Oh God. That was *you*?' She looked acutely embarrassed. 'I had a vague memory somebody had. Sorry.'

'Happens to us all.'

She made no effort to continue the conversation. Then she closed her eyes as if in pain.

'You all right?'

'N-no,' she winced. 'Not too well at the moment as it happens.'

Still hungover, Sam suspected. 'Can I do anything for you?'

She shook her head. A bus drew up, but she made no effort to board it.

'Where are you heading?'

'N-nowhere just now. This is the only place I could find to sit.'

'You were on the demo?'

She nodded.

Sam looked over his shoulder.

'There's one of those coffee chain places down the road. Be warmer there. I'll buy you a latte.'

Melissa fixed him with a stony glare. 'Don't you *know* those places exploit people? – Guatemalan farmers, their own employees.'

'It just happens to be near,' Sam answered apologetically. 'You look in bad need of something to warm you up.'

A warm drink might help ease the pain in her stomach, she decided. Anything was better than freezing out here.

'Perhaps there's somewhere else.' She stood up stiffly and peered along the pavement.

'I can see a place with an Italian-looking name,' Sam said, pointing. 'Prepared to risk *that*?'

'I guess so. Thank you.' As they began to walk from the bus shelter, she pooh-poohed his offer of an arm. 'I'm okay, really. Just the usual female trouble.'

In the warm fug of the café they sat opposite one another with cappucinos. She eyed him warily, trying to guess from his expression whether she'd said things she shouldn't have done on Saturday.

'How d'you think it went, the protest?' Sam asked as an opener.

'All right. Disappointing turnout though. People put off by the stuff in the press about violence. The trouble with anti-globalisation is that everybody's got their own agenda.'

'What's yours?'

'Simply to make people aware of the fact that our lives are increasingly controlled by unelected bodies called corporations who exploit the poor of the third world,' she said in a monotone, fixing him with a disparaging look. 'They dictate what we eat, what we wear, and how we spend our free time.'

'You don't strike me as being a person who'd let herself be dictated to.'

She ignored his attempt at flattery.

'Perry Harrison not with you this time?' he asked innocently.

Melissa felt a frisson of alarm. He'd asked a lot of things about Perry on Saturday night, she remembered. Suspected him of being a policeman or reporter. She shook her head.

'Did you come from Bordhill all by yourself, then?'

'There's three of us.' She held out her arm to look at her watch. 'I said I'd meet them back at the minibus at three. We left it in North London and came into the centre on the tube.' She did a quick mental calculation and decided she was okay for time. Despite her suspicions about him, she found she was quite liking the attention she was getting from this man. Nice to have someone interested. Because it didn't happen that often.

'You work near here, Geoff?'

'Yes. In finance.' He smiled self-deprecatingly. 'I guess I must be the sort of person you've been protesting against.'

Melissa was far from sure he wasn't really a journalist, but decided she didn't care. The vapours from the coffee, the general warmth of the place and his friendly presence across the table were making her feel a lot better.

'I hear Perry Harrison's very ill,' Sam said. 'Sad news.'

Now she was *really* worried. This was *very* sensitive information he'd come out with. 'Who told you that?' She had a horrible feeling it must've been herself, letting it slip on Saturday night.

'His son told me. I met him this morning at some City do. Quite by chance. Extraordinary thing.'

She gulped with relief.

'Said his father had terminal cancer.'

Melissa nodded solemnly. She'd always found it hard to talk about serious illness and death and her eyes began to water. 'He didn't want anyone at Bordhill to know,' she whispered, extracting a tissue from a pocket in her jeans.

'But *you* knew?'

'Well yes. Because he confided in me. About most things actually,' she added, dabbing her eyes.

'He tell anyone else?'

'Ingrid, I imagine.'

'Was he having a relationship with her?'

Melissa gasped. 'What on earth makes you think that?' Despite trying not to, she began to blush, then gabbled on rapidly to cover it up. 'He'd have told Ingrid because she's his deputy and has to plan for the future. She's effectively in charge now that Bordhill's become a trust. Perry made it over to them a fortnight ago. The house – everything. Ingrid is one of the trustees *and* general manager, so she has enormous power.'

Melissa had been warned not to talk about this, but she *wanted* people to know about the iniquity of what was happening. Didn't care anymore whether this man was a reporter or not.

'Who are the other trustees?'

'Perry himself, until he passes on. A man calling himself Aung Shwe who leads a Buddhist order in the West Country. He's actually an Englishman. And Robert Wetherby who's a very old friend of Perry's. Lives in Suffolk. They were in the war together. Aung Shwe's been making eyes at Ingrid, so I suspect he has some protégé in mind for Bordhill.'

A lifetime's work being picked over by his underlings – another possible reason for Harrison's disappearance, Sam surmised.

'What does Perry say about that? You must still be in touch with him – you said you were closer than anyone else at Bordhill.'

'He's very unhappy about it, of course.' Melissa bit her tongue, aware she needed to exercise *some* restraint. 'I know that, because I've been his PA for the past couple of years.'

'When did you last see him?'

'Nobody's seen him since the end of the year.'

'Oh yes. I read that in the papers. What did it involve, being his PA?'

'Helping with admin. Lots of letters that needed answers. And there were odd things I sorted out for him, like the Internet.'

'*Internet?*' Naïvely, Sam had never imagined seventy-seven year olds tapping into the web. 'He was online a lot?'

'I don't actually know,' she replied. 'Once I'd shown him how to use the browser and e-mail and set up some newsgroups for him, I left him to it.'

'What sort of newsgroups?'

'Anything to do with Burma.'

She closed her eyes in disbelief. Had she actually said that? Let the word slip out as if it had no particular meaning?

'Because of being born there,' she added in a rapid effort to fudge things. 'He loved that country. Hated the fact the military rulers had changed the name to Myanmar. And was awfully exercised by what the regime's done to suppress the will of the people.'

Sam's suspicions multiplied. 'He contacted other people interested in Burma? On the Internet – is that what you're saying?'

'I don't really know. All I did was set up an anonymous email post-box for him – *Myoman* he called himself.' She allowed herself a little smile, unable to resist the chance to show *how* close she'd been to her Master. 'Apparently *Myo* is a name the Burmese give a child born on a Thursday. And Perry was.'

Myoman. Sam memorised it. 'This was recent, him being on the Internet?'

'Since learning he didn't have long to live.'

'D'you know why he suddenly took it up?'

'To find out about Burma, I assume. He wanted to put things right, you see. Before he passed away. With the family. Hoped to make his peace with them.' She kicked herself for telling him that. Engaging mouth before brain, as usual.

'Was he still in touch with . . .' Sam snapped his fingers. 'I've forgotten the name of the Burmese wife.'

'Tin Su. No, he wasn't in touch. Which is partly what he was upset about. Not knowing what had happened to her and their two sons.'

'So is that where he's gone, d'you think? To Burma?'

Melissa's insides turned over. This was absolutely not the conclusion she'd wanted him to draw, yet by letting her tongue run away with itself it was inevitable that he would.

'Oh I wouldn't have thought so. It's the other side of the world and he's very unwell.'

Watching Melissa's face was like seeing curtains move on a stage. Sam couldn't decide if anything meaningful was going on behind them.

'My own, rather sad feeling is that he may have just slipped off somewhere to die,' she declared, eyes widening with the ingenuity of her fantasy. 'Well away from all the fuss over his succession at Bordhill. You know, like animals do. He's always been close to nature. What does Charles think?'

'Charles was concerned about what his father might do to that Japanese bloke . . .'

Melissa blinked. 'What Japanese bloke?'

'Kagata, Kamata or whatever his name is. The one who's buying the Walsall car plant.'

There was still no sign she'd understood.

'The man Perry mentioned in his book,' he explained. 'The Jap who tortured him.'

Melissa wrinkled her brow. 'Yes, yes, I know all about that. But I still don't understand. What might Perry *do* to him?'

'You didn't know about his letter to *The Times*?'

She felt incredibly stupid all of a sudden.

'On New Year's Eve. Saying Britain shouldn't accept financial support from a man with blood on his hands. It wasn't published but there was stuff in the Sunday papers about it yesterday.'

'I don't read newspapers,' she said, defensively. 'They're so full of lies.' But she was shocked that something as significant as this could have passed her by. And that Perry hadn't told her. 'But I still don't understand why Charles should be so worried.'

'It's because of what the letter said at the end. That now Mr Kamata had come into the open it wouldn't be long before one of his former victims did away with him.'

Her eyes widened. For several seconds she couldn't speak. Her world had just turned upside-down.

'The implication being that Perry himself might be the one to do it,' Sam added, so she wouldn't miss the point.

'I . . . I have to go,' she stammered. 'The others . . . they'll be waiting for me.'

Sam hunched forward, realising he'd touched a button.

'Perry needs help, Melissa. If you know where he is . . . '

She stood up and backed away, recalling all the stupid things she'd let slip in the last few minutes.

'I have to go now,' she whispered. 'Oh . . .' She started digging in the pocket of her coat. 'Can I give you some money for my coffee?'

'Forget it.' He stood up too and grabbed hold of her arm. 'Where's Perry gone, Melissa?'

'I honestly don't know.' She jerked herself free and headed for the door.

Sam followed close on her heels, but as they reached the pavement there was a squeal of brakes and a bus drew up. Melissa ran to board it. She stood on the platform as it pulled away, staring back at him as if he'd set the devil on her tail.

12

Less than an hour later Sam was back in the Ealing flat, with two new leads to check out – the Internet sites and Harrison's friend Robert Wetherby. It had begun to rain on the walk back from the tube. He hung his dripping coat on a hook in the hall and stuck his collapsible umbrella in the kitchen sink. It'd be another hour before Julie was home.

He powered up his laptop and was about to plug it into the phone socket to search for Burma newsgroups on the Internet when he noticed the answerphone flashing. He touched the replay button.

'*Hello Julie. I'm around for a few days. Love to see you. Could you ring me on my mobile?*' A man's voice. Foreign accent. Eastern European by the sound of it.

Sam stared at the machine as if it had bitten him. There were east Europeans in his past who wanted him dead.

He played the message again, listening for anything familiar in the voice. Then he drummed his fingers on the table, realising it wasn't his safety he was worried about.

He was jealous.

They'd had an understanding, he and Julie. An agreement that if they had the odd fling while apart, they wouldn't let it intrude on their relationship. But this cock crow from inside that damned plastic box, had done exactly that.

No name given – no need to, because the voice would be familiar to her. No number either, because she could doubtless dial it from memory.

He jabbed the modem plug into the wall socket and connected his laptop to the Internet. His email contained another message from Midge. It made him swallow his anger. What right did *he* have to get uptight about Julie's shenanigans – if that's what this was? He was hardly guiltless himself.

There'd been a couple of women he'd slept with in the last year. Business execs he'd met in hotels, away from home territory. Clever women hungry for the whiff of adventure. No surnames. None given, none sought. No numbers exchanged. No risk of conflict with their normal lives.

Which was why he resented that damned voice breaking into *his* space. His and Julie's.

He forced himself to concentrate on the screen. The email from Midge was to tell him that another cargo of cheap Burmese heroin had just hit the Sydney streets.

The man we suspect of pushing the stuff is ex Australian SAS. Name of Marty Hebble. Military records show that a couple of years ago he was on a joint training exercise with your lot. We've asked your MoD in London to find out if Jimmy Squires was in the British unit involved. Seems impossible to believe he wasn't.

We need to nail these creeps before any more suckers die, Steve. Don't know what you're up to now, but please don't give up on me.

Yours till the cows come home,

Love

Beth

Despite having been drunk at the time, he could still recall the taste of her mouth.

'God Almighty . . .'

He had no damned right to get worked up over Julie's phone message, yet he couldn't help himself and touched the play button on the machine one more time. It was the familiarity of the man that irked him. He sounded so at ease. So chummy. So bloody intimate.

He turned back to the PC, punching the keys to select 'newsgroups' on his mail browser. Then he ran a search for ones dealing with Burma. A couple came up which seemed promising. The machine downloaded scores of messages, but most were gabbles, a waste of time and space. Distractedly he clicked the 'find' icon and typed in *Myoman* to see if anything appeared. Nothing did. He tried hyphenating it and altering the spelling, but with the same result. Had Melissa remembered wrongly, or could he have misheard? Or maybe Harrison simply hadn't used these particular sites.

He jumped the cursor to the top of the list, pursuing a new thought. The date of the first message was a week ago. Anything Harrison contributed would have been earlier than that. He clicked on the options menu to see if he could reset some filter or other to reach further back in time, but failed to find a way.

He knew a whole government department that wouldn't fail, however. Disconnecting from the Internet, he rang his controller at Vauxhall Cross. Waddell promised to get back to him within a couple of hours.

Sam stood up and crossed to the window, staring down at the street. By now the pavements were covered by a thin film of slush. This was the worst part of an English winter. However hard it was to cope with the heat and humidity of the Far East, he preferred it to this.

He felt calmer now. More rational. It was being separated from Julie that was causing the problem. They *had* to spend more time together. He decided to have another go at persuading her to join him in Singapore.

As much as anything, to get her away from the bloke with the east European accent.

On the A1(M) north of Hatfield

Melissa Dennis sat at the front of the minibus next to Toby who was driving. The wipers cut smeary arcs out of the filth kicked up by the trucks and cars in front of them. She stared through the murk, seeing nothing, her mind preoccupied with the startling twist to events that she'd learned a few hours ago. Instead of trying to make peace with his family as she'd imagined, the man she admired most in the world could well be bent on murder.

When she'd got back to the vehicle in West Hampstead, after a pre-planned detour to an address off Berkeley Square, there'd been no sign of the others. She'd fretted, fearing the demonstration might have become more impressive after she'd dropped out, with them all being invited into 10 Downing Street to make their case.

She'd arrived at the van shortly before the agreed hour, at ten to three, but it was nearer four when the others turned up. Half-frozen by then, she'd been far from amused to learn that when the rally broke up her companions had spent an hour warming themselves in a pub. She'd demanded a seat at the front on the way back home, to be near the heating vents.

As she stared ahead, mesmerised by the sweep and creak of the wipers, her mind was an aviary of ideas. Ever since Perry revealed he hadn't long to live, she'd known his approaching death would mark the end of one phase of her own existence and the beginning of the next.

She'd decided to write a book. A memorial to him. To pick up the story of his life from where his autobiography had left off twenty-five years earlier. She'd even thought of a title – *The Path Back From Hell* – *a biography of Peregrine Harrison written by his intimate friend and confidante Melissa Dennis*.

Ever since she was very young, Melissa had believed she would write a book one day. Books had played such a part in her life. Her schooling had been conducted in the confines of her own home under her parents' tutelage – an isolated house in the depths of the country where books had provided the only window into the wider world. Under the critical eye of her mother she'd studied their construction. Later, at university, she'd listened to authors spelling out the joy and pain of creation. And she'd continued to read widely. Biographies, histories, novels. She knew she could create a written work herself. Knew she had to now. Because even though Perry would die soon, the memory of him mustn't.

At first, the one thing she hadn't been able to decide was how to set about it. Whether to remain at Bordhill after Perry's death and write about him from within the community, or take herself far away in the hope of doing it with a clearer head. The problem was she had nowhere to go. Her only relatives were her parents. They lived at the far tip of Cornwall and she'd had almost no contact with them since the 'great upheaval' eight years ago.

The thought of rebuilding those links purely to get a roof over her head while she wrote was anathema to her. And the atmosphere would make work impossible. They would want to control what she did. Want to deconstruct her every sentence until the very pith had been sucked out. And at some point they would turn on her as they had in the past. Focus on her all that energy and pressure which *they* thought of as positive and beneficial, but which had driven her to the breakdown that had ended her university studies in 1992.

No. No more of that.

The minibus turned off the motorway onto the A505, climbing over the downs that joined Hertfordshire to Cambridgeshire. It was a landscape she loved. Sweeping empty skies above huge fields of furrowed grey earth, speckled with chalk and flint. Rolling grassland with small copses of wind-bent beech and blackthorn. In the three years she'd lived at the Bordhill community she'd often come here on summer weekends, striding up to the highest points and marvelling at the distances she could see. Now it was mid-winter and dark, but with her eyes closed she could visualise it all exactly.

Twenty minutes later, as the minibus dipped towards the plains of Cambridgeshire, all Melissa could think about was Perry's tortured soul. Could he really be bent on revenge? It went so against her perception of him. Peregrine Harrison was a force for good, a man who believed his position in the next life depended on the merits he'd scored in this. And however much of a pick-and-mix attitude he'd had to the *dhamma*, reincarnation was something she knew he believed in. Surely he would never willingly harm another living creature? It would be his own acts of inhumanity he'd need to attend to, not those of others.

In the weeks before his sudden disappearance she'd watched Perry become preoccupied with the fate of his Burmese family and after much cogitation had convinced herself that it was to the present-day state of Myanmar that he must have gone.

Despite the hot air blasting at her thighs, Melissa shivered. From fear – not of what might be happening to Perry, but of the alarmingly adventurous plan she'd spent the last few days working out.

If she was to write authentically about his final moments, then she knew she had to experience them with him. At that very moment her passport was sitting in a grubby cubby hole at the Myanmar Embassy off Berkeley Square, awaiting its visa stamp. But the idea of actually travelling to such a far off place terrified her. Her furthest venture abroad so far had been to Paris for a weekend. And *where* in Burma would she find him, particularly now it appeared his journey there might have a double purpose?

The headlights picked out the gateposts to Bordhill. Toby braked gently and turned in. Melissa looked up at the half-lit old manor, knowing the only place to find an answer to her questions was in that darkened wing of the upper floor which until a few days ago had been Perry's secure domain. A place sealed off by a combination lock whose code she wasn't supposed to know.

But she did know it.

13

West London

SAM'S CONTROLLER RANG at ten to six to tell him to look at his email. 'I've sent you the list of Matsubara's global interests. And IT have come up with a clutch of newsgroup postings involving your man's login. They've copied them to you.'

'Excellent. There's something else I need. The address and phone number of a man called Robert Wetherby. He's a friend of Harrison's and lives in Suffolk. I've checked the directories but there's no record.'

'We'll find it. Oh, and we're moving on the search of the premises.' He cleared his throat. 'Should have a result in the morning.'

A couple of minutes later Sam was online downloading.

Then Julie walked in.

'Hi, lover!' She kissed him softly on the mouth. A supermarket bag swung from her hand.

'Hi, sweetheart. Message on the machine for you.'

She didn't ask who from, but went straight to the recorder to play it. Sam tried to concentrate on the screen, but when he heard the contorted vowels from the loudspeaker again he glanced across. Julie had her face turned away. He watched her press the erase button, stand up, then walk towards the door.

'Going to take a shower,' she announced without meeting his eyes.

Sam bit his tongue. This was a game he didn't want to play. He stared determinedly at the screen.

The first of Harrison's *Myoman* messages had been posted to the Burma newsgroups at the end of November. It was a request for information about a political prisoner in Myanmar and seemed to have been a response to earlier mailings by others. The prisoner was called Khin Thein. Harrison had wanted to know where he was being held, his profession and his alleged crime. Sam clicked through the responses but found nothing relating to it.

The more he read, the more he realised the one-sidedness of what the cybersnoops had uncovered. Several replies to Harrison's missives had been missed. Sam typed a list of the correspondents' logins and e-mailed it to the IT men so they could expand their search.

As he sorted the mailings into chronological order he found Harrison's concerns diversifying in late December. Early outpourings about the stifling of democracy in Myanmar had been replaced by anger at plans for some foreign-funded diesel truck factory to be built at Mandalay.

Foreign investment does almost nothing to improve the life of ordinary Burmans. Instead, it encourages the junta to believe it can go on ruling for ever. And don't be fooled when they claim the factory is for trucks and buses to improve the transport infrastructure. The vehicles will be for the army, and a good share of the investment money will end up in the pockets of the generals.

Diesel trucks. An odd issue to get worked up about. In search of a connection, Sam opened Waddell's file on Matsubara's global activities, skimming through the country list to see if Myanmar featured. It didn't.

The sound of Julie splashing in the shower was making it hard for him to concentrate. Then the noise stopped. He stood up. He couldn't work like this. Had to have it out with her. But halfway to the door he halted, fearing he was about to make a complete ass of himself.

He sat down again, dithering like a teenager. Then he dialled into the Internet one more time. He'd had an idea.

The archive of the Singapore-based *Straits Times* opened on the screen. He tapped *Myanmar* and *diesel* into the search bar and hit return. Ten seconds later he had his answer.

NIPPON CAR GIANT PUTS OUT FEELER TO THE GENERALS
   Kyoto, Japan   *28 December 1999*
   Reports that the Matsubara Corporation and Myanmar's military rulers are in talks about building a diesel engine plant at Mandalay are not being denied in the Japanese motor giant's home town of Kyoto. Rumours of the plan which first surfaced last month have triggered protests from Burmese pro-democracy movements in Thailand and the United States. The objectors want an international ban on all foreign investment in Myanmar (formerly Burma), claiming the generals use slave labour for construction projects and divert foreign funds into their own pockets.

'Gotcha,' he murmured.

The article went on to reprise the story of Kamata's past and his desire to make amends to Britain through a car factory investment and concluded, 'Now it's his fellow Buddhists in Myanmar who are in line to benefit from an old man's wish to improve his karma before his next reincarnation.'

Sam felt a buzz of satisfaction. The case for Harrison having gone to Myanmar was building. If they could discover Kamata was due there soon it would be as good as certain.

He printed the article, then logged off, reaching for the phone to ring Waddell. But before he could pick it up, Julie walked back in. She was dressed in a grey sweatshirt top and track-suit bottoms. Her hair was wet and the expression in her eyes was combative.

'What are you looking so serious about?'

'Am I?'

Bare-footed, she flopped onto the sofa, stuck a heel on the arm and unscrewed the top of a nail varnish bottle.

'You don't mind, do you?' She held the brush poised over her toes.

'As long as *you* don't,' he told her. 'Solvents make me randy.'

'Tell me something that doesn't.'

He watched her spread the dark crimson gloss onto her nails.

'Julie . . .'

'What's that you've just printed?'

'Oh, a newspaper article.'

'About?'

'Tetsuo Kamata.'

'The car factory man.' She applied a few more brush strokes.

The fumes from the varnish were getting to him. Her very presence was challenging. She was trying to provoke him into asking the goddam question straight out.

'Who was your message from?'

She stopped painting.

'What — on the answering machine?'

'Ye-es.'

'It's not important.'

'Then you won't mind telling me.'

'You don't need to know, Sam.'

'Yes I do.'

'No. Believe me, you do *not*.'

He swung his chair to face her. She reddened under his glare, but continued to defy him.

99

'Obviously someone you know well,' Sam pressed, 'because he didn't leave a number.'

Julie put the brush back in the varnish bottle, despite there being two toes to go.

'So I know his number – so what?'

Sam looked for guilt on her face but saw only anger.

'Does he have a name?'

'What's your problem with this, Sam? We have an agreement. What we do when the other's not around is our own business.' She stared fixedly at her toes, then with great deliberation reopened the bottle and applied the brush again. 'His name's Jack, if you must know.'

'Jack.' He nodded, as if the name told the whole story. 'Odd name for an east European.'

'He anglicised it. He's from Latvia originally.'

'And you've seen a lot of him?'

'I've seen him a few times, yes.'

'Slept with him?'

'I shan't even dignify that with a reply.' Glowing with fury, she finished the little toe, swung her leg off the arm and placed the foot squarely on the floor. 'It's none of your damned business, Sam. I don't ask about the women you've fucked in Singapore . . .'

'They don't leave messages on our answerphone.'

'So you're admitting . . . Whadyamean *our* answerphone? God almighty! In the last nine months you've spent less than two weeks here. I know you pay half the rent, but to you this is just where you doss down in London. To me it's my *home*.'

He'd hurt her, yet he didn't feel bad about it.

'And no, I haven't seen him that often.' She was having to work on her voice to keep it under control. 'He's well aware I have a partner and would never have rung if he'd known you were here.'

'In *our* bed?'

'*Sa-am!*' Her face flushed. 'It's none of your fucking business. Can't you understand that?' She stormed from the room.

Sam bit his lip. Stupid. Incredibly stupid. She was right. A man called Jack . . . He'd have been better off not knowing.

He picked up the *Straits Times* article again, but the words were a blur. He got to his feet, knowing it was lunacy to leave things like this.

'Julie . . .'

No response. He stopped in the hall to listen. The bathroom door was open and she wasn't inside. He went to the bedroom and found her sitting on the duvet, painting the toes of her other foot.

'I'm sorry . . .'

She ignored him.

'I'm sorry,' he repeated.

'You had no damned right to interrogate me like that.'

'No.'

'We're not married.'

'No.'

'You don't have any long-term plan for us, so far as I know.'

'Well, I . . .'

'I mean you can't have, can you? The life you lead.'

She looked up at him, damp-eyed.

'It won't always . . .'

'Yes it will, Sam. It's the way you are. The way most men are . . .'

'Including Jack?'

'Bugger Jack!' She let out a long, exasperated sigh. 'There's nothing there, Sam. Can't you get it? He's just someone I happen to have spent a few evenings with for reasons I'm not prepared to explain at this point in time, and I'm simply not going to talk about it.'

'Okay.'

'The person I want to be with is *you*. Can't you understand that?'

He felt wretched. But relieved too. Her sincerity seemed beyond doubt, but he was on the spot again. The onus on him to tell her when they could live together instead of just having visiting rights. He approached the edge of the bed and squeezed the back of her neck.

'I'm a jealous idiot,' he muttered, trying to glide over the issue. She reached behind her neck and pressed a hand onto his.

'Where are we headed, Sam?'

He ran his tongue round the inside of his mouth.

'I was going to ask you to think again about coming out to Singapore. There are some great schools . . .'

'You know I can't do that. Liam's settled where he is.'

He swallowed hard. That little plan hadn't got far.

'Then I'll try and get a posting back here. The dust should've settled.'

'Is that what you really want?'

'To be with you? Of course it is.'

She squeezed his hand.

'I wish I was certain you meant that,' she whispered.

He kissed the top of her wet head and wrapped his arms around her.

'Let me . . . let me just finish what I'm doing in there. Then I can concentrate on you. On us.'

Back in the living room, he felt in need of a breathing space before ringing Waddell again, so he reconnected to the Internet. There was new mail from the IT men. More responses to Harrison's postings. And two of them talked about Khin Thein.

The man had trained as a lawyer, it transpired, then become a part-time official of Aung San Suu Kyi's National League for Democracy. Arrested three years ago, charged with speaking ill of the regime – and with illegally owning a modem. A ten-year sentence. He was forty-five.

But why did Harrison care about Khin Thein?

He had an idea. Grabbing hold of *A Jungle Path to Hell*, he turned to the section on Harrison's life in Burma in the '50s and '60s, looking for names. Flicking through the pages he found very few that were Burmese and none of them was Khin Thein. Disappointed, he put the book down again.

Julie poked her head round the door. 'I picked up some lamb chops on the way home. Suit you?'

'Great. I'll open some wine in a minute.'

But he wasn't done with the book. Another thought had come to him. After a short search he found what he was looking for.

George, Peregrine Harrison's first child with Tin Su, had been born in 1955.

Khin Thein was forty-five. Born the same year.

It fitted. The pieces were clicking into place.

He disconnected from the net and phoned his controller.

'It's Myanmar,' he told him.

'Explain.'

Sam did.

'I could get on a plane tonight.'

For a few moments Waddell stayed silent. Sam imagined cogs turning.

'We need harder evidence than this, Sam. Remember, we checked all the flight manifests. Harrison wasn't listed heading in that direction.'

'He could have travelled under another name.'

'False passport? He's an old man for Christ's sake, not a character out of *Day of the Jackal*. No. Let's see what happens tonight. In a few hours time the burglars will be in. With a bit of luck . . .'

'Instinct tells me we'll need more than luck if we're to stop him, Duncan. A hell of a lot more.'

'Changed your tune, haven't you? No longer the doubting Thomas? You actually believe he's going to do it?'

Sam hesitated, but only for a moment.

'Yes. Unfortunately I do.'

Bordhill Manor
Around midnight

Melissa Dennis listened to the nocturnal noises of the long, red-brick house known as Mandalay Lodge, which stood about 50 metres behind the manor. She was biding her time.

She heard a cough from the room next door – the walls separating the spartan single bedrooms were of thin plasterboard. Her neighbour had a cold. She worried it might keep the woman awake. The last thing she wanted was for anyone to hear when she stepped into the corridor in a short while from now.

Melissa was already well acquainted with every loose floorboard on the way to the stairs, having learned to avoid them when returning late from being with Perry. Despite his years, he'd been extraordinarily fit two years ago when he'd asked her to become his new personal assistant. Not an ounce of excess flesh and still doing regular 10-mile walks. She'd known his reputation, known exactly what the role was likely to involve and had been more than ready for it. When he'd failed to make the expected advances, however, she'd been disappointed, and so, she'd sensed, had he, having to acknowledge that age was finally catching up with him.

Melissa looked at the luminous clock glowing on her bedside table. How long should she wait? One o'clock? Two? *That*, she'd heard, was the hour when most people were in their deepest sleep. Yet if she waited too long she risked nodding off herself.

She heard the distant clock on Sidgefield church tower chime once. Half past midnight. She'd give it another thirty minutes.

Three hundred metres away, down the lane heading out of Sidgefield, a dark Vauxhall Astra turned off the tarmac into the muddy entrance to a field. The two men inside wore black trousers and trainers and thick black pullovers. As they prepared to leave the car they donned balaclavas and tied thick waterproof canvas bags over their shoes.

They'd checked out the area earlier in the day, investigating a footpath running along the side fence of the Bordhill estate. Easy access to the grounds. Soon they'd be lifting the sash at the back of the house, whose security lock they'd disabled that afternoon.

The phone company had been as good as gold, disconnecting the lines so they could bowl up in a telecoms van to look for the fault. A short-circuit they'd said. Often hard to find. They'd insisted on checking every extension. Even those in the private quarters of the community's absent founder. The Madsen woman had watched them like a hawk as they'd done their business there, but they'd already got what they needed – the combination she'd used to open the door.

The ground crunched gently under foot, a sharp frost having encrusted the damp soil with ice. They moved steadily forward, relying on starlight to see the path. Both men had excellent night vision.

In a few minutes they were at the back of the house, crouching and listening. From some far away copse an owl hooted. Behind them the residential block was in darkness – the Bordhill Community was at rest.

They removed the black bags from their feet and stuffed them into pockets, then pulled on thin latex gloves. Finally, with a flick of a screwdriver the bottom sash was lifted. One after the other they rolled over the sill and dropped soft-footed and clean-shoed onto the floor inside.

Impatience got the better of Melissa. There had to be *something* in the apartment – some scrap of information that would reveal Perry's intentions, and she was desperate to find it.

As she swung her legs to the floor the bed springs twanged. Cocking her head she listened for anyone else stirring. Nothing. Even her neighbour's coughing had stopped.

She stood up and put on the fur-lined boots and long, quilted coat left ready at the end of the bed, then edged towards the door. The starlight was just enough for her to see by. She'd left the curtains open deliberately. The handle turned easily – none of the rooms was ever locked. And in fact several were empty, the result of the community going through a lean patch with recruits. Holding her breath she crept along to the staircase and a few seconds later was outside in the cold night air.

A door slammed somewhere causing her to jump. Not in her own block, nor the main house. The sound had come from the stables area where Ingrid lived in style amongst a handful of old farm cottages used mostly by couples.

She heard a distant cough – a man's. Her mind took off. There'd been gossip that one of the couples was on the verge of breaking up. Perhaps they'd had a row and the chap had gone outside to cool off. She decided to stay put for a few moments in case he took it into his head to go wandering about. Hugging herself in the doorway, she was glad of her coat. The moon was up, its light illuminating her breath.

The combination lock had clicked softly when the men tapped in the numbers. Once inside, they turned on narrow-beamed torches. The layout they knew from before. A self-contained flat with a small kitchen and bathroom. Comfortable. Pleasantly furnished. The bedroom had a kingsize and a bookcase holding works on Buddhism and Hinduism – and a copy of the *Kama Sutra*, one of them had noticed that afternoon. Next to the books was a TV with built-in VCR.

Their instructions were clear. The visit was to be undetected. In the far corner of the living room stood a small table with a computer. One man made a beeline for it, swinging the small rucksack from his back and placing it next to the keyboard. He turned the PC to get at the connections. After unplugging the printer cable, he extracted a portable hard-drive and a small scanner from his rucksack and connected them up.

While the computer specialist loaded software, the other man shone his torch looking for papers. Finding none, he set to work on the filing cabinet beside the computer desk.

Melissa hurried towards the south wing of the manor where the kitchens were, her fingers gripping the mortise lock key in the pocket of her coat. There was a white dusting of frost on the path. Her instinct was to run, but with her luck she knew she would fall on her face.

The key turned easily in the lock. Inside, the kitchen smelled of fried onions, a warm, comforting odour. The cooks did a good job at Bordhill and she would miss them when she'd gone. And she *had* made up her mind that evening. When she left here in two days' time she would never be coming back.

Moonlight filtered through the high windows of the great hallway. She turned towards the grand staircase. Some of the treads creaked but it didn't matter because there'd be no one else in the house. At the top she paused, listening. There'd been a noise outside. A fox perhaps. There was a plague of them locally. She still hadn't got over the sight of that poor goat kid a few days ago, its belly ripped from one end to the other.

She walked past Ingrid's darkened office towards the wing which had been Perry's domain. She touched her forefinger on the number pad. Typical of Perry to have sealed his private world with a combination lock. Enhancing the mystique which had drawn so many young women to him over the years. She remembered the feeling when given the code for this secret portal. That she was becoming a part of his exclusiveness. But they were just his tricks and she'd seen through them eventually. Seen that at the bottom of it all he was just a man, one who was making the most of his charisma and his still relatively youthful looks. And that would be the theme of her book. Not a debunking of Perry Harrison. Far from it. There was no one she admired more. A portrait, warts and all. But unless she could find him and share his last days, the book might never be written.

She tapped in the number.

Inside the room the burglars heard it. A rattle like a mouse gnawing at a loose piece of wood.

The man at the computer was halfway through copying the hard-drive. He switched off the screen and waved his companion to the bedroom, then crouched behind the desk, heart thudding like a road drill.

The second man pressed his back against the bedroom wall. The apartment door opened, then closed again. The sound of breathing. Female. Laboured, like someone overweight. He heard feet pass, moving towards the living room. Then they stopped as the woman held her breath. She'd seen or heard something. Nothing for it. He reached into a pocket and closed his fingers round a small plastic tube.

Melissa knew something was wrong, but not *what*. There seemed to be a noise from the computer and it shouldn't have been on. She stared into the corner where she knew the machine to be, but the screen was dark. And the rest of the living room too. Surprisingly dark. No moonlight coming through, the curtains tightly drawn, and they weren't normally. A shiver ran up her spine. Was it . . . could it be possible that the man she admired most in the world had come back?

'Perry?'

She fumbled for the torch in her pocket. Then, right behind her, a floorboard creaked.

'Ingrid?' she squeaked, beginning to turn.

Suddenly a hand clasped her mouth and nose, jerking her head back. She tasted latex. Then another hand hooked round her front, tugging at the buttons of her coat.

She tried to scream, but her voice wouldn't work.

The hand wrenched open the quilting and began probing her nether regions. She groaned inwardly. She was to be raped. Her first sexual experience with a man and it would be an act of violence

She began to struggle, but too late. Something pricked the top of her thigh. She felt a sharp, stabbing pain, followed by a burning inside her leg. A second pair of hands was grappling with her now, pulling her off balance, tumbling her to the floor. She lay prone, feeling a heavy weight pressing on her knees. She wanted to kick but couldn't. A slow wooziness came over her, like a sudden onset of drunkenness. Then a creeping numbness. A steady loss of feeling throughout her body.

Then nothing. Absolutely nothing.

The man who'd administered the injection pushed fingers against the artery in her neck. When he was sure her pulse was steady he breathed a sigh of relief.

'Okay,' he whispered. 'Let's get this fucking job over with.'

14

West London
The next day, Tuesday, 11 January, 7.30 a.m.

SAM STOOD BY the living-room window looking into the street as Julie made her way to the tube. She was wrapped in a dark overcoat, collar up against the stiff breeze. They'd made it up last night. Agreed that all big decisions should be put on hold. She'd even withdrawn her ultimatum, admitting it had never really been serious anyway.

He retreated to the kitchen to make toast and fresh coffee. For now it was the job he had to concentrate on. Late last night Waddell had rung with a phone number for Robert Wetherby. It had been too late to call it then and it was still too early this morning. Not too early though for a report back on what the burglars had found at Bordhill Manor.

Sam was just finishing shaving when the call came from his controller.

'There was a problem,' Waddell began. 'The team were disturbed.'

'By whom?'

'They don't know. Some woman. They gave her a shot to knock her out.'

'But who was it?'

'Someone from the commune, they assumed. Aged about thirty. Rather overweight, with wiry hair.'

'Oh God . . . Melissa probably. Harrison's PA. She'd have had access to his flat. What did your psychos hit her with?'

'A cocktail including rohypnol. So with a bit of luck she won't remember anything about it.'

'Hope they didn't kill her.'

'Don't . . . What I'd like to know is what she was doing there.'

'Same as us probably. Looking for evidence. I told her about Harrison's letter to *The Times* and it shook her rigid. What did our guys get?'

'Nothing.'

'What?'

'Sod all of any use. Copied his computer hard-drive only to find the thing had been spring cleaned. The disk had been formatted then reinstalled with just the basic programmes on it like it was a new machine. No document files or email software anywhere. Same with the stuff in his filing cabinet – they scanned a whole bunch of pages on the off-chance, but there was nothing of interest.'

'Shit.'

'Harrison was thorough,' Waddell declared mournfully. 'Extraordinarily thorough. And his disappearance clearly wasn't a spur of the moment affair. But where he's gone is as much a mystery as ever.'

'It's Myanmar,' Sam declared. 'Burma.'

Waddell grunted. 'Find me proof and we'll get you on your way.'

Sam waited until nine, then rang the number in Suffolk. It was answered by a dithering female voice. The woman, sounding elderly and a little confused, said her husband had taken an early train to London. Something going on at the Imperial War Museum. Burma veterans, but more than that she couldn't remember.

He rang the Museum's press office, claiming to be a stringer for the *Straits Times*. They told him of a reception at midday to mark the opening of an exhibition of war paintings.

He homed in on the green cupola and colonnaded portico of the Imperial War Museum at a quarter to twelve. The last time he'd come here was as a child with his submariner father. He remembered climbing on the 15-inch naval guns on the paved forecourt.

Inside, the building had been refurbished. An airy atrium held the hardware of conflict, ancient tanks vying for space with an omnibus used by troops in the First World War. Far above, fighter planes hung from wires beneath a glass roof. Sam made his way to the stairwell and pressed the button for a lift.

The glass-fronted art galleries were on the second floor. Above one of them a banner bore the words *The Jungle War*. Beyond the glass he could see caterers putting finishing touches to a drinks table in the centre of the room. The walls were hung with pencil drawings and watercolours. A poster told him they'd been done from sketches made during the Burma war.

Sam moved away and leaned against a balcony to wait for the guests to arrive. Before long two men emerged from the lifts, their dark blazers glittering with regimental badges. Guided by a museum assistant, they walked with the aid of sticks. Each looked about eighty. Harrison's age.

Doubts crept in again. How could *any* man of that vintage travel halfway round the world to kill someone?

He approached the pair.

'Excuse me. I'm looking for Robert Wetherby . . .'

'Oh he'll be along.' The old man's voice was surprisingly strong. 'Never misses a free drink. Know him, do you?'

'No. No I don't.'

'Purple birthmark on the side of his face. Spot him a mile off. What's it about?' The old soldier's eyes burned with curiosity.

'Oh, a family matter.' Sam saw the gallery doors being opened behind them. 'Enjoy the reception.'

The old men turned to look. 'Kicking off, are they? Come on Frank. Let's get at it.' They marched unsteadily towards the drinks table.

The lift disgorged a steady stream of war veterans. Most could walk unaided, but two were being wheeled by fitter colleagues.

It was a quarter past twelve before the man he was looking for emerged. Straight-backed and with a thin slick of grey hair, he wore a thorn-proof suit of brown and green. Sam stepped forward.

'Mr Wetherby?'

The man's birthmark made his smile appear lopsided.

'How d'you do . . .'

'My name's Stephen Maxwell. I work for the Foreign Office.'

Wetherby's face darkened, his eyes flickering with alarm. 'Nothing to do with this?' He swung an arm towards the gallery.

'No. I wanted to talk to you about Perry Harrison. We're very concerned about him.'

'Are you?' Wetherby sounded wary.

'I've been told you were one of his oldest friends and hoped you'd know where he was.'

'I'm sure Perry will make his whereabouts known if he wants to be found.'

Sam gritted his teeth. This wasn't going to be easy.

'I spoke to his son Charles. He told me his father hasn't long to live, Mr Wetherby. Would you mind – after the reception – if we had a chat?'

'There's no point. I can't tell you anything.' The old man waved at another veteran and called across to say he'd be joining him in a minute. 'What did you say your name was?'

'Maxwell. Stephen Maxwell.'

'How did you know I'd be here?'

'Your wife . . .'

Wetherby's eyes registered annoyance. 'All right. We can talk. In about an hour. After this shindig's over. Where will you be?'

'Here. I'll be waiting for you. And there's a café on the ground floor we could go to.'

'Very well.' Wetherby turned and made a beeline for the drinks table beyond the glass doors.

Sam took the lift to the ground floor and whiled away the time looking at the displays.

It was one o'clock when he returned to the upper level. The frailer veterans were already leaving. Wetherby was still inside however, laughing with a couple of comrades at the far end of the room.

Ten minutes later he emerged, pausing by the door to compose himself before coming across to Sam.

'They must mean a lot, occasions like these,' Sam ventured as they took the lift to the ground floor.

'It's a chance for a laugh. But there are fewer of us each time.' He said it quite matter-of-factly.

'Would Perry normally have come to a do like this?'

'Probably not. He wasn't good at reunions.'

Sam led the way into the café, found them a table, then queued at the counter. Wetherby had asked for tea. When he returned with the tray the old soldier cocked his head and narrowed his eyes.

'Look, it's no good asking me where Perry is,' he said, 'because I don't know.'

In terms of his precise location it was probably true, Sam guessed. 'When did you last see him?'

Wetherby thought carefully about his answer. 'Sometime around Christmas.' The eyes flickered when he said it. Sam suspected it was more recently than that.

'You've known each other since the war?'

'We were prisoners together in Rangoon. Before that we'd each been held at different internment centres. Fought with different units too. My lot fell into Jap hands when they invaded in 1942, so I had a year more of being locked up than Perry. We knew of each other's existence in the prison but weren't friends particularly. That came later.'

'When?'

'Oh, long after the war.' He picked up his cup and sipped the tea, beginning to look more at ease. 'Nineteen-sixty-three to be precise. We bumped into each other – at Green Park tube. Literally. At the top of the steps. He nearly knocked me down them. Apologised profusely for his carelessness, then we both recognised each other.'

'And that was it?'

'Well, yes. We've been friends ever since. I suppose we discovered we had more in common than we'd thought.'

'Your past, you mean?'

'And our present. The same sort of problems.' He picked a sugar lump from the bowl on the table and rolled it across the surface like a dice.

'Nightmares? That sort of thing?'

'Well, yes. Most of us had those, although Perry's seemed more persistent than mine. And there was guilt – you'd seen your mates being used for bayonet practice or wasting away in prison, and you sort of felt bad about surviving. Hard to talk about except with somebody else who'd been through it.'

'You'd had similar experiences after the war?'

'No. Very different. I'd been a regular soldier before '39 and stayed in afterwards for another five years. And I got married soon after coming back. Both of those things gave stability to my life. I mean Perry got hitched too, but it didn't work out. He's like a man suffering from tinnitus, you know. Or with a mosquito in his ear. Some irritation in his head that's always made it hard for him to settle. Never worked out if it's because of what he went through in Burma or whether it's in the genes.'

'But after that reunion you saw each other regularly?'

'Perry was of no fixed abode at that point. He'd just left Dorothy for the second time. Full of grandiose plans for founding his commune. I invited him to stay with us until he got himself somewhere permanent.'

'Were you living in Suffolk then?'

'Yes. I'd set up an electronics business in Bury St Edmunds. Servicing and spare parts for hi-fi and TV sets. Employed 135 people at one stage,' he added proudly. 'We'd moved into computers by the time I sold out.'

Sam's antennae twitched. 'You must be quite a techie.'

'Trained in the Royal Signals.'

So he would almost certainly know how to format a hard-drive, Sam surmised.

'Did he talk to you about his illness?'

'Not much.' Wetherby leaned back and folded his arms as if deciding he'd said enough. 'Look, I'm sorry I can't help you.' He looked at his watch. 'Need to be on my way in a minute. There's a train at a quarter past the hour.'

'Charles said his father had unresolved issues from his past.'

'Wouldn't know about that . . .'

'In Burma. His ex-wife. And a son who's a political prisoner. Khin Thein?'

'I couldn't say.'

'He talked to you about them?'

'If he did it'd have been in confidence.'

The loyalty of Perry Harrison's friends was getting on Sam's nerves.

'That Jap who tortured him . . .'

Wetherby put a hand up to his birthmark.

'. . . Perry wants him dead. Yes?'

'I don't know about that.'

'And he's gone to Burma because he thinks he'll find Kamata there.'

Wetherby shook his head. 'It's no good making all these wild allegations.'

'There's a man's life at stake, Mr Wetherby. Maybe several lives. If you know something . . .'

The old soldier licked his lips. The shutters had come down.

'Ever been back to Burma?' Sam asked in a desperate attempt to get him to say something else.

'Never. England's good enough for me.'

'You mean you don't like travelling abroad?'

'Don't even have a passport.'

Sam's throat went dry.

'You've never had one?'

'Nope.'

So there'd be no record of a Robert Wetherby at the passport office. Which meant that if Perry Harrison happened to have applied for a travel document in that name a few weeks ago, the powers that be would have had no reason to deny it to him.

Wetherby pushed his chair back and got stiffly to his feet. 'That train . . .' he muttered uncomfortably. 'I'll miss it if I don't go now.'

'Yes of course.' Sam stood up too.

'Sorry you've wasted your time.'

Sam gave him a kindly smile. He hadn't.

15

Bordhill Manor
1.15 p.m.

MELISSA DENNIS HAD been found on the floor of Ingrid Madsen's office soon after 7 a.m. by Ingrid herself. She'd been quite unable to explain how she'd got there and had no memory of what had happened the previous evening. She'd hardly been able to stand and her voice was slurred. Despite the absence of alcohol on her breath, Ingrid had chided her for yet another episode of drunkenness.

Eventually, after Melissa's voluble protests of innocence, a doctor had been called. He could find no reason for her state and proclaimed her to be perfectly fit but suggested she should spend the day lying down.

Now it was lunchtime and Melissa was fed up with her bed. She felt fine again, apart from a headache and the strange inability to remember what she'd done last night. She recollected her intention to enter Perry Harrison's private quarters and had a vague memory of setting out to do so. But how she got into the manor and ended up in a drugged sleep in Ingrid's office she had no idea.

Drugged. She was sure that's what had occurred. No other explanation. But how and at whose hands she couldn't imagine. She'd read in the papers about date rape drugs which made you forget, but there was nothing to suggest her body had been interfered with sexually.

She was experiencing the vaguest of recollections, merely a tickle, that she'd actually opened the door to Perry's apartment and stepped inside. Suppose, *just* suppose, Perry hadn't disappeared at all but had been hiding in there . . . All her plans for travelling to Burma the next day would be a waste of time.

So she had to find out. And there was no other way but to go back in and look. Not in the night this time but during the supper break when everybody else would be in the dining room and the top floor deserted.

And this time she would go armed with the battery-powered rape/attack alarm which she'd bought a year ago on a visit to London.

West London
3.15 p.m.

Sam put down the phone.

Waddell had just confirmed it. An 'R. Wetherby' had travelled alone to Bangkok last Saturday, the 8th of January. Then yesterday – Monday the 10th – he'd flown on to Yangon, the Myanmar capital, the return flights left open.

Sam himself was now booked on a Qantas to Bangkok at half past ten that night.

He'd asked Waddell if Tokyo had anything on Kamata visiting Myanmar, but the answer was negative. Wheels were in motion, he'd said. The station head would be given a fresh kick up the backside and the SIS rep in Myanmar would be ordered to check the Yangon hotels to see if a Wetherby was registered. But because of the time difference and communication problems it'd be morning before they heard anything.

Sam stared blankly at the walls of the flat. There was something very basic about the emerging scenario which still didn't make sense to him. Harrison was seventy-seven and terminally ill. It was inconceivable to him that he could mount a murderous assault in a far off land without help. The man had been away from Burma for thirty-eight years.

The phone rang again.

'Hello?'

Silence. Then a click as the line cut.

'Shit.'

He banged the receiver down.

Jack, no doubt. Expecting to get the answerphone and being surprised by a male voice. Fresh doubts set in about Julie's protestations of innocence.

This was a mad time to be disappearing. Daft to be heading for trouble on the other side of the world when there was a personal battle to be won right here.

The phone rang one more time. He decided to leave it. Let the machine pick it up.

'*Sam. Ring me straight back.*' Waddell's voice.

He snatched up the receiver.

'Ah. Caught you in the bog, did I?'

'Something like that.'

'Listen. IT have broken Harrison's email password. There's a stack of messages sent and received that didn't appear on the newsgroups. They've downloaded the lot and are sifting them. Anything interesting'll be copied to you. Give them five minutes then go online again.'

'Brilliant.' He pondered for a moment. 'Out of curiosity, did you try to get through a few seconds earlier?'

'No. Why?'

'Doesn't matter.'

'Transport have arranged a car to take you to the airport at seven. Ring me when you get to Bangkok and keep checking your email. And good luck.'

'Thanks.' He was going to need it.

He rang off, then went to the bedroom to get his suitcase together.

Five minutes later with the task uncompleted he returned to the living room and logged on. The cover note from IT was brief.

The four attachments are all to the same bloke and look highly relevant. We're having a crack at breaking 'Rip's' password, but no success yet. We'll keep you posted.

When Sam opened the first of Harrison's emails the last of his doubts disappeared.

From: Myoman
Date: 28 December 1999
To: Rip
Subject: Past conversations
Dear Rip,

I have recently gone 'online' as I believe it's called, and have decided to contact you via the email address you gave me some time ago. Ever since we first met at the Chindit reunion in 1995, you have repeatedly offered me your help in any counterstrike venture I might eventually contemplate. Such a moment has now come and I should like to avail myself of your assistance. I'm not as strong as I was and need someone who knows the ropes. You told me in your last letter that your work now takes you to the Far East. I shall be travelling to Bangkok shortly, and would like to meet and discuss what I have in mind.

For security reasons I am not signing my normal name, but I'm quite certain I have said enough for you to know who I am!
Yours ever,
Myoman

December 28th. Two days before Harrison's disappearance from Bordhill. Sam clicked on the next attachment. Dated the 29th, it was the reply.

Myoman. Bangkok is a city I pass through frequently and will make sure one of my visits coincides with yours. I am intrigued to know what you plan to do. Email me your flight dates as soon as you have them. Rip

The third attachment was from Harrison again. A week later. Detailing the BA flight he was on and the name of a hotel he'd booked in Bangkok.

The fourth, dated January the 9th, the Sunday just past, bore a more plaintive message.

Dear Rip,
Sorry not to find any word from you at the hotel in Bangkok when I arrived. Realised I forgot to tell you I was travelling in the name of Robert Wetherby. Please do get in touch if you can. I'm rather relying on you.
My plan is to fly to Rangoon tomorrow. (They'll never make me call it Yangon.) Time is of the essence. Please join me in Burma if we don't meet here in Bangkok. When I'm sure about where I'm staying I shall email you the details.
Yours in hope,
Myoman

Sam stroked his chin. Harrison's 'plan' seemed long on aspiration but short on strategy. And did '*time is of the essence*' refer to his failing health, or to the imminence of Kamata's arrival in Burma?

The former, he suspected, because if SIS was having a hard time discovering Kamata's plans, it'd surely be almost impossible for an elderly pensioner.

He wondered for a moment if they were panicking over nothing. Looking at the bungle he'd got himself into, there was a good chance Harrison would fail of his own accord.

He heard the key in the lock. Julie was back.

'Hi. I'm home,' she called.

He got up and walked into the hall. She was standing by the open bedroom door, her sopping coat halfway off. She'd seen his suitcase.

Julie turned to him, her face crumpling with disappointment.

Sam put a hand on her arm.

'I'm terribly sorry sweetheart. It won't be for long. I promise.'

Bordhill Manor
7.00 p.m.

Melissa found it ridiculously easy to creep up the stairs to the first floor without being seen. Heart thudding and with a quick glance back to the main stairwell to ensure the coast was clear, she tapped in the numbers on the lock to Perry's apartment. Clutching the battery-powered screecher, she stepped inside, closed the door and listened.

Nothing. Not even the distant clink of cutlery from the dining room downstairs. These quarters had been designed for Perry to be able to shut out the community he'd founded.

Melissa tiptoed to the bedroom. The door was wide open and the bed showed no signs of having been slept in recently. She checked the bathroom and kitchenette. Clean, tidy and unused. Perry always left his imprint. He couldn't have been living here in secret. So who *had* attacked her last night?

She walked warily into the day room, crossed to the corner and switched on the computer. While waiting for it to power up, she opened the filing cabinet and began checking folders. What exactly she was looking for she didn't know. Something under 'travel' or 'family', but there was nothing. She turned her attention to the computer, clicking through his file folders in My Docs.

Gone. Everything deleted. The emails too.

The finality of it shocked her. It was as if all trace of his existence had been purged from the place. The action of a man who knew he would never return.

She switched off the computer and looked round the room, memories flooding back. She'd been nervous the first time she'd come here, but all they'd done was talk. *She*, mostly. He was a good listener. A few little prompts from him and before long she'd spilled out the story of her life, including the extraordinarily personal fact that she was still a virgin and didn't much want to be.

Instead of taking advantage of her obvious readiness for sex, he'd talked fondly about her predecessors. *Handmaidens*, he'd called them. Spoken of them in a way that deconstructed them, never using their real names. The 'Jenny wren', 'The vole'. Always animals and birds. What did he call *her* behind her back, she'd wondered?

In the ensuing weeks and months she'd come here nearly every day, whenever he requested it. And every evening she'd expected him to make his move. Sometimes they'd lain on the bed together watching TV or reading books. But he'd never touched her. Not in the way she'd wanted.

The bedroom.

She'd remembered a place where Perry kept things. An odd, schoolboy-ish hiding place. A hollowed-out book on the shelf next to the TV. She had a feeling – although where she'd got the idea from she didn't know – that he used to keep contraceptives in it. Imagined that a part of his *usual* ritual with new ingenues had been to take the *Kama Sutra* off the shelf, excite the girl with some exotic illustrations, then open the book's secret cavity and pluck out a little foil pack.

Melissa entered the bedroom, flushed with vicarious excitement and a touch of resentment. She took the book off the shelf and opened it up. There *was* something in the hiding place, but it wasn't a prophylactic. Gingerly she extracted a little scrap of paper, half expecting some tawdry item of pornography. She sat on the bed.

It was a cutting from a magazine. A colour picture of a smallish stone obelisk. Some memorial or other with oriental writing on it. And standing in front of it was a tall, straight-backed but elderly man.

She read the caption, saying where it was.

And it identified the person.

A Japanese name. One which had recently taken on a terrible new significance for her.

'Oh Perry,' she gasped.

Suddenly there was a noise.

Melissa's heart missed several beats as she realised it was the clicking of the combination lock. She struggled to stuff the cutting down the front of her pullover, but Ingrid appeared in the doorway to the bedroom and saw her doing it.

'What have you found?' she snapped.

'Don't know what you're talking about.'

The Danish woman's face went a vile shade of puce. 'You fat bitch!' She hurled herself at Melissa, snatching at the hand that was still buried in the pullover. 'Give it to me. You have no rights in here.'

Melissa tried to roll clear, but Ingrid crashed down on top of her. She reeked of wine. Melissa dug at the hated woman, her elbow making contact with soft flesh.

'Give it to me!' Ingrid screamed, tearing at Melissa's jumper.

'Get off!'

She managed to slide off the bed and away from her attacker, making a dart for the door, but Ingrid was too quick for her. She was taller than Melissa and blocked her path.

'You think you're so special,' Ingrid hissed. 'But you're so stupid. You believe Perry cared for you.'

'He did! He did!'

'So why did he never make love to you?' She smiled as she saw Melissa's embarrassed reaction.

'Who says he didn't?' The words *how does she know* shrieked inside her head.

'*He* says,' Ingrid smirked, trying to mimic her voice. 'Perry. He told me. *Me*, Melissa. There.' She pointed at the bed. 'Between those sheets. Told me you were the only one of his handmaidens he couldn't bring himself to *fuck*.' She flung the word at Melissa, like a slap across the face. 'Now, silly little girl, whatever you've found, give it to me.'

A scream burst from Melissa's chest. She charged forward, punching Ingrid's breasts like a prize fighter. The woman retreated under her blows, clawing at Melissa's eyes. But Melissa ducked. Head down, she charged again, ramming Ingrid against the door frame. The woman's shoe caught against it and she went down, cracking her head on the polished wood floor.

Melissa stood over her. Panting for breath, she waited for her to get up again. When she didn't, when she saw Ingrid wasn't moving at all, she panicked, hurling herself through the open door and down the grand staircase to the ground floor.

Back in her room in Mandalay Lodge she fought to calm herself. To gather her thoughts. Lies. It had to have been lies what Ingrid had said.

Her rucksack lay on the bed. She'd already packed most of the things for her flight tomorrow night. She couldn't stay here, that was clear, even if Ingrid was merely unconscious rather than dead. The bitch would come after her. She stuffed the last items of clothing into the bag, swung it onto her shoulders and ran down the stairs into the cold night air.

Listening to check there were no noises from the manor, she began to walk. Towards the drive. Then the village. And a phone box so she could get a taxi to the station and a late train to London.

16

Yangon, Myanmar
Monday, 10 January 2000, 11.40 a.m.

ONE DAY EARLIER and five and a half thousand miles away from where Melissa had made her shocking discovery, Peregrine Harrison was collected from Yangon's Mingaladon airport by a driver sent from the hotel in a taxi.

It was an uncomfortable journey into the city where he'd lived thirty-eight years ago. The doctors had warned him the pain and exhaustion would increase towards the end, but he had never imagined it would worsen so fast.

He sat wedged in the back of the car trying to minimise the effects of the bumps and jolts, trying at the same time to recognise places – faces even. But although the town felt familiar, like an old jacket discovered in a loft, there was a strangeness about it too. Trees had grown in places where there'd been none before. Old landmarks were half obscured by new buildings. Only the people seemed not to have changed – men and women still wearing *longyis* and sandals, their placid faces which had accepted rule by colonialists now tolerating the strong arm of their own military.

Harrison had picked the Inya Lodge Hotel from the pages of the *Lonely Planet Guide* because it was in the northern suburbs, away from the noisy centre of the city he still thought of as Rangoon. Also because it was close to where he'd lived last time he'd been here.

The taxi turned off a broad, tree-lined avenue into an area of large colonial mansions, many in a state of disrepair. The hotel was of bungalow style, set in its own leafy compound. A young man in white shirt and black trousers erupted from the entrance to open the car door. Inside the small, dark lobby, the eager faces of the three reception staff made Harrison suspect he was the first foreign visitor they'd seen for weeks.

A boy carried the small suitcase to the bedroom, its white walls speckled here and there with the red and brown of squashed insects. High up near the ceiling an air-conditioner hummed and rattled. The boy pulled back the curtain to show off the garden, revealing windows covered with a rusting wire screen.

When he was alone, Harrison lay on the bed and let out an exhausted sigh. The strain of the long flight to Bangkok and the seven-hour time difference were not things a terminal cancer patient could be expected to tolerate well. During the first part of the journey, the pain from the spinal tumour had become excruciating. He'd hobbled to the aircraft's toilet to stick the first of his Fentanyl patches to the side of his chest. As effective as morphine, the doctors had said, when they'd prescribed them a few days ago.

Rather than continuing immediately from Bangkok to Yangon, he'd scheduled a night in the Thai capital, partly to recover from the journey and partly to keep the appointment he'd made before leaving England. When Rip failed to make contact at the hotel, it had been a bitter blow.

He stared up at the ceiling. A plastic lampshade hung from it. He knew he'd left far too much to chance coming here. In the interests of preserving secrecy he'd made no checks that Tin Su was still alive, even. Nor that Tetsuo Kamata had booked his annual pilgrimage to Burma this year, for fear that by doing so he might alert the authorities to his plans. All that work was still to be done.

And the pain and exhaustion he was now suffering made that prospect a daunting one. Particularly the thought that he might need to confront Kamata on his own. It had been stupid to forget to tell Rip the name he was travelling under.

He smacked his forehead – he was about to forget something else. He raised himself into a sitting position, picked up the phone and pressed the button for the reception desk.

'I need to send an email,' he announced when the man answered.

'Yes sir.'

'Can I do that from here?'

'Oh no sir.'

'Then where?'

'We do not have Internet in Myanmar, sir.'

The news stunned him. He'd naïvely assumed the technology was universal. It was the only means he had of telling Rip where he was.

'But surely *somebody* . . .' he protested. 'I'm happy to pay.'

'Sir, I think some people telephone to Thailand to make Internet connection. But for us it is not permitted.'

It was a disaster. Madness not to have checked before leaving Bangkok.

'Thank you,' he whispered and put the phone back on its cradle. The thought of trying to find a sympathetic person with a computer who would connect him up through Thailand defeated him utterly.

He lay back again, feeling foolish and wrecked. The journey had been too much for him. He had an overpowering need to sleep. Maybe in a couple of hours he would feel fresher. Ready to begin the process of confronting his past.

North-east of Yangon
12.10 p.m.

A Hilux pickup truck crammed with bags and bodies hummed southwards towards the Myanmar capital. The road was good by Burmese standards. A dual-carriageway. Every so often the driver stopped to pay a toll of a few kyat. Road tax – except the money went towards brighter uniforms for the military, the passengers believed. As the vehicle lurched on again from one such stop, Daw Tin Su clutched for support at the rail which surrounded the open back. Hardly necessary, for the press of bodies held her firmly in her seat. Above the roof of the driver's cab, a crate of ducklings was wedged between sacks of rice.

Tin Su wore a *longyi* of rust-coloured cotton. Her greying hair had been drawn back behind her neck and curled into a bun. A rush bag holding some fruit for her son lay on her lap. She was tired already and the day was only beginning. She'd slept little last night or the night before. The days preceding a visit to the prison were always anxious ones.

They passed rice paddies, squares of glinting water and a few of yellow-green where the new crop was taking root. Here and there little figures crouched, their heads shaded by coolie hats. A different climate, a different landscape from the hills and orchards of her former home a long way north in the cool Shan hills. She longed for it often, when the humidity of the plains wore her down.

The name 'Tin' meant 'gentle' and as a girl it had suited her. The apple of her father's eye, she'd been much loved for her sweet nature. She was aged sixty-eight now, and during the long, hard years of her life, her once-smooth, pale-brown skin had become taut and lined.

Burma had been British when she was born in the small hill town of Mong Lai. Her father, a strong, forceful man, had taught her to treat their masters with respect but not affection. He'd been employed by an English trader exporting rubies and jade for women on the other side of the world. Responsible work that had paid well, enabling her and her older brother to have a better education than many of their peers.

In 1942 when the Japanese invaded, the English trader had fled, leaving behind his stock of precious stones. Her grateful and startled father had hoarded it, then sold the gems to Japanese officers so he could minimise the family's hardships during the lean years of the war.

After it was over, and the country was rushing towards independence, Tin Su had continued to study the departing colonialists' language and literature. A lending library established in the town decades earlier by the British had somehow survived the war and she planned to work there.

Then her mother died of malaria. Tin Su had just turned eighteen. Her older brother had gone abroad to seek his fortune, so she'd had to care for her heart-broken father alone. Three years later, he too had died.

The shock of being without immediate family at such a young age had turned her thoughts inwards. For months she'd hidden away, hardly speaking to anyone, before finally deciding to make a life for herself. She'd persuaded the old scholar at the English library to take her on as his assistant. The work was far from arduous and she'd loved being surrounded by books.

Then, in 1953, a foreigner had visited Mong Lai, changing her life forever.

A particularly deep pothole sent a bone-jarring jolt through the chassis of the pick-up. Tin Su was shaken awake. She'd been dozing and her head had flopped onto the shoulder of the tall young man beside her.

'I'm sorry,' she whispered, hiding her mouth behind her hands, embarrassed at such intimate contact with a stranger.

The young man said nothing, staring across the paddies as if he hadn't noticed. Tin Su looked around. All the passengers were younger than her. She wanted to know their stories, yet dreaded them asking for hers. Had they guessed where she was going? They would know soon enough when the line bus stopped outside the bleak walls of the prison.

Her stomach clenched at the thought of those twin layers of wire-mesh inside, reaching out to her son with her soul because he was beyond the reach of her touch. He'd looked thinner last time she'd seen him two weeks ago, his not-quite-Burmese face pale and drawn, his spectacles with a crack in one lens. He'd told her he was all right. What else could he say when every word was listened to.

The brakes squealed. She glanced up, sick with nervousness.

They'd arrived.

The Inya Lodge Hotel
2.20 p.m.

Perry Harrison had slept for nearly two hours and felt a little better. He asked reception for a taxi, then tidied himself and made his way to the lobby, sinking into a chair to wait. The man behind the desk smiled unwaveringly, watching his every move.

'Not many tourists coming?' Harrison remarked.

'France, German some. England – not many. You are most welcome *thakin.*'

Thakin. The servants had called him that in the family home near Mandalay a lifetime ago. It meant master.

'This first time in Myanmar?'

Harrison wondered whether to lie.

'First time for a very long time,' he answered eventually.

He picked up an English-language newspaper from the table called *The New Light of Myanmar*, whose content was summed up by its banal headlines.

Secretary-1 attends skill demonstration by outstanding students.
Secretary-2 visits traditional apparel show.

The job titles the junta had invented for themselves sounded like something out of George Orwell.

The taxi came and drove him towards the centre of the city, where he hoped to find the man who could lead him to Tin Su. As they passed the gilded hilltop splendour of the huge Shwe Dagon Pagoda he remembered taking his new wife there on their first evening in Rangoon more than forty-six years ago. She'd never been to the capital before.

The centre of Yangon looked little changed from its time as colonial Rangoon. The warmth and smells of the place slipped round his shoulders like an old cardigan. The car dropped him at the smaller Sule Pagoda and he looked about to get his bearings. Two young children ran up, one with a basket covered with fine lace through which the beaks of wild birds poked. Smiling at their expectant faces, Harrison pulled out a 50-kyat note and gave it to them in payment for the creatures' freedom. Buddhist tradition said such an act improved a man's chances of a good reincarnation. As he watched them flutter away he knew that securing freedom for his son was going to be infinitely harder.

He began to walk, stiffly conscious of the pain in his pelvis and back.

The analgesic patch appeared to be losing its efficacy, despite the doctors saying they lasted three days.

At the junction with Merchant Road he stopped to catch his breath outside a grey ministerial building, guarded by watchful soldiers. When the military junta took power in 1988 it had called itself the SLORC, he remembered. State Law and Order Restoration Council. Today it was SPDC – State Protection and Development Council, a softening of the acronym but not of the regime. It irked him that within a few short days, fate willing, he'd be doing business with these strutting demagogues.

The pavements were crowded, men as well as women dressed in the skirt-like *longyis*. He passed shops selling electric fans and aluminium pots, and side-stepped tea shop customers crouching on low stools by the kerb. An ancient bus clattered past, gushing blue fumes, its rusting bodywork disguised by bright green paint.

Central Yangon was laid out as a grid, the numbered north–south roads crossing named streets at right angles. The house Harrison was looking for was on a junction, but he couldn't remember which, though he recollected a wrought-iron balcony overlooking the main road. The address had been on the faded yellow letter his friend had written twelve years ago, but he'd destroyed it because it reminded him so chillingly of all he'd turned his back on.

Than Swe. Still living in that corner house in 1988, but today? Harrison hoped he wasn't dead. Because however shamefully he'd neglected their friendship, he was the key to the past. The one key he had.

When they were children Than Swe was the only Burmese friend he'd had. They'd played in rivers and streams and frightened one another with tales of wild beasts from the jungle. At the age of thirteen Perry had been sent to boarding school in England, but the friendship had continued in the summer holidays. After the war they'd met again in Rangoon when he returned in 1953 to work for a timber exporter. Their conversation then was of politics, books and women.

Harrison walked on along Market Street, peering up at every corner house, hoping to recognise it. After six blocks, he began to think he must have missed it. The heat was getting to him. He needed a rest and stepped into a tea shop which seemed to be staffed by cowed boys no older than ten. As soon as he sat down, one of them hovered for his order.

'*Lek peq-ye,*' Harrison mumbled, hoping he'd remembered the right Burmese words. The boy scurried away and returned with a brimming mug.

As he sipped the sweet and milky tea, he watched the children scurry from table to table, snapped at by a fat slave-master perched behind a counter stacked with pastries. At the next table a middle-aged man was studying him intently. Eventually he leaned forward.

'Where you from?'

'England,' Harrison replied. He drank up quickly wanting to avoid conversation.

'Yes,' the man nodded, as if he'd guessed all along.

'Tell me,' said Perry, having an idea, 'do you know the house of U Than Swe?'

The man's face lit up. 'Oh yes. You walk one more street.' He beamed with pleasure at having been of service.

'Thank you very much.' Harrison stood up. The tea had done its work. He was ready to move on.

At the next junction he looked up and there it was. He experienced an extraordinary sensation of coming home. The familiar balcony, still the dark green colour he remembered. And the french windows behind it, open in the way they'd always been.

Insein Prison

Tin Su squatted in a long corridor, waiting in line with scores of other inmates' relatives. She kept her eyes averted.

There was a Buddhist saying that people don't own their children, but are given them temporarily to take care of. She'd done her best for hers in the years past and was still doing so now, but the fact that she was here in this place to see her son made her think she'd failed.

She sighed wearily. Whenever she came it was the same. The long wait for her name to be called. The all too brief interlude with Khin Thein.

Her first born, he was the only flesh and blood she had left. Her other son had vanished on the eighth day of the eighth month in 1988, when the Burmese people rose up to demand a return to democracy. A million people on the streets believing the dictatorship could be overthrown. Then the soldiers had opened fire. She'd looked for her son for days after. In the hospitals. Tracked down his friends, but all they could do was shake heads and wipe away tears. She'd never found him. Never learned his fate.

She looked up. A prison officer had appeared at the end of the corridor. He called out five names, but not hers.

She slumped back into her memories, the stepping stones that had brought her to where she was now.

Her journey had begun forty-seven years ago when the Englishman had walked into the library in Mong Lai. He'd had wild, fair hair and a proud face. She'd likened him to a lion. His eyes had been startlingly blue, and the sensation of knowing they were exploring her slender back as she'd reached up for a volume of Dickens had caused her to wobble on the ladder. There'd been an extraordinary intensity about his gaze, a look which conveyed desire, with a directness no Burmese man could ever contemplate. But a look which had burned with something else. Something dark, which in all the years she knew him she'd never understood.

She remembered trembling when signing the book out to him, blushing over her inability to spell his name. At first she'd thought he'd said 'Pelican', then he'd taken her hand with the pen in it and traced the letters for her in her ledger. P-E-R-E-G-R-I-N-E. Peregrine Harrison.

His forwardness in touching her like that had shocked her. In fact everything about him had left her breathless. His physique was rugged yet he'd moved in a graceful way. Not effeminate, yet devoid of the brutishness common amongst Europeans. He'd said he was in the hill resort for a week, taking a break from Rangoon.

The next day he'd reappeared, not to return the book or seek another, but to talk to her. With no sense of shame he'd told her he couldn't get her out of his thoughts. She could still feel the heat of her blushes. He'd asked if she would join him for dinner that evening at the hotel where he was staying, a colonial mansion by the edge of the town's small, artificial lake. She'd refused, of course. It was unthinkable for an unmarried Burmese girl to be seen alone with a man. And even if she'd been tempted to break the rules of her society, she'd had nothing suitable to wear. When her father died she'd given away her finer clothes, because their bright colours had seemed to mock at her grief.

She remembered how her rejection of his invitation had startled him, as if he were unused to being denied something he'd set his heart on. Then a twinkle had come to his eyes and he'd left the library, telling her he would be back.

Several hours later 'Per-grin', as she'd called him, had returned with a parcel. He'd placed it before her, saying she couldn't possibly refuse to dine with him now. Inside the package was a *longyi* of Mandalay silk. She'd blushed to the roots of her hair, startled that a man could have such insight into a woman's mind. He'd stayed there talking, telling her about his life, as if to prove there was nothing unwholesome about him, charming her, until she'd given in.

She'd been nervous that evening. More nervous than ever before. Per-grin had offered his arm as they walked up the steps of the hotel, but she'd refused, not daring to touch him. The table he'd reserved was on the terrace overlooking the lake, and as they'd taken their seats she'd been conscious of the disapproving stares of the staff and other guests.

Eventually she'd begun to feel sufficiently at ease to tell him about herself. He'd listened, and he'd smiled – except when she'd talked of the war years living under the Japanese. It had felt wonderful to have a man *listening* to what she said rather than rebuking her foolish thoughts as her father had done.

The next day Per-grin had been waiting outside the library when she arrived for work. And in the days that followed, with no family to caution her, she'd allowed herself to fall in love with him.

One day he'd hired a car and driver and asked her to accompany him to a pretty waterfall 30 kilometres away. After a hot and dusty journey, they'd climbed up past the torrent and looked down on the valley from the ruins of a monastery. She could still remember the sun glinting off a distant stupa. He'd talked about the life of the Lord Buddha, as if the stories were more familiar to him than to the shaven-headed monks who begged in the streets every day.

They'd watched the sun set beyond the distant peaks, and then he'd asked her to marry him. It had shocked her. Shocked her too when she heard herself say 'yes'. As the car rattled and banged its way over the stony road back to the town, she'd let him hold her hand. He'd told her about the home they would set up in Rangoon, with servants – a gardener and a cook. Of the beautiful babies they would have, to whom they would impart all their wisdom. And in time, if they wanted, they could travel the world. Even to England, to the land she'd read about in Trollope, Jane Austen and Dickens.

That night she'd let Per-grin come into her home. And there, in a room filled with her treasured books and with photos of those no longer with her, they'd embraced. At first he'd done it the Burmese way, a nose pressed to a cheek and a little sniff. But then he'd put his lips against hers. She'd felt the hard press of his flesh and her physical desire for him had been awakened. He'd taken her into her sleeping room and they'd lain down on her mat. A part of her had wanted him to open her up as a woman there and then, yet deep inside she'd feared it. Feared this might be a dream after all. Again that night, his intuition had been good. He'd held back, understanding her caution. Told her they'd be married as soon as they reached Rangoon, and then they would make love. Every day and every night, and never be parted.

The prison guard was back. More names called out.

This time hers was one of them.

Market Street, Yangon

Set into the side wall of Than Swe's house, a stone staircase led up to the first floor. Perry Harrison gazed at it, remembering the indentations in the treads and the scar along one wall where something metallic had been scraped. The last time he'd walked up them was in 1963, the day before being expelled from the country, along with all foreign workers. They'd said their goodbyes, he and his lifelong friend, believing the generals' nationalisation programme would be disastrous and short lived and it wouldn't be long before he could return. They'd been right on the first point but wrong on the second. Burma's crippling socialist isolation had lasted twenty-five years.

Harrison began to climb, full of trepidation about what he would discover at the top. The stairs gave access to a small terrace where clothes hung to dry. He paused to regain his breath. The door to the apartment was open. It always had been, he remembered – for visitors and to let a cooling breeze pass through.

A middle-aged woman in a dark patterned *longyi* and short-sleeved white top emerged, with a baby in her arms. She looked at him without curiosity, as if it were perfectly normal for strangers to turn up here. Even Europeans.

'Is this still the home of U Than Swe?'

'Yes.'

'Could you tell him Perry Harrison is here?'

She looked as if she'd seen a ghost.

'We used to be close friends,' he explained.

'Yes. I hear him say you name. You please to wait here.'

She turned towards the large, airy dayroom where he and Than had talked so often, so many years ago. On the threshold she glanced back, as if checking he was real.

It was a couple of minutes before she reappeared, still holding the child. With her free hand she beckoned him in. 'My father not well,' she whispered. 'Please, not stay long.'

Her father. There'd been two girls and a boy, Harrison remembered. The woman had a beautiful face and her oiled black hair shone like polished ebony.

Inside the room a very old man sat in a book-lined alcove, the skin clinging to his skull like crumpled paper. His hands clasped some ancient volume which was held together with black tape.

Harrison hardly recognised him. He felt tears welling up and choked them back.

'Than? My old friend?'

The Burman stared at him without smiling. The face was so lifeless Harrison wondered if he'd had a stroke.

'So it is you . . .' The voice when it came was as dry as a husk.

The daughter placed a chair behind Perry's legs. He sat down gratefully.

'Thank you.'

For a while the two men looked at one another, slowly taking in what time had done to them.

'You'll be surprised to see me, I expect.' Harrison's voice trembled. 'I've been a poor friend to you.'

'Yes.' Despite the immobility of his face, Than Swe's eyes burned like gemstones.

'I regret that. I'm sorry.'

'It comes with age, regretting things.' The Burman spoke with a light accent.

Harrison's tears welled up again. 'But it's damned good to see you . . .' He leaned forward and took hold of Than Swe's hands, prising them away from his book.

'You don't look well,' his erstwhile friend remarked, unmoved.

'I'm not. It's cancer. I don't have long.'

The Burman nodded. 'And I suppose you've come here to try to clear your conscience. To be reconciled with the people you turned your back on.'

Harrison felt wretched. Stupidly he'd expected instant joy at being seen again, instant forgiveness for the past.

'Yes.'

'You have come to see Daw Tin Su?'

'Well, yes . . .'

'And because you have not contacted her for thirty-eight years, you don't know how to find her.'

'Help me Than Swe . . .'

'I don't know if I should. She won't want to see you, you know.'

'She is . . . still alive, then?'

Than Swe's contemptuous glare made him blanch. This man had once loved him but now it felt like hate.

'I know I have a lot of ground to make up,' Harrison mumbled.

'You have left it very late.'

'I'm aware of that.'

Than Swe began to stir, like a moth emerging from a chrysalis.

'You see . . . I am struggling to comprehend, Perry. Is it simply *regret* that has brought you all this way? Ahhh . . .' His eyes widened as he perceived the truth. 'Of course. You are a believer still. Afraid of what awaits you in the next life. You want to improve your standing. To obtain merit before you die. Like the generals in the SLORC who spend their stolen money on new Buddhas.'

Harrison felt winded by Than Swe's scathing sarcasm. 'It's more a matter of being able to die in peace,' he mumbled defensively.

Than Swe's daughter returned, carrying a thermos of green tea and two cups on a small tin tray. She poured some for them, then left again.

'You've been unwell too,' Perry commented, wanting to turn the focus away from himself. 'Your daughter said so.'

'I got ill in prison. A long time ago. By the time they released me I was very weak.'

'Prison?'

'You didn't know . . .?' He said it scoldingly. 'It was because of my writing. I was an enemy of the state.'

'How long?'

'Six years. Three of them alone in a cell. Amnesty International campaigned for me. In *England*. Perry . . . How is it you didn't know?'

Harrison shook his head, his wretchedness growing. 'Solitary confinement,' he murmured, flinching at his own memories. 'You had books?'

'Nothing. Reading and writing were not allowed.'

'How did you survive?'

'I walked. Around my cell. It was only a few paces. But I counted them. All day long. Every day when I wasn't sick. Counted my footsteps until I reached ten thousand, then I knew the day was over and it was time to sleep again.'

Harrison bowed his head in admiration. He wondered about Than's wife. There wasn't even a photograph in the room. 'May Kyi . . . ?' he asked.

'She died two years ago. My daughter looks after me now. Because I cannot do anything by myself.'

Suddenly he spread his hands in a gesture of welcome.

'I *am* happy to see you, Perry.'

Harrison's eyes began to water again.

'Now, please tell me *exactly* why you have come.'

'To see Tin Su,' he said, huskily. The main reason for his visit was one he could never reveal. 'To ask for her forgiveness and to help her if I can. Perhaps some money . . .'

Than Swe drew in his cheeks as if preparing to spit venom.

'Do you know *anything* about what happened to her after you went away?'

Harrison knew his shame was about to be immeasurably deepened.

'No.'

'Then I have a story to tell you. And I hope it breaks your heart.'

17

Insein Prison

THE VISIT TO her son was brief. It should have lasted an hour, but today it was less. No explanation why.

Tin Su felt a terrible emptiness as she climbed into the back of the pick-up for the journey home. There seemed so little hope. The political accommodations between the military regime and Aung San Suu Kyi's National League for Democracy that would allow Khin Thein's release looked as remote as ever. And as far as she could tell, the outside world had turned its back on her country just as resolutely as her husband had on her.

With a crunching of gears the truck drove off.

It was nearly thirty-eight years since she'd last seen Per-grin. No way of knowing if he was alive or dead. There were many days when she wished she'd never let her head be turned by him. If she'd settled with some dependable school-teacher in Mong Lai, she might have had children to care for *her* needs, instead of having to care for theirs.

The first years of their life in Rangoon had been happy. A fine house, with a gardener and cook, even if the pair despised her for marrying outside her race. And beautiful children.

When the military ordered the foreigners out, she'd wanted to go with Per-grin to England, happy to uproot their children and start a new life in a land she only knew from books. But the authorities had refused them exit permits. Per-grin had promised to return as soon as he could and send money through the firm where he'd worked.

At first the arrangements had run smoothly and she'd convinced herself they'd be together again soon. There'd been letters saying he'd got work in the timber firm's London offices and was making efforts through the Burmese Embassy to secure travel permits for her and the boys. Then the letters had stopped and after a few months it had dawned on her he might never write again. The money had come for another ten months. Then one day when she'd gone to collect it she'd been told the young man responsible for passing it to her had been arrested for stealing. His job had been taken by an older man with slicked hair and greasy skin called Myint Aung, who'd claimed there was no record of payments from abroad for her. In response to her pleadings he'd promised to look into it.

A few days later he'd come to her home. Admired her furniture and possessions and flattered her over her looks. Then he'd claimed he was having difficulty tracing the money, but it might help if she were to do something for him. From his awkward demeanour, she'd guessed immediately what he wanted and, horrified, had sent him away. But as the weeks passed with no income she'd become desperate, resorting to selling treasured possessions to keep her family fed.

One evening, after the children were asleep, Myint Aung had returned, bringing money with him this time. He'd told her very pleasantly that it would be hers if she would perform some sexual favours for him. She'd burst into tears and sent him away once more. A week later however, she'd gone to the timber office to tell him to come and see her again.

For the next year her income had been restored. His demands upon her had not been excessive. Nor had they been as physically unpleasant as she'd expected. Once or twice a month he would come to see her late in the evening and leave before dawn. But the money he brought began to decrease. Exchange rates, he'd explained. Weeks later he'd told her the remittances from her husband had actually stopped some time ago and that he, Myint Aung, had been paying her out of his own pocket. True or not, she'd had no way of telling. But the money he offered no longer fed and clothed her children or paid for their lessons.

Myint Aung had been sympathetic to her plight. He'd mentioned other 'gentlemen' who would happily give her money for her favours. He'd brought them to visit one at a time, taking care to ensure their arrival would not be observed by neighbours. There'd been nothing unpleasant about them. Like Myint Aung himself, they were middle-ranking officials. One had never been married. The other had a wife who he claimed was cold.

And so she'd sunk into a discreet form of prostitution. Myint Aung had become her 'manager', vetting clients and handling the financial arrangements. He'd taken a percentage for himself, but she told herself he deserved it for making sure the clients he sent weren't types who would do her harm. Over time she'd even grown fond of him.

For ten years she'd lived like that. And she'd even managed to retain her self-respect, telling herself she was only doing it in order to bring up her fatherless sons. Then gradually the customers had stopped coming. Age had caught up with her. Eventually Myint Aung himself had found some younger woman. Tin Su's career and her income had petered out. By then her sons had been nineteen and twenty-one, both studying law. As a parting gift, one of her clients arranged a job in the government department where he was a manager. One that would suit her and provide a small income. Working with books again – in the censor's office.

And so, for the next decade, she'd helped stifle her countrymen's faint cries for freedom, in the interests of helping her own sons become lawyers, a profession that might one day help restore liberty to the country. The job had lasted until that dreadful day in 1988, when her younger boy had disappeared. For weeks afterwards she'd not felt strong enough to return to work. And as soon as she had she'd been sacked for being the mother of a man who'd dared defy the regime.

Now, today, as she rode that rattling truck back to the place where she lived, her whole life seemed so pointless. She'd lost everything. Her home, her children, her standing and her happiness.

And all because of an Englishman she'd met when she was very, very young.

Market Street

Perry Harrison sat very still. It wasn't just the story of what had happened to Tin Su that had shaken him. It was the realisation that he felt no responsibility for what had come to pass. Regret, yes. But no blame.

'I have never loved another woman as much as I loved Tin Su,' he confessed, mystified that after such a love he could have given so little thought to her fate.

'Did you not ask yourself what happened to her?' Than Swe pressed, peering at him as he would a creature that was not quite human. 'When you stopped sending the money, what were you thinking? A wife and two children . . .'

Perry felt his face burning.

'At the time I needed every penny I had for setting up the Bordhill Community.' It was the excuse he'd given himself then. And at the time it had seemed justified – using his limited resources to help *hundreds* of people with problems rather than to support one small family in a faraway place, whose needs were very simple anyway.

'I suppose I thought she would find someone else,' he explained lamely.

As indeed she had. And the non-emotionally-engaging sex which circumstances had forced her into shouldn't really have done her any harm, he told himself. It was, after all, precisely what he'd coached his Bordhill disciples in for the past thirty-five years.

He could see the disappointment in Than Swe's eyes, but he'd come here for a purpose and was determined to fulfil it.

'Look. They've been on my conscience recently, she and Khin Thein. I know it's late, but it matters to *me* that I do something about it. So . . . tell me. Do you know where Tin Su is?'

'Yes. But may I know what *exactly* it is you want from her?'

'Forgiveness I suppose,' he answered eventually.

'Then I think you will be disappointed. She has tried very hard to forget you after so many years, but to forgive is a lot to ask. She told me once that everything she does *not* have in life is because of you, and all that she has – her fine man of a son – is in *spite* of you.'

Harrison dropped his gaze.

'You've seen Tin Su recently?' he asked humbly.

'About six months ago. She came here to talk about Khin Thein. There is very little of you in him, you know,' Than told him quickly. 'His looks and his gentle character come from his mother. It was your other son who resembled you more. Mo Win was a wilder, less balanced person than Khin Thein, but he disappeared in 1988. The military killed him when the people rose up. Did you know this? I wrote you a letter about it. Gave it to an Englishwoman who was here and asked her to try to find your address.'

'I got your letter.' It had troubled him so much he'd had to shut it from his mind. 'You think they'd let me visit Khin Thein in the prison?'

'*Why* do you want to see him?'

'Because he's my son.'

'He's been your son for forty-five years.' Than Swe ruminated for a few moments, then made up his mind. 'You can ask Tin Su about going to the prison. She will know the procedure.'

'How will I find Tin Su?'

'My grandson can take you to her. It's an hour's drive from Yangon. He will use his father's car. You must pay him. He is a student, but since the SLORC closed the universities he has to do his study by correspondence. And that costs much money. So he drives tourists around. The few that come here. Twenty dollars a day.'

'I'll willingly pay double that.'

'No. Twenty dollars is enough. It will spoil him if you give more. He will expect it from others.'

'Whatever you say. When? When can he take me?'
'This evening, maybe. I will call him on the telephone.'
'Thank you. Thank you so very much.'

The road north of Yangon

The sun was getting low in the sky as the pick-up neared its next stop. Tin Su could smell the smoke of cooking fires. She saw a man walking in the dust beside the road, broken-necked chickens dangling from his hands.

The town where she lived sprawled along the main road. Two other passengers got down with her, gingerly easing the stiffness from their legs. Then with a cloud of blue exhaust the pick-up continued on its way.

Tin Su was taller than the local women, despite the bend to her back that had come with age. Many Shan people were that way. Her mother used to tell her it was the mountain air that made them grow more.

She walked along the main road for a minute or two, tempted by smells from a curry shop but knowing she couldn't afford to buy anything. The line-bus had taken all she'd been able to save in the last month.

She turned into a side street, past a covered market and walked on towards a small temple with a *zedi* from which the gold leaf was peeling. Finally she reached the alley that led to the little house where she'd lived for nearly ten years. She stopped outside, slipped her feet from her sandals, and turned the handle. Nobody locked doors around here. Theft was unknown in the town, and in truth she had little for anybody to steal. Inside it was dark. The light didn't work because the power was off. Cuts happened all the time. She moved towards the little cupboard at the back of the room, groping for the matches she kept there. Then by the light of the spluttering flame, she lifted the glass of an oil lamp and touched the match to the wick.

She preferred its light to the electric. A kinder glow that revealed less of the shabbiness of where she lived. With a sigh she lowered herself onto one of the two rush-seated chairs that together with a small table were the only furnishings of the room.

Holding her hands to her stomach, the bones of her pelvis pressed hard against her wrists. She knew she should eat something but she had little inclination.

For more than an hour she sat there in the gloom, preoccupied with her thoughts. Then she stirred, telling herself this wouldn't do. She liked to read, the same old books over and over again, but her eyes couldn't see the print anymore in the feeble light from the oil lamp.

She decided to go to bed, taking off her clothes and carrying the lamp into the bathing room. She squatted over the toilet, before washing all over with cold water scooped from a cistern. Then she dried herself on a towel, extinguished the light and settled onto her sleeping mat. She checked there were no gaps in the mosquito net then lay down and covered herself with a thin cotton sheet.

Her hands went up to her breasts, remembering how those flat pouches had once been filled with milk. She remembered too how Per-grin had kissed them on that first night in Rangoon after the long journey south. Kissed them and the rest of her firm innocent body until all of her fear and shyness had been blown aside by her overwhelming need for him to make her his own.

It was good she could still remember those tender moments, because they softened her anger and made it easier to bear. There was something else about him she would never forget – his body twisting and shuddering beside her every night, in the grip of the evil dreams he would never explain.

For some time, Tin Su lay there, unable to sleep. Her body was exhausted but her mind wouldn't let her rest.

Suddenly she heard a noise. Footsteps outside. But instead of passing on to one of the other homes further up the alley, they'd stopped outside her door.

She pulled up the sheet, holding her breath. The footsteps moved on, but hesitantly. She breathed again.

Moonlight filtered through the sackcloth curtains covering the one small window at the front of her room. The footsteps returned. More determined this time. Soft padding on the earthy ground right in front of her door. A shadow moved in the window. Someone trying to see inside.

Tin Su was afraid all of a sudden. She imagined dacoits – armed bandits. The knob rattled. She heard the creak of latch springs as it turned.

The door slowly opened, letting in a faint quadrant of light, just bright enough to show that her visitor was large. Shan people were tall. Someone from her past? The brother she hadn't seen for fifty years? Her younger son?

A thin beam of light shone from the visitor's hand, swinging round the room until it found the white veil of the mosquito net.

'Tin Su?'

Her heart quivered as if it were about to stop. This couldn't be. Not *that* voice.

Then the visitor turned the torch on himself. The face was deeply lined. Haggard even. The hair that had once flowed like a mane was cropped short, its colour like snow.

'Per-grin,' she croaked. 'You have come to kill me?'

18

HARRISON HARDLY RECOGNISED her. She'd become skin and bone. Seeing her there in the flesh, cowering on the sleeping mat, stirred up emotions he'd spent most of his life suppressing.

He closed his eyes, feeling he was about to unravel.

'You have come to kill me?' she repeated, her voice thin and tremulous. She clutched the sheet to her chest.

'How can you say such a thing?' he croaked.

'Because you must hate me,' she told him.

'How can you think that?'

He swung the torch beam until he found a chair, then sat on it, hunching forward in the vain hope it would ease the pain in his back. He'd put on a new patch before leaving Yangon but it had not yet reached its full effect.

'Why you have come here? How do you find me?'

'Than Swe.' He indicated the young man standing in the doorway. 'This is his grandson Saw Lwin.'

She was still clutching the sheet to her chest. 'Please . . . you turn away so I put clothes on.'

The youth went outside and Harrison swung the chair round, happy not to see how emaciated her once fine body had become.

'You want I find place to stay for tonight?' Than's grandson called out.

'Yes please.'

There was no room in Tin Su's tiny abode and he was in no physical condition to sleep on the ground. He heard the boy scuttle off down the alley.

Harrison took measured breaths, switching on his defence mechanisms to choke off his feelings of guilt and shame. He made himself visualise the

141

vile men who'd paid Tin Su to have sex with them, so he could feel disgusted by her.

Tin Su's shaking hands made it hard for her to tie the knot in her *longyi*. Once dressed, she lit a small oil stove to heat some water for tea. Then she just stared at him, her arms limp at her sides.

'I did something wrong?' she asked. The question had tormented her for nearly forty years. 'Why you don't write to me and don't want to see me again.'

'No, Tin Su. It was I who did something wrong. I've come to say sorry.'

Her face creased in a frown. She didn't understand.

'Please,' said Perry, beckoning her towards the table. 'Let us sit together.'

Still not certain this wasn't a bad dream, Tin Su complied, sitting upright on the rush-seated chair with her hands clasped tightly on her lap.

'How are you, Tin Su?' It was a stupid question but the only way he could think of beginning.

She didn't answer. He didn't expect her to. She wouldn't know where to start.

'Tell me about our sons. I . . . I never really knew them.'

For a while she didn't reply, fearing her voice would betray her feelings.

'They were beautiful children,' she whispered eventually. 'Not often fighting. Khin Thein put up with very much from Mo Win who was like you, Per-grin. Always worries in his head. Could never say what. Very like you . . .'

She talked of the hardships of bringing them up alone. The difficulty of earning money. Then she looked away, wondering how much Than Swe had told him.

'I know what you had to do,' Perry said. 'The shame is mine, Tin Su, not yours.'

She got up from the chair to make the tea.

'Tell me about 8.8.88. The last time you saw Mo Win.' It was the first time he'd called him by his Burmese name. 'Michael,' he murmured.

As she poured water into the pot, she began to tell him about the people's anger at their incompetent military rulers in the sweltering summer of 1988. The eighth day of the eighth month of that year had been chosen as an auspicious date for the masses to take to the streets in protest.

'Khin Thein suspecting the military only sleeping. He stay at back of crowd,' she whispered, carrying a tray back to the table. 'But Mo Win won't listen. Always in front, close to people who speaking. And when the tanks come, when the soldiers start shooting, he can't get away. We don't know what happen to him. Ask at hospitals. Then I ask the army. Where is he? Have they taken him? They question me. All day. Wanting to know name of his friends.' She sniffed back tears. 'Our son want to change Myanmar, Per-grin. To make it better after long sickness. Like doctor – that's what he say last time I see him.'

She searched her former husband's face for some sign that he felt what she felt, but all she saw in his eyes was the confusion and mania of an old man.

'And Khin Thein?' Harrison asked. It was his surviving son he had to be concerned about. The only one he could help.

'I see him in the prison. Insein. Today. He very thin. Food no good. I take fruit for him.'

'Tin Su, I want to go and see him.'

His bald statement knocked the breath from her.

'Not possible,' she whispered, full of fear.

'We must *make* it possible, Tin Su.'

The intensity of his insistence took her back to the first time they'd met. His refusal to take no for an answer.

Reluctantly she told him of the mechanics of visiting the prison. Two visits per month for members of the family. Next visit not due for another couple of weeks.

'I can't wait two weeks.' There was another way. There always was. And in Myanmar the bribe wouldn't need to be large. 'To whom do I give a present?'

Tin Su told him that 100 kyat slipped quietly to the officer in charge of the prison guards might be sufficient for a Burmese to secure an extra visit. The equivalent of twenty pence, he calculated.

'You've done that?'

'No. But I hear people talk.'

Harrison saw her lips flicker. Some little story had occurred to her. She liked stories, he remembered. Used to garner them from her friends to amuse him when he returned from work.

'This officer – the bell to his house is at the back door, not the front. And down low. Close to ground. Because visitors always come on their knees. And they carrying heavy presents.'

He smiled condescendingly. 'We will go there tomorrow, you and me.'

The protest in her eyes died quickly, as he knew it would.

Than's grandson returned. He'd found two rooms in a small guest house. Ten dollars a night for Harrison because he was a foreigner and one dollar for himself. The rooms were simple but clean, he said.

Harrison stayed on with Tin Su long enough to make arrangements for the morning, then, feeling utterly drained, he hobbled down the alley to where they'd left the car.

Five minutes later he lay in a narrow bed with a lumpy mattress, longing for sleep to deaden the pain. In his mind as well as his body.

19

Myanmar
The next day, Tuesday, 11 January

IT WAS DAWN WHEN they began the drive back to Yangon. Against her will, Tin Su guided them to the township on the outskirts of the capital where the prison officer lived. Then, quivering with embarrassment at being seen with a European, she led her one-time husband to the door – it *was* at the rear of the house – and explained on his behalf what they wanted.

The prison officer was in his uniform and appeared to be about to go to work. He spoke no English, but the alarm their request created was evident on his thin, light brown face. An Englishman arriving at the jail would stand out like a sore thumb. There'd be questions from above. Reports would be filed to Military Intelligence. No. It would be very hard to arrange – Harrison understood his drift even before Tin Su translated.

Then he produced a fifty-dollar note. Tin Su had told him not go above twenty but the situation was desperate. The man's eyes doubled in size at the sight of the money. He pocketed it quickly and told them to come back the same time the following day.

Harrison twitched with frustration. There was a clock ticking inside him whose spring was about to run down. He suggested Tin Su remain in Rangoon until tomorrow, fearing that if he let her go she wouldn't come back. He offered her a room at his hotel, but she begged to be allowed to return to her home alone.

In fact he was relieved. Conversation in the car on the journey to Yangon had been a strain. Than Swe had been right. Forgiveness was not in Tin Su's gift. After the initial confused emotions of seeing him again, she resented his presence here, telling him there was nothing he could do to make amends for having abandoned her. And she wanted nothing from him. Not even the belated benefit of his money.

He got Saw Lwin to arrange for another student friend to drive her home, with instructions to collect her again early the following morning. Then Than's grandson took him back to the Inya Lodge Hotel. Inside the lobby there were still three people behind the desk and still no sign of other guests.

He retired to his room and lay on the bed, telling Saw Lwin to wait for him. It wasn't the pain that was troubling him this morning but a feeling of impending failure. In his bones he knew he would not be allowed to see his son, and even if he were, Khin Thein would probably be embarrassed to see him rather than glad. And as to the other purpose of his journey, without the physical assistance of Rip it seemed impossible that he'd be able to complete it.

He rested for thirty minutes then forced himself to get up again. There *were* things still to do, because however deep his despair he had to press on. And hope for a miracle.

Back in the car again, Saw Lwin drove him beyond the northern outskirts of Yangon. Nondescript industrial sprawl gave way to agricultural land, orchards and water buffalo. Then, coming up on the right, Harrison saw a denser, darker patch of ground. Trees had been planted in an orderly way, surrounding a compound bounded by a perimeter wall. Emotions welled up. He began the measured breathing tactics he'd learned years ago, to keep them under control.

Saw Lwin pulled up outside a wrought-iron gateway. There was one other car there, its driver waiting patiently for his passengers to return.

'Not quite sure how long I'll be,' Harrison mumbled as he eased his legs out of the car.

'I wait here. No problem.'

Straightening his painful back and placing a soft bush hat on his head as protection from the sun, he stepped across the threshold, then stopped to catch his breath. He'd forgotten how large the cemetery was, line upon line of stone tablets set out in the grass, the morning light glinting off their polished granite. Twenty-seven thousand Allied soldiers who'd died in Burma and Assam were commemorated here, including several Harrison had counted as friends.

Fighting for self-control, he began moving between the rows. The orderliness of the place struck him as a terrible deceit when he thought of the vile circumstances in which the men had met their ends.

He faltered as he read the names, ranks, regiments. He'd been twenty-one years old. Picked because he knew Burma. A lieutenant in charge of men much older than himself. And a couple of them lay here in front of him. He could smell the jungle again. The damp earthiness, and the pungent mix of stale rice, sweat and human waste that he'd come to know as the whiff of Jap.

The date on the stones, 29 March 1943, was etched in his memory as deeply as into these pieces of polished granite. That day their infantry column had been picking through dense thorn to avoid a swamp not marked on maps. They'd been exhausted when the ambush happened, their spirits frayed by eight weeks of short rations and long marches. Two men cut down beside him.

These two, in front of him now. Corporal Dent.

A smiling face, a heart of gold,
No dearer one this world could hold.

And Private Billings.

Beloved Tom. Forever in our memory.

Harrison's chest quivered. He clamped a hand to his mouth. He'd shut out these feelings for so long, but he needed to experience the pain of them again, if he was to have the steel to achieve his goal.

He walked on, reading more inscriptions. Then he stepped up to the colonnade in the centre of the cemetery and stared at the huge stone tablets. Indians, Australians, New Zealanders were listed there, their remains lost forever. Also reading them was an elderly Sikh. For a moment the two men's eyes met in mutual acknowledgement. Then they bowed to one another and continued with their sad and solitary business.

At the end of the colonnade Harrison stepped onto the lawn again. The air was heavy with scent. Beneath the trees that edged the cemetery, two young girls in white shirts and dark *longyis* were making garlands from fallen blossoms. They were laughing. This solemn place had become their playground. Harrison felt a rush of anger. He wanted to tell them of the awful things he'd experienced in their country in a bygone age, but knew they wouldn't want to hear. He turned away, shutting them from his sight.

He felt desperately alone. Wished he'd died in the jungle with the others. Been laid out here, with his suffering flagged for the world to see, instead of it staying buried in his soul.

He faced the plaques again and saluted, then headed back to the road. Saw Lwin helped him into the car.

'Where you want to go now, Mr Harrison?'

The old man took in a deep breath. It wasn't where he wanted to go, but where he *had* to.

'The Japanese Embassy, Saw Lwin.'

20

IT TOOK THEM twenty minutes to reach the north side of Kandawgyi Lake where the Japanese government had its mission, by which time Harrison was in a cold sweat. The war had not only left him with an undying hatred of the Japanese, but a fear of them too. He knew it was irrational. They couldn't harm him now. But ever since his release from internment, the sight of a Japanese face could send him into a panic.

'I wait around next corner,' said Saw Lwin, drawing up in front of the building. 'Not allowed to park here.'

When there was no response from the back he turned round. The pallor of his passenger alarmed him.

'You want go back hotel?'

Harrison didn't answer, preoccupied with trying to control his stupid terror. In a burst of determination he reached for the door handle and tugged. Saw Lwin swung himself out from the front to help.

'How long you stay here?'

Perry put a hand on the roof for support. 'Not very long, I can assure you of that.' Feeling unable to move, he focused on the entrance. 'This is ridiculous . . .' With a supreme effort he willed his legs across the pavement and reached for the buzzer. The lock clicked and the embassy's entrance door swung back automatically.

He froze again. 'Ridiculous,' he repeated, forcing himself to step into the small lobby. On one side was a window with a guard behind it and at the far end a door with a swipe-card entry system. There was a grille in the glass to his left. He steeled himself to look beyond it, expecting to see the kind of eyes that haunted his dreams. But the face was Burmese.

'I . . . want to talk to someone about the war.'

He heard his own words as if they'd been spoken by someone else. And realised how nonsensical they'd sounded.

'I mean I want to talk to someone about the memorials in Myanmar to Japanese soldiers who died in the war.'

Not much better. The Burman stared uncomprehendingly, then replied in Japanese.

The harsh sound of the language made Harrison shudder. He remembered the barking of the guards, the chanting of *ichi, ni, san, shi, go* . . . numerals learnt so you could shout your prison number at roll-call. He gripped the counter beneath the grille. This wouldn't do.

'Can you find me someone who speaks English please?'

The man at the desk picked up the phone and dialled. His conversation with the person at the other end was brief. 'Please to waiting,' he said, when he'd finished.

There were two straight-backed chairs in the little lobby, black lacquered and upholstered in green. Harrison lowered himself onto one of them.

He'd come here out of necessity, not choice. There was no other way he could think of to get the information he needed. The location of remote Japanese war memorials in Burma was not something the government-controlled tourist information centres in Yangon were likely to know. And he suspected that any out-of-the-ordinary enquiry from a foreigner would be reported to Military Intelligence anyway, a risk to his plans that he couldn't afford to take.

Coming to the Japanese Embassy also risked drawing attention to himself, he realised, particularly if he failed to keep a grip. But there was no other way.

The space where he sat was horribly claustrophobic. He examined the ceiling for evidence of ventilation and was relieved to see a grating. After a few minutes he heard the inner door click and turned to see a young woman standing there. Straight black hair and small spectacles. Very oval-eyed. Neat dark skirt and white blouse. Flat chest. She bowed to him, holding the door open in case of the need to dash back inside.

'Can I help you?' She pronounced 'help' as if the 'l' was an 'r'.

Harrison gazed at her. She looked so fresh and innocent, this girl. Straight out of the box. She would know nothing. *Nothing* of what her forefathers had done in this country.

'I . . . wanted to find out about Japanese war graves in Myanmar. For reconciliation.'

She looked at him without blinking.

'Scuse me?'

Harrison felt incapable of explaining things coherently, despite having rehearsed what to say. He stuffed his fingers into his shirt pocket and pulled out the photocopy of the *Newsweek* press cutting which he'd brought from England.

'I saw this in a magazine,' he blurted out, handing it over. 'Made me realise we have something in common.'

The girl took the piece of paper from him and studied it. Her face was doll-smooth. Expressionless.

'This is Japanese Embassy,' she told him, looking up again.

'I know.'

'Could you please explain me what you want?'

'Information, girl. Information.' Anger surged, but he controlled it quickly. 'I want to know where that place is.'

'Ohhh,' she sighed, understanding him at last. 'Where this memorlial is in Myanmar?'

'Yes.'

'I don't know. Can you please to tell me why you want to know this?' She said it as if she were dealing with a mental case.

Perry told himself he had no need to fear her. She was only a girl. And yet and yet – she was *Japanese*.

'I was in the war. A prisoner of your army.' He pointed to the cutting. 'Seeing that made me realise we do the same things, them and us. We honour our dead.'

Her expression remained quite detached, as if he were relating events of no importance to her which had taken place a very, very long time ago.

'I've come to Myanmar to pay my respects to my own comrades. The ones who didn't survive. They're buried here. And I thought I'd try to meet some Japanese doing the same thing. So we could each express our regrets about the past. D'you see?'

'Mmm. You want to go to Japanese memorlial?'

'That's right. At the same time as some Japanese. So we can pray together.'

'Uh-huh. You want to pray with Japanese people.' She still seemed puzzled.

'Only, first I have to find out if any Japanese veterans are in Myanmar at the moment. You understand? That article talked about a party coming here every January.'

'Tetsuo Kamata,' she murmured, reading.

'Doesn't have to be him,' Harrison lied, desperate to conceal his purpose. 'Do you know if *any* old soldiers are here at the moment?'

'Mmm.' She became inscrutable again. 'I ask someone. Wait here please.'

He feared he might have set alarm bells ringing. The terrors gripped him again. She was going higher up the ladder. To the level where they took decisions. Decisions that could wreck a man's life. His instinct was to run. To put as much space as he could between himself and those unsmiling eyes before they plunged him back into the past. But he sat down again, not having the strength to go anywhere at that point. He sensed the man behind the glass watching him. Watching in the cold, incurious way the Japs' Korean guards had done as he'd lain out in the sun, chained to a post, half dead after a beating.

It took five minutes, then the girl returned.

'Please to come inside.' This time she smiled. And even looked interested. He fought off the suspicion that he was being drawn into a trap.

As he stood up, he staggered, groping for the wall to support himself. 'I'm not well,' he mumbled.

A man had appeared at the woman's side.

'May I?' He took Harrison's arm to steady him.

They led him to a reception room furnished with a dark veneered table and four chairs.

'Would you like some tea?' The man had short, straight hair, pale cream skin and a prominent beard shadow. The same age as the woman or a few years older.

'Yes. Yes I would.'

As the woman went to organise it, the man introduced himself as the cultural attaché and said he'd acquired his American accent as an exchange student in Los Angeles.

'You were a British soldier in Burma during the Second World War?'

'A POW.'

'My grandfather was also a prisoner. Of the Americans.'

Harrison wanted to say there was a world of difference between the ways they'd been treated, but restrained himself.

'We think we've been able to identify the memorial in this picture,' the man said chirpily. 'It is near the town of Mong Lai in the Shan hills.'

'Mong Lai . . .'

The town where he'd met Tin Su. Not far from the ruined shrine where he'd been captured in 1943. And where hundreds of Japanese troops had fought to the death rather than surrender to the advancing Allies two years later.

'And are there some Japanese veterans in Myanmar at the moment?' he queried, trying not to sound too eager.

'Such visits are private. At the embassy we wouldn't know that.'

The young woman returned with a Burmese servant carrying a tray. She set it on the table, poured tea into small cups and left again.

'You would have many things to talk about, if you can meet with Japanese soldiers,' the cultural attaché suggested.

'Yes. But first I have to find them.'

'Maybe you can try some travel agents. Ask if they've arranged any visits by Japanese parties to Mong Lai. We can give you some names.' The young woman immediately set off to find the information. 'This is the first time you come to Myanmar?'

'Since the war, yes.'

'It's very backward.' The diplomat laughed. 'No Internet!'

'So I've discovered.'

Within a minute the woman returned with a piece of paper.

'I find these two companies,' she told him. 'They are better than the others, I think. More efficient.'

Efficiency wasn't what concerned him. It was who they dealt with that mattered. He thanked her and got to his feet. The walls were closing in.

The two Japanese stood up and bowed.

'We hope you find what you're looking for.'

The attaché bowed again, took his leave and disappeared. Then the woman showed Harrison back to the entrance lobby.

'Enjoy your stay in Myanmar,' she said, bidding him goodbye.

Outside, the sweat began to pour off him. He spotted Saw Lwin crouching in the shade of a large tree, and waved to him. The young man stood up languorously, refastened the knot of his *longyi* and turned towards where he'd left the car.

Harrison sank onto the rug-covered rear seat and closed his eyes, shaking from his ordeal.

'Saw Lwin . . .'

'Yes, Mr Harrison. Where we go now?'

'The hotel. I need you to make some telephone calls for me.'

For the next twenty minutes Perry lay on his bed, listening to his driver babbling on the room phone. Eventually the boy put the receiver down for the last time.

'These travel agents don't know anything 'bout what you ask. They never hear of Mr Kamata.'

Harrison despaired. Without confirmation that his tormentor was in Myanmar he was stumped. He became aware of Saw Lwin studying him with something like pity.

'If you like I can take you meet my aunt,' the young man mumbled awkwardly. 'Maybe she fix something for you.'

'Your aunt?' Harrison's despair deepened, imagining she'd be some quack herbalist who claimed miracle cures for cancer.

'She know all about tourism in Myanmar.'

Harrison blinked.

'And she speak Japanese,' the boy added.

Harrison swung his legs off the bed and sat up. 'I don't understand. What exactly does she do, this aunt of yours?'

'She make vacation for peoples.'

'You mean she works for a company, like the ones you've been ringing?'

'No. Work alone.'

'Well . . . can you ring her? Ask her the same things you've been asking the other agencies.'

'Better we go to see her. Her phone not working at home. I see her last night and she make big noise about it.'

The car passed beneath the gleaming bell of the Shwe Dagon and on to a township where the houses were smaller and more densely packed than in the area around his hotel. Tall, grey-barked trees gave shade to the busy streets. It was midday. Shiny-haired children in green *longyis* and gleaming white shirts were pouring from a school, their day's study over. Dilapidated buses scooped some of them up for transportation to remoter parts of the city.

Saw Lwin turned off the main road into an area of small bungalows. After two blocks he turned again down a lane just wide enough for a single car and stopped in front of some wire-mesh gates.

'She is here,' he announced, seeing the front door open in the house beyond.

Saw Lwin's aunt was a matronly figure who reminded Perry of Imelda Marcos. Unlike the Filipino dictator's wife however, her clothes lacked gloss, and instead of wearing silk shoes, her feet were bare. She beamed fondly at her nephew, then with eager anticipation at Perry.

'You want me to arrange something for you?' she asked as soon as they'd been introduced. 'A tour to Mandalay and Bagan? I can make the best price for you.'

The living room of the house was small and in need of decoration. A map of Myanmar hung on one wall next to a photograph of a huge reclining Buddha. At the far end a door opened into what looked like a bedroom, but the curtains were drawn and the space was dark.

'Please. Sit down.' She spoke briskly and with little trace of an accent. 'I

154

speak many languages, which is a great help in the travel business. Not all the agents do, you know.'

Harrison lowered himself onto a wooden-armed sofa whose springs were weak with age. 'I'm afraid you'll find me a disappointing client.'

'I can arrange anything you like,' she insisted, beaming.

But as he began explaining what he wanted to know, her face darkened with the realisation there'd be little in it for her. He showed her the press cutting. 'I believe this place is near Mong Lai.'

She looked briefly at the picture, then put it down. 'I make many tours for Japanese people.'

'To this memorial?'

'I can do it if they ask. You want me to arrange for you?'

'No . . . At least, not yet. You see I want to meet that man there. The one in the picture.'

She looked at the cutting again. 'Tetsuo Kamata?'

'Yes.'

'You know him?'

'We met a long time ago. That article says he comes here every January.' She frowned.

'Not one of your clients, then.'

'No. But you want me to find out if he is here now. Not easy, I think. Maybe he doesn't use a travel agent.' She pulled a face.

'I would pay you a fee,' he told her quickly.

'Dollars?' she queried.

'Of course.'

'Then I try.' Her eyes began to scheme. 'Where you stay in Yangon?' He told her.

'That's not a good hotel. It is better you stay at the Pansea.'

'I'm really perfectly happy . . .'

'You must stay at the Pansea. I will arrange a very good price for you.' He understood. She would get a commission for bringing him there.

'They won't be very happy at the Inya Lodge. I'm their only guest,' he protested.

'We can tell them you fly to Bagan this evening. I will go with you now to arrange everything.'

The upheaval of moving hotels filled him with dread, but he knew that if she was to help him, he would have to go along with her wishes.

And hers was the only help on offer.

21

Bangkok
Wednesday, 12 January, late evening

LESS THAN TWENTY-FOUR hours after Sam Packer discovered the name Perry Harrison had been using for his travels, he flew into Bangkok feeling he'd probably arrived too late. The man had a forty-eight-hour start and it'd be another twenty-four before the Myanmar embassy would issue a visa so he could follow.

On the flight out from London he'd read a partial transcript of Kamata's 1947 trial for war crimes. Harrison's case hadn't featured at the hearing. It had surprised him until he remembered Perry hadn't known the name of his torturer until Kamata came clean about his past a few weeks ago.

He'd been charged with maltreating prisoners in contravention of the Geneva Convention. His defence counsel had pointed out that since the Japanese Empire had never been a signatory to the treaty, its soldiers couldn't be in breach of it. There'd been statements from soldiers of several nationalities who'd been his victims. Also some gruesome evidence that wounded prisoners in his care had been left to die in cages, with their eyes being eaten by maggots.

A second charge of ordering his men to rape the women in the villages they'd passed through had been dropped through lack of evidence. Despite that, Kamata had told the hearing he believed the Emperor expected his soldiers to father at least four children each in the occupied countries, in order to ensure their future populations had Japanese blood.

Kamata had got five years, but with two already served while waiting for the trial and time off for good behaviour, they'd repatriated him in January 1949. For the next fifty years the details of what he'd done had been buried. Until Kamata's own conscience made him reveal them again.

A decision he might already be regretting, Sam suspected.

The Thai capital was hot and hazy. Sitting in the back of an airport taxi heading for his downtown hotel, he drummed fingers on his knees, not entirely comfortable with being back here. Midge's fear of Yang Lai's Burma Triangle mobsters had got to him.

An hour after leaving the arrivals terminal he was at the hotel. Five hundred rooms and no shortage of European faces to lose himself amongst. He took the lift to the eleventh floor. The elevator car had an unpleasant smell – stale food seasoned with cleaning fluids.

He dumped his bag in the room, freshened up, then returned to the ground floor.

Avoiding the smiles of a pair of women, who he suspected were probably transsexuals, he headed for the computer centre next to the reception desk, which advertised Internet access.

There was a message from Waddell.

Yesterday our rep in Yangon identified the hotel where 'Wetherby' was staying. Found he'd checked out p.m. Hotel staff said he'd gone to Bagan. Our girl's bashing the phones. Hopes for news by the time you arrive. Suggests you meet at 49th Street Bar and Grill, Thursday 20.30.

K scheduled back in Japan same time as you arrive Bangkok. No official duties for next two weeks. Vacation. Trying to find out if at home or abroad.

Some background: Fifteen years ago K's name involved in scandal surrounding death of call girl. Not a suspect, but on her client list. She popular with businessmen who liked to humiliate women. Nice bloke. Good hunting.

Sam sent an acknowledgement giving his room number, then messaged Julie, saying he'd arrived safely and that he loved her. He was about to log off when he thought of Midge. Sydney would be three hours ahead, he calculated. Mid-evening. The little workaholic might still be at her desk. He clicked on New Mail.

Hi Beth,
Passing through Bangkok again and thought of you.
Moving on tomorrow, but if you feel like a long-distance call I'm in room 1106.

He gave the phone number of the hotel.

Be nice to catch up.
Steve.

He logged off and wandered over to the bar for a beer. There was little he could do to advance the operation until tomorrow, and he resigned himself to an evening on his own. Minutes later a gong sounded and he turned to see a porter carrying a paging board with his room number on it. He marched over to the house phone.

'Hello?'

'Steve?' Midge's Aussie twang.

'That was fast. I guessed you'd be chained to your desk. What sort of night is it in Sydney?'

'No idea. I'm here. Round the corner from you. Got into Bangkok in the small hours and was doing my evening mail check when up you came like the proverbial. We need to meet.'

'Excellent idea.' Sam felt a flutter of unease.

'Things are moving fast, Jimmy Squires-wise. That's not the reason you're here, though?'

'No.'

'Sodding well ought to be. You guys get a share of the blame for that arsehole.'

'Because we trained him?'

'Exactly.'

'You're a hard woman.'

She hesitated before responding, as if uncomfortable with his description of her. 'Only when I want to be,' she said eventually. 'Tell you what. Fancy a plate of crustaceans? Or did they stuff you on the flight out?'

'Er, no. I'm ready to eat something.'

'There's an ace place on the river. May have to wait a while for a table but it's worth it. We can get there by boat from the Taksin bridge. That's at the end of the Skytrain line.'

'Sounds great.'

'Good. I have to go see someone just now, but I could meet you at the station exit in an hour?'

'Fine.' He checked his watch then headed back to his room to take a shower, making a firm resolve to behave himself that evening.

7.10 p.m.

She wasn't there.

As he descended the stairs from the overhead track there was no sign of her. The boat jetty was a hundred metres away and he began to head for it, wondering if he'd misunderstood where they were to meet.

Then she grabbed his arm.

'Christ! Where'd you spring from?'

He hardly recognised her. A shoulder-length peroxide blonde last time, Midge had cut her hair short and coloured it mouse. She wore a blue denim skirt, a yellow tee-shirt and dark glasses.

'Keep moving, Steve.' Her voice was husky and tense. She hustled him towards the pier.

'Overdoing it, aren't we?'

She clicked her tongue. 'Two days ago I was nearly flattened by a hit and run in Sydney. The Wa tribes of the Golden Triangle – Yang Lai's lot – were headhunters until a few years back.' She said it with grim earnestness. 'Did you check if you were followed?'

'Didn't see anyone.'

'Did you look?'

'Of course I bloody did.'

There was an awkwardness about her manner which made him wonder if all this security paranoia was to cover up her embarrassment over their near miss two weeks before.

'Like the hair colour,' he said.

'Same as the tree trunks. Makes it easier to hide.' There was a hoot from the jetty. 'Quick. With luck that'll be our boat.'

They half ran to the quay. Midge shouted the name of their destination to an official and he pointed them on board just as the crew were untying the warp.

'Nice timing,' Midge breathed, pausing under the canopy to look back at the jetty. The tension slipped from her shoulders. 'Sorry about all that. Coming a hair's breadth of being crushed by a Holden makes a girl jumpy.' She removed her sunglasses.

They found seats at the side and looked out at the river, which was teeming with lit-up craft. The sun had set forty minutes ago.

'I like it best at night,' Midge breathed.

'So do I,' Sam murmured, leaning closer. ''Cos after doing it I'm always ready for a zizz.'

She dug him in the ribs.

'*Bangkok*, dickhead. I meant Bangkok.'

She smiled, shaking her head at him. The ice was broken.

As the boat accelerated up river they passed gleaming hotels and towering offices, their glass sides ablaze with light.

Midge turned from the view and eyed him curiously.

159

'Just for the record Steve, why the hell *are* you in this neck of the woods again?'

Sam told her he was looking for somebody, but gave no details.

'The bloke you should be after is Jimmy Squires,' she needled. 'We've got the bugger on the run. Haven't they told you?'

'I'm off the case, love. Totally. Orders from on high. Why don't *you* tell me about it.'

She glanced round to ensure they wouldn't be overheard, then moved close enough to whisper.

'We've just had amazing luck. Help from a most unusual source.' She turned away again to look at a motor boat passing in the other direction. A floating restaurant junk, with diners at tables and a waiter serving them.

'You going to tell me who, or do I have to guess?'

The hair colour she'd adopted matched her eyes, giving her a softer look. Everything about her seemed softer than before.

'Can't remember how up to speed you are on the Triangle,' she said. 'Try me.'

'I mean you've been out of the loop a few days. Mind on other things. How's that girlfriend of yours by the way?'

'Just tell me about Jimmy.'

'I'll go over the background first, because it's relevant. The Golden Triangle is the fiefdom of the United Wa State Army, right?'

Sam looked away, suppressing his irritation at being treated like a rookie.

'And for a long time the Wa were fighting for autonomy from the Myanmar government, but in 1989 the junta bought peace with them. The trade-off was to let them grow poppies down as far as the Thai border. The insurgent army, the UWSA, became the protection force for the drug traders.'

Midge stopped. The boat had pulled in to another pier and a European couple had settled immediately in front of them. She gave Sam a glance which said 'tell you the rest later'.

'How many stops?' he asked as the boat accelerated away again.

'Not sure. Hope I can recognise the place when I see it. The restaurant's right by the jetty. You're going to like it.'

They watched the shoreline pass. The thick, brown river water was striated by lotus leaves torn from their mother plants by the current, turning it into an exotic mulligatawny, stirred by the brightly lit ferries and the dark hulks of barges. There was a sinister, teeming beauty to the place. A city that wrote its own rules.

'How *was* London, by the way?' Midge let her shoulder rest against his.

'Cold and wet.' He had a feeling it wasn't the weather she'd been enquiring about.

'Nice of them to send you back here, then.'

'Wasn't it, just.'

'Julie must have been thrilled,' she said pointedly.

'She wasn't best pleased.'

'Don't you just love the smell of this place,' she enthused, quickly changing the subject. 'So goddam *basic*.'

'Like a sewer, you mean.'

She pulled a face. 'Where's your sense of romance?'

The ferry's gears clunked into reverse as it nudged another jetty.

'Christ! This is us.' Midge sprang to her feet.

Half-a-dozen others were ahead of them over the gangway, straight-haired office workers in white shirts heading for home. One by one they stepped across the black planks of the pontoon, which dipped and sagged under the weight of each new passenger.

Midge led the way, moving with the feline fluidity he remembered from Phuket. She paused for a moment, pretending to fish something from her eye while she checked the faces of those following them off the boat.

Soon the stench of the river was replaced by the more appetising smell of stewing shellfish. The restaurant was a wooden chalet with a deck over the water supported on piles. It was packed, each table lit by a small oil lamp. Midge could speak a few words of Thai, enough to encourage a stunningly pretty waitress to scuttle round the terraces looking to see if a table was about to come free.

'Fingers crossed,' Midge whispered, eager to impress him with the place.

Within half a minute the waitress returned and led them through the ranks of diners to a corner near the bar. 'You wait here. Two maybe three minute.' She pointed to a table where a couple were settling up.

Midge beamed at Sam. 'How about that for timing? Twice in one evening.'

He wondered if there'd be a third moment that evening when the timing felt right. Her perfume was making mincemeat of his resolve.

As soon as they were sitting down, Midge leaned forward on her elbows and systematically scanned the other diners' faces.

'Finish telling me about Jimmy Squires,' Sam prompted.

The return of the waitress prevented her from answering. They ordered Singha beers, then the girl left them to study the menu.

'Okay. We know that what happened in Phuket was bad news for him. One thing we can say for definite about Yang Lai is that if any of his associates attracts the attention of the likes of us, he dumps them fast.'

'I see. When did that happen?'

'Twelve days ago.'

'How do you know that?'

'The Thai Narcotics Squad picked it up on the border. Hot gossip.'

Sam straightened his back. 'So what are you saying? Jimmy's out in the cold now? Finished? Game over?'

'It's complicated. Yang Lai didn't drop him altogether. And anyway, Jimmy's sharp enough to know the Wa aren't to be trusted. So he hedged his bets. Made new friends.'

'Who?'

Midge lifted an eyebrow. 'They wore military uniforms.'

'Thai?' There was corruption everywhere in the border area.

'No . . . Burmese.'

Sam sat bolt upright. 'Go on.'

'From what we can make out, Jimmy's contacts with the Wa were at two levels – the people who supplied and those who shipped in bulk. The side of the business Yang Lai was most sensitive about was transportation. So that's the part they shut Jimmy out of. But they were still happy to sell him packs of the stuff, if he could find his own means of getting it out of the Triangle.'

'And he did a deal with the Myanmar military to achieve that?'

'Yep.' She grinned triumphantly.

'Is that just gossip again?'

'No. It's from that highly unusual source I told you about. The very best of authorities.'

'Tell me.'

'Secretary-2.'

His jaw dropped. 'The junta itself?'

'Exactly.' She was enjoying his reaction.

'Explain.'

'Okay. The Myanmar regime has just gone through one of its regular exercises trying to convince the outside world it's doing something to curb the drug trade. Secretary-2 held a press conference in a place called Mong Yawn a couple of days ago. That's in the Triangle. Then the Tatmadaw – the Myanmar military – took a truck load of carefully chosen foreign media to a poppy farm and burned the crops for the cameras. After that they stuck an army officer on a charge to demonstrate their determination to stamp out corruption and drug trafficking.'

'But where's the Jimmy connection?'

'This is the amazing bit. The officer they nailed admitted having dealings with someone travelling on an Irish passport. Name of Vincent Gallagher.'

'The alias Jimmy Squires used in Phuket.'

'Exactly. The Tatmadaw notified the Thais and the Thais told us.'

'So is that enough? You could get a warrant?' Then he frowned, realising the unlikelihood of it. 'The Burmese officer's testimony would never stand up in an Australian court.'

'Highly improbable. Anyway the junta wouldn't allow their guy out of the country – in case he spilled the beans on how many of the military commanders flesh out their pay packets with drug money.'

Sam leaned back in his chair. 'Poor old Jimmy. Shafted from both ends.'

'Couldn't have happened to a nicer bloke.'

'So, let me get this straight. After Phuket, the Thai military dropped him from their payroll.'

'Too right. And put him on their wanted list.'

'So he really is out of business now?'

Midge scowled. 'What do *you* think? That bloke's probably got half-a-dozen different aliases. More than likely has someone else lined up already to ship his stuff out of Myanmar. But we're getting closer, Steve, that's the point. The tomcat's lives are running out.'

She said it with passion – or desperation. Sam wasn't sure which.

The beers arrived. Large glasses alive with condensation. The waitress hovered for the food order.

'You choose,' said Sam. 'You've been here before.'

Midge selected fish, prawns, noodles and vegetables and the girl went away again.

'What exactly did the junta say?'

'Simply that the Tatmadaw officer – he's a Major Soe Thein – was using military transport to move Jimmy's heroin down to Rangoon. Nothing about how it was shipped out of the country.'

Sam sat back and folded his arms. 'So what's the next step?'

'Nailing the bastard.' Midge pulled a long face. 'That's the trouble. We still don't have the hard evidence to put him away. Don't even know where he is right now.'

'*I'm* going to Yangon tomorrow.'

'You are?' She looked as if she'd seen a vision. 'That's incredible. That's the third time this evening. Things clicking into place, I mean.' There was a childlike wonderment about the way she said it.

'Yeah, but I've got a job to do there. Finding Jimmy Squires isn't in my brief.'

'*Make* it your brief.'

'He who pays the piper . . .'

She gave him a withering look.

'How are you going in?'

'On a tourist visa. I pick it up tomorrow.'

He could see she wasn't going to waste her breath asking what he was being sent there to do, but from the calculating look in her eyes he knew she would use his visit if she possibly could.

'This lot get through five hundred million tabs a year now,' she announced out of the blue, gesturing towards the affluent young Thais at the tables nearby.

'*Tabs?*'

'Methamphetamine tablets. Speed. Half a billion produced in the Triangle this year. On top of the heroin. The Wa make 'em in a couple of huge sheds just inside the Burma border. You can see them from a military observation post in northern Thailand. Most of it comes here. But we're getting some in Oz too.'

'And you're telling me this because you think Jimmy's into that trade as well?'

She shrugged. 'More a fear he might get into it at some future date, I suppose. His smack trading is what matters for now. Because it's so lethal.'

A veil seemed to slip across her face and she looked away from him as if to prevent him seeing into her mind. He suspected she was thinking of the boyfriend who'd died from contaminated heroin, the man she'd told him about when drunk on New Year's Eve.

'You said his name was Barry?'

She glared at him, angry with herself for giving him an opening into a domain she liked to keep private. 'The man we were talking about was Jimmy Squires . . .'

'. . . who supplied the dope that killed your boyfriend.' He knew he had no right to dig into that area of her life, but there was a part of him which wanted to see her vulnerable again, like the last time they'd had a meal together.

Midge bit her lip and stared at the table as she got a grip on herself.

'Now look, Steve,' she grated. 'Don't you try and make anything out of that. No snide, pommy suggestions that I'm letting my personal history interfere with my professionalism. I want Squires nailed because he's a crook. Nothing to do with Barry. Okay?'

Sam raised a disbelieving eyebrow.

'All right. Shit . . . Maybe Barry *did* have something to do with it.' She smiled self-consciously. 'But Christ . . . What d'you expect? I was only fifteen when I fell for him. You fall pretty deep at that age. Took ten years for the rose-tinting to fade and for me to realise what a damaged creature he was.'

Sam knew it would be kinder to stop there, but his curiosity wouldn't let him.

'Tell me about it.'

She shot him a glance that he thought said *mind your own effing business*, then surprised him by answering.

'It was in Cabramatta that he died. Heard of it?'

'No.'

'A suburb of Sydney where the druggies hang out. I worked on the squad that made arrests there. We got a call to a squat and there he was, splayed out on the floor, stark naked. Thin as a skeleton – I think he'd given up on food. No money. There were abscesses on his arms, a couple of syringes and an empty vodka bottle on the floor beside him. The autopsy showed the heroin he'd used had been cut with brick dust. Two of his fingers were black with gangrene because the dust caused blood clots. But they reckoned he just stopped breathing. The mix of booze and smack paralysed his chest.' She gulped in a lungful of air, then let it out again. 'Hadn't seen him for the best part of a year and there he was, dead as a rat.'

'I'm sorry.'

'Yeah. So was I. Waste of a great body.' She said it with a bitter smile, but kept her eyes looking down.

'And there's been nobody else for you since then?'

She looked up startled. 'Aw, shit! I've had my fair share of blokes, Steve. Don't get some idea I'm in love with a ghost.'

'I meant nobody else you've loved in the same way.'

'Yeah, but that was the sort of sick love you have when you're in plaits and tooth-braces. Doesn't happen when you're older, does it?'

'You had plaits?' Sam tried to imagine it. 'And the boys pulled them?'

'Now you're piss-taking.'

'No. I'm interested. What colour were they?'

'My natural hair's pretty fair, if you really want to know. Used to go blondish in the summer . . . Heck, that's enough! Watch it, or I'll start on you as a kid. Bet you had loads of spots and stuck your fingers into your nose like it was a bag of sweets.'

Sam laughed. 'Okay. I was intruding. Sorry.'

'I should bloody well think you were.'

She looked fetchingly vulnerable all of a sudden.

'It's just that I like to know as much as possible about my dinner dates,' he explained.

She pulled a face. 'I think it best if we stick to talking shop this evening. Don't you?'

He shrugged. 'Whatever you like.' The waitress appeared behind

Midge's head bearing a tray. 'Only trouble is, if we keep talking about Jimmy Squires, it'll spoil the food.'

She'd been right about the restaurant. The shellfish were sensational. They ate in silence for a while, Sam noticing how she kept glancing towards the end of the restaurant where the door was. He could sympathise. He knew what it was to be hunted.

Midge's mind wandered off somewhere for a few moments. Then, as if she'd thrown a switch, she was back with him again.

'Changed my mind. Tell me about you as a kid. I want to know.'

He shrugged and began talking about his upbringing in a south coast town. A philandering, submariner father and an uptight, moralistic mother.

'There was a lot of hate at home, which created what I suppose you'd call an anxious childhood. I was glad when it was over.'

Midge nodded sagely, as if the conflicts he was describing went a long way towards explaining the defects she'd spotted in his character.

'There must've been something good about it, though. What's your happiest memory?'

'Sailing with my dad.'

'Ah yes. The love of boats.' She said it as if it were a sickness. 'Got you into the navy – I remember that from New Year's Eve.'

''Sright.' He told her about his days in RN Intelligence during the dying years of the cold war. 'Throwing up on stinking trawlers, taking photographs of Soviet warships.' He grimaced at the memory. 'And you? I suppose your upbringing was like something out of *Neighbours*. Mum in the kitchen and endless horny teenagers dropping by.'

'Oh yeah. *All* Aussies live like that.'

Her jaw set firmly, her mouth in a thin line. He had the impression she was trying to decide how much to tell him.

'Actually it was more like something out of *Alice Doesn't Live Here Anymore*,' she said, taking in a deep breath. 'My mum worked in shops or cafés – and occasionally did other things she wouldn't talk about. We lived in a slum in Sydney and I never knew my father. Not sure mum did either, except for the few minutes it took him to jerk his stuff into her. She claimed the johnnie broke, but I suspect she was pissed as usual and didn't check he was using one. Then when I was eleven she married a real arsehole she happened to have fallen in love with. A couple of years later he started abusing me when my mum was too drunk to notice. Always used a condom so there'd be no evidence of having sex with me. A sly bastard. Real criminal type. And I was too scared to do anything about it. Mum was out of it most of the time and when I eventually told her, she accused me of lying. So at sixteen I ran away from home.'

Sam gulped. It had come out so pat, he thought for a moment she was making it up. But from the look in her eyes he knew it was no lie.

'Christ . . .' he grunted, feeling humbled. 'Where . . . where did you go?'

'To stay with Barry's family.'

'You told them what had happened?'

'Not about the abuse, no. Couldn't talk to anyone about it then, because I didn't think anyone would believe me. But Barry's folks were aware of my situation at home. And they were great. Got me into a new school so I could finish my studies. Barry's dad was a policeman and he encouraged me to give it a go in his profession. I liked the sound of the training – and the idea of putting people like my step-dad behind bars – so I did. And here I am.'

'Did Barry sign up too?'

'No way. Whatever his dad did, he was going to do the opposite. Which was fine in principle, only he never settled at anything for longer than a few weeks. Always had a good reason for giving things up.' She bit her lip. 'Yep. He was a master at that.'

'Didn't give *you* up, though?'

'Oh no. I was his fairy on the Christmas tree. Trouble was, that's where he wanted me to stay. But I moved on. Wanted to do something that mattered. And although he did too in theory, he just couldn't work out where he fitted in. Couldn't even *find* a ladder, let alone get his foot on it.'

'But you went on loving him.'

'Oh yeah. To bits. And hated myself for not being able to help him find his way. For not being able to stop him sliding into addiction . . .' The sense of failure was written on her face. 'But sometimes we're powerless to help the victims, Steve. I've learned that.'

'Of course.'

'Which is why we go for the people who damage them instead.'

'People like Jimmy Squires.'

'You've got it.'

They ate on in silence for a bit, Midge's gaze drifting repeatedly towards the door.

'Bloody wonderful,' said Sam, pushing his plate away.

'Glad you approved.'

The softness of her smile made him wonder if she was a little in love with him.

'When are you going to Yangon?' she asked.

'Tomorrow evening, so long as the visa's through.'

She narrowed her eyes. 'Give me a clue.'

'Why I'm going?'

She nodded.

'To try to prevent a killing.'

She pursed her lips. 'Take care of yourself.'

'I will.'

'Otherwise that girl of yours'll be broken-hearted.'

'Maybe.'

His less than certain reply caused her to lift her eyebrows.

'You're not sure?'

He shrugged. 'There seems to be another man on the scene.' He kicked himself for telling her that.

'Oh. I'm sorry.' But her eyes said she wasn't sorry at all.

'I guess it's the price one pays for not being there all the time,' he said, ignoring the alarm bells clanging away in his head.

'I guess it is.'

She didn't say any more. And that was the last either of them spoke about their private lives. They talked a little about London and Sydney and the beats they worked. About friends who did normal jobs and led predictable existences. And about how, despite all the hassles, they couldn't imagine themselves doing anything else.

'We ought to go,' she announced eventually. 'It'll have to be a taxi. The river buses will have stopped for the night.'

They paid up and began to walk towards a main road. To their left a Buddhist temple gleamed under spotlights, its gold stupa rising above an explosion of red and blue. Beside the road, small, savoury-smelling food stalls glimmered under oil lamps, their customers crouching on benches to eat. The night air was still very warm, but pleasantly so, with less humidity than earlier. Sam found himself putting an arm round Midge's shoulders. She didn't object. He wondered uncomfortably if Jack might be doing something similar with Julie back in London.

The main highway when they reached it was busy with tuk-tuks and cars. Within a couple of minutes a cab was pulling into the kerb.

Midge used her Thai to ask the price of a ride back to the city centre, then scornfully waved the driver on his way.

'They're robbers, some of these guys. Total con men.'

Another car stopped soon after and this time the fare was acceptable. They sat in the back not speaking, aware of the decision they would each have to make in a few minutes time.

Midge's hotel was only a couple of blocks from Sam's. Walking distance. They both got out there and he paid off the taxi.

'So . . .' he said.

'So . . .' she replied.

They smiled awkwardly.

'Feels like we've been here before,' he told her.

She laughed and looked down at the ground. He put his arms round her waist.

She looked up and it seemed only natural that he should kiss her. She let him, parting her lips and drawing him in. Then she put a hand on his chest.

'I don't know . . .' she breathed, pulling back a little and resting her forehead against his chin. 'I mean I like you a lot. But . . .'

He bent to kiss her neck.

She shivered at the feel of his lips on her skin and pressed her hips forward instinctively. Then pulled back again.

'Not drunk enough,' she mumbled.

'You have to be drunk to make love?'

'No . . . not if the circumstances are right.' She frowned and banged a hand against her head as if trying to get a grip on what she felt. 'I mean . . .' Her eyes rolled for a moment. 'I'm not saying things *aren't* right, Steve. It's just that I don't know you very well yet.'

'I know a good way to remedy that.'

She pulled a face. 'Need a good night's sleep. I'm flying to Chiang Mai for a conference tomorrow. Runs through Saturday. And . . .' She gave him an apologetic smile. 'And also, I don't know what's going on in your head.'

Which was fine, because he didn't either.

'Then it's goodbye, I guess. Until the next time.'

'Make it soon, Steve.' She gripped his hands.

'Goo'night.'

He turned and began to walk.

'Steve . . .'

He swung round again.

'There *is* something you could do that would kind of clinch it next time round.'

He detected mischief in her eyes.

'What's that?'

'Get me Jimmy Squires.'

22

Yangon
Earlier that same day

THE HOTEL WHICH Saw Lwin's aunt had transferred Perry Harrison to the day before was costing him eighty dollars a day, four times what he'd been paying at the Inya Lodge. But he'd passed an extremely comfortable first night there and he'd told himself he could afford it.

Early that morning, when the sun was still low in the sky, Saw Lwin had driven him and Tin Su back to the jailer's house. His former wife's dislike of him and her annoyance at what he'd persuaded her to do had been more apparent than ever. In the car she'd kept her face turned away, and when they reached the prison officer's home she'd walked several paces behind him.

As soon as the door opened Perry had known the answer. The man was full of self-justification. Tried his best. Passed on part of the Englishman's 'present' to other officials further up the chain. But in the end the request for a special visit to a political prisoner had been refused. The best he could suggest was that Harrison apply for a permit from the Ministry of Foreign Affairs. It might take months, but if he could prove he was the father of Khin Thein, then there was every possibility of success.

Tin Su had touched her hands in gratitude for the man's efforts and walked quickly from the door. As they returned to the car she'd told Harrison he shouldn't have come back to Burma. Should've left them all in peace.

Then Saw Lwin had taken them back to his hotel. Harrison had got out, with Tin Su remaining in the car, waiting to be taken home. He'd lifted a hand, half salute, half wave, but she hadn't been watching. As the car disappeared at the end of the drive he'd felt a terrible loss. For several years she'd been his life, and he'd thrown it away.

Back in his hotel room he'd sunk into a deep depression. If he'd had the courage he might have ended it there and then. The medicine bottles he'd brought from England contained quite enough to kill him. It was fear that stopped him. Fear of what death would be followed by.

He'd believed in reincarnation since he was a teenager, because it made better sense to him than concepts such as heaven and hell. In general he reckoned he'd done more good than harm during his present existence, so hoped for a reasonable placing in his next life. Even his plans for the Japanese Lieutenant amounted, in his view, to a long-delayed triumph of good over evil. But his confidence in his standing had been eroded now by the knowledge of the suffering he'd caused Tin Su. His prospects beyond the grave would have dimmed.

He spent the rest of the day in his hotel room, drifting in and out of sleep, waiting for the call from Saw Lwin's aunt that might or might not bring news. By the time it came, the shadows were lengthening outside the windows of his ground-floor room and the fierce daylight was beginning to mellow.

'It has been *very* hard, Mr Harrison,' she stressed. '*So* many phone calls. I have to make them from my sister's house because my phone still not working. In the end I have some luck. Mr Tetsuo Kamata has reserved two rooms at the Jade Palace Hotel in Mong Lai tomorrow night and Friday night.'

Harrison's heart somersaulted. He scrabbled for the pad and pen which he kept on the bedside table.

'You would like me to arrange things for you? Book you into the same place? They have beautiful suites for thirty dollars. And the flights I can do at a very good price. When you want to go?'

'I need to think about this.' His heart was thudding uncontrollably.

'Yes. But you must think quick. There is a flight to Heho every morning about seven-thirty but it always full. Another flight at eleven. You want me to try book you on it?'

'Yes. Yes. Book it please.'

'I will do it in the morning. Airline office closed now. And the hotel?'

He hesitated. 'Is there another place?'

'Golden Lion. Not so nice, but clean.'

'Then please book that.'

'I will come round to your hotel tomorrow morning. Eight o'clock. All right?'

'Yes. Yes, that'll be fine. And thank you. Thank you very much.'

He replaced the receiver and smiled for the first time that day. Fate was beckoning. Challenging him. Somehow he would have to do the deed alone, but if he could achieve that it might earn him extra merit. The trouble was he had no idea *how* he would manage it.

Time to resort to prayer, he decided. Not to the Christian God who'd ignored his pleas for release from suffering in 1943 and 1944, but to whatever amorphous force it was up there that controlled the destiny of humans.

He looked out of the window at the reddening sky. There was only one place to be when the sun set over Rangoon and a man wanted to commune with the heavens.

He made his painful way to the lobby.

'How quickly can you get me a taxi?'

'One waiting outside Mister Wetherby. Where you want to go?'

'The Shwe Dagon Pagoda.'

'You pay taxi 300 kyat. I tell him.'

The clerk ushered him through the door and into the car, speaking briefly to the driver.

Harrison slumped in the back as they accelerated down the drive. Within minutes they were entering the car park at the base of the temple, drawing up outside the entrance for tourists.

There was a freshly painted notice beside it:

Entrance fee for foreigners $5. Includes camera.

Last time he'd come here he'd walked up one of the long, covered ramps that took Burmans to their place of worship without charge.

In the entrance hall he took off his shoes and placed them in a rack, then paid his fee and began moving to the lift that would take him to the platform. A studious but attractive young woman waylaid him, asking if he wanted a guide.

'Five dollars,' she said.

A few years ago he'd have taken her on, in the hope that in the hour or so of the tour he could work his spell on her and get her to share his bed for the night. He smiled at the memory of what he used to do. Memories were all he had left.

'No thank you.'

He stepped into the lift and half a minute later the doors opened onto the main platform of the temple. The bell-shaped *zedi* towered nearly a hundred metres over the mound, its gold-plated bulk picked out by floodlights against a purple-red sky. To his right, in a corner of the courtyard, a banyan tree towered, its aerial roots encircling the trunk like creepers.

Harrison stopped beneath the *zedi* and looked up. Somewhere nearby a guide was reciting numbers. Thirteen thousand plates of gold on the banana bud at the top. Thousands of diamonds and other precious stones on the decorations above that. Fifty tons of gold leaf on the bell itself.

Such statistics were repulsive to him. The unacceptable face of Buddhism – of any religion adhered to by the poor. He began to walk around the platform, clockwise as custom demanded. Despite the glitz, for him the place radiated spirituality. Dozens of smaller shrines surrounded the main one. Everywhere he looked people kneeled in prayer or sat in quiet meditation.

Prayer was what he'd come here for and he turned towards a side pavilion that looked empty. The significance of the shrine was unimportant to him. All he sought was an atmosphere in which to focus his thoughts. He climbed the steps.

Inside, an elderly woman and a young girl knelt before an unsmiling Buddha, a photograph of a young man placed on the ground between them. Their eyes were closed, their hands pressed together. Perry dropped stiffly to his knees behind them.

He looked up to the face of the Buddha. Then he cast his eyes down and closed the lids. To concentrate. He tried to ask for a boost from above in these last, frail days of his life, but the words wouldn't come. His thoughts simply wouldn't mould themselves into prayers. For several minutes he remained where he was, yearning to connect with the superior force. Soon his knees began to hurt so much that he had to get back to his feet. He stood in solemn silence for several more minutes, then finally admitted defeat.

As he stepped back onto the paved courtyard beneath the *zedi*, the pain in his back was like a bayonet slicing through his vertebrae. He sat on a low wall, despair and weariness engulfing him.

How, *how* could he do this thing on his own? This act he'd waited over fifty years to carry out. It wasn't the issue of applying sharp or blunt instruments to living flesh that worried him – he'd proved himself still capable of that by disembowelling a goat kid at Bordhill a few days before leaving the place. It was the lack of strength. He simply didn't have enough any more. Not in his spirit nor in his body.

Yes, he could make it to Heho. Yes to the hotel at Mong Lai. Yes even to confronting Kamata at the memorial. But then what? Without the support of a man of Rip's local knowledge, contacts and sheer bloody bravado, he would fail. And worse than that, would risk humiliation again. He felt close to tears after coming so far.

He looked at the placid Burmese faces gathered to witness the sunset. Old and young. Men and women. Accepting what the religion taught them, that they should put up with their lot without protest. Something he had never been able to do.

He watched a quartet of young monks squatting by a small Buddha, chatting like schoolgirls. Shaved heads, maroon robes. They'd rejected worldly goods. Rejected sexual pleasures. And looked happy with their choice, a choice he could never have made.

A sense of peace began to descend on him. Shwe Dagon was working its magic. It was dawning on him that he was finished. That he'd reached the end of the road and this was as good a place as any to die. Here. Tomorrow evening, he could do it. With the rest of the morphine patches plastered to his skin, a box of pills and a bottle of water to swallow them with.

His life would end, fittingly, as the sun went down.

He felt extraordinarily calm, having decided that, and let his eyes wander. Above him bats flitted blackly against the gold of the *zedi* and the purple of the sky.

He studied the others who'd come here. The flat-faced Burmans from the central plains. Those with Chinese features from the north of the country. And a few Europeans. A handful only. Elderly mostly. Independent-minded travellers impervious to international calls for a boycott of this place.

Then he saw a face that looked startlingly familiar.

The man it belonged to was a European in his early forties, but wearing a *longyi*. Talking with an unusually tall and burly Burman. Curly hair. A small v-shaped scar on his left cheek, which Perry Harrison happened to know was from a knife wound inflicted during a skirmish in the Omani desert.

He rose to his feet as if propelled by springs. The miracle had happened. His prayers, such as they were, had been heard after all.

As he walked, his hands reached out in greeting.

'Rip . . .'

The European turned to him and gaped.

Then, very slowly, a smile spread across his face.

23

Yangon
The following evening, Thursday, 13 January

SAM CHECKED INTO a city centre hotel just before 8 p.m. His rendezvous with the SIS rep was in thirty minutes.

The guidebook had described the place as recently built, Chinese-owned and good value at twenty dollars a night. It was on nine levels and when he left the lift he found the floor sloping alarmingly.

He had a quick wash, then studied a street map. The 49th Street Bar and Grill was five blocks away. The SIS woman he was to meet there gloried in the name of Philomena and had been described by Waddell as frighteningly bright.

It was a sultry night. The tea shops and food stalls were busy. Walking amongst these slight, brown-skinned people, he was the only European, yet there were few of the hostile stares that would be normal in many parts of the Orient. The avenues he passed along had been given Burmese names after independence, but some of the old street signs persisted – Fraser Street, Godwin Road, echoes of Empire and the Raj.

He turned into 49th Street, an alley whose darkness was punctuated by a scattering of feeble lights. On one side of the road were businesses repairing motor bikes or selling household goods. On the other, tenement blocks reminded him of the Peabody Buildings which dotted the east end of London. Windows were wide open in the hope of catching some movement of air. TV screens glowed inside and clothes hung on lines suspended over the street. Here and there children played, delaying the moment of bedtime.

A familiar tune caused him to slow his pace for a moment. Lillibullero. At the side of the street, squatting on the ground by a parked car, was an elderly man listening to the BBC World Service on a small short-wave radio. The wizened face turned to look up and smiled graciously. Sam smiled back and went on his way.

The 49th Street Bar and Grill was a brown brick warehouse conversion. Inside, its rough walls were hung with posters and photographs of colonial Rangoon. A horseshoe bar filled the centre of the space and a broad, iron staircase led to an upper floor. The staff were both European and local, but the few customers were ex-pats and male. Three sat on their own at the bar and a few more hugged a billiard table. They glanced briefly at Sam, then returned to their preoccupations.

He perched at the counter and ordered a beer, placing a copy of *Time* magazine beside him.

'Here working?' The woman's accent gave her away as Australian.

'No. Just visiting for a few days. I was in Bangkok on business and thought I'd take a look.'

'Hope you enjoy it. Are you planning to eat here tonight? Like to see a menu?'

'Er, no. I'm meeting someone. Daughter of a neighbour of mine back in England. Works at the British mission. Said I'd get in touch when I was here.'

'That'll be Phil. Been here about a year. The only female at the embassy – amongst the ex-pats anyway. Popular girl.'

'Sounds about right.' In truth he knew nothing about her. He glanced at his watch. Three minutes to go.

The manageress turned to deal with another customer and Sam began flicking through the pages of *Time*. But his mind had flipped back to Bangkok, the woman's accent making him think of Midge.

She'd turned up at his hotel that morning. He'd been on the point of leaving to take his passport to the Myanmar Embassy and had told her jokingly that if it was sex she'd come for, her timing was lousy. But she'd been deadly serious. Pressed a small black box into his hand, the size of a cigarette lighter. Told him it was a satellite tracker.

'In case you bump into Jimmy Squires. Plant it in his luggage or whatever. It has a strong magnet too, so you can stick it to a car.'

He'd told her she was out of her sweet little mind, but took it anyway.

'The conference I'm going to is at the Empress Hotel in Chiang Mai,' she'd said. 'The tracking of that thing's done back in Oz, but I can dial into it through the net from my PC.'

'So you can check what I'm getting up to.'

'Well I did say I don't know you well enough . . .'

He'd packed the device in a pocket of the small rucksack which he carried as hand baggage.

'Hello.' A woman's voice right beside him.

He looked up from the magazine.

'Philomena?'

'Yes.' She was a big girl, dressed in a linen skirt and jacket. In her twenties with a jolly face. 'Recognised you immediately from my dad's description. Nice to meet you.'

'Get you a drink?'

'A coke thanks. Then we can go over there and natter.' She pointed to a small round table next to a hearth which Sam suspected had never been lit.

'Was that a coke, Phil?' the manageress checked.

'Please.'

As they ambled to the table Sam remarked on the cosiness of the place.

'A haven for lonely Europeans,' she murmured, nodding a greeting to the group round the billiard table.

'Many Brits amongst them?'

They sat down.

'Not a lot. Most UK companies respect the trade embargo and don't do anything in Myanmar. A few blokes are here with Premier Oil – there's a new gas pipeline operating. And a handful of others who don't reveal what they're up to.'

Sam leaned forward. 'Any luck with finding Perry Harrison?'

Philomena leaned in too. ''Fraid not. We know where he *was* staying but he checked out on Tuesday. The hotel said he'd gone to Bagan, but I've rung all the main hotels there and there's no trace.'

'Bagan's where all the temples are.'

'That's right. Thousands of them. It's the jewel in the crown for tourists.' She had big round, guiltless eyes. A good card player, Sam guessed.

'No Burmese officials who could help? They must keep track of tourists.'

'They do, but it's not exactly done in real time. Anyway our policy is not to collaborate with the regime in any way. The Tatmadaw are illegally in charge of this country as far as UK government is concerned. The State Protection and Development Council tolerates our presence here, but we're highly suspect because we're always rattling on about freedom of speech and democracy. Our phones are bugged, our domestic staff are paid to inform on us. It's not the easiest country to work in.'

'So where was Harrison staying in Yangon? Sounds like my only starting point.'

'And not much of one, I'm afraid.' She handed him a scrap of paper with the address on it. 'I doubt you'll get any more joy than I did.'

'Is this your first posting?'

Her self-confidence cracked, but only momentarily. 'Does it show?'

'No, but "father" said you were only twenty-five. So I assumed . . .'

'Rightly, as it happens. It's an interesting brief, if of limited significance.' She spoke with the dismissiveness of someone who was highly ambitious. 'I'd have preferred Beijing, I must admit.'

'This place where Harrison was staying . . .' He glanced down at the piece of paper. 'Tell me about it.'

'Small. Off the beaten track. Not doing much business. God knows how they survive, these places.'

'How long to get there in a taxi?'

'At this time of night? Ten or fifteen minutes. You're thinking of going now?'

'Unless there's somewhere else. You've no other information for me? On Harrison's ex-wife for example?'

'Nothing. Sorry.'

'And London hasn't messaged you with Tetsuo Kamata's vacation plans?'

'Negative again.'

He leaned back in the wooden chair and drank from his glass. There was a desultory sociability about the bar. People came here because they had nothing else to do. He was keen to leave it.

'You get much of a social life here?' he asked.

'Pretty limited. Mostly with the other ex-pats. The Americans keep to themselves, but the Australians are fun. Fortunately our ambassador here and his wife are both great characters.' There was a girlish enthusiasm about the way she said it.

'Any Burmese friends?'

'A few. But you don't get very close. They're too scared of being arrested for consorting with foreigners.'

Sam finished his beer.

'You'll want to be on your way,' she ventured.

'It'd make sense if we left together,' he told her.

'Of course.' She abandoned most of her coke. 'Look, if there's anything else I can do . . . You've got my numbers. Just ring and say where you want to meet.'

As they moved towards the door, she gave a wave to the woman behind the bar.

Outside, Philomena guided him to the right.

'You probably won't be watched while you're here unless you do something that catches the attention of MIS, the Military Intelligence Service, but it'd be worth keeping an eye open. They're sometimes obvious, sometimes not. Rickshaw drivers are quite often informers for the Tatmadaw. Beware the ones who speak English well.'

'I will.'

'To find a taxi you'll do best in Strand Road. That's where our embassy is. Don't pay more than 600 kyat to get to the Inya Lodge and make sure you fix a price first.'

'Thanks. Can I drop you anywhere?'

'That's kind, but I have a car and driver waiting for me.' She smiled grimly. 'And there's a cook/housekeeper and a gardener back at the place where I live. When I was at Cambridge I never dreamt my first job would come with three servants.'

Twenty minutes later the battered taxi dropped Sam at the Inya Lodge. Lights were on but the place seemed deserted. He opened the glass-panelled door to the lobby. Behind the desk a young man woke from a doze and leapt to his feet, staring at Sam expectantly.

'I'm looking for a friend. I think he's staying here.'

The boy stared uncomprehendingly.

'Mister Wetherby?'

Mention of the name propelled the youth into a back room. He reappeared a few seconds later with an older man who spoke English.

'You look for Mister Wetherby?'

'Yes. I believe he was staying here.'

'He gone sir. Day before yesterday.'

'D'you know where he went?'

'He say he go to Bagan, but I think maybe he gone back to England. Mister Wetherby very sick. Another English person ask for him today.'

Sam tensed. 'You know his name?' His first thought was that this was the mysterious 'Rip' whom Harrison had hoped to meet in Bangkok.

'A lady, sir. She arrive from England this afternoon. Very unhappy that Mister Wetherby not here.'

'A lady?' Could Rip be a *woman*? 'What's her name?'

The man scrabbled amongst the papers behind the counter.

'Miss Dennis, sir. Her name is Miss Dennis.'

Sam gaped in disbelief. Melissa was here.

'You know her, sir?'

'Met her a couple of times.' And on the last of which she'd claimed not to know where Perry had gone. 'Is she here in the hotel?'

'No, sir. Gone to restaurant.' He pointed towards the main road.

'What's the place called?'

'Music Café. Very nice. I tell her, because a lot of young people go. She can talk with them. Make her feel less lonely.'

'She's by herself?'

179

'Yes. So, so unhappy.' He shuttled his head with the misery of it.

Sam thought of asking whether she'd been clutching a duty-free gin bottle when she set off, but restrained himself.

'You need room tonight sir?'

'Already have one, thanks.'

He saw the man's disappointment and felt sorry for him.

'How do I get to this restaurant?'

The man explained. Sam thanked him and left.

The thought of another misleading conversation with Melissa filled him with dread, but there were questions he needed answers to. The fact that Perry had moved on the day before Melissa turned up here suggested she hadn't told him she was coming. Unless she *had* and the old man had done a bunk to get away from her. Whatever, if she'd ventured all the way out here to be by Perry's side, she had to have good reasons and he needed to know what they were.

The main road was unlit. He'd had the foresight to bring a small torch. Traffic was light and he crossed to the other side where there was some sort of pavement. Using the flashlight to pick his way over broken stones and drainage gullies, he passed bungalows set back from the road, heading for a cluster of neon lights. As he got nearer he heard the thump of a woofer and a high female voice.

Twenty paces from the café, he stopped to rally his thoughts. He wasn't ready for this. And neither would she be.

Melissa sat alone at a corner table. She'd finished eating but was delaying her return to the hotel room because she knew its smell of stale insecticide would remind her how alone she was.

The band had been playing familiar tunes from the seventies, which had had a soothing effect on her – a lifeline from home in a place that felt incredibly alien. Dark faces, dark eyes staring all the time.

She'd arrived at the hotel that afternoon full of anticipation and in a high state of anxiety after having her bag taken at the airport by some native insisting she use *his* taxi rather than anyone else's. The price to the hotel had been much more than that quoted in the guidebook but she hadn't had the nerve to argue with him. The Inya Lodge had seemed an oasis of calm when she'd arrived. But when they'd told her 'Mister Wetherby' had gone, she'd wanted the ground to open up. Things worsened when they took her to her room. There'd been a lizard on the ceiling.

For an hour she'd sat on the bed and cried. If someone had offered to take her straight home she'd have leapt at the chance.

Then, gradually, she'd pulled herself together. She was an author after all. And a writer's lot was to face obstacles and surmount them, time and time again, until the finishing line was reached. She liked the image of creator as long-distance runner.

Bagan, she'd decided, must be where the Japanese war memorial was which she'd seen in that cutting – she could think of no other reason why Perry would have gone there. But before following him north she would have to make sure. After a good night's sleep she would find a library, show them the magazine clipping and see if they could pinpoint the obelisk for her. Then she would employ an English-speaking guide, preferably one who was young, male and good-looking, to take her there.

When she'd stepped inside the café, it had reminded her of night spots in small English market towns. Trying to be with-it, but without knowing how. The place was very dark with candles flickering on the tables. She'd hovered on the threshold afraid to go further in. Three young males whom she took to be waiters had stared at her from the bar area, as if they too were unable to bridge the cultural divide. Eventually, two older boys had nudged a younger one into action. He'd approached with a bemused grin, touching his hands together in greeting.

'I'd like to eat,' she'd told him.

'Yes.' He hadn't moved.

'Where shall I sit?'

'Yes.'

It had dawned on her that 'yes' was the only word of English he knew or understood.

'Food,' she'd repeated, miming action with a knife and fork.

For some reason her play-acting had galvanised the youths. All three had clustered round and ushered her to a small table by a wall, incongruously adorned with Manchester United tee-shirts and scarves. They'd vied to be the one to pull the chair out and present her with a menu, but all the time she'd felt they were laughing at her.

The menu was mostly incomprehensible, particularly the cranky English translations stuck next to the Burmese text. Seeing her struggling, one of the youths had pointed to a photo on the menu's cover.

'Yes,' she'd said. 'Rice.' Couldn't go wrong with that.

'Chicken?'

'No. Vegetables.' She hadn't touched meat for years.

Having come straight from an English winter she was finding the heat oppressive, so she'd asked for a cold beer which tasted all right and was refreshing. Then she'd waited for her food to come, aware all the while of the giggling in the corner where the three waiters had gone to linger. *Surely* they'd seen lone females before? The guidebook had a section giving advice to such travellers.

One of the young men had a face that wasn't quite so foreign as the others, with eyes like plump, plain chocolates. She'd wondered, as she often did with nice-looking males of almost any age, what it would be like to be deflowered by him. Would he be gentle and knowing? Or all thumbs – a creature as inexperienced as her?

Deflowered. She always used that word when thinking about the act, because it sounded earthy. And literary too.

She'd read in the guidebook about the shyness of the Burmese. How a young man wasn't allowed to spend time alone with a young woman unless already betrothed to her. From that she'd deduced there'd be a high frustration level amongst the young men here, and had toyed with the idea that her own readiness for intimacy might be quite an asset.

Having her first experience of intercourse had become a matter of great importance to her. She'd decided that in her biography on Perry Harrison, she ought to describe her relationship with him as a sexual one. It'd be more interesting for the reader, and once Perry was dead there'd be no one around to deny it. Apart from Ingrid. And *she* wouldn't talk for fear of revealing that the upright moralistic character she projected was only a mask. But to write about such a thing without actual personal knowledge of what sex with a man felt like, might risk giving herself away.

She'd thought about the matter a great deal before setting off for Burma. The whole adventure of coming out here was clearly going to be packed with life-changing experiences. So, she'd decided, there was no better time or place to have her first fuck – that was the cruder, more basic word she also used when describing it in her thoughts.

The choice of man for the event wasn't particularly critical, so long as she fancied him of course. She glanced at the corner again. The boy with the beautiful eyes was smiling at her. She smiled back, but rather uncertainly, realising that however attractive he was, his foreignness might be a problem for her.

Sam stepped onto the terrace in front of the café. Three sprawling youths and three cross-legged girls sat at plastic tables drinking cokes together. One of the young men was jangling keys and keeping half an eye on a black 4-wheel drive parked ostentatiously at the side of the road. Sons and daughters of the military, Sam suspected.

Through the plate glass window he saw a small combo playing, illuminated by a dim spotlight which picked out the girl singer. She was pretty and young, with short black hair and an intelligent face. The song was by Eric Clapton.

Inside he didn't see Melissa at first because the room was quite dark. Then, as his eyes adjusted, he spotted her on the far side, hunching forward with her head in her hands. Her hair spilled over her fingers in a shaggy mane. In front of her was a half-empty glass.

Sam planned to keep his encounter with her as short as possible. As soon as he'd discovered whether she knew something he didn't, he would be off. Taking a deep breath, he walked over to her table, pulled out a chair and sat down opposite her.

It was a few moments before Melissa realised she was no longer alone. She gasped when she saw who it was.

'*You*. I don't *believe* it! What . . . what on earth are *you* doing here?'

'I was going to ask you the same question.'

She sat up dead straight, laying her hands flat on the table as if to steady herself. Sam guessed she couldn't remember his name.

'Geoff,' he reminded her.

'Yes. And Ginny.' She glanced past him for some sign of his partner. 'What on earth . . .?'

'Charles asked me to come,' Sam declared, brazenly. 'You remember I told you I'd met him?'

'Ye-es . . .'

'Well, he and I had a drink the other day and I mentioned I had some leave owing and wasn't sure what to do with it. Then out of the blue he said, did I fancy a trip to Myanmar? He'd had a tip-off his father had come out here. Desperately worried about him, but he was in the middle of a huge case at the Bailey and couldn't get away. Well, to cut a long story short, I said I'd have a go at finding his father if he paid my fare. And he agreed. So here I am.' He grinned broadly, watching to see if she believed him.

'But how did Charles know Perry had come to Myanmar?' Her eyes brimmed with suspicion.

'I think Robert Wetherby told him.'

She gaped. 'I can't believe that.'

'It wasn't in so many words, apparently. But enough of a clue to justify the expense of the air ticket.' He smiled again, working hard on his charm. 'Can I say how glad I am to see you?'

'God, me too.' She grinned back, wondering if he realised *how* glad. 'Welcome to Myanmar.' She stretched out a hand and he shook it.

'Infuriating to find that Perry checked out yesterday,' he prodded.

'Ghastly.'

'You hadn't arranged to meet him here.'

'Not at all. My arrival was not something he was expecting.'

'Where d'you think he's gone?'

'Well, they said Bagan.'

'Why would he go there?'

'I'm not entirely sure. Tomorrow I'm going to . . .' She was on the point of telling him about the cutting, then realised that if he *was* a journalist after all, she would be handing him an exclusive on a plate.

'You're going to what?' he prompted.

She shook her head. The music had got louder, giving her a convenient excuse for not continuing. Her mind was running out of control, suddenly imagining him on top of her, kissing and thrusting. 'Are you staying at the Inya Lodge too?' she shouted above the din.

'No. At some dump in the town centre with sloping floors.'

'Sounds lethal. Ginny with you?'

'No. She couldn't get time off work.'

'Poor you. All alone. Just like me.'

She quickly stared down at her half-empty glass. She hadn't meant to say those last three words. A case of brain engaging mouth before going through the filtering process of judgement. Yes, of course it was fate his turning up like this without his partner. And he was obviously a far more suitable candidate for her to lose her innocence with than some native boy with dubious hygiene routines. But if it was to happen, she'd have to catch him first. Which would require subtlety rather than blundering about like a pubertal teenager.

She looked up again, shook her mane of hair and eyed him coquettishly from between its strands. 'You know, I'm finding it terribly hard to believe any of this.'

Sam feigned surprise. 'What exactly are you finding hard to believe?'

'Your being here now. I mean, talk about coincidences. You sure you're not following me?'

He peered through her straggly mane, trying to decide if she was winking at him or merely blinking hair from her eyes.

'Absolutely sure.'

'I mean there was the pub in Sidgefield. Then that rally in London on Monday. And now here. Extraordinary.' She raised one eyebrow. 'I bet you *are* a reporter . . .'

'I can assure you I'm not.' He adopted what he hoped was a modest and slightly affronted smile. 'Good at stringing figures together but lousy with words.'

Her manner was beginning to alarm him. The teasing looks, the nervous fluttering of her hands – he could imagine the fantasies sprouting in her mind. Two lone travellers meeting in romantic Rangoon . . .

Deciding to play on it, he narrowed his eyes to suggest she'd been a bit naughty with him. 'You're the one who's been telling porkies, pretending you didn't know Perry was coming here.'

'He wanted it kept a secret,' she protested. 'No one was to know.'

'He tell you what he planned to do here?'

Melissa's head spun as she wrestled with what was safe to tell him and what wasn't. The dark-eyed waiter was hovering a few feet away, his white shirt glowing in the UV lighting and a menu clutched in his hands like it was a holy scripture.

'I think he wants to take an order,' she said, glad of the distraction while she got her thoughts together.

'I'm going to have a beer. Like another one?'

'Why not?' Melissa drained her glass. She'd have preferred a G and T, but at least it was alcohol. 'A drink to celebrate this extraordinary twist of fate.'

Sam didn't like the sound of that. 'You've eaten already I take it.'

'Yes. And the rice and veg wasn't bad.'

He browsed the menu and chose the same but with the addition of chicken. The boy took his order and hurried away, grinning like he'd just caught a fish.

'So . . .' Sam persisted, determined to get something from her, 'what did Perry tell you about his plans, exactly?'

'Nothing. Nothing at all. It was all an accident my finding out he was coming here. You see, a few weeks ago I lent him some Internet printouts – stuff about Nike clothing workers in third-world countries. And when he returned them I saw he'd jotted notes on the back. Flight numbers and quotes for air tickets. And then there was the name Inya Lodge with a phone number and the word Yangon.'

'Did you ask him what it meant?'

'Certainly not. If he'd wanted me to know he'd have told me.'

'You knew he'd got a passport in the name of Robert Wetherby?'

'Well . . .' This was an issue Melissa felt a little foolish about. 'I did and I didn't. Quite by chance I saw a passport application in Robert's name on Perry's desk a few weeks ago. Assumed he was witnessing it for him. It was only when I rang the Inya Lodge from London before setting off – to check he *was* staying there – that they told me the only elderly Englishman on their books was called Wetherby. Then it all sank in. I was quite shocked. I mean, that's *illegal*.'

'Why are you here, Melissa?' It was time to cut to the chase.

'Because I felt he needed me. And I couldn't bear the thought of him dying alone out here.' Her eyes began to glisten.

Sam blinked. If that simple, self-indulgent motive really was the reason, he could keep this meeting blissfully short. 'He didn't tell you his plans? Where he was going? Who he was seeing?'

She shook her head. 'None of that.'

'And you came all this way in the hope that somehow you would manage to find him?'

She nodded forlornly. She looked so self-conscious about it, Sam believed her.

Melissa was quite used to seeing a look of incredulity and pity in other people's eyes. And usually it was followed by them making their excuses and leaving. She'd trained herself to accept it with resignation, but in this case she couldn't. She'd felt frighteningly alone a short while ago and now she didn't. She needed him, in all sorts of ways. The idea that he might walk out of her life so soon after walking into it was unbearable.

'There's another reason I've come here,' she announced, desperate to make herself more interesting.

Sam's expectations rose about a millimetre. 'Tell me about it.'

'I'm writing a book.'

'How fascinating.'

'Not got far yet. Just starting really. I'm telling you this in confidence, by the way.'

'Of course. Won't breathe a word. What's the theme?'

'Perry's life. The things that shaped it and how much he's meant to other people. Picking up from where *Jungle Path to Hell* left off. And, of course, giving the outsider's view. Although a very *inside* outsider, if you see what I mean.'

'Absolutely.' Sam tried to look respectful.

'I'll be revealing something pretty sensational about his reasons for coming here.'

'Will you now.' He wondered what new game she was conjuring up.

'I worked out that it was partly to see his family of course. But there's also the little matter of Mr Kamata . . .'

Her words were like a kick in the butt.

'Go on.' He leaned forward.

Melissa feared losing control of the situation and giving away the Crown Jewels before she'd fixed her price. She looked up and saw the beers arriving. Then a second waiter came with Sam's food. She was grateful to the boys for providing her with a breather.

'Hope you enjoy it.'

Sam didn't touch his plate. 'Go on,' he repeated. ' What about Mr Kamata?'

'Eat up. You must be hungry after your long journey.'

There was something cloying about the way she was looking at him. Like a maiden aunt who'd won custody of a child for a day. It repelled him.

'Look,' he snapped, losing patience. 'The reason I'm here is to try to stop Perry committing a murder. If you know anything . . .'

'Oh no,' she protested. 'That's not right. I've been thinking a lot about it and I really can't believe . . .'

'You'd *better* believe it, Melissa. Perry hates Kamata and wants to get his own back. It's in the book and it was implied in his letter to *The Times*.'

Melissa felt her insides knotting into a ball. He was defacing her idol. 'Look, hasn't it occurred to you that what Perry's actually seeking at the end of his life is reconciliation, not revenge?'

'He ever tell you that?'

'No. As I said, he hasn't told me anything. But I don't care. He's come here to build bridges. To lay ghosts. I read a book by some other Burma veteran who did that. Worked on the Railway. Met up with his Japanese guard fifty years later and became friends.'

'Perry's different.'

If this was what she believed, the sensational details she'd been promising were likely to be a damp squib. He picked at the food but it was greasy and cold.

Melissa saw she was running out of time. It was pointless prevaricating any more. A busted flush, hoping she could interest him in her as a person. But she had something he wanted. One vital piece of information. And she had every reason to believe he was well equipped to pay for it.

The music stopped. They clapped politely. Then in the silence that followed she made her pitch. It would have to be a straight trade, now. There was no other way.

'I found something of Perry's. In his private quarters at Bordhill. I think it's the sort of thing you'd be interested in.'

Sam stared disbelievingly at her. There was a distinctly odd look in her eyes now. Anticipation mixed with intense unease.

'What is it?'

'It . . . it's something I was going to look into tomorrow. At a library. We could do it together.'

'Tell me about it.'

She didn't immediately, because the band began to play a Stones number. She knew the tune but waited to hear the words before she was sure. Then she smiled. The song was 'Let's spend the night together'. Yes, she thought, fate works in the most mysterious of ways.

'I *will* tell you what I found,' she said, leaning forward and half closing her eyes in an attempt to look seductive. 'And I can promise you you'll be incredibly glad that I did. But . . . and I know this may sound rather forward, there's something I want in return.'

She looked intensely vulnerable. Sam sensed that if he refused whatever she was about to ask of him, she'd be cut to the quick.

'What is it?'

Melissa took in a deep, deep breath and pressed a hand to her racing heart.

'I want you to fuck me, Geoff.'

24

Central Myanmar
Friday, 14 January, late morning

THE FRENCH-BUILT turbo-prop delivered him efficiently to the narrow landing strip at Heho. Philomena had advised him to fly with one of the country's small independent airlines because the state-run company had lost half its fleet through accidents. The tiny, ramshackle terminal building had a cafeteria attached. There were staff in attendance but no customers.

Outside stood an olive-skinned man in his thirties, holding a card with the name Maxwell on it. Sam raised his hand to acknowledge him.

'Are you Tun Kyaw?'

'Yes.'

'Philomena said good things about you.'

The man's polite smile didn't disguise his nervousness. He took hold of Sam's bag and led the way to his car, a small Suzuki off-roader that had seen better days.

Tun Kyaw had a lean, bony face with a sculpted jaw. A thin moustache marked his upper lip like a scar and on his head he wore a dusty blue baseball cap. As they drove from the airport, two soldiers in helmets waved them through a barrier after checking who was at the wheel.

'You have money for me?' Tun shot him a sidelong glance.

'Yes.' Five hundred dollars which the embassy woman had given him that morning. By Burmese standards, a fortune. 'I was planning to pay you when we're finished,' Sam said firmly.

Tun slowed the car. 'No. You must pay me now. Because I take the money to my home. For safety.'

Philomena had said this man was reliable, but she'd only used him once. The last thing Sam needed was to be deprived of his money, then taken to the hills and abandoned when the going got tough. But he had little choice. Tun Kyaw was the only person likely to be his friend up here. Sam reached into his small rucksack. The driver took the envelope from him and hid it under the seat.

They drove in silence for about fifteen minutes, then pulled up outside a rambling two-storey house on the outskirts of a small town. A peeling board above it said *Good Feeling Guesthouse*.

'You wait please.' Tun took the envelope and hurried into the building.

Half a minute later he was back, carrying a coolbox and some insulated canisters of food. He stowed them in the back, then accelerated onto the road east, trailing a vortex of dust.

'You run that place as a business?' Sam asked, pointing back.

'For wife and me. Many tourists come to Inle Lake. You know it?'

'Yes. I know.' Again it was Philomena who'd briefed him. The lake was famed for its beauty, and Tun's normal income came from driving visitors around it, most of them French.

Pausing for a moment on the edge of town to buy a bunch of jasmine blossom which he hung on the driving mirror for luck, the Burman drove on fast, hammering the horn whenever they overtook. There was little traffic, most of it pick-ups jammed with local travellers and the occasional heavily laden truck.

'How far to Mong Lai?' Sam asked.

'Two, maybe three hours.'

'Philomena told you what we have to do when we get there?'

Tun half-smiled. 'She say you look for two old men. Japan and English. Have bad memories. Maybe they kill each other.'

A muscle in the side of his jaw twitched.

Sam had phoned the SIS woman at six that morning and they'd met for breakfast at the restored colonial Strand Hotel.

'You look dreadful,' she'd said. He didn't tell her why. He had every intention of erasing last night's episode from his mind.

Unaware of how he'd obtained it, Philomena had taken Melissa's magazine clipping back to the embassy, telling him that one of their Burmese staff had an encyclopaedic knowledge of his country's geography. Ten minutes later she'd returned with the news that the memorial was at Mong Lai.

'I rang the main hotels there,' she'd announced excitedly. 'Tetsuo Kamata is registered at the Jade Palace. And Perry Harrison, in the guise of Robert Wetherby, at the Golden Lion. They both checked in last night.' She'd glowed with satisfaction at what she'd discovered.

Sam had expressed a fear it might be over already. Kamata dead and Harrison under arrest.

'I didn't get that impression just now,' she'd said. 'No indication of anything abnormal from the people I spoke to on the phone.'

Then she'd told him about Tun Kyaw.

'I recruited him when I was doing my intensive language training at the beginning of my posting here, up in Mandalay. There's nothing very political about him, as far as I could tell. Like with most Burmese, his main interest is survival. He's made it his business to be friends with local Tatmadaw commanders and claims to be able to get to parts of the country normal mortals can't reach.'

'Ever put it to the test?'

'A couple of times.'

'So you trust him?'

'Up to a point. His big ambition is to get out of the country with his wife and kids and he needs plenty of money to achieve that. So he'll do most things if you pay enough. But I imagine he's a bit of a whore, taking money from anyone who offers it.'

'Including the military?'

'Probably. I saw no evidence of that, but it's likely he informs for MIS. So if it comes to a choice between his own survival and yours, I wouldn't rate your chances.'

'Thanks. Any chance of the loan of a satellite phone? Sounds like I could be lonely up there.'

'Not on, I'm afraid. They'd stop you at the airport. Arrest you for spying. This is not a country where people trust one another. And it'd be wise for you to do likewise.'

'I'll remember that. And Mong Lai – how close is that to the Golden Triangle?'

'Let me put it this way. If you try to drive east from there you won't get far. The military and the UWSA keep foreigners out. You know the recent history of that area?'

'Give it to me.'

'It's the eastern Shan State, and the Shans are one of the many groups in Myanmar wanting autonomy from Yangon rule. Last year the SPDC began muddying the waters by resettling Shan areas with Wa tribespeople from an inhospitable mountain terrain further to the north-east. We don't know the numbers relocated, but it may be as many as 200,000. Back in their old homeland the Wa's main harvest was opium – they claimed the land wasn't fit for growing anything else. So to persuade them to raise more benign crops like sugar cane, the Tatmadaw resettled them in the Shan lands. Many Shan villagers lost their homes as a result. The other aim behind the move was that in exchange for letting the United Wa State Army virtually run their new domain, the Wa agreed to do battle with the Shan separatists and put them down on the SPDC's behalf. Following this?'

'Just about. So the Tatmadaw get peace in the area and a cutback in the opium trade at the same time.'

'That was the idea. The SPDC told the UN it would stop all drug production in Wa areas by 2005. Only it's not quite working out that way, because the Wa don't seem able to kick the habit. Instead of cash crops, they've been planting poppies in their new lands. And not only that, they've built factories near the Thai border to produce speed pills by the million. *Ya ba*, the Thais call it. Which translates as *crazy drug*.'

'I've heard about those sheds. One final question. How far advanced is this diesel factory Kamata's building for the military?'

'We know very little about it. But as far as I can tell it's only on paper so far.'

Time had been pressing. He'd needed to return to his hotel, to collect a bag and get to the airport, but before leaving Philomena, he'd asked her a favour.

'There's a Ms Dennis staying at the Inya Lodge Hotel. First name Melissa. In a rash moment I said I'd see her this evening. Tell her I've been called away, will you? Say I'll be in touch in a day or two.'

'Who is she?'

'A friend of Perry Harrison. Writing a book about him. She knows me as Geoff, by the way. Just . . . just make sure she's okay, will you? And . . . a word of warning. She's a bit of a fantasist. If she tells you any weird stories about me, don't believe them.'

Because they wouldn't be true. It had taken all his ingenuity last night to extract the cutting from her without giving in to her demands. In the end he'd resorted to claiming he'd recently been tested HIV positive.

They reached Mong Lai after a twisting climb up a roughly tarmacked road. At a couple of points on the way they'd passed cars with bonnets up to let engines cool. The outskirts of the town reflected its former existence as a summer escape from the sweat of colonial Rangoon. Set back from the road were fine mansions, built in the style of an English resort, their verandas spattered with red from giant poinsettias. Amongst them huddled smaller ranch-style houses, wood-framed and raised on stilts. Somewhere here, Sam remembered, Perry Harrison had fallen in love with a Burmese girl.

'Where you want to go, boss?'

'The Jade Palace Hotel. Know where that is?'

'Yes, boss.' Tun Kyaw drove into the centre of the town. An imposing clock tower stood at a crossroads. They turned right and followed a road fringed by flower-filled gardens. It could almost have been Sussex.

Tun Kyaw slowed.

'Hotel here.'

He indicated a large house coming up on the left which looked recently renovated. On a curving gravel drive a handful of cars were parked at the far end. Tun Kyaw was about to turn in when he suddenly swerved away again.

'What's the matter?'

'Police there, boss. I know the cars.'

Sam's heart sank. He'd arrived too late.

'I need to know what's happened.'

'No boss. Anybody coming in asking questions they arrest. Specially European.' The fear on Tun's face was palpable. He drove on up the road, then stopped when they were well clear of the hotel. 'You don't know these people,' he stressed. 'They very bad.'

Sam considered getting out and walking back to the Jade Palace, but Tun's fear was getting to him. Being thrown in a Burmese jail wouldn't help.

'Where we go now?' Tun enquired, eager to get away.

There was one other place where he had a chance of learning something.

'There's a Japanese memorial somewhere near. From the war. You know it?' He found the magazine cutting in his rucksack and showed it to him.

'Yes boss. I take Japan man there last year.'

Tun turned the car and drove back to the main street. They passed along its dusty length, then out into the country. Soon they were amongst fields of maize. Banana plants grew in clumps and eucalyptus trees gave shade for workers resting from their labours.

Tun stopped to ask the way of a couple of wan-faced women wheeling bicycles. They jabbered at him, each pointing in different directions.

After a while Tun drove on, but Sam could see he wasn't confident.

'I thought you said you'd been to this place?'

'Yes, boss. Hard to find last year too.'

They paused for directions a couple more times before Tun drove into a field and stopped. White buffalo grazed, tethered to stakes by long ropes.

'Where is it?' Sam asked.

There was nothing here that looked remotely like the picture in the cutting, but Tun pointed to a fence at the end of the field, beyond which a cherry tree blazed with blossom. Beneath it was a rough canopy of sun-bleached corrugated plastic supported by white-painted posts.

They got out. Beyond the fence, beneath the canopy, was the memorial, a spike of white-painted stone little higher than a man, with Japanese script painted on it in black. The site was deserted. A table and chair stood at one end of the canopy, and on the table lay a book of remembrance. Sam opened it and turned to the page for today. There was an unsigned entry in English which chilled him to the bones.

We said we would never forget. And we haven't.

Sam looked around. He peered beyond the fence but there wasn't a soul in sight. The stillness of the place was eerie. Then the gate in the fence creaked open and an elderly woman entered the memorial ground, dabbing her nose with a handkerchief. She eyed them with deep suspicion.

'You speak English?' Sam asked.

The woman made some angry noise which he took to be 'no'. From her looks he guessed she was Japanese.

'Tun. Ask her what happened here today.'

The Burman began speaking to her. Her reaction was hostile but eventually he coaxed it out.

'This morning Mister Kamata come here to pray. Alone. Come by taxi.'

'What time?'

'She say nine-thirty.'

Sam checked his watch. Seven hours ago.

'Two Englishmen already here, one as old as Mister Kamata, the other younger. They come in a big jeep with two . . . she call them dacoits. Have guns.'

Two Englishmen. Had the elusive Rip finally turned up?

'They take hold of Mister Kamata and drive away with him. Mister Kamata very angry. He shout to this woman to tell the police what happen. She go to Mong Lai in Mister Kamata's taxi and say it. Then police come here. She show them this book which the Englishman write in. Then they go away again. This all she know. Very unhappy woman,' Tun added. 'She say Mister Kamata come here every year.'

'Has she any idea where they took him?'

Tun asked and it was clear the answer was no.

Sam stared at the memorial. 'How many Japanese died around here in the war?' he asked.

Tun checked. 'More than one thousand.'

So many casualties and yet the memorial was so simple. No tablets. No lists of names. So different from the massive commemorations of human sacrifice made by the Commonwealth War Graves Commission. It was as if the memorial had been erected in a hurry by people who didn't want to remember what had happened here.

They made their way back to the car, Sam fighting off a sense of hopelessness. If Kamata had been kidnapped seven hours ago, the chances were he would already be dead.

'How well do you know this area, Tun?'

'I been here some time, but it not my home. What you want to know?'

'Some ideas about where they could've taken Mr Kamata.'

'I cannot tell that.'

Of course he couldn't. Sam swung himself into the passenger seat of the 4-wheel drive. If there was an answer to his question, *he* had to find it. He tried to think himself into Perry Harrison's mind. The man was controlled by the past. So perhaps it'd be *in* his past that he'd locate the answer.

Something niggled at the back of his mind. He dug into his rucksack for *A Jungle Path to Hell*, turning to the chapter where Harrison described the day he'd decided to marry Tin Su. He fingered through the pages until he found the section he was looking for.

I was totally infatuated with this young woman, and wanted to be alone with her. I realised that if I was to get her to submit to me I had to move her away from her familiar surroundings. To knock her off balance and crack that veneer of self-control that many Burmese women affect to disguise their shyness. I knew she would not be able to resist me so easily if I could destabilise her a little. And my determination to have sexual intercourse with her was extremely strong.

I hired a car and driver for the day and we took off into the hills. It is a pretty landscape around Mong Lai. Because of the altitude there is no thick jungle in this part of Burma. Temperatures at night can drop below freezing. The earth is red and fertile and in the lower-lying areas much of the land was richly cultivated. The place I instructed our driver to take us to was a pretty waterfall called Pak Chin, which even in the driest parts of the year had crystal clear water passing over it. I knew it from when I was a child. In those days an expedition there from my home in another hill town had involved a three-day trek with mules.

I had had more recent experience of the place, however, because in 1943 my platoon used the falls as a source of drinking water. We had been there on the day before my capture by the Japanese. The village where we were ambushed was not far from the falls and the place where I had hidden after being wounded was a ruined temple at the top of an escarpment above them.

I felt a certain sense of trepidation as we neared the place. There were ghosts to be laid and I was not sure I would be able to cope. The falls were accessible by a bumpy track. When we reached them the driver parked in the shade and proceeded to go to sleep. My desire to make love with Tin Su was extremely strong and I am sure if she had been a European woman nothing could have stopped us. But I was very conscious that simply by being alone with me in such circumstances Tin Su had already cast her culture's social customs to the four winds. To try to take her further down the Western road of intimacy without her believing that I was strongly committed to her, would have been grossly unfair.

We had our picnic by the waterfall. It was a late lunch because our departure from Mong Lai had been delayed by problems finding sufficient petrol for the journey and then by a puncture. It was already mid-afternoon, and the more we talked the more I became both enchanted by her and, unusually for me, determined to control myself and respect her ways. In the back of my mind, unsettling me, was the knowledge that not far from where we lay in the shade of a tree was the place where my descent into hell had begun ten years earlier.

I knew I could not leave that place without seeing the ruins again. The sun was beginning to get low in the sky when I suggested we climb up to the ridge to watch it go down. Heart in my mouth, we set off. There was no track as such, so we scrambled diagonally up a bank of loose stones. Twice she lost her footing and I had to reach out a hand. Necessity made her take it, and it was the first actual physical contact we had had that day, so mindful had I been about her sensitivities.

At the top of the ridge we stopped to catch our breath. The old temple was not as I had remembered it. More dilapidated. More overgrown. And it felt a place of great peace, whereas ten years before I had lain there in fear, a throbbing wound in my side, listening to the rustlings in the scrub around me, terrified that every crack of a twig marked the footfall of the approaching Japanese.

The main zedi had been constructed of mud bricks, the paint and plaster that had originally coated it washed away by centuries of rain. The bell shape had collapsed on one side, creating a small cave. This was where I had hidden in 1943. It was strangely liberating to see the spot again, because, as I said before, the place felt so peaceful now. I thought for a brief moment that I would tell Tin Su of the last time I had been here, but quickly stopped myself, knowing that her questions could lead to a territory I could not bear to revisit.

We stood on the edge of the zedi's base watching the sun go down. The magic of the moment overwhelmed me and before I knew what had happened, I had asked Tin Su to marry me. Not only that, but she had accepted. The power of that place must have had a remarkable effect on us because for my part I had had no intention of marrying again. I was not even divorced. And I *suspect that until that moment Tin Su had also never considered marrying a man not of her culture.*

We made our way down the slope again, so the driver could negotiate the worst of the track before darkness enveloped us. Tin Su let me hold her hand in the car. I can remember to this day its smallness and its delicacy, but as we bumped our way back to Mong Lai, a part of my mind was still up there at the old temple. I recall resolving never to visit it again until all my ghosts had been laid to rest. Which meant being certain that the man who had tortured me would never be in a position to harm me again.

Sam snapped the book shut and beckoned to the driver. 'Pak Chin, Tun Kyaw. Know where that is?'

The Burman slid onto his seat, his brow furrowed.

'It's a waterfall near Mong Lai. You know it?'

'No boss.'

'Then ask someone.'

Tun Kyaw drove the Suzuki from the field and back onto the rough track leading to the town. On the outskirts was a tea shop where he stopped to consult the customers. While he went inside, Sam watched three young girls walk past. Dressed in white blouses and carrying woven bags for their schoolbooks, their smooth-skinned faces were caked with *thanakha* paste as a protection from the sun. They smiled shyly at him, then quickened their pace, turning to one another to giggle.

Tun climbed back behind the wheel.

'How far?' Sam asked.

'Maybe one hour.'

Sam clicked his tongue. Sixty minutes on a gamble that might prove fruitless.

'They all talk 'bout Mr Kamata,' Tun said suddenly.

'In there? What are they saying?'

'That he taken away by two Englishmen and police not know where they gone.'

'Then we have an outside chance of finding them first,' said Sam, grimly.

Tun Kyaw drove for twenty minutes on the road east, heading ever closer to the Shan lands controlled by the Wa. Twice they were halted at military roadblocks where Tun's connections came up trumps. At each he produced a paper which turned scowls into smiles and salutes. But Sam's relief at the strength of the Burman's contacts was tinged with unease. To be *that* close to the military who ruled this divided land, Tun Kyaw *had* to be working for them too.

'They grow poppies around here?' Sam asked, after the second roadblock.

'I don't know, boss.'

'The Tatmadaw still seem to be in charge.'

'For thirty kilometres more. Then Myanmar soldiers finish.'

'We're going that far?'

'No, boss. Very dangerous. We turn off road very soon. You see the *paya*?'

He pointed ahead where a *zedi* stood incongruously in the middle of a small field to their left. Its bell looked recently gilded and garishly out of place in this seemingly empty landscape. Tun slowed down, searching for the track which he'd been told was just past it. The lane when they found it was the width of a single vehicle. The Suzuki bounced and banged over its stony surface. The first stretch was on level ground between rice paddies worked by women wearing coolie hats. Then the road began to climb and the ground on either side became rougher. Cultivation was replaced by scrub peppered with wild flowers and punctuated by stands of bamboo and eucalyptus.

Sam looked behind as they climbed. A plume of dust lay in their wake, its colour warmed by the late afternoon light. They'd be visible from miles away.

'Stop, Tun.'

The driver braked, then turned to him expectantly. 'What matter, boss?'

'You've never been here before, right?'

'No boss.'

'So you have no idea of the layout of this place. What other roads there may be.'

Tun appeared not to understand. 'In the restaurant they tell me waterfall is five kilometres from main road.'

'The place we need to get to is above the waterfall. On a hill. A ruined *paya*. And if the people we're looking for are there, it's better they don't see us coming.'

'Then when we get close, maybe it better you walk, boss.'

Sam noted he'd said it in the singular. He couldn't blame him. This wasn't his fight.

'Okay. Drive on. But try to keep the dust down.'

The ground undulated, an inhospitable landscape of boulders and outcrops of rock. At times the track became all but invisible and Tun slowed the Suzuki to crawling pace to negotiate the stones.

Sam felt appallingly unprepared. He had no idea what to expect. If the

Englishman with Harrison was the elusive Rip, then the man must have significant contacts to have conjured up two armed local men as escorts.

And *he* was unarmed, his sole weapon his tongue. His only hope lay in trying to talk Harrison out of whatever he planned to do – if he hadn't already done it. That's if he could get to him without being shot to pieces first.

Ahead of them the skyline was marked by an almost continuous escarpment. Sam scanned it for evidence of a ruined temple but couldn't see any. A lookout up there would have had a perfect view of their approach and there was nothing they could do about it. As they neared the place, the track began to follow the course of a stream. Most of its bed was dry, but a thin sliver of water wetted the middle. White wading birds pecked in the shingle for grubs.

Sam clasped his hands until the knuckles went white. Uncertainty gnawed at his belly. He had no instinctive feeling this time, nothing to tell him this *was* the place Harrison had come to with his prisoner. He looked around at the terrain they were crossing, trying to visualise Japs and Brits bayoneting each other half a century ago.

Soon they reached a denser clump of trees and the track petered out. Tun Kyaw stopped the car.

'Now you walk, boss.' It sounded more a command than a suggestion.

'You're not coming with me?'

'I stay with car. In case someone steal it.'

Sam smiled cynically. They hadn't seen another human for miles. He opened the door and got out.

'Don't go away,' he cautioned.

Over to his left the sun was nearing the horizon. He reached onto the back seat of the Suzuki and undid the side flap of his rucksack. There was a torch in it which he stuffed into a trouser pocket.

He set off into the trees, lured by the sound of water splashing. The waterfall, when he came to it, was a thin rope of silver, dropping thirty metres onto a slope of polished rock. A tranquil place. Perfect for the seduction Perry Harrison planned all those years ago. He looked up. The face of the escarpment behind was almost vertical. Wherever the couple had made their climb, it couldn't have been from this spot.

There was the semblance of a path heading off to the right. He followed it and soon reached the edge of the trees. The cliff stretched ahead of him, still impossible to scale. He looked for some break in its profile which might indicate the start of a steep track to the top. But there was nothing visible.

From now on there'd be no more cover. He peered up at the ridge for signs of being watched, conscious of his vulnerability – if anyone *was* up there. Seeing nothing untoward, he stepped into the open and continued across the stony ground.

A few moments later he stopped abruptly. In front of him were tyre tracks, faint marks in the dust revealing some other vehicle had come here, which must have skirted the trees at the waterfall to strike out across the rough terrain. Suddenly this was for real. Anxiety racking up, he followed them until they turned sharply left, passing through a fissure in the rock face. Beyond it was a steep incline.

Full of trepidation he began to climb. In places the tyre tracks were smudged where the wheels had fought for a grip. Every so often he paused to listen, but heard nothing other than the thudding of his own heart.

Soon the tops of trees appeared over the escarpment edge. Somewhere amongst them birds were shrieking. The slope began to level out. A stationary car came into view and he stopped, crouching down while he tried to see if there was any movement in or around it. He listened again. Still nothing. The vehicle was a large Mazda jeep and seemed to be empty. Beyond it was dense bush, the reason, he presumed, why it had gone no further. He took a chance and ran across to it, crouching by the rear wheel arch. Then he raised himself to look inside. On the back seat was a piece of apparatus like an oversize notebook computer. A satellite telephone.

Suddenly there *were* voices. From deep in that scrub which began a few metres away. Or rather a single voice – speaking in some local tongue but with an accent that was unmistakably English. And it was getting nearer.

He ducked behind the rear door of the Mazda. Footsteps crunched towards him. With nowhere else to hide and no means of defending himself, he slid beneath the car, his head scraping the hump of the rear differential.

From beneath the chassis he watched the feet approach. Dark green jungle boots with black trousers tucked into them. The man dumped a rifle onto the ground, leaning its barrel against the bodywork. Then he opened the rear passenger door and took out something heavy, which Sam assumed to be the satphone. The feet moved to the front and the equipment was lifted onto the bonnet.

Sam heard expletives as the man fiddled with the antenna. The voice – it sounded disturbingly familiar.

He eyed the rifle. If his suspicions were confirmed he was going to need it. As he eased himself closer to the vital weapon, he heard the beeps of the satphone's dialler.

The man cleared his throat to speak.

When he did so Sam knew that the search for Harrison had just taken a most extraordinary turn.

'Jan. It's Jimmy. I'm in one fuck of a mess here. This bloke Harrison's gone off his rocker.'

25

JIMMY SQUIRES.

Sam's brain corkscrewed. Why? What possible connection could that man have with Perry Harrison?

Then it dawned on him. Of *course* Squires was 'Rip'. The clues had been there and he hadn't seen them – the background file saying the former SAS sergeant was obsessed with World War Two – Harrison's email talking of meeting Rip at a Chindit reunion. And even the name. Squires had been brought up in *Rip*ley. Midge had told him. Ripley, Yorkshire.

The ex-soldier was talking again. More urgently this time.

'Listen, Jan, I need a lift across the border. Tomorrow. And a stamp in my passport. Talk to them, eh? You can fix it.'

Jan. The woman Squires had been with on the boat at Phuket. Linked to Yang Lai's heroin gang. Squires was still plugged into the system, just as Midge had said.

Sam's brain went into overdrive. His missions had fused, suddenly. He faced the incredible possibility of saving Kamata's life *and* delivering Squires to Midge in one fell swoop. *If* he could get control.

The rifle was within touching distance now.

He listened, waiting for his moment. Squires was speaking again, agitatedly.

'I know your friends don't fucking like me anymore. But you can fix it, Jan. And you've got to. No. It'll be me on my own. I'm going to leave the old men here.'

Men. Sam's hopes rose. It sounded like confirmation that Kamata was still alive.

'Soon as I'm well clear, in a couple of hours say, I'll get word to the Tatmadaw telling them where to find 'em.'

Squires cleared his throat again, with annoyance. Sam had the impression the woman was questioning him more closely than he wanted.

'I'll tell you what's changed, darlin'. Harrison asked me to negotiate a deal with the SPDC, that's what – saying they can have Kamata back if they release his son from prison. The daft old bugger wants a swap. I've told him there's no way I'm going to stick my head in a noose on that score.'

Stifling his incredulity that Harrison could have had such an ambitious scheme, Sam concentrated on the timing of his emergence from beneath the car. It was critical. Too soon and Squires could use his phone call to rally help. Too late and the former soldier would have repossessed the gun. In readiness, he eased his body from under the sill of the car, checking that Squires' view of him was blocked by the broad spread of the bonnet. The rifle butt was inches from his head.

'Anyway, just fix me a way out of Myanmar, okay?' Squires ordered. 'I'll call again in a couple of hours.' The phone clicked back on its rest.

The time had come. Sam rolled clear, grabbed the gun and levelled it at the former SAS man.

Squires gaped in astonishment. 'What the fuck . . .?'

For several seconds they stared at one another. Then Sam got to his feet.

'Move away from the jeep. Over there.' He gestured with the rifle. 'I want you down on the ground facing the trees.'

For a couple of moments Sam thought Squires would rush him. Then, very slowly, the man complied. When he was sitting on the stony earth he twisted his head round.

'What the fuck are *you* doing here, shitface?'

'Harrison,' Sam growled.

'*What?*' He looked utterly confused. 'Who the hell *are* you?'

'I work for the government.'

'Whose?'

'Yours . . .' Sam kept an eye on the tree line beyond Squires, fearing the sudden intervention of the two 'dacoits'. 'Where are your men?'

'No idea.'

There was a thwacking noise from deep in the thicket. Like someone knocking in tent pegs.

'What's happening here?'

Squires ignored his question. 'That blonde tart with you? Beth?'

'Maybe.'

Squires eyed him coldly. 'I said I'd kill you if I ever saw you again.'

'So you did.'

Sam knew his hold on this situation was perilously weak. At any moment one of Squires' gunmen could take a shot at him. The rifle aimed at the small of their master's back might or might not deter them.

'What's Harrison done to Kamata?'

'Let's see. What's the best way to put it?' Squires ruminated for a moment. 'I'd say he's been making him understand how he feels about life.'

'How?'

'Oh, knocking him about a bit. And helping him get a suntan.'

Staking prisoners out in the midday heat until sunburn and dehydration drove them mad – it's what the Japs had done to their POWs.

'And before you ask, this wasn't my idea,' Squires added quickly. 'Anyway, what are you – SIS?'

'Something like that.'

'And why do you care about Harrison?'

'Because if Kamata dies, so does a whole load of Anglo-Japanese trade.'

'Yeah, but in Phuket you weren't . . .'

'That was different. I was helping the Aussies out. Now, where's Harrison?'

Squires fell silent. He seemed to be digesting the situation. Calculating his next move. Quietly racking up the pressure on Sam.

'On your feet again,' Sam snapped. 'Hands on head.'

He faced an almost impossible task. Even if he managed to resolve the immediate situation, he knew it'd be a marathon undertaking to get Harrison and Kamata back to civilisation. *And* to persuade the Jap to tell the Myanmar authorities his abduction had been a misunderstanding. And *then*, to get Squires into Midge's little hands in Thailand. Simply handing the man over to the Tatmadaw wouldn't work. The chances were they'd give him safe passage out of the country. No. By one means or another he was going to have to hand Squires over to Midge in person, and at this point he hadn't a clue how.

The thwacking in the trees intensified. With a surge of horror he realised the object being hit was a human being.

'Move.' He prodded Squires with the barrel.

'Perry won't be pleased to see you.'

'Too bad. Where are your men?'

'Around.'

'I want them disarmed. Any farting about and you get a bullet in your back.'

'You wouldn't dare. Fucking boy scout . . .'

'Don't tempt me.'

They elbowed their way through the bush. Then Squires stopped and turned.

'Tell me something, *Steve*, or whatever your name is. Just curious. How the fuck did you find us?'

The man was far too composed for Sam's liking. As if knowing damned well it'd be him holding the gun again before long.

'Harrison told me about this place,' said Sam cryptically.

Squires scowled. 'Do me a favour.'

'It was in his book. Ever read it?'

'Course I have.' He began parting the foliage again, swiping at branches with his arms. 'That book's what made me a fan of his. Blokes like Perry – they're the forgotten heroes of World War Two.' He said it with a bitter edge to his voice, as if Sam were part of the establishment that had turned its back on the veterans. He stopped one more time, glaring at Sam with narrowed eyes. 'Look Mr SIS man. Let's get one thing straight. It's like I said – all this that's going on here is Harrison's idea. He asked for muscle, so I provided it. That's all. But I didn't know he was terminally ill. Nor that he'd lost his marbles. So this is not exactly what I was expecting. Okay? I was just trying to give a good friend a helping hand.'

'Such a good friend that you're now running out on him.'

Squires looked pained, as if unjustly accused. 'Only because he's lost it.' Then the ruthlessness returned. 'Anyway, he'll be dead in a few weeks.'

'Just keep moving.' Sam disliked the man more intensely than ever.

A few seconds later they reached a clearing. Something dreadful was happening on the far side of it, but Sam's eyes were locked on the two bandit-like figures squatting on the ground a few paces away, drinking from beer bottles.

'Fuckers,' Squires hissed. 'Turn your back for five minutes . . .'

The men looked very young. They had brown faces with wary Chinese eyes and hair that was long, black and straight. Assault rifles were slung across their backs, which they swung onto their laps as soon as they saw Sam.

'Tell them,' he hissed, his forefinger slipping through the trigger guard. 'It would give me real pleasure to blow your guts out.'

Squires muttered something in the men's language and they laid the guns on the ground, their faces expressionless. One of them had a cowboy hat jammed on his head. Both had spare magazines stuffed into webbing belts. Sam guessed they were Wa fighters from the tribal militia Yang Lai used to guard his drug empire.

'Tell them to chuck their guns and spare rounds over there.' Sam pointed to the open ground to their right. 'Then to stand up with their hands on their heads.'

Squires spoke to them again. Reluctantly the men did as they were bid. Only then did Sam lift his gaze to take in the scene at the far side of the clearing.

'Jesus!'

Silhouetted against the glow of the sunset was the ruin of a small Buddhist temple. To one side of the half-collapsed *zedi* was a banyan tree. Hanging by a rope from its branches was the naked body of an elderly man, his hands bound above his head and his feet just inches from the ground. His shins and ribs were red and black from the beatings he'd been given.

Sam jabbed the gun into Squires' back again. 'Move! And your boys.' He pushed them closer to the tree.

Peregrine Harrison, dressed in a sweat-stained bush shirt and khaki shorts, stood staring up at his victim, looking for some sign that his one-time torturer had at last been broken. He'd heard nothing of what was happening on the other side of the clearing, his mind locked in a private nightmare.

His legs were akimbo and he was resting on the log he'd been using as a club. Adrenalin had kept him on his feet long after his condition would normally have permitted. But now the very act of breathing was causing him pain. It was Kamata's silence that was fazing him. Apart from initial protests when they'd seized him at the memorial, he'd not spoken once. Yelped with pain when Rip's men had hoisted him up to the branch, shed tears as the bruises had spread up his legs and torso, but hadn't spoken. His refusal to answer Harrison's anguished questions had been a potent weapon.

Harrison was taller than Sam had expected. Nearly six foot, despite the shrinkage that must have come with age. He still hadn't noticed their approach.

'We have a visitor, Perry,' Squires announced.

Harrison spun round. His face bore little relation to the Teuton-eyed war hero Sam had seen smiling from the back cover of *A Jungle Path to Hell*. The deep lines and demented eyes belonged to a man crippled by the pain of the disease that was killing him – and by the torment inside his head.

'Who's this?' The voice was husky, but officer class.

'A spook, Perry,' Squires announced. 'From Her Majesty's Secret Intelligence Service.'

'*What?*' To Sam he looked like a schoolboy caught smoking. 'How the heck did he get here?'

'You left a trail, Mr Harrison.'

Perry looked at their visitor with bewilderment. His first thought was that Rip had brought him here. That his betrayal by the man he'd thought of as a friend had been complete. History repeating itself. Like the Burma Rifleman who'd given him away to the Japs. The enemy once more at his door.

For Sam the sight of Tetsuo Kamata's bruised and battered body dangling from the tree was shocking. He found it hard to accept that the damage to this aged human being had been done by a man who'd spent most of his life preaching peace and goodwill. Keeping half an eye on Squires and his guerrillas, he looked for signs of life on the Jap's face, but saw none. Eyes closed, head slumped forward, his almost hairless skin as pale as paper and his genitalia shrunk to the size of acorns, Kamata could well be dead already, for all he knew.

Sam felt an urge to grab Harrison and rub his nose in what he'd done. Instead he told himself to take things gently. Because even when *old* men went mad they could still be dangerous.

'I think you've done enough, sir. Don't you? Take him down, shall we?' He found himself speaking as he would to a child subject to tantrums.

Harrison recoiled at the suggestion. He couldn't let it happen. If the man was cut free before he'd been brought low enough to beg for mercy, he would have won. And he, Perry, would have lost.

'Rip!' He spread his arms to shield his prisoner. '*Do* something.'

'Take a look at who's holding the gun, Perry,' Squires murmured, making no effort to disguise his exasperation with the old man.

Only then did Harrison grasp what had happened. Panicking, he spread his legs and folded his arms in defiance.

'Take Mr Kamata down, Jimmy,' Sam ordered.

'Over my dead body,' Harrison growled.

Squires shook his head. 'Do it yourself, Steve.' He began to back away, smirking. 'I'll hold the gun for you, if you like.'

Sam had half a mind to shoot the bastard full of holes, together with his two lads, but seemed to recollect there were laws against that sort of thing. He threw another glance at Kamata. Still no sign of life from the man. He feared his chance to save him was slipping away.

One thing was clear. He couldn't get Kamata down from that tree with four men determined to stop him. Persuasion was his only chance and for that he needed more time. But the longer they took to resolve things here, the greater the danger of the Myanmar police and army finding them – possibly with the help of his own driver. They were perilously unprotected here. Not even a lookout in place. He pointed to the ruined *zedi*.

'Up there, Jimmy. Put one of your boys on watch before we *all* end up in the shit.'

Squires smirked condescendingly. 'Good move. We'll make a soldier of you yet.' He sent one of his guerrillas scrambling up the pile of bricks.

Sam turned to Harrison. The man's eyes were like tunnels. He saw fear there, but no readiness to concede.

'Look, I know what you've been through, sir.' Treading on eggshells. 'I've spoken with your son.'

Harrison's eyes widened with astonishment. If this were true, things were taking an extraordinary turn. 'You've seen Khin Thein?'

'No. Your son Charles.'

Harrison's disappointment was acute. Charles was an irrelevance.

'And I've talked with Robert Wetherby,' Sam continued, desperately seeking a point of contact. 'And with Melissa.'

'Oh God . . .' They were all conspiring against him. Every last person he'd thought of as a friend had turned. Suddenly he was engulfed by despair. There was no way they'd let him continue with his punishment of Kamata. No way now that he'd be able to reduce the monster to the level of self-hate he himself had been taken to fifty-seven years ago.

Sam detected a weakening of resolve on Harrison's part. He watched the old man lower himself onto a large stone in front of the *zedi*, then bury his face in his hands as if trying to shut out the besieging demons.

'They're all very concerned about you, sir,' he soothed, still keeping a wary eye on Squires.

Peregrine Harrison felt utterly drained. The adrenalin that had let him overcome the pain and weakness of his condition in the past hours had evaporated. He stared at this strong-jawed young man who'd gone to such trouble to find him and felt strangely humbled. He looked so confident. So capable. Like he himself had been in days long gone.

'The Prime Minister himself . . .' Sam continued.

Anger shot through Harrison's veins.

'Don't talk to me about politicians!' he exploded, suddenly reinvigorated.

'Look, if any lasting harm comes to Mr Kamata . . .'

'What? Is this some bleat about six thousand car workers looking for other jobs?'

'Not just them. The implications for the economy . . . the UK's relations with Japan.'

'God Almighty! It irritates me beyond measure hearing politicians care so much *now* about a Japanese sadist, when they cared so little for his victims after the war.'

'The war ended fifty-five years ago.'

'Not for me it didn't. Nor for my comrades. And remember, it wasn't *six* thousand men who's lives were wrecked by the likes of Tetsuo Kamata, but *sixty* thousand. You . . . *people*. You live in your little boxes in Whitehall. You have no *idea* . . .'

Harrison turned to face the purpling western sky, using its beauty to calm himself. The trouble was *nobody* had any idea, except those who'd been there. And even most of *them* had learned to forget and forgive. He knew that in essence he'd become a dinosaur. A rogue creature whose time had finally come. The chance to fight the battle he'd longed for had been given to him too late. *They* were going to stop him winning it.

'You know,' he murmured, half to himself, half to the man beside him, 'every time the sun goes down these days, I'm never sure I'll see it rise again.'

Sam squatted beside him, still with half an eye on Squires. He was beginning to feel sorry for Harrison. 'We're going to get you home, sir.'

Harrison didn't hear him. 'The awful thing is . . . it hasn't helped,' he whispered, eyes watering with self-pity.

'What hasn't?'

'What I've done to him.' He wiped his eye sockets with the back of his hand. 'I thought I would feel some kind of release. You know? Some escape from the hatred. But . . . there's been nothing.'

'Then for heaven's sake let's take him down. He's suffered enough.'

'Oh no! He hasn't suffered enough at all. He's nowhere near the mental condition I want to reduce him to.'

For a moment Sam saw Harrison as a child, given all his Christmas presents, who couldn't understand why he was *still* unhappy.

'What d'you want from all this, Perry?'

'Peace. Respite from the voices in my head.'

The voices of insanity, Sam wondered, or the man's conscience talking? 'What do they say?'

Peregrine Harrison looked sideways at this man who'd hunted him down. It felt oddly like the arrival of a confessor. And there were things he did want to unburden himself of, but others he couldn't. Like the terrible full truth of why he was doing this. A truth far too dark to be revealed to *anyone*.

'It's the uncertainty, you see. That's what's . . . niggled away. Not being able to understand . . .'

'Understand what?'

For a few moments Sam thought Harrison wasn't going to answer.

209

When he eventually turned his head and looked at him, the eyes belonged to a dead man.

'I don't understand how any man can do such things to another human being.'

After what he'd just done to the man in the tree.

'But surely . . .' Sam protested, gesturing vaguely at Kamata, 'what you've done is the same thing.'

To Harrison it wasn't the same at all. The injuries he'd inflicted that afternoon had been done with none of the cool detachment Kamata had shown back in '43 but in a frenzy of rage and frustration. Done too with the purpose of creating a noise. A racket in his head to drown out the voices that had driven him to the brink of insanity so many times. Voices reminding him every second of every day that fifty-seven years ago in a Japanese encampment not far from here, *he'd told this monster what he'd wanted to know.*

Told this bastard where his unit of brave Chindits was heading. Put in jeopardy the lives of the men who'd become his brothers. Ever since that day, he'd buried this terrible truth deep inside his soul, where, instead of eventually disappearing as he'd hoped, it had burned on and on like molten lava.

He'd lied in his autobiography. Said that although the torture had been so horrific he'd been ready to talk, a slide into unconsciousness had made it impossible. But the truth was he *had* talked. Easily. The beatings had been enough. No need for water torture. That most vivid part of his maltreatment had never happened. He'd made it up to conceal his own cowardice. His own treachery. That terrible weakness in his character which Tetsuo Kamata had so casually revealed.

Only one other person knew the truth. The man hanging by his hands a few feet away. It was why he'd dreamed of killing Kamata, so it could never be revealed. Then, a few days ago, it had dawned on him that the demise of the Jap would solve nothing.

'Do you believe in anything, Mr . . . ?'

'Maxwell,' said Sam. 'Stephen Maxwell.'

'You believe in God? Heaven and hell? An afterlife?'

'I'm agnostic.'

Harrison nodded. 'It's easier that way. Because if you're a believer, you can never win. You see . . . I thought that by killing this man I would rid him from my life forever. Then I realised he'd be there in the next life. Waiting for me to arrive. Waiting to point the finger again.'

'No point in killing him, then,' Sam said, seizing his chance.

Harrison let out a long sigh. 'No.'

'No point in carrying on with the beatings, either.'

Harrison didn't respond this time, his eyes focused on the darkening horizon. His thoughts began drifting beyond it.

'What did she say about me?' he croaked.

'Who?'

'Melissa. The spaniel . . .'

'Why d'you call her that?'

'I don't know. Always gave my girls the names of creatures. Mel was always so ridiculously pleased to see me – I think that was it. What did she say?'

'She wanted to be with you when you died.'

'Of course. For her book.'

'You knew she planned to write one?'

'She never actually said it. But she was the type, so I just guessed. Is she here? I left a clue for her, but I wasn't sure she would have the courage to come.'

'She's in Yangon. You could see her tomorrow.'

Harrison shook his head. 'I don't think I'd like that.'

'You never felt anything for her?'

'Not really. The trouble was I never found her physically attractive.'

'And the others? Did you love any of them?' It was irrelevant to the matter in hand, but he wanted to know and wanted to keep the old man talking.

'Oh yes. Most of them at some time or another.'

'And when you ended the relationships, you never felt guilty?'

'Never. I felt nothing. No remorse, no guilt.'

Harrison turned his gaze towards Tetsuo Kamata. The questioning had led him to the nub of his concerns about who he was and what he'd become.

'What I have never understood is why that man expressed no emotion while I was being beaten. Why he felt nothing. And yet . . . my women must have asked themselves the same about me when I told them I didn't desire them any more.' He turned to Sam, hoping for some look or word of comfort, but knowing he didn't deserve it. 'So does that make me the same as *him*? Because I too could be cruel without feeling the least bit uncomfortable about it?'

Harrison's eyes filled with tears. He'd been forced to look deep into his own soul in the last few days and hated what he'd seen.

From the body in the tree there came a groan. Kamata's chin lifted from his chest. Sam felt a huge sense of relief at this confirmation of life.

'It's over now, Mr Harrison. All over. Let's take him down.'

Harrison lowered his eyes. 'Yes.'

Sam stood up. 'Okay, Jimmy. We're ready now. Take him down.'

Squires glanced at Harrison for confirmation, then told the second of his bodyguards to untie the rope, while he himself grasped the body round the middle to support the weight.

It took a minute before the old man was lowered, flinching from the fresh pain of being moved. Squires backed away when he'd laid him on the ground, his face twisting with disgust.

'Bastard's just shit himself,' he hissed, ripping up some grass and wiping the front of his clothes.

Sam realised Kamata's arms were so numb he couldn't move them. Checking Squires was keeping a safe distance, he laid down the rifle and rubbed at the scrawny flesh to make the circulation restart.

'You'll be okay now, Mr Kamata,' he said, speaking softly. 'I work for British security. We'll get you out of here as soon as we can.'

Kamata didn't reply. His features were scrunched up like a bag. He looked broken by what he'd gone through. With such loss of face, if they gave him a knife he would probably kill himself, Sam guessed. And maybe it'd be a kindness.

Night was drawing in fast. And night was dangerous. He was increasingly concerned about Tun Kyaw, anxious to wrap things up here and get the two old men down to the car – if it was still there. But first he had to work out what to do with Jimmy Squires and his bandits.

Harrison sat on his rock, disturbed at the speed with which he was becoming an irrelevance. He felt he'd opened himself up too much to this man and needed to justify himself again.

'You know, all I really wanted was to be able to die with a clearer conscience,' he explained. 'That's all. That's why I came to Burma. Why I tried to help my wife. And free my son.'

Sam could think of nothing comforting to say. But there was another question that niggled him. He asked it in a voice low enough not to be overheard.

'Tell me, how did you persuade Jimmy to help you with all this?'

'Rip, you mean?' Harrison cleared his throat, then let out a long sigh. 'There was a deal.'

'You don't say . . .'

'You see, there's a suitcase of his. In the jeep. I promised to take it to Yangon when this business was over.'

Sam ground his teeth. Squires had planned to use his 'old hero' as a courier.

He rounded on his prisoners, noticing from the corner of his eye that they'd drifted back towards the guns.

'Get away from them, Jimmy!' He levelled the rifle.

Suddenly a shot rang out, cracking over their heads like a whiplash.

'Christ!' Sam ducked instinctively.

A fusillade of rounds smacked into the trees around them.

'Down!' Sam pushed Harrison to the ground as rounds ricocheted off rocks and chipped splinters from the trees. He glimpsed Squires and his gunman scampering away, the snatched-up weapons in their hands.

'Shit!' The guns attacking them were to his left, but they seemed to be aiming high. Squires however was to his right, and *his* aim would be straight to the heart. He darted towards the *zedi* for cover.

Suddenly he was felled to the ground, his breath exploding from his chest. A heavy weight, smelling of beer, pinned him to the earth. He heaved the body off him. It belonged to the Wa guerrilla who'd been on sentry duty on top of the ruins. The man lay lifeless beside him. Ludicrously, his hat was still in place, but the head below had taken a bullet through the front and was pumping out blood.

'*Perry*,' Sam hissed. 'You okay?'

'All right,' the old man croaked, inching his way painfully towards him.

The crack of incoming rounds was matched now by the heavier thump of returning fire. Jimmy Squires and his surviving henchman had opened up on their attackers. Burmese soldiers, he guessed. A Tatmadaw rescue party, summoned no doubt by his trusty driver.

'Stay here Perry, and keep your head down.'

He crabbed left through the trees surrounding the clearing, looking for new cover. There were muzzle flashes to the west. The soldiers had come out of the setting sun. Sam was tempted to shoot back, to help hold them off so they could escape the other way. But he knew it would draw fire onto himself and reveal to Jimmy Squires where he was hiding.

It was a mess. Even if they held off the rescuers, he had no chance of regaining control of his prisoner.

Suddenly the attack stopped. There were cries from the woods to the west. The Tatmadaw soldiers had taken hits.

Peering back at the *zedi* from beneath a thorn bush, Sam could just make out three shapes lying on the ground at its base. Harrison, Kamata and the dead Wa sentry. No sign of Squires or his other gunman.

The night had become deathly still, even the wildlife shocked into silence by the shooting. The rifle he'd been gripping all this time was unfamiliar. He felt for the cocking lever and the safety, hoping to God he'd be able to fire the thing if he had to.

'*Steve!*' Squires' voice rang out suddenly, hoarse and urgent. Not far away and behind him. It chilled his heart.

Sam lay still, hardly daring to breathe. He heard footfalls, half turned and saw a figure run past a few metres away, crouching low.

Squires.

The man stopped at the *zedi* and crouched over the bodies, checking who was who. Then he stood up and pointed his gun.

With a sickening jolt, Sam guessed his intentions. He jammed the rifle against his cheek, but in the gloom couldn't see the sights to aim it.

And it was too late. A shot rang out. Then a second.

'Christ Almighty . . .' Sam's stomach turned over. The men he'd come to save were dead.

Parakeets screeched in the trees above as Squires crouched down to check his work. Two targets. Two hits at point blank range. No witnesses to say he'd been here.

Except one.

Back on his feet, Squires peered into the darkness towards where Sam lay.

Silence returned. It was as if the place had been blanketed by snow.

Sam took up first pressure on the trigger, then eased it, knowing if he opened up he'd probably miss. But Squires wouldn't.

A second man appeared, darting from cover. For a moment Sam thought the rescuers had broken through, but it was Squires' surviving bodyguard. He grabbed his dead comrade's arm and tried to pull him away.

'Leave him there,' Squires hissed, his eyes sweeping the darkness.

The gunman began tugging the corpse towards the trees.

'Leave him!' Squires knocked the youth away from the body, then shoved him into the undergrowth. 'Start the car. We get the fuck out of here.'

He repeated it in the local language, then swung back, looking straight at where Sam lay. Levelling the rifle, he fired a wild burst. Bullets kicked close, spattering grit into Sam's face. Then the gun jammed. Cursing, Squires drew something from his belt and began heading towards him.

Sam squeezed the trigger.

Nothing happened. The safety had stuck. He jabbed it with his thumb.

Then guns opened up from the west again. Three rounds snapping overhead. Squires spun round and sprinted for the trees and safety.

Silence once more, except for the slamming of car doors. Sam crawled to the foot of the *zedi*. Shading the beam with his fingers he shone his torch on the ground.

Kamata had a dark red hole in the centre of his chest. He swung the flashlight until he picked out Harrison's sandalled feet. In the head this time. Smack in the middle of that troubled brow. A life of torment ended in a second. A double murder, carried out with a ruthless precision learned in the service of the Crown.

Sam charged towards the woods. From beyond the trees he heard the Mazda start up. He smashed his way through the scrub, ignoring the thorns ripping at his skin and his clothes. Emerging on the other side, he found the car gone. He ran to the edge of the slope and looked down. There, near the bottom, were the tail lights speeding away.

He slithered and slid down the escarpment, then ran in the direction of the waterfall. Tun Kyaw was his only chance, but Philomena's words taunted him. *If it comes to a choice . . .*

The Suzuki would be gone, he guessed. That was the reality. Particularly if it was his driver who'd directed the Myanmar military to this place.

He stopped, fearing he'd be running into the arms of the Tatmadaw. The soldiers had come from the west, from further along the escarpment. He shot a glance over his shoulder. Squires' vehicle was still heading east. Open, flat ground for a kilometre or two.

He pounded on again, relying on starlight to avoid tripping over rocks. It was a disaster. Total mission failure. And he'd come so close. Now he was alone – probably. Without wheels, in an alien land. When the sun came up, he'd stand out like a boil on a baby's backside.

He stopped for a moment. There was shouting up on the hill. The 'rescue party' had found the carnage. Would they see him if they looked down? Night sights on their rifles?

He began to run again, not sure where he was heading, but knowing this wasn't a place to hang around in.

Then a blast of light blinded him.

'Shit!' His first thought was that Jimmy Squires had doubled back. He waited for the shot, wildly pointing the rifle.

But the shot didn't come. Instead, the light went out and a hand grabbed his arm.

'Quick, boss! Get in car.'

26

'WE NOT GO road,' the driver muttered as the Suzuki set off over the stony ground. 'Army close it. Shoot first then ask who we are.'

Sam could just make out the shape of Tun Kyaw's head in the glow of the dashboard lights. Impossible to see what the man was thinking.

'Too damned right we're not going on the road,' he muttered. 'We're going after that car.'

The tail lights of Squires' jeep kept disappearing and reappearing as the vehicle dipped through gullies and wove through the scrub.

'Tun . . . you're a good man,' Sam growled, emotional with gratitude all of a sudden. At that moment he didn't care if it was the Burman who'd alerted the military. The man might well have saved his life.

Tun Kyaw didn't respond for several seconds. When he did, his voice was squeaky with tension.

'What people in that car, boss?'

'Bad people. An Englishman who's just murdered two old men.'

There was the sound of sucking teeth. 'Where they go, boss?'

'To the Thai border, I think. The Englishman has a suitcase of heroin. Needs to get it out of the country.' He was thinking aloud. 'How far is it?'

'Maybe seventy kilometre. But he can't go there. Army. Many, many roadblock. Fighting.'

'Over poppies?'

'Yes, boss. Many, many. Control by Wa State Army, you know?'

'Yes. I know. But the man who's with the Englishman, driving that car – he might be one of them.'

More sucking of teeth. 'This vahry dangerous, boss.'

He wasn't backing off though, Sam noted. Still pressing on, driven by the dual need to earn his dollars and to get away from whatever was going on up on the escarpment.

Tun switched the lights off and slowed right down, hunching forward, as if being nearer the screen might boost his night vision.

Soon there was no more sign of the other car. Jimmy Squires had disappeared into the night. Sam remembered Midge's tracking device in the lid of his rucksack and wished he could have stuck it on the Mazda.

Tun Kyaw was worrying him again. He wanted to know where the man's loyalties really lay.

'How come the military knew where to find us, Tun Kyaw?'

Silence. Then after a while, 'Boss?'

'You tell them about us going to the waterfall?'

Silence again.

'Maybe somebody hear me when I ask how to find it, boss. In restaurant in Mong Lai. In every place is army spy. Man who listen.'

It was a plausible explanation. Just. And all he was going to get. He told himself to be on his guard.

The Suzuki rattled on into the night, slowing and accelerating according to how far Tun Kyaw could see. Swerving now and again to avoid clumps of scrub. Sam searched the darkness, praying for another glimpse of red.

'Any idea where this takes us?'

'No boss.'

Suddenly Tun slammed on the brakes, letting out a gust of garlicky air. They'd reached a line of trees.

Two choices, left or right. Because straight ahead was impenetrable.

'Switch off,' Sam ordered. He got out.

The night was windless. Sound would travel. He listened, turning his head like a directional antenna. From the way they'd come there was nothing, which was a relief. But there was nothing from any other direction either.

Squires' jeep had several minutes' start on them. And it had been driving with lights, faster than Tun. They'd lost the buggers.

Then he heard a faint rumble somewhere to their right. Engine noise.

'Over there, boss.' Tun had heard it too.

'Let's go.'

The scrub grew thicker. Tun Kyaw needed the lights to pick his way through it. They bumped on for five minutes with no sign of the other car. Sam feared the noise they'd heard could have been military reinforcements moving in. He visualised Squires back on some tarmacked road by now, tyres humming as he raced for the frontier. And he thought of Midge

Adams attending her conference on the other side, blissfully unaware that the man topping her most-wanted list was heading her way.

'What's that ahead?' Lights on the horizon, moving left to right.

'I think road,' Tun announced.

'Where's it go to?'

'From Mong Lai to Chiang Mai.'

In Thailand. The place Midge had flown to for her conference.

'There'll be army checkpoints?'

'Oh yes. Many, many.'

'And will we be able to . . . ?'

Tun made a noise like a cat in pain. 'I will try. But it is better you hide. On the floor at back. I put cover over you.'

'They'll find me. What's the point?'

'Because if they see foreigner sitting in car in this part of Myanmar they must arrest him. But if they don't see, maybe they don't bother look.'

Particularly when blinded by banknotes, thought Sam.

Five minutes later they bumped over a drainage gully and joined the roughly metalled road. After a couple more minutes Tun stopped the car, got out and began clearing space in the back for Sam to lie on the floor behind the rear seats.

'Soon there will be army. It better you don't have gun, boss. If soldiers find . . .'

Sam understood his logic but was reluctant to part with the weapon. The men they were chasing were armed to the teeth.

'Can't take gun, boss,' Tun Kyaw insisted, making it clear they wouldn't be going any further if Sam resisted.

Stifling his fears that Tun Kyaw wanted him unarmed for his own reasons, Sam chucked the weapon into the scrub at the side of the road, then lay on the floor at the back of the Suzuki. The cover which Tun placed over him smelled of sweat.

He was desperately uncomfortable as they set off again and appallingly vulnerable. The back of his neck felt as if it had the rings of a target painted on it.

Within minutes they were slowing again.

'Roadblock,' Tun whispered. 'Stay very still.'

Like the grave, thought Sam, except for his heart which had developed a mind of its own.

They stopped. He heard voices. Fierce, aggressive tones, followed by mollifying noises from his driver. Sam held his breath. Tun Kyaw sounded genuinely scared. Whatever this man's relationship with the military, it wasn't universally smooth.

The engine revved and they were off again.

Before long they slowed once more. This time Sam heard the tooting of other cars. A town. He wanted to lift his head and look, but decided to wait for Tun Kyaw's reassurance. The Suzuki slowed to a stop, then turned round. After a few seconds they stopped again.

Another roadblock? No voices this time, just the creak of the driver's seat as Tun Kyaw leaned into the back.

'Boss. You must look here.'

Sam raised his head. They were in the barely lit street of a small town. Buildings down each side, two or three floors high. A Chinese feel to the place. Nasal voices. A smell of wood smoke and cooking which reminded him he hadn't eaten all day.

'There is jeep,' said Tun tensely. 'Two men, one European. They filling with petrol. Maybe is the man you look for.'

Hopes racking up, Sam struggled onto the seat squab. Tun Kyaw pointed to the opposite side of the road, but he saw no sign of a petrol station.

'Where?'

'On the left. Fifty metres.'

There was a jeep, but no pumps. Instead a line of jerry cans stood in the dirt. One was being emptied into the vehicle through a large, orange funnel.

'Black market,' Tun Kyaw explained. 'For government petrol you need paper.'

'Drive past them so I can see.'

Sam sank lower as they approached the Mazda, his eyes panning. In the back sat Jimmy Squires. Just visible. Doing the same as him. Keeping down.

'Yes boss?'

'Yes.'

Sam's mind raced. He wished to God he still had the rifle. Somehow he was going to have to stick with Squires until he was across the Thai border. Which wouldn't be easy, because the closer they got to it the less influence Tun Kyaw was going to have.

They drove on a little further, then stopped.

'What we do, boss?'

'Good question.' Sam racked his brains, frowning. There was something here that didn't make sense to him.

'How'd he get through the army checkpoint, Tun?'

'Don't know, boss. Maybe same as me. Know people in Tatmadaw.'

'But that guy with him, he's Wa.'

219

Tun didn't answer immediately. 'Maybe this Wa and this Tatmadaw do business together, boss.'

'So if he's got army friends and Wa friends, he could get to the Thai border with ease?'

'Don't know boss. That depend on what friends. Maybe he know military commander here, but not other soldier down the road.'

'What about you? How many commanders do you know?'

This time Tun didn't answer. 'What you want me do, boss?'

There was only one thing they *could* do.

'Follow them. Keep a distance, but for God's sake don't lose them.'

Tun Kyaw looked hesitant. He held out his arm and pointed to the watch on his wrist. 'I think we stay here tonight, boss.'

Sam stared disbelievingly at him.

'It vahry dangerous to drive more down this road in the night. Dacoits, boss. They kill us and take everything.'

Sam pointed back at the Mazda jeep.

'They also will stay here,' Tun Kyaw predicted. 'Big, big danger.'

On the opposite side of the road from where they'd stopped sparks flew in a small forge. An ancient motorbike was being taken to pieces in a garage next to it and in front of the two premises watermelons were stacked for sale.

The Mazda began to move.

Tun restarted the engine and swung round to follow it.

'How are *we* for fuel?' Sam checked.

'Plenty, boss. Plenty. I make sure this morning.'

A little way down the road the jeep pulled up outside a restaurant, dominated by a large neon sign for Myanmar Beer. Tun Kyaw swerved into the kerb, stopped abruptly and doused the Suzuki's lights. From thirty paces away they watched as the Wa fighter went inside.

'Ask if they have room for sleeping,' Tun Kyaw suggested.

Sam doubted it. Squires wouldn't want to hang around.

After half a minute the Wa fighter came back out and spoke through the open window of the car. There was an argument, then Squires himself got out. They locked the jeep and went into the restaurant together.

'What we do, boss?'

'You go inside and see what they're up to. Ask to use the phone or something. Give your wife a call.'

Tun Kyaw's jaw muscles flexed. 'Yes, boss.'

He loped along the road, moving with the wariness of a wild dog. Sam stayed in the back of the Suzuki, keeping low. He thought of Midge, visualising her sitting in a hotel room with her laptop, watching a dot move across a map of Myanmar and wondering what the hell he was up to.

Now would be a perfect time to stick the tracker on the Mazda, he realised. Then he decided against it. It was Squires they needed to follow, not the car.

One way or another though, he had to let Midge know what was going on. And talk to his own masters too. Break the bad news about Kamata.

He glanced up and down the main street of this small town. For all its third-world roughness, there were new buildings amongst the old. And maybe one of them had a phone with an international connection.

It was ten minutes before Tun Kyaw returned.

'He make telephone call,' he announced, climbing in behind the wheel.

'The Englishman?'

'No, boss. The Wa man.'

'You overhear anything?'

'No. I think he waiting them call him back.'

'How d'you know that?'

'Because when I ask to make call they tell me be quick.'

The Wa fighter would be reporting the death of his buddy, Sam guessed. And Squires would be finalising arrangements for his exit from the country across some remote part of the border.

'So what were they doing?'

'Eating.'

Sam felt intensely hungry all of a sudden.

'I bring some food this morning. You like to have?'

'Yes, but first I too need to make a call. Anywhere in this town with an international phone connection?'

Tun pondered for a moment. 'There is hotel.' He pointed further up the road, then started the engine. 'We have plenty time,' he added reassuringly. 'I think they stay there tonight.'

Thirty seconds later they reached the hotel. It was modern and Chinese run. The woman behind the counter found the number of the Empress Hotel in Chiang-Mai and dialled the call for him.

When Sam asked for Ms Adams room, he was told there wasn't a guest of that name. Of course there bloody wasn't. And the silly bitch had forgotten to tell him what cover she was using.

'There's a conference at the hotel?'

'Yes sir. Narcotics Suppression Bureau.'

'Then take this message and address it to Inspector M. Adams of the Australian Federal Police. Got that?'

'Yes sir. What the message?'

'"*Keep an eye on me, Beth. I'm bringing our friend out.*" Sign it – "*Steve*". Hand it to whoever's running the conference.'

'Okay, sir.'

Midge would kill him for breaking her cover, but she'd forgive him if he delivered.

Outside the hotel again, he found that Tun Kyaw had unpacked some of his food boxes and set up a picnic table beside the Suzuki.

'What the fuck are you doing? We need to be back down the road watching the Mazda.'

'Plenty time, boss,' Tun insisted, making it plain he had no intention of moving. 'If I not eat I not drive.'

Sam stared down the road. In the gloom he could just make out the neon beer sign, but nothing to say the jeep was still there.

'We see if they come past,' Tun Kyaw assured him. He pointed to the plates of rice and vegetables which he'd rustled up from the containers taken from his house that morning.

Sam sat on a camp stool, conscious of the ridiculousness of the situation. A short distance away a murderer had paused in his flight for a bite to eat. Now he, his pursuer, was doing exactly the same.

They ate hungrily and in silence. But Sam's uneasiness grew. He sensed Tun was waiting for something. Moments later he discovered what it was.

From down the road came a squeal of tyres. Then shots rang out. As Tun Kyaw ran for cover inside the hotel, Sam crouched by the Suzuki. The Mazda howled towards him, with Jimmy Squires leaning from a window, blasting away with a rifle at the army jeep that was following.

Within seconds the circus had passed. The shooting continued, its volume receding into the distance.

'Tun Kyaw!'

Sam ran into the hotel. His driver was standing by the desk trying to calm the woman behind it.

'Let's go,' Sam snapped.

'No, boss. We stay here.'

'We have to follow,' Sam insisted.

'No boss. Vahry dangerous. Shooting. Maybe you want die, boss, but not me.'

No, he didn't want to die. Just wanted to keep that damned murderer in his sights.

'It wasn't your wife you rang, was it?'

Tun Kyaw's eyes hardened. Sam took it as an admission. The Burman turned to talk to the woman behind the desk, stuffing his car keys firmly into his trouser pocket.

Sam toyed with the idea of pounding Tun Kyaw's head until he yielded them up, but knew that if he turned up at any sort of a roadblock on his own he'd be as good as dead.

A few moments later the Burman swung back towards Sam.

'She have rooms for us, boss. We stay here tonight. No more drive tonight.'

10.35 p.m.

The room was rudimentarily furnished − a table, a chair and a cupboard, a thin layer of dust covering every surface. Sam lay on the narrow bed staring up at the ceiling. A small beetle was making a slow, meandering transit of it, as if trying to work out what the hell it should be doing next. He found himself identifying with it.

Tun Kyaw had fixed him. Firmly in control now. When he'd tried calling Chiang Mai again, the hotel receptionist had claimed the international line had failed and wouldn't be repaired for days. Servant turned master, as Philomena had predicted. At dawn the man would want to drive him back to Heho and put him on the first plane to Yangon.

Sam had one final weapon which he intended to deploy in a last-ditch effort to prevent that happening.

One thousand dollars in new notes which Philomena had given him, concealed in the false bottom of his rucksack.

27

Shan State, Myanmar
Saturday, 15 January, 6.10 a.m.

THE DAYLIGHT WOKE him, although he'd hardly slept. Throughout the night the fear that Jimmy Squires was slipping away to freedom had smouldered within him like a fire in the tundra.

He swung his legs to the floor, pulled on shirt and trousers, then hammered on the door of the room along the corridor. After a few moments Tun Kyaw opened it, bleary-eyed.

'Time to move,' Sam said, walking in uninvited.

Tun Kyaw's breathing was thick and wheezy. He flopped back onto the edge of the bed with his head in his hands.

Sam stood over him.

'We're going after that Englishman.'

The Burman let out a weary sigh.

'Ring your army friends, Tun Kyaw. Ask what happened last night.'

'Boss . . . not possible.'

'Why not?'

'They not tell me.'

Sam believed him. Informers were people the military *took* stuff from. A one-way traffic.

'Then we'll bloody drive and you can ask at the roadblocks.'

'We go to Heho, boss,' the Burman insisted.

'No. I've paid you a lot of money,' Sam reminded him.

'I earn it yesterday.' The eyes were rock steady.

Sam couldn't deny it.

'There could be more, if you do what I ask.'

He saw what looked like a wince of pain as the man was tempted to do something against his better judgement.

'How much you pay me?'

'Another five hundred.'

Tun Kyaw gave an appraising look, trying to judge the depth of his purse. 'We go to Heho, boss.'

'Six hundred, then.'

'Boss, these Wa peoples vahry dangerous.' A long pause. 'One thousand.'

'All right. But you take me all the way to the border.'

The Burman grimaced. 'I try boss.'

Trying was better than nothing.

Ten minutes later they were on the road, with the British Embassy's banknotes stuffed into a concealed safe beneath the driver's seat. Sam lay on the floor in the back again.

The first roadblock came after a few miles. He heard a short burst of uneasy conversation, then the sound of Tun Kyaw reaching into his pocket. Money changing hands.

They drove on. After a short while, Sam risked raising his head to look. The landscape was more rugged. Thickly forested hills rose up on either side. The road was pitted. Here and there gangs of workers filled holes with stones broken by hammers – men and women, with armed guards watching over them. Prison labour.

It was getting unpleasantly hot in the car and the air-conditioning was on the blink. Tun Kyaw kept turning it on and off to try to make it work. Sam stayed upright. Lying down was making him nauseous.

After half an hour the road dipped towards a rusting girder bridge across a deep river gorge. As they bumped onto its planked surface Tun Kyaw slowed down. The water far below was thick and green, swirling strongly with the force of the current.

A little further on, poppy fields appeared on the lower slopes to their right, the first of the winter's flowers dotting the cabbage-green plants with white.

'Soon there will be Wa checkpoint, boss,' said Tun, his voice reedy with anxiety. He pointed ahead where pitched roofs and a gilded temple erupted from the hillside. They were approaching another town.

'Ask them about the Mazda that came through here last night.'

Tun Kyaw ignored the suggestion. 'Stay on seat, boss,' he said, as Sam prepared to squeeze onto the floor again. 'They always search car. Not good to hide.'

They rounded a bend and saw a pole across the road. The uniforms of the soldiers guarding it were a darker green than the Tatmadaw and the men wore Chinese forage-caps. They stared at the approaching car with malevolent interest. As if they were expecting it.

'This not good, boss,' Tun warned through clenched teeth, hunching his shoulders.

They stopped at the guard post. Soldiers took up positions each side of the car, opened the doors and barked instructions. Their faces were absurdly young and totally uncompromising.

'They tell us get out,' Tun Kyaw translated. His fear was infectious. Sam began to sweat profusely. The rock in his stomach told him things were about to go badly wrong.

Hands grabbed as they stepped onto the tarmac, spinning them round and pushing them against the vehicle. Intrusive fingers probed their bodies for weapons. All the while Tun was bombarded with questions. His answers were curt. Little more than grunts. Then two of the soldiers took him away, round the back of the guardhouse. Sam heard slaps and voices rising to a pitch of anger.

'Look, he's just my driver,' he protested. The boys in uniform stared sullenly at him, keeping their rifles aimed at his stomach.

He could hear Tun Kyaw talking now. A torrent of words. Humble, cringing sounds, which suffused him with guilt at having bullied the man into this. When, after a few minutes, they brought him back to the car, Tun Kyaw's nose streamed blood.

The soldiers pointed at the ground, indicating they should sit. Their hands were wrenched behind their backs and tied with plastic cable ties.

A soldier who looked senior to the others retired to the guardhouse. Through the open window they could see him pick up a phone.

'You all right?' Sam whispered, turning to Tun Kyaw. A sentry kicked him in the back to silence him.

It was several more minutes before the senior soldier re-emerged. When he did, they were jerked from the ground and pushed into the back of the Suzuki. Two soldiers occupied the front and one of them began to drive.

'You speak any English?' Sam asked. The men in front ignored him.

He turned to Tun Kyaw and asked if he knew where they were going, trying to sound calm. The Burman was trembling and ignored him too, his face taut with fear.

The road twisted its way steadily upwards. Sam had visions of being taken to a ravine and pushed over the edge, a bullet in the brain. He told himself they were probably driving to a headquarters, however. Somewhere where there might be an English-speaker.

The road surface improved as they headed further east. Paved with drug money, Sam guessed. Orchards had been planted along it, as if to convince visiting UN inspectors that the switch from opium into other crops was actually happening.

Soon there were signs of a town ahead, a modern place of flat roofs and satellite dishes. On the outskirts they passed a small industrial zone, two large sheds which matched the description Midge had given him in Bangkok. He imagined *ya-ba* pills being churned out in their millions inside.

Then they passed a large barracks, as neat and tidy as that of a regular army. Tucked away on a parade ground, artillery pieces were lined up. The fiefdom of the UWSA was a state within a state.

One of the soldiers kept turning to stare at him, as if wanting to make the most of the opportunity to eye up a foreigner. Sam felt like some rare but doomed species, soon to be examined in more detail on a pathologist's slab.

They entered a downtown area of shops and markets. The people on the streets were mostly young, many of the males in uniform. The Suzuki swung left and stopped at a striped pole guarding the entrance to another military base. Words were spoken with the guard, a report filed on a walkie-talkie and the pole lifted. Inside, neat roadways were interspersed by swards of well-watered lawns. They stopped outside a white, two-storey building guarded by sentries.

'You come,' the driver snapped. He got out and opened the rear door, grabbing Sam by the arm as he stepped onto the road. Then he frogmarched him inside. The air-conditioning beyond the doors was icy.

Sam was propelled along a corridor whose floor was impossibly shiny. Through open doorways he saw desks and banks of phones and all the quiet activity of a military HQ. At the end of the corridor they stopped in front of a portico of polished teak. The soldier knocked. When it opened, he saluted and took a pace back.

On the far side of the room was a desk, towards which Sam was pushed. The man behind it wore a plain green uniform with no insignia of rank. He looked up, his face square and Chinese-looking, with slicked-back hair.

Sam had seen it before. In the marina in Phuket.

Hu Sin.

He felt the blood drain from his face. Sensed rather than saw the small wooden chair he was being guided towards. Was aware of others in the room, all watching as unseen hands pushed him down onto the seat. His eyes focused on the middle of the desk. An automatic pistol lay there, with a silencer attached.

The ties round his wrists seemed to tighten, along with the muscles in his throat.

'What is your real name, Mister Steve?' Hu Sin's accent was light, his voice softly threatening.

'Stephen Maxwell.'

He heard footsteps, then his belongings were dumped on the floor beside him. The holdall for his clothes and the small rucksack. Hu Sin went for the backpack first.

He found the passport. Saw that the name was the one Sam had just given, then dropped it on the floor. He went through the wallet – credit card and driving licence in the same name. A handful of dollar bills and some grubby kyat notes. Then he upended the bag, dropping books, torch, water bottle, medical pack and a few odds and ends on the ground.

Sam willed him to move on to the holdall, to get stuck into his dirty underwear and not discover the one thing that mattered. But the willing didn't work. Hu Sin fingered the rucksack flap, opened the small zipped pocket and extracted the tracer Midge had given him.

'Who you work for?' Hu Sin demanded, holding it up.

'Guess.'

Hu Sin put down the tracer and picked up the pistol, pulling back the hammer with his thumb.

'You want I kill you?'

'No. But you're probably going to anyway.'

The Wa commander glared at him as if he were a piece of meat that had gone off.

'You answer question – then maybe I don't kill. Who you work for?'

'I'm a police officer. I'm looking for your murdering friend Jimmy Squires.'

'England?'

Sam shrugged. 'You've seen my passport.'

'*A valueless document . . .*'

It was a different voice this time. From behind him. A voice that was both plummy and oriental, which for some reason made Sam think of Calcutta.

He turned his head to see who'd spoken. Seated in an armchair behind him and to his left was a soldier in a different uniform. Pips and swirly bits on the shoulders. The insignia of a senior officer in the Tatmadaw. A Brigadier, Sam guessed.

But why here in a command headquarters of the Wa state army?

'You are a man for all seasons, Mister Stephen Maxwell . . .' the officer brayed. 'Also calling yourself *Geoff*, I believe.'

Sam swallowed uncomfortably. Melissa was the only person he'd used that name with.

'Miss Dennis contacted us yesterday,' the officer explained smugly, smoothing his neatly trimmed moustache. 'In Yangon. She was worried about Mr Harrison – or Wetherby as he called himself.' He clicked his tongue mockingly. 'You English. So many identities. Unfortunately the young lady contacted us too late to stop this savage tragedy from taking place.'

The officer stood up and glared down at him. Sam felt like a condemned man about to be sentenced. Hu Sin watched with the pistol still in his grip.

'There is only one word that can be used to describe you, Mr whatever-your-real-name-is,' the Tatmadaw officer declared. 'You are a *spy*.'

'Rubbish. I came here to try to save a man's life.'

'You are in a part of Myanmar which is forbidden to foreigners. You will be charged with spying.'

'I came here in pursuit of the man who killed Harrison and Kamata.'

'Spies are executed in Myanmar,' the officer continued, as if it was the only thing he could think of saying. He fingered his moustache again, then stepped forward, placing himself between Sam and Hu Sin. 'What do you have to say for yourself?'

'That I'm not a spy,' Sam repeated. He was thinking fast, a desperate plan developing in his head. 'And that Myanmar and Britain have a common interest here.'

'The only thing your country and mine have ever shared is an unhappy history,' the army officer sneered.

'Think about it. The death of Tetsuo Kamata is a terrible setback to your country as well as to mine.'

The Brigadier pursed his lips and stepped to one side, walking away with his hands behind his back. Behind his desk Hu Sin seethed with annoyance at being upstaged in his own headquarters by a strutting officer of the Myanmar army.

'Setback?' The Brigadier spun round to give thrust to his question. 'Why do you say that?'

'Because we both stand to lose out in a big way if Matsubara cancel their plans for factories in our countries,' Sam explained, a little breathlessly.

The Brigadier studied him with what looked like renewed interest. 'You have something to propose?'

'First thing is to limit the damage from this tragedy.' He was thinking as he went along.

'Absolutely. And punish the perpetrator . . .'

'Of course.'

'*You*, Mr Maxwell.'

Sam's heart missed a beat as he read their miserable minds. They intended charging *him* with Kamata's murder. Concocting some mad motive which might smooth things with the Japanese. And if he 'confessed', he'd be rewarded with a jail sentence instead of being shot.

'They were killed by Jimmy Squires,' Sam growled, 'the man your soldiers gave chase to last night.'

'Your word against his, Mr Maxwell.' The Brigadier turned away again.

Sam digested what he was saying. They'd got Squires. And the bastard had blamed him.

Hu Sin laid the gun down on the desk and began fingering the tracer device, as if by so doing he might confirm his suspicions about the recipient of its signals. His impatience seemed to be growing. Sam guessed the Wa gangster had his own simple answer to the problem. Kill them both.

'How about if the deaths of Kamata and Harrison could be shown in a different light?' Sam suggested, suddenly remembering what Melissa had said. 'Then maybe both of the motor projects could be saved.'

'What sort of different light?' The Brigadier kept his back to him.

'If we pretend Harrison came to Myanmar to effect a reconciliation with his former enemy instead of taking his revenge on him.'

'I am not following you.' The Brigadier walked back to where Sam was seated. He leaned over him with his hands clasped behind his back.

'We could say the two old gentlemen met at the Japanese war memorial in Mong Lai with the intention of turning their backs on the past,' Sam explained. 'They shook hands there, shed a few tears and agreed to let bygones be bygones. But then, in a dreadful twist of fate, they were snatched by dacoits – this region is famous for them, after all. The bandits took them to a remote place, stole everything of value they had, then beat Kamata halfway to death, before finally shooting the two of them.'

'And how would that help our mutually problematical situation?'

'The British and Myanmar governments could then propose to the Matsubara board that they continue with Kamata's two pet projects as a memorial to him and to Mr Harrison, and to the great act of reconciliation they'd brought about.'

The Brigadier perched on the edge of Hu Sin's desk and folded his arms.

'Ingenious,' he said. 'But there is always a problem when rewriting history.'

From his icy glare, Sam guessed where the problem lay.

'In this case *two* problems. You are one. And the other is Mr Squires. You both know the real truth about how Mr Kamata met his end.'

A vein in Sam's neck began to twitch.

'One solution would be to kill you both, and burn your bodies,' the Brigadier added nonchalantly.

'That won't help,' said Sam. 'To convince the Matsubara board you'll need a witness. Me. I saw the reconciliation, the handshakes, the tears. Even saw the two men being seized by the dacoits. And Jimmy Squires? I agree he's a problem. Yes, a bullet in his brain might be appropriate, but I've a better idea. You give him to me. Then you take us to the Thai border with a couple of soldiers as escort and we cross into Thailand. The suitcase of heroin which he's carrying as personal baggage will be enough to get him locked away in a Thai jail for the rest of his life. And by doing that, Brigadier, you'll have shown the world that the government of Myanmar really is ready to do its bit to stop the drug trade.'

Sam glowed with the ingenuity of what he'd come up with. The Brigadier swung round to look at Hu Sin. Then the two men got up and walked to the window, talking in low voices. Hu Sin still had the tracer in his hands, fiddling with it as if it was a cigarette lighter.

It was a couple of minutes before they turned back towards Sam.

'You would make your testimony to Matsubara jointly with Miss Dennis?' the Tatamadaw officer asked. 'She would be an important witness as to Mr Harrison's intentions.'

The idea of doing *anything* with Melissa filled him with horror, but Sam agreed. 'One other thing. Jimmy Squires won't go willingly with me.'

'On the contrary, he won't give you any trouble. One of my soldiers put a bullet in his leg yesterday. The femur is shattered. The UWSA have an excellent hospital here, but they don't have the experience for such a fracture. They have made him comfortable, but he should be treated by a specialist as soon as possible. In Bangkok they have such people.'

Sam felt euphoric. A chance to salvage something from the catastrophe of yesterday and make Midge happy too. Now all he had to do was cut her in on it. He stared longingly at the tracer which Hu Sin was playing with. When the drug baron saw his interest, he closed his hand round it.

'Everything can be ready very quickly,' said the Brigadier briskly. 'A car will take you twenty kilometres towards the border, then it will be by mule over the mountains. The main crossing is closed, you see. There has been some fighting.'

'How long will it take?'

'By nightfall you will be in a village in Thailand.'

'What about Tun Kyaw, the man who drove me here?'

'He will be looked after. They will fill his car with petrol and give him an escort out of Mong Yawn district.'

'I'd want a guarantee of that.'

'Don't worry. Tun Kyaw is useful to us, Mr Maxwell. We'll keep him safe. And Miss Dennis? You surely want to know about her?'

Sam didn't. He was dreading the thought of what she might demand in exchange for her co-operation.

'Tell me.'

'We will deport her to Bangkok and tell her to go to the British Embassy. She can wait there until you make contact.'

'Fine.' Sam felt dangerously optimistic all of a sudden. Victory snatched from the jaws of defeat. He pointed at Hu Sin's fist.

'I'd like that piece of kit back if you don't mind.'

The Wa leader's face bore no expression whatsoever. Then he shook his head.

Sam remembered what Midge had said back on the boat at Phuket.

People who get in Hu Sin's way tend not to live long.

Things were still far from over.

28

Mong Yawn
11.30 a.m.

JIMMY SQUIRES LOOKED terrible. They'd shot him full of morphine to dull the pain for the journey and he looked out of it. He'd lost a lot of blood in the shooting, Sam was told. Pale-faced, eyes flopping about like a cheap doll, it was clear he'd be no trouble. The injured leg was encased in bandages and held out straight in some sort of traction cage. It gave Sam a bitter satisfaction to see the man so incapacitated.

Although suffering from the after-effects of the anaesthetic, Squires was conscious enough to acknowledge Sam's presence as they loaded his stretcher into the back of a large, green 4-wheel drive, placing the suitcase of heroin beside him. The eyes flickered defiantly and he looked as if he were about to speak, but exhaustion defeated him.

Three soldiers piled in with Sam, a uniformed driver and two others wearing grubby tee-shirts and camouflage trousers that made them look like ravers on a club night. The pair in mufti carried rifles and had belts heavy with ammunition pouches. As they set off from the barracks Sam checked his watch. It was just before midday. They'd need to make rapid progress if they were to cross the border before dark.

The jeep left the town and began climbing towards the wooded peaks that marked the start of Thailand. Soon it left the metalled road and jolted over a stony track between poppy fields. Sam heard an expletive from the back and guessed the morphine was beginning to lose its effect.

He tried to make eye contact with the man sitting next to him, hoping for some sign of friendliness, but the Wa soldier would have none of it. He was bigger and broader shouldered than the two in the front, and looked as if he spent his free time doing weights. He smelled of sweat.

'Any of you speak English?' Sam asked.

The passenger in the front turned round. He had a glass eye. But there was no verbal response. Sam and Squires were no more than cargo to them. Bodies to be moved.

He began worrying about how he would handle things on the other side without Midge being on hand to smooth his way with the Thai authorities. Hu Sin's refusal to hand over the tracer meant she would have no idea he was there. He visualised the man using the thing as a paperweight or showing it off to his underlings.

To any Thai border patrol that intercepted them, he and Squires would be two Europeans slipping across from the Triangle with a suitcase of heroin. Rich pickings. All the evidence they needed to prosecute for a capital offence. He worried how long it'd be after they arrested him before the Thais let him contact Midge and the Embassy.

After the best part of an hour the 4-wheel drive bounced into a village of wooden huts, thatched with attap leaves. In the centre was a more substantial breezeblock building with a corrugated roof, the radio masts beside it marking it as a military post. The jeep stopped and the three Wa soldiers got out. Half-a-dozen uniformed fighters gathered around them. For several minutes there was disgruntled chatter. Then an argument broke out, which was suppressed by a man Sam took to be the local commander.

'Wass goin' on? Where are we?' Squires voice slurred from the back of the jeep.

'Changing cabs,' Sam answered.

He got out to stretch his legs and avoid further conversation with Squires, but the two plain-clothes soldiers gestured for him to stay where he was. A small crowd was gathering, villagers curious at the arrival of *big nose* foreigners.

Suddenly decisions were being taken. The rear of the jeep was opened and the stretcher eased onto the ground.

Far more alert now, Squires winced at the pain the movement caused him. 'Would someone tell me wha' the fuck's going on?'

Sam heard hooves. A trio of mules appeared from behind the military building, led by a muleteer who looked about fourteen. A couple of the animals had bamboo poles stretched between them, with straps attached.

Squires understood the purpose of the rig at the same moment that Sam did.

'No way,' he croaked. 'They're not putting me on that.'

Ignoring his protests, four soldiers in fatigues picked the stretcher up, one on each corner, and lifted it over the first mule's back. Squires howled as fresh pain shot through his leg.

'Jesus . . . I can't take this. *Steve*, or whatever your fucking name is. Tell 'em I need another shot.'

Sam turned to the village's military commander, a thin-faced man with bloodshot eyes.

'You have any morphine?'

The man stared straight through him.

'Sorry Jimmy.'

Squires began slurring in pidgin Burmese, but the soldiers affected not to understand.

'Looks like you've run out of friends, old son,' Sam breathed.

The baggage from the jeep – Sam's holdall and the case of heroin – were balanced on the third mule's back and strapped in place, together with a water carrier and some stores.

Sam hoisted the small rucksack onto his shoulders. The local commander slapped the rump of the nearest mule and they were off, led by the two men in tee-shirts from Mong Yawn. The muleteer walked by the head of his pair of animals, Sam a few paces behind. Three uniformed soldiers brought up the rear.

The path climbed steeply out of the village. Sam glanced back at the palm-thatched roofs below. An ordinary agricultural settlement. Children playing. Chickens pecking in the dirt. Women grinding seeds and pulses. But instead of sugar cane or tea, this little community's export crop was opium.

As they moved on up the slope he watched Squires brace himself against the rolling of the beasts.

'How much of this have I got to take?' he gasped.

'Thought *you*'d know the answer to that,' Sam responded. 'Must have come this way before.'

'Spare me the clever stuff. I'm in fucking agony.'

'You mean you *didn't* use this route to get your gear out?'

Squires took hold of a loose end of webbing and clamped his teeth on it, like a soldier from an earlier century awaiting the surgeon's knife.

Soon elephant grass was towering above their heads. Then a little later the path opened out and followed a rocky ridge, the ground falling away on either side. A thin veil of cloud dulled the heat from the sun. Over the not so distant peaks through which they would have to pass, thicker clouds gathered.

As they trudged on, Sam found himself daring to believe the operation was almost over. Barring some disaster, he'd soon be handing responsibility to others. Midge, Waddell and the machinery of diplomacy would take over. Yes, he would talk to the Matsubara board, to give substance to the 'reconciliation' story. Even hold Melissa's hand if he had to. But then he could go home.

Before long they were amongst trees, the well-worn path climbing ever higher. Gibbons screeched in the branches and unseen birds gave mocking cries. Squires had his eyes closed and the strap had fallen from between his teeth. A drift back into unconsciousness had eased his pain.

After a while the path became steeper however, and the mules began struggling for a footing. Jimmy Squires came to with a jolt. Then one of the animals fell, pulling the stretcher and the other beast down with it.

'God . . . Oh Jee-sus!'

The muleteer hissed at the creatures, trying to encourage them back on their legs, but it was clear they'd have to unload the cargo if they were to get them moving again. The straps were undone and the stretcher lifted onto the ground.

Sam crouched down. Despite his loathing of Jimmy Squires, he could see the man was in excruciating pain. And he did have a means of relieving it, he realised. But there'd be a price to pay.

'I could help you.'

'*Yes* . . .'

'The smack in that suitcase . . .'

'Yes . . .'

'I could make a solution and inject it. I have a syringe.' It was in the medical pack in his rucksack.

'Do it . . .' Squires' voice was barely audible.

'But first you tell me what I want to know.'

'Oh God! Anything . . .'

'What route were you using?'

Squires panted like a birthing mother.

'This . . .' he gasped. 'This was the route.'

Sam stood up again, shaking his head. 'It isn't going to work.'

'Waddya mean?'

'You're fucking lying.' He began to walk away.

'*Steve* . . . Come back.'

Sam glared over his shoulder. 'What's the point?'

'I'll tell you everything. Just get the gear outta that bag.'

Sam walked to the third of the mules and began unstrapping the suitcase. The tee-shirted soldier with the glass eye rushed over to stop him.

Sam pointed at Squires, then at the bag and mimed making an injection with a syringe. The soldier shook his head, but the wail from the stretcher persuaded him to relent. They lowered the case to the ground and opened it.

The heroin was packed in thick polythene bags, each the size of a pound of sugar. Sam picked one up and walked it back to Squires.

'How much do I use?'

'No bloody idea.' His face was in permanent spasm by now.

'So tell me,' said Sam. 'The route. Names, places, the lot.'

'Jee-sus . . . Just give me a shot, for pity's sake.'

'Tell me about Yangon.'

'Okay. Okay. There's a furniture-maker. 39th Street. Name of Myo Tin. The smack gets concealed inside the containers he uses to ship the stuff abroad.'

'And it was Major Soe Thein who got the gear to Yangon for you.'

'*Yes*. Shit, man! Just give me a shot will you?'

Sam took a water bottle and the medical pack from his rucksack.

'Can't vouch for it being sterile,' he commented. Squires grunted non-committally. 'Still . . . that's not a detail you'll have given a second thought to, in relation to your customers.'

With a knife he cut a corner off the polythene and poured a small amount of the powder into the cap of the water bottle. Then he added some water.

'I'm guessing on the dose. This may kill you.'

'Right now I don't care.'

'Keep talking.'

'I've told you . . .'

'Next to nothing.'

'Jesus! What else . . . ?'

'The shipping on from Yangon. Your contact in Oz.'

'Okay, okay. It goes by boat to a furniture distributor in Port Klang, Malaysia. He ships it on to Sydney. That's all there is.'

Sam clicked his tongue. 'This is going nowhere.'

'Wha' you mean?' Squires gibbered.

Sam tipped the heroin solution onto the ground.

'Fuck . . .' Squires bit his lip.

Two uniformed soldiers bent to lift the stretcher.

'No-oo!' Squires yelled. 'Jesus, Steve. What are you made of?'

'Same as you, Jimmy. Same as you. Your last chance. Tell me about Australia.'

'Man, there's nothing to say.'

'Try. Who gets the stuff when it's removed from the furniture shipment?'

'Not my area. I don't deal.'

'Who does?'

'I honestly don't know.'

'You couldn't be honest if your life depended on it.' Sam backed away.

The soldiers bent to lift the stretcher, but Squires' howl stopped them in their tracks.

Sam looked down at his prisoner.

'Two names, Jimmy. The furniture-dealer who strips out the heroin and the man who cuts and pushes it. Two little names, then I'll give you a shot that'll put you onto a nice pile of cotton-wool clouds . . .'

'The pusher's called Marty. He's ex-army.'

'Hebble,' said Sam, remembering the name Midge had emailed him back in London.

'Jesus! You knew . . .'

'Wanted the pleasure of hearing you say it. And who's the furniture man?'

'Bartholomew. Runs a warehouse in Newcastle. Now help me for fuck's sake.'

Sam was being hassled by the soldiers but persuaded them to wait a few minutes. He poured more of the powder into the bottle cap and swished water around until the solution became clear. Unpeeling the sterilised wrapper from a syringe pack, he dipped the needle into the liquid and drew it into the chamber.

'Never done an intravenous before,' he cautioned, easing up the plunger to expel the air. 'But I've watched "Casualty" a few times.'

Squires stretched out a forearm in eager anticipation. Sam removed a shoelace from one of Squires' boots and used it as a tourniquet.

'Nice veins.' He punctured the blue line of skin and slid in the needle. Then he pushed the plunger home.

Gradually, the tension eased from Squires' face. Sam withdrew the syringe and pressed a finger on the dribble from the vein.

A few minutes later the convoy was ready to move again, its cargo drifting back into unconsciousness.

'Just don't die on me, Jimmy,' Sam muttered as he fell in behind the mules. 'You're a present for someone, so just don't fucking die.'

It was another two hours before they reached the pass through the mountains, the soldiers' increasing jitteriness indicating their proximity to Thailand with its hostile army and police.

Evening was drawing in and the insects were starting to bite. Sam watched a mosquito settle on Jimmy Squires' forehead, idly wondering if the heroin in the man's blood would make the creature incapable of flight.

The path began to descend. Ahead of them, some way down the valley, a vertical smudge of brown suggested smoke from a village. Sam pointed and asked if that was their destination, but got no response. He felt increasingly uneasy, sensing the men had an agenda which involved more than simply delivering him and Squires to the other side.

As they drew nearer to the village, he could make out the shapes of low houses. The back of his neck prickled. He glanced behind. The three uniformed soldiers bringing up the rear of the caravan were gone.

Covering their retreat, he guessed. Which meant the buggers were expecting trouble.

The two at the front, the weightlifter and the man with a glass eye were no longer carrying rifles, he noted. He spotted one of the barrels protruding from a saddle pack on the third mule and felt irritated with himself that he'd allowed his mind to wander and hadn't noticed them put it there. The civilian-dressed pair must be hoping to pass at a distance for local people, he guessed. He felt increasingly anxious. His goal was in sight, yet still beyond his reach.

They emerged from the last of the trees and the track widened. The two soldiers spread out, as if wanting to make themselves a harder target. Their shoulders hunched with tension. A handful of people were standing at the edge of the village watching. As if they'd been expecting them.

About a hundred metres to go and the soldiers stopped suddenly. The man with the glass eye gestured for the muleteer to wait. They came back to the animals, pretending to adjust the loads, but it was to provide cover for the weightlifter who produced binoculars and worriedly scanned the edge of the village.

Logic told Sam the pair would still be armed. He eyed their baggy trousers, looking for the bulge of handguns, but all he saw was a small rectangular outline in the back pocket of the weightlifter's pants.

The glasses were passed from one man to the other as if a second opinion was needed. Sam peered past them, trying to identify what was concerning them. The people on the edge of the village did not appear to be in uniform.

That box in the man's back pocket . . . Matches?

They began to move again.

At fifty metres he could clearly see it was three people on the village edge. One looked to be a woman. Brown hair and a slim figure. Wearing something yellow.

Midge wore yellow.

With a surge of horror he realised what Hu Sin had done.

Not matches. That lump in the Wa soldier's back pocket was his tracer. The bastards had used it as a lure. And there she was, a pistol shot away.

Brought here by a transponder beep so that Hu Sin could have her killed.

And here she came. Marching out of the shelter of the village, a grin splitting her face, and with two white-shirted Thais beside her.

So stupid of him. So totally fucking stupid to have believed in happy endings.

'*Midge! Get away!*'

His yell stopped her in her tracks.

But too late. The soldiers pulled out pistols and began firing. Sam cannoned after them, rugby tackling the weightlifter and bringing him down onto the rough grass. Midge and the Thais threw themselves flat. Shots rang out from the village behind them, flashes across a wide arc of the perimeter. Midge had brought the cavalry.

The weightlifter kicked himself free and scrambled to his feet. Bullets zipped through the scrub as he began to run back to the cover of the trees. He was felled within seconds.

Sam felt a kick in his side. He knew immediately he'd been hit, but looked up, more concerned about Midge than himself. He saw the yellow of her shirt, prone on the ground, then his view was blocked by the mules trotting towards the village, delivering their cargo as if on autopilot.

Feeling his strength draining away, he reached down to his side. The ground beside him was sticky with his blood.

He tried to get up, but his arms gave way and he slumped forward again, face flopping against the earth.

Then he heard a voice. Far, far above him.

'Sam! *Sam!*'

Midge. As he slipped towards blackness he had a weird, out-of-body vision. She was standing over him. Then crouching down and pressing her hand against his side.

The last thought in his mind before passing out was that for the first time in their acquaintance she'd used his real name.

29

Maharaj Nakorn Hospital, Chiang Mai
Sunday, 16 January

WHEN HE'D COME round from the anaesthetic it had been the middle of the night. They'd told him he was okay. Lost a lot of blood, because the bullet had ruptured his spleen. They'd removed the thing. Told him he would manage fine without it. A few days' recuperation in the hospital and he could be on his way.

He'd slept some more, on and off, and now it was morning. He studied his surroundings for the first time. It was a private room and an outrageously pretty nurse had just come in to check his dressing and take his pulse. Her English was poor but she could be a deaf mute for all he cared, so long as she stayed where he could look at her.

She told him not to try to sit up. Anyway, the pain in his side when he tensed his muscles was an instant deterrent. When she'd made him comfortable and given him some water to sip, she handed him an envelope that had been left on his bedside table.

He let her open it for him but declined her offer to read it aloud. It might be personal. Even confidential.

It was both.

My Hero!
You're amazing. Saved my life back there.
I've gone with Jimmy to Bangkok. Military air ambulance. They don't know if they can save his leg. Couldn't happen to a nicer bloke. We have the 'H'. The Thais will prosecute. Death sentences aren't often carried out here, more's the pity, but if he gets fifty years in a Bangkok jail that's fine by me. All my ghosts laid to rest. The police will want to interview you in a day or two, so don't go away. I'll get back up to Chiang Mai as soon as I can myself.

I want to hear everything. And to see if there's something I can do to speed your recovery . . .

Business first. The SPDC in Yangon have put out some extraordinary story about two old war vets being murdered by bandits after an historic reconciliation. One Jap, one Brit? What the hell's that all about?

Anyway, I contacted your people in London and at the Embassy in Bangkok. They're very concerned about you and agitated about the two deaths in Myanmar. Urgently wanting your version of events. Mutterings about 'the bugger better make it good.' I assured them you would. Someone's on their way to see you. Should be with you mid-morning. And they mentioned a distraught Englishwoman turning up at the consulate. Expelled from Yangon and expecting to meet you in Bangkok? They're worried about her mental state and are looking for a nice clinic to keep her in until they've worked out where she fits into the story. Quite curious to know myself . . .

Now for the rest. I took the liberty of phoning Julie. Hope you don't mind. Duncan Waddell gave me her number. She sounded quite shocked, but I assured her you were okay and would be in touch today. Hope that wasn't too presumptuous. She was really upset, Sam. Didn't sound to me like a girl who was giving up on you. She also sounded a real understanding type, which is great, because you and I had a deal and I wouldn't mind keeping my side of the bargain before you disappear from my life! So get your strength back . . .

Love,
Midge
P.S. Don't do anything stupid.

Like running around getting shot at and losing bits of his body. It was going to have to stop. And so was getting into situations with loose women.

Sam asked the nurse what day it was.

'Sunday. You want to see priest? We have many Christian church in Chiang Mai.'

'No, I don't want a priest.' He'd been trying to work out whether Julie would be at home or at work. 'I want to make a phone call.'

She moved the instrument closer to him and showed him how to get an outside line.

'Where you want to call?'

'London.'

Julie gave a little squeal of delight when she heard his voice. 'I've been so worried . . .'

'I'm fine. Coming home in a few days.'

'The woman who rang said you'd been shot.'

'Nothing serious.'

'Who was she, Sam?'

'An Australian policewoman. Ugly as sin . . .'

Julie laughed. 'But are you really coming home soon?' She sounded as if she didn't believe it.

'Soon as they let me out of here.'

'Then I've some news for you.'

He felt a fluttering of unease. 'Tell me.'

'I passed,' she said.

'Passed what?' He had a dreadful feeling he ought to know what she was talking about.

'My Day Skipper sailing exam.'

'*What?*'

'I've been doing the theory course at evening classes. You know that phone message that upset you? From Jack? He was my instructor.'

Sam tried to grasp what she was saying. 'I don't understand . . .'

'Thought I'd better learn a few tricks, because you love boats so much. More use to you if I know something about it too. But I didn't want to tell you in case I failed . . .'

'So Jack . . .'

' . . . was helping me understand all that estimated-position stuff.'

'Christ! Never heard of it being called that before!'

'You bast . . .'

'Sorry darling. I got it wrong. Utterly, stupidly wrong.' He felt absurdly emotional all of a sudden.

'Actually I was rather flattered afterwards. Realised you cared.'

'I love you, Julie.'

'Love you too.'

There was a pause. They both knew the moment had come for him to say something else.

'I've made up my mind,' he told her, having done so a split second ago. 'What I've been doing is a bloody stupid way to earn a living.'

He waited for her to respond, but she didn't. Holding her breath, he suspected.

'I'm giving in my notice.'

'You mean that?'

'Absolutely definitely.'

But as he said it, the doubts crept back in.

'What'll you do instead?'

He looked up. The nurse was watching him from the half-open door.

'Well just at this moment there's a stunningly pretty Thai girl in my bedroom . . .'

'Sam! You're a rotten sod.'

'But you love me.'

'That could change.'

'See you in a day or three.'

Sam put down the phone and stared up at the ceiling. This time, he was glad to say, there was no beetle crawling across it.